Odin Rising

Written by: Axl Barnes

© 2019 by Axl Barnes. All rights reserved.
Find out more at:
axlbarnes.blogspot.com

No part of this publication may be reproduced, distributed, or transmitted in any form or by any means, or stored in a database or retrieval system, without the prior written permission of the publishers.

This is a work of fiction, names, characters, places and incidents either are the result of the author's creative exploration or are used only in a fictional manor. Any resemblance to actual persons, living or dead, business establishments, events, or locales is entirely coincidental.

Paperback ISBN: 978-1-9992556-0-2
Editor: Mercy Borne
Cover Illustrator: Brittany Cardinal
Graphic Designer: Konn Lavery

Printed in the United States of America.
First Edition 2019.

"How I would love one day to see all people, young and old, sad or happy, men and women, married or not, serious or superficial, leave their homes and their workplaces, relinquish their duties and responsibilities, gather in the streets and refuse to do anything anymore. At that moment, let slaves to senseless work, who have been toiling for future generations under the dire delusion that they contribute to the good of humanity, avenge themselves on the mediocrity of a sterile and insignificant life, on the tremendous waste that never permitted spiritual transfiguration. At that moment, when all faith and resignation are lost, let the trappings of ordinary life burst once and for all. Let those who suffer silently, not even uttering a sigh of complaint, yell with all their might, making a strange, menacing, dissonant clamor that would shake the earth."
Emil Cioran, On the Heights of Despair

"The true sense of agony seems to me to lie in the revelation of death's immanence in life"
Emil Cioran, On the Heights of Despair

"To defy heredity is to defy billions of years, to defy the first cell."
Emil Cioran, The Trouble with Being Born

"Something I study is how people react when my blood is streaming everywhere…"
Mayhem vocalist Per Yngve Ohlin aka "Dead"

"Against boredom, even gods struggle in vain."
Fredrich Nietzsche, The Anti-Christ

Odin Rising by Axl Barnes

Table of Contents

Chapter 1 The Bleeding Boredom	1
Chapter 2 Alex's Open Eye	43
Chapter 3 Ave Satanas!	61
Chapter 4 Midday Mutilation	95
Chapter 5 The Storm of Bones	141
Chapter 6 The Enemy Inside	157
Chapter 7 The Wild Hunt	213

Odin Rising by Axl Barnes

Chapter 1
The Bleeding Boredom

Despite having masturbated before falling asleep, Tudor woke with a bulging erection.

His excitement shrank gradually as he contemplated the day ahead. Math homework. Plane geometry. Mr. Stan.

And then physics.

Thursdays were tough. Both math and physics.

Tudor hated them. He loathed school in general, but he especially dreaded those two classes.

Sighing, he saw the clock on his desk blink 8:54 as he dragged himself from bed.

He went to the bathroom, urinated and washed his face. In the kitchen, he ate the ham and eggs and the strawberry jam on toast his mom had prepared for him.

Tudor was in ninth grade. He was supposed to prepare for high school entrance exams. National exams. That *national* made him cringe. Exams were in Math, History, and Romanian Lit. But Tudor didn't want to think about those exams or what high school he'd end up in. Those were things *they* talked about, of no concern to *him*.

Renovations at his school had shunted most junior high students to the "Industrial High School," one of three high schools in the small town of Tatareni. Their names echoed the communist obsession with planification: "The Theoretical High School," "The Industrial High School," and "The Agricultural High School."

Future tradesmen and factory workers attending "The Industrial High School" went to school in the morning. Tudor and other junior high schoolers had classes from two till eight.

This meant mornings were for homework.

Back in his bedroom, Tudor sat at his desk and fished his Math books from his backpack.

He leafed through his notebook looking for the last geometry lecture. But then he remembered he took no notes.

Fuck me, what do I do now? Tudor asked himself bitterly, staring at the band logos, skeletons, and satanic symbols doodled on the page in front of him.

For the last geometry class, he had written only the date and the title, "The Postulates of Congruent Triangles." But there followed not postulates of geometry but of demonic imagery: a few versions of Slayer's pentagram logo nested among inverted crosses and the number *666*, in various styles but always in red or black.

What if Mr. Stan sees this? Tudor shuddered.

Below the satanic symbols, he had scribbled the details of the homework exercises. Then he wrote, "Pythagoras' Theorem."

Did Mr. Stan talk about that theorem too? Tudor couldn't remember.

He opened his textbook and browsed the chapter on congruent triangles.

He wrote down the first exercise.

Prove that, if two angles of a triangle are congruent, the sides opposite these angles are also congruent.

Tudor carelessly scrawled the diagram. The triangle

Chapter 1 The Bleeding Boredom

looked like an Indian teepee.

A good diagram means the problem is half-solved, Mr. Stan was fond of saying.

Tudor marked two of the angles as congruent.

Studying the picture, he thought, *It's obvious! The opposite sides must be congruent. How can they not be? Since the angle dictates the length of the side opposite to it.*

But Tudor knew this intuition wasn't proof. Saying "It's obvious" wasn't good enough. Proving it had steps.

But how can I break something so clear and evident into steps? Tudor wondered in frustration.

Feeling helpless, he sighed deeply.

"Fuck, this shit is stupid!" he said out loud. Half-heartedly, he searched the chapter for some relevant information but found none.

His feeble motivation melted away.

I'll just ask Edi for his homework before class. His friend Edi was a math and physics wiz. Mostly because his dad was one. Mr. Manea had a hands-on approach to his son's education. The bruises on Edi's arms, back, and thighs testified to that.

Tudor envisioned Mr. Manea whipping Edi and the boy yelping like a dog as he tried to dodge his father's whistling belt. Tudor shuddered in disgust.

Gazing back at the triangle, Tudor bisected the opposite angles and transformed the figure into a pentagram. He felt the familiar fog of boredom enshroud his brain.

If he didn't do his math, there was no point in doing his other work. Only his math grade hovered near failure. On the ten-point grading scale, he usually scored five or six. Rarely seven.

With Edi's help.

On his own, he would score three or four. Failing grades. Summer school. Maybe repeating the ninth grade.

Tudor didn't want to think about it.

For today, he needed an excuse in case Mr. Stan decided to test him at the blackboard, in front of the entire class.

Tudor played with a strand of hair from his mohawk, a new hairstyle he copied from Phil Anselmo of Pantera.

I'll tell him my grandma suffered a stroke and was hospitalized.

It was actually true.

They had to take her to Bucharest. We were all afraid she'd pass away.

Tudor smiled. *Yes, that might work. So what if the stroke happened last month? Who the hell knows? Mr. Stan surely doesn't.*

Maybe he'd catch up on his math homework on the weekend.

Pleased with his idea, Tudor finished the pentagram and began to fill its empty space with the horns, ears, and pointed beard of a goat's head.

Heil Satan!

Heil Master!

He considered drawing something more complicated. He looked at the large poster above his desk. Night. A monstrous skeleton rising from the hollow of a tree, ready to pounce on its prey.

The poster was the cover of Iron Maiden's *Fear of the Dark*.

Tudor hated Iron Maiden and mocked Edi for digging their style of metal.

But Eddie the Head, Maiden's emblematic monster, was cool. The same couldn't be said, Tudor thought, about Edi the Nerd.

Tudor smiled at his private joke.

Edi was okay, but just a follower with no personality.

Edi was no Alex.

Suddenly, Tudor remembered Alex's pentagram. The one Alex sliced into his arm with a razor, adding a Slayer logo next to it.

Tudor and Edi thought that was rad.

Alex was the coolest, most awesome guy, no question.

A flash of inspiration brightened the morning gloom.

Chapter 1 The Bleeding Boredom

Tudor would cut himself too. But he didn't want to blindly imitate Alex.

Monkey see, monkey do, the others would say.

But cutting band logos and satanic symbols into your skin was rad. And worrying about imitating others was a sign of weakness.

He just needed to find a symbol that characterized him, that would let him retain his semblance of authenticity.

After a moment's reflection, Tudor decided: the inverted cross. That was *his* symbol.

During one of their first incursions in the local cemetery, it was he, Tudor, who began uprooting wooden crosses and implanting them upside down.

Tudor pictured Jesus crucified upside down, screaming in agony, his face red as if about to burst.

Then he thought of an angry black goat goring the martyr's stomach.

Suddenly excited, Tudor tossed aside his math notebook and opened his sketchbook. He scribbled, "Jesus crucified upside down, disemboweled and pissed on by a goat."

Nice. This day is not complete shit.

A principle from philosopher Emil Cioran emerged vaguely from Tudor's memory, "Smoking by the side of the grave is better than reading the Gospels."

Tudor had never read the Gospels, but he agreed. Nothing was as good as smoking, especially smoking in the cemetery.

Tudor's focus returned to self-mutilation. He decided to cut the symbol on his stomach. The sides of the cross would intersect around his navel, the longer part reaching all the way to his solar plexus.

The morning didn't seem so empty. He had a project and something to look forward too: impressing Alex and Edi.

Extreme music would create a proper atmosphere for such art.

Tudor opened his desk drawer and scanned his cassette collection: Sepultura, Sodom, Slayer, Napalm Death, Pantera.

Pantera was his new favorite.

But they weren't really Satanists. Just a group of pissed-off rednecks from the southern U.S.

Tudor deemed Slayer's *Show no Mercy* appropriately satanic. He loaded Side B into his player. "Black Magic." A hypnotic guitar riff filled the room, followed by frenzied bass and drums.

Tudor removed his shirt and rushed to the bathroom for a razor. The sharp object between his fingers, he admired himself in the mirror. He was handsome. The mohawk crowned an oval face with intense, blue-green eyes, an elegant nose, and full lips. The bridge of his nose was slightly crooked, from eating a flying knee in a particularly violent street fight. But despite a few close calls, he had triumphed in many brawls and never lost an arm-wrestling match. He was strong for his age and usually liked to challenge older opponents. The thought of fighting made him curl his upper lip like Billy Idol, revealing a sharp incisor. His body was perfectly proportioned, tall, athletic, and slender. He flexed his biceps, triceps and pectorals. Unfortunately, his muscles were not yet bulging like Van Damme's or Stallone's. He needed to lift more weights.

Looking at the razor between his fingers, Tudor thought of using it as a weapon. He pretended to slap someone quickly with his right hand.

Maybe a girl. Slap the bitch and run. Leave her crying, bleeding, disfigured.

Or maybe first take her clothes off and then...

Tudor slapped again at his reflection in the mirror.

Pleased with his idea, he went back to his bedroom.

A frantic guitar solo erupted as Tudor returned to his room. He sat in his armchair, leaned back and looked at the pale, smooth skin of his abdomen, with its tufts of blond hair above and below the navel.

He brought the razor close to his skin.

But, in spite of the violent music, Tudor realized he

Chapter 1 The Bleeding Boredom

couldn't cut himself.

He recalled the nasty sensation of being cut by accident. His friend George had cut him once by mistake. They were devouring a watermelon with only one knife between them. Tudor reached for the knife, and George snatched it instinctively, eager for another sweet slice. The blade slit Tudor's index finger. Tudor felt the edge breaking his skin, then saw the blood seeping through the cut.

The pain started throbbing.

"Shit, I hate that," Tudor muttered.

How could Alex have done such a thing? He must have an iron will.

Or maybe he was drunk.

Yes, Tudor decided, Alex must have been drunk when he cut himself. Alcohol numbs the pain and makes you careless. And Alex loved to drink.

But it doesn't make sense for me to get drunk now. Especially before school. That's what afterschool parties and weekends are for.

Tudor imagined going to school hammered, being summoned to the blackboard, stumbling toward the front of the class, and vomiting on everything: teacher, classmates, maps, equations, the anatomical models of the human body. Everything covered in his stinking puke.

That would be rad, even legendary. Maybe some other time.

As "Tormentor" followed "Black Magic," Tudor focused again on his project.

A nail clipper might work better than a razor. Clipping bits of skin would yield constant yet less intense pain. Tudor returned to the bathroom, put the razor back in its place and fetched the nail clipper.

In the bedroom, he blasted power chords from an air guitar, pounded his chest, and banged his head to Slayer's demonic riffs.

Slayer was the shit.

Maximum brutality.

Back in his chair, Tudor pinched his skin with the clipper. Each agonizing pinch created a red dot. Dots coalesced into a line. As he finished the bottom of the cross, the doorbell chimed over the rock music.

Donning his shirt, Tudor stopped the cassette and hustled to the door. Through the peephole, he saw George's round and smiling face.

George, a.k.a. Rude Pig or Fat Stuff was a fixture of Tudor's mornings. Usually, the two friends followed their whims in the fight against monotony. They would drench passersby with water balloons lobbed from Tudor's balcony or record impromptu death metal songs with Tudor grunting the accompaniment to his acoustic guitar riffs and George's pot-and-pan blast beats or atmospheric flute lines. Sometimes they looked at porno mags. In short, they did whatever.

Tudor opened the door.

"Hey there, bro," George said, coming in.

"Hey, man" Tudor mumbled.

"I brought your cassettes back." George handed him two tapes: Slayer's *Divine Intervention* and Kreator's *Pleasure to Kill*.

"Thanks."

As he removed his sneakers, George asked, "What the fuck were you doing? Jacking off?"

"No, I was waiting for you to give me a hand," Tudor said, smiling.

"Oh, so your mom's not home?" George grinned.

Tudor gave his guest a solid shot in the arm. "You fucking pig!"

"*Rude* Pig."

George pretended to kick Tudor's ass as they headed for the bedroom.

"Fuck off, or I'll beat you up Piggy!"

"Okay, okay. Seriously, what the fuck were you doing?" George sat on the armchair, the place of Tudor's self-

Chapter 1 The Bleeding Boredom

mutilation. "Don't tell me you were doing your homework."

"Oh! God no," Tudor said as he sat on his bed and crossed his legs under him. "Fuck homework, man! I'll get it from Edi later at school. That's what friends are for."

"I'm not going to school today," George boasted. "My dad is taking me to Bucharest. You know the Big Expo? He wants to buy a few more arcade games."

"Oh, sweet," Tudor said.

After the Romanian revolution in '89, George's dad had opened a bar with arcade games. Tudor and George used to play there a lot until George went crazy after losing a car race and punched a hole in the monitor. He sliced his wrist and had to be taken to emergency.

That happened shortly after George's mom had died from cancer, and Tudor often wondered if the two events were related. George had always been weird, but after his mom died, he approached insanity. The strongest indication of George's mental instability came when Tudor saw him playing with kittens in front of his building. George was caught in a demented soccer game, attempting rainbow flicks and keepie-uppies with tiny balls of fur. His sneakers were red with blood and guts. His face was frozen in an alien grin. He killed them all, including their mother, and then side-footed their bodies against the wall till they exploded into chunks of fur and pink meat.

Tudor and George were both fifteen, but George was only in the seventh grade. He had repeated kindergarten when the teachers said he wasn't ready for school. They diagnosed him with A.D.D. Then, after failing a few classes, he had to repeat the seventh grade. But now, the second time around, he claimed he was doing better.

George asked, "How are Alex and Edi? Are you guys doing something this weekend?"

"We'll probably get smashed as usual," Tudor said, smiling. "Alex cut a bunch of satanic symbols on his arm. He showed us yesterday. It looked awesome!"

"Oh, my God. He is a crazy Satanist."

"Yeah," Tudor said and lifted his shirt.

George's eyes widened.

"It will be an inverted cross. It's a work in progress," Tudor explained.

"You motherfucking Satanist!" George exclaimed again. "That is so extreme!"

Pleased with his friend's reaction, Tudor didn't dispute the label of "Satanist." But he doubted George understood its significance. You couldn't have deep conversations with George. He didn't know there was no God. Although he could say it or agree if Tudor asserted it, he was unable to really grasp the fact. Tudor knew it made no sense to talk about serious issues with most people. It was like explaining colors to the blind. They would just give you a sad and shamed smile.

True knowledge isn't for everyone, Alex had told him. *Spiritual power is for only a select few, the initiates.*

Tudor had discovered there is no God by accident. One morning, boredom drove him into his dad's office seeking porno movies—he knew his dad's stash—and money—he habitually paid himself an allowance with his dad's leftover change.

But then his eyes started scanning the rows of books lining the wall. His dad, Claudiu Negur, was a librarian and passionate bibliophile. Tudor noticed a few skinny ones. It was better to start with the smaller books which didn't require a huge commitment. Several spines bore the same name: Emil Cioran. Tudor knew from TV and discussions with his dad that Cioran and Mircea Eliade were Romania's most renowned intellectuals. One title intrigued him: *The Trouble with Being Born.* He grabbed a stack of the slim books and sat at his dad's desk. *The Syllogisms of Bitterness* had a cool cover. A man in a chair, slouching in infinite sadness and lethargy. He looked like a marionette with its strings cut; a body devoid of will and purpose. Tudor opened the collection of aphorisms. Although he didn't understand most of the

Chapter 1 The Bleeding Boredom

author's remarks, Tudor reacted to the tone: an aggressive yet melancholy quality. Cioran's intended message resonated in Tudor's depths. Later, while reading through *On the Heights of Despair*, Tudor recognized Cioran's central insight into two simple words.

"Nothing Matters." It was the title of one of the chapters.

Nothing matters, Tudor repeated the magical formula to himself.

When his dad had come home for lunch, Tudor asked what a syllogism was. Washing his hands in the bathroom, Mr. Negur answered that a syllogism was a form of argument. Like, when one concludes that Ion is mortal because Ion is a man and all men are mortal.

Later that day, Tudor revealed to Alex and Edi that there was no God and nothing mattered. He was excited to learn they were also atheists. And Alex knew about Cioran. Alex confessed that, although he had read many books supporting atheism, he had realized, deep in his heart, that there was no God when he found a chick in the kitchen garbage can. It was alive and chirping anemically. Alex's mom had wanted to raise chickens in an incubator on their balcony. But many of the chicks died shortly after hatching, and Alex's mom assumed the deformed bird dead and discarded it with the others. The sight of the dying bird, stuffed between potato peels and apple cores, killed Alex's appetite. Disgusted and angry, he stormed into his parent's bedroom and spat on the crucifix on the wall.

Edi said he discovered long before that existence was just a cosmic accident and the Bible was all bullshit. "They say that, on Judgment Day, our bodies will rise from the grave. But what if you were incinerated?" Edi adjusted his glasses and looked at his friends with sparkling eyes. "Or what if you were dismembered or smashed in an accident? Or a grenade exploded in your hand? What is this, the Judgment Day of mangled meat? That's retarded."

At that point, a special bond united the three youngsters. They weren't only metalheads, but rebels with a cause. Alex, the most well-read of the group, began lending the others books like Hitler's *Mein Kampf*, Cioran's *The Transfiguration of Romania*, Nietzsche's *Twilight of the Idols*, and LaVey's *The Satanic Bible*.

At first, Tudor showed interest but couldn't finish any of the books. After the revelation that nothing mattered, it seemed any book that didn't acknowledge the futility of everything was worthless. Why should anyone follow Hitler and sacrifice himself for the glorious destiny of a nation? What should a people, whether German or Romanian, go to war and conquer others? In Tudor's view, *all* people, whether German, Romanian, Chinese, Paraguayan, were equally worthless and ridiculous when seen against the background of cosmic chaos. Humanity was a mound of ants about to get squashed. Similarly, Tudor had asked himself why anyone should worship Satan or conduct any of LaVey's stupid rituals. Why should anyone worship *anything*? All these books, Tudor had realized, assumed *something mattered*. The assumption condemned them to banality.

Tudor had concluded that the vast majority of people were hypocrites, hiding like cowards from the obvious truth that nothing was important. They came up with projects and goals and dreams as if the universe cared. But it didn't. So why have projects? Why try to do anything? Acting wasn't only stupid but also ugly. Being enthusiastic and full-hearted about your job or whatever society made you do was revolting and humiliating.

Tudor swore he'd never be enthusiastic about anything, never aim at anything.

After a month or so, even Cioran had started to bore Tudor. He turned his attention to drawing and painting. He enjoyed reproducing the artwork of metal albums, band logos, and various occultist symbols. His room slowly became both workshop and canvass. He wrote 666 in each corner on the inside of his door, and in the middle, he painted a masked headsman ready to strike with his axe. The cover of Sodom's

Chapter 1 The Bleeding Boredom

Obsessed by Cruelty.

Gradually, Tudor stopped copying and started painting the morbid visions of his imagination. Closing his eyes and listening to heavy music, he watched mental pictures develop into short films. The images were a mixture of movies, album covers, his most vivid dreams, and daytime musings. He drew muscular monsters with skeleton heads torturing, strangling and decapitating innocent people such as his teachers, his parents, and classmates he hated. Sometimes Tudor wasn't sure about the source of mental images or what they meant. Once he drew a warrior with long, dark hair framing his skeleton head. The warrior clutched a spear in his mighty right hand. His forehead was smashed. The hole in his skull was a broken window revealing an identical spear-wielding soldier. The tiny inner warrior had thrust his weapon through his larger counterpart's head.

Unlike Tudor, Edi had shown a genuine interest in the books borrowed from Alex. Unfortunately, Mr. Manea, had caught him reading Nietzsche's *Twilight of the Idols or How To Do Philosophy With a Hammer.* Mr. Manea snatched the book and read its title. A bulging vein tugged on the temple of his reddening face.

"Eduard, what is this crap? Can you explain how reading this book can help you? Who gave you this junk? When was it written?"

Strangled by fear, Edi shook his head. Mr. Manea frantically turned to the front of the book. "First published in 1889. 19th century. Eduard, do you know what century you live in?"

"20th," Edi murmured.

"So, how will this ancient book help you adapt to our new world, a world that's always changing?"

Edi shrugged. "I don't know."

"Well, it won't. Do you know in what century humanity made the most technological and scientific progress?"

"20th?" Edi answered feebly, looking up at his dad.

"Damn straight. And you know what? You either adapt or get left behind. Just like Darwin said. Progress doesn't wait for slackers and dreamers and poets. That's what these philosophers are, lazy dreamers! Weak, sick people! Do you understand?"

"Yes."

"Yes, what?"

"Yes, sir."

Mr. Manea leafed through the book harshly, almost ripping out the pages. Then he raised it in the air. Edi ducked his head, fearing a blow. But Mr. Manea only threw the volume against the wall. It landed open on the floor like a dead bird.

"If I catch you again wasting your time with this junk, I'll show you discipline with a hammer. Understood?"

Edi managed a tearful yes.

Despite having failed to enlighten his friends, Alex had still felt united with them. He hadn't given up on them. The death of God was now their religion. But George wasn't one of his disciples. George didn't see the light. George imitated them and hung out with them as much as possible. Yet, on a deep level, he was always far away, worlds apart.

But Tudor didn't mind George's hopelessness. He enjoyed George's flattery and imitation. Having shown his work in progress, he began boasting about his other extreme goals.

"I'm thinking of getting some animal blood, like a dog or cat or something, and writing 'Heil Satan' on a church or some crosses in the cemetery. Wouldn't that be cool?"

"Hell yeah!" George agreed. "I think I can help you."

"Really? How?"

George didn't register the question, his attention fixated on Tudor's books. He grabbed a couple of volumes and started leafing through them and sniffing them with his bulbous nose. Tudor was used to his friend's attention lapses.

Idle curiosity satisfied, George returned the books, stood up abruptly and scratched his ass vigorously. It was a nervous tic. He sat back down and smelled his fingers. A light

Chapter 1 The Bleeding Boredom

appeared in his black eyes.

"Boy oh boy, I meant to tell you! I went to the cemetery with my grandma yesterday. To my mom's grave." George spoke the last sentence in a low voice. Then his enthusiasm picked up, "And I saw an open tomb. And the coffin inside was broken, so you could see the corpse!"

"Wow, awesome!" Tudor exclaimed.

"Hell yeah! I thought you'd be interested, you sick fuck. Anyway, I think maybe a gypsy or something broke the lock and got inside looking for jewels and stuff like that."

Now, it was Tudor's attention that lapsed. He noticed spittle forming around his friend's lips as he talked. It was almost like George was foaming at the mouth. Tudor wondered whether George noticed. He hadn't done it before, at least not as much. The more George talked the more spittle beaded on his lips, till he ended spitting on his shirt and pants.

He ended up spraying it, not saying it.

But this happened mostly to old people wearing dentures. Like Tudor's grandmother.

Returning to the conversation, Tudor said, "Dude, that's stellar. So, was it like a newly buried corpse or just bones?"

"Fuck, I'm not sure. I only managed a glimpse. He was wearing a dusty suit and I only saw his hands. I think there was some meat on them, they weren't just bones. But they weren't like normal hands either."

"Hmm," Tudor uttered thoughtfully, stroking his chin. "I'm curious to see for myself."

"Wanna go now?" George jumped with excitement.

Tudor raised his hand. "Not now. Maybe tomorrow after school. So Alex and Edi can come too. We'll turn it into a fucking party in the cemetery."

George sank back into the armchair. "That sounds cool. I just hope they don't put the lock back before then."

"It's okay, maybe we'll find some other ones. Fuck it, we'll break them open if we need to," Tudor said, grinning.

Warming up to the idea, George blurted, "I can bring my

cassette player. And wine. Now I know how to get it from my dad's barrel in the basement."

"Stellar! What kind of wine?"

"White, sweet I guess."

"Ah, and how much?" Tudor asked, all business as he organized the party.

"Two litres. I can bring two bottles if you want."

"If Edi and Alex come along, that would be half a litre each," Tudor calculated, stroking his hair. "That might be enough. We'll see what Alex says."

"I can get more…"

"No, it's okay. We'll either buy some beer or move the party to your basement. You know, at midnight. Is that okay?"

"Sure. Why not? My old man goes to bed early. We can suck the wine through the tube directly from the barrel. I heard you get really wasted that way."

"Why do you always dream of sucking, Piggy?" Tudor smiled. He was pleased. Now he had something to look forward to.

"I don't know. I might be turning into your mother," George said, and started sucking and slobbering over an imaginary phallus. He pretended to choke on it and spit on the floor. "Fuck, I swallowed the wrong way."

"Oh, speaking of blowjobs, maybe you can show us your porn stash," Tudor said excitedly.

"Yes, I have cards with naked babes on them. We should play."

"Sweet! Maybe we can invite your slutty neighbor."

"Which one?" George asked with a grin, saliva still dripping on his chin.

"The one with big tits," Tudor said.

"Sure, we'll bring her with, whether she wants it or not," George said, spittle flying. He reminded Tudor of Sylvester the Cat.

The two friends were silent for a while, as if contemplating the upcoming evening, considering whether they had covered

Chapter 1 The Bleeding Boredom

everything.

George broke the silence. "You know the school where my grandpa lives?"

"Uh-huh."

"I heard there are hookers around there. And they show you their tits for free."

"Do you get to grope them too?"

"Yes, you can play with them all you want. Till you get bored."

"Wow, really? Are you fucking serious?"

"Yes, man, but they only come out on Friday nights. Fridays and Sundays, I think."

"We should fucking go for sure. Oh, my God!"

Tudor was very pleased with his friend. George was truly useful for a meathead.

"Oh, before I forget," George went, "I want to show you something cool in my attic. I'm sure you'll like it. Got a minute?"

"Yep," Tudor said. He had nothing else to do. The inverted cross project could wait. And he trusted that George wouldn't waste his time. There must be something interesting in his attic. And the fact that George didn't specify what it was intrigued Tudor and quickened his heart.

"Okay, let's go!" George said and stood up again.

Tudor glimpsed the clock on his desk. It was eleven. His dad would be home for lunch at noon. Plenty of time.

Tudor fetched his apartment key from the top of the dresser in the hallway, stowed it in his shorts' pocket, and slipped into his sandals. George's apartment was across the street, on the second floor of a three-story building, right beneath a tall, red-shingled roof.

Tudor locked the door and followed his friend down the stairs. As George opened the building door, Tudor grabbed him by the shoulder, stopping him abruptly.

"Wait, man!" Tudor said and pointed toward the street. "Look, the walking corpse."

Mr. Schmidt lumbered toward the dumpster, dragging his garbage bin. He walked slowly on skinny, pale, atrophied legs. It was probably his day's big adventure, taking out the trash. Two stray dogs scavenged through the refuse near the dumpster, amid clouds of flies.

Tudor couldn't resist taunting the old man, "Hey old fart! The Grim Reaper's at your house looking for you!"

George yelled in turn, "Stray dogs fuck your wife."

Mr. Schmidt's head turned slowly toward them.

Cackling, the kids ran back up the stairs, two or three at a time. They stopped on the second floor and looked out a window. The old man was still inching to the dumpster, seemingly undisturbed.

"Maybe he didn't hear us," George said with disappointment.

"Yeah, he's probably deaf." Then, looking at his friend Tudor asked, "Hey man, is his wife still alive?"

George shrugged.

"You said she fucks dogs, but I'm pretty sure she died a few years ago."

"Maybe that's *why* she died," George smiled, then added as an afterthought, "Who gives a shit anyway? That's what old people do. They die. It's their job."

"Yes, except they always seem to die too late," Tudor mused, watching Mr. Schmidt trying to feed leftovers to a growling stray dog.

The old man dumped the rest of his garbage and turned to hobble away. Once the coast was clear, the youngsters left Tudor's building and crossed the street toward George's apartment.

It was a beautiful, sunny May day. High above the red-tiled roofs, the sky was blue and clear. On the other side of the street, a chain-link fence enclosed one of the neighborhood's soccer fields. Bright green grass flourished everywhere except the dusty areas in front of the goalposts.

Before getting into heavy metal and Satanism, Tudor

Chapter 1 The Bleeding Boredom

had ruled that field. Actually, he had been king of junior high soccer in the whole town. In the 7th grade, when he was captain of his class' soccer team, they won the City's Junior High School Soccer Tournament. Tudor's sublime skill carried the team to the championship. And when he wasn't powering through opposing defenses, he was a general in the center of the pitch, organizing the team, boosting morale with his unflagging effort, and enticing his teammates to emulate his ardent lust for victory.

Tudor thought they could win the tournament again if he got involved. But he didn't care about soccer anymore, to the disappointment of his gym teacher, who thought of him as the Romanian Marco van Basten. Without Tudor, none of his classmates bothered to take charge and organize the team. Also, Tudor figured, drinking and smoking didn't help his athletic ability. He was so out of shape, he probably couldn't even play a full game.

Soccer was a thing of the past, something he had grown out of.

Thinking about his transformation, Tudor silently followed George up to the second floor. George asked him to wait outside his apartment. He soon emerged with an empty jar and a black garbage bag.

The objects amplified Tudor's curiosity.

They climbed the last flight of stairs and opened the door to the attic. Tudor smelled a mixture of fresh-cut wood and bird droppings. It reminded him of his grandma's chicken coop, a smell both sweet and nauseating. Light spilled through a large window near the ceiling, shining a triangular section of the gravel-covered floor but leaving the corners of the room in shadow.

That's where the pigeons had their nests, where the slanted roof met the floor. Tudor heard them scurrying atop the shingled roof.

Tudor knew about the pigeons. He could see them from the window of his dad's office. Dozens of them would gather on George's roof and fly in circles when scared by a sudden noise, a car's engine or a yell. They flew in perfect coordination, sometimes landing on Tudor's roof, out of sight, or on the top of the apartment building to the right. Eventually, they always flocked back to their home on George's roof.

Home sweet home!

George placed the jar and the bag on the floor and walked toward one of the corners. Alarmed, two pigeons flew away, one of them landing on the window sill. The bird tilted its head and stared at them with black, beady eyes.

George crouched and scooped something from the corner.

"Look at this shit!" he said, turning back to Tudor and showing a baby pigeon with puffy feathers, yellow and grey. "You wanna hold it?"

Tudor looked at the bumpy, black beak, stepped back, raised his hands, and exclaimed, "God no, take it away from me!" He hated the feel of bird feet on his palms or the pecking at his skin.

George, aware of Tudor's phobia, chuckled.

Once, Tudor had to make a small insect collection for his biology class and had ended up asking for George's help. They went to the river valley to catch locusts, butterflies, and other insects. George did all the work. Tudor couldn't even touch the nasty creatures, especially the locusts. He hated their tiny, rigid bodies squirming between his fingers. Hated their constant buzzing. Dreaded their claws scratching his skin. To George's delight, Tudor would scream girlishly whenever a grasshopper jumped his way.

Now George was holding a baby pigeon instead of a buzzing locust. Still grinning, he lifted it to Tudor and teased, "Come on man! What are you, a pussy?"

"Fuck you! I'm not touching that winged rat."

"It's just a baby, man."

Tudor shook his head. "They carry fucking diseases, you stupid fuck. Viruses and shit."

George shrugged off Tudor's refusal of the bird, stepped

Chapter 1 The Bleeding Boredom

toward the empty jar, uncapped it with his free hand and set it on the floor. Then, with a single practiced motion, he tore the bird's head off and casually tossed it aside. Tudor watched George's hands move in opposite directions, wringing the carcass like a dishrag. When this technique bore no fruit, he suspended the matted wad of feathers above the jar and forced out a few red drops, ketchup from the squeeze-bottle bird.

A few red drops slid toward the bottom of the jar.

"This might take a while," George mumbled.

Tudor watched intently, hands crossed on his chest. George was now in one of his sadistic trances, dull eyes blind to all but his grisly task.

"I need a fat one," George said as he lurched toward a group of adult pigeons. He leaped into their midst and snatched one just as it spread its wings. "I got you, fat fuck!" he exclaimed while the plump bird struggled in his grip. No ceremony, just casual violence, George ripped the bird's head from its body and squeezed.

This time a jet of blood erupted from the victim.

Tudor noticed that the pigeon's head kept blinking and staring, watching its body's blood fill the jar.

George completed his task in merciless silence. There were two heaps on the floor, one of the pigeon's heads and one of the decapitated bodies. Some of the heads were bigger than others. Some eyes were closed, some open and blinking weakly. The bodies were drained of blood, their wings paralyzed. Crazed survivors screamed and desperately beat their broken wings. The cool air, a breeze of pigeon panic, fanned Tudor's skin and fed his growing unease.

This might turn into Hitchcock's The Birds any minute now.

When the jar would hold no more blood, George screwed on the lid and handed the container to Tudor.

"There you go! Blood for writing!"

"Thanks," Tudor mumbled. He saw white and grey feathers floating in the thick crimson liquid.

George shoved the pigeon carcasses into the garbage bag. With his foot, he covered the traces of blood with pebbles. Job done, he turned to Tudor and asked, "Do you want a bag for that?"

"Good idea. I don't want people seeing me with this."

"Okay, let's go! I'll get you a bag, and then I'll come with and throw this in the dumpster."

Tudor nodded.

As he walked down the quiet stairs, Tudor felt relieved for getting out of the attic safely.

Outside, the neighborhood was still calm, almost deserted. Tudor took a deep breath of fresh air.

George emerged from the building and handed Tudor a bag. Tudor placed the jar inside and held the bag tightly, making sure it wouldn't tip over.

Tudor remembered George was going to Bucharest. "Hey dude, if you see any metal tapes, make sure you buy some. You know the bands I like."

"Sure thing. I'll keep an eye out for that."

"Oh, and t-shirts. Let me know!"

"You bet, brother."

George threw the bag of dead pigeons in the dumpster. It dropped with a muffled thud.

"Well, I'll see you tomorrow evening, man. Be careful with that blood, it might start smelling. Maybe you should put it out on the balcony."

"Yes, sure," Tudor replied. "Don't forget, tomorrow after class. Let's meet by the school soccer field."

"I'll be there. Oh, Tudor, before I forget, don't let your mom sip the blood through a straw! I hear she sucks whatever she can get her hands on, at least when she's not too busy picking cucumbers with her ass."

Tudor wanted to reply with his own mom joke but recalled in time that George's mom was dead.

He just stood there grinning, watching George go back to his building.

Chapter 1 The Bleeding Boredom

Stupid fat ass.

Then, still holding the jar carefully, he went back to his apartment.

Back in his room, Tudor stowed the jar under his bed and sat in his armchair, hands folded under his head. He thought of tomorrow's party in the cemetery. He loved getting drunk in that place. No one else had ever thought of partying there. The other kids went to nightclubs like Queen, or got hammered in the park downtown, or threw house parties. Only him and his buds would get drunk in the forest at the edge of town, or down the river valley, or in the cemetery. The graveyard was so much fun, such a solemn place to explore and desecrate.

A party at night in a local church would be good too, Tudor thought. *Destroying everything inside and then setting the damn place on fire.*

Tudor thought of the fresh blood under his bed. He would write on the walls of the cemetery chapel with the syringe George had given him. Tudor mused that George had lifted the large syringe from the hospital during one of his mom's chemo treatments.

A wave of excitement washed over the youth. He couldn't wait to tell Alex about his new plan.

Tudor's dad arrived home from the library at noon, and father and son lunched together. As usual, his dad read the paper, and the radio droned in a woman's monotone about the levels of the Danube's tributaries. The two dumplings in Tudor's soup looked like the brains of a giant mutant pigeon. His appetite vanished.

When his dad went for his post-lunch nap, Tudor returned to his room and put on his new favorite album, Pantera's *Vulgar Display of Power*. While putting his schoolbooks in his backpack, he remembered he didn't do any homework.

His heart sank.

I'll tell them my grandma had a stroke and had to be taken to Bucharest.

He rehearsed the excuse in his head: "I'm sorry, Mr. Stan,

but my grandma suffered a terrible stroke, and we had to take her to emergency and then to Bucharest. She's paralyzed. My family is devastated."

Tudor thought the excuse might work if he looked heartbroken and confused. He wouldn't go as far as other students did, eating a piece of chalk to look pale and sickly. But at least he could look sad and vulnerable.

At half-past one, Tudor changed into his school outfit: tight blue jeans, Napalm Death t-shirt, and black leather boots.

The shortest way to the high school was through a nearby neighborhood. The buildings here were older than the ones on Tudor's block. Built before the revolution, their flat roofs suggested a mass of grey, weathered cubes. Ceausescu's urbanization hadn't achieved much, except, as Tudor's dad used to joke, raising the suicide rate. Rusted metal framed the windows. A few clotheslines dangled laundry in the afternoon air. The downspouts leaked at the joints, leaving dark circles of damp on the cement walls. Hundreds of television antennas sprouted from the roofs like the rigid legs of upturned roaches.

Hands in his pockets, Tudor navigated the desolation, skirting packs of scavenging dogs. His mind turned to the usual, nagging questions that always popped into his mind on the way to school.

Why do I have to do this shit? Why do we need to go to school? Why doesn't any teacher explain why we should learn his stupid crap if we hate it and don't give a shit about it? What's the use of this torture?

Tudor's view was that he was going to school to meet his friends, Edi and Alex. He didn't care about anything else.

Walking past the soccer field, Tudor spotted Alex strutting toward the high school gates.

"Alex, wait up!" he shouted and accelerated to catch his friend.

Alex turned, smiled, and took a drag of his cigarette. He was wearing his usual denim vest, with its Slayer patch and

Chapter 1 The Bleeding Boredom

SS logo in parallel lightning bolts. The strap of his satchel divided his chest diagonally. Alex was burly but not fat. Bangs of straight blond hair framed his long face. He wore his hair long in front and shaved at the back. His blue eyes were cold and arrogant. A long, straight nose joined his tall forehead. He reminded Tudor of the Minotaur, half-man, half-bull.

"Hey man, can I bum a smoke?" Tudor asked as he neared his friend.

"Sure, bro." Alex produced a pack of smokes from his vest and handed one to Tudor.

"Danke Schön," Tudor said. He lit the cigarette, took a deep drag and fell into step beside Alex.

"How goes it, brother?" Alex asked.

"Good, good. I hung out with George again today." Tudor told Alex about the broken tomb George saw in the cemetery and how the Rude Pig had slaughtered a dozen or so pigeons for their blood.

"Oh, brother! George is fucking nuts," Alex said. He flicked away his cigarette butt and stomped it out. "But it's good having a servant doing the dirty work for you." Alex grinned at Tudor, displaying a set of yellow teeth.

Tudor smiled back. "Anyway, we were thinking of going to the cemetery tomorrow evening and using the blood to desecrate the chapel and some graves. Wanna come?"

"Sure, bud. After class?"

"Yep. And George said he's gonna bring some wine and his tape player," Tudor added, feeling another wave of excitement.

"Cool," Alex said. "I'll bring some music. We should tell Edi about it too."

"You bet," Tudor said.

As they rounded the corner toward the students' entrance, Tudor remembered another episode with crazy George. And Alex loved stories about Piggy.

"Oh, man, speaking of George being nuts, did I tell you about the time we pissed on those girls?"

Intrigued, Alex grinned and shook his head.

"Oh, brother, Piggy does *everything* I ask him. Once we were playing soccer on our block, and some girls came and started playing volleyball in the corner of the court. They kept giggling and looking at us, begging for some attention. I told George, 'Man, these girls are so disgusting; I want to piss on their stupid, ugly faces.' It just happened he was drinking a Coke. Next thing I know, he gulps it down, turns his back to the girls, pulls his dick out, and starts pissing in the bottle."

"Oh no," Alex said. "Don't tell me!"

"Oh, but I will. He filled the bottle with piss. Some dripped onto his hand, but he didn't care. And then, hiding the bottle behind his back, he went up to the girls. At first they stopped their game and smiled at us. They started laughing when George doused them with the yellow liquid, probably thinking it was orange juice. But then they somehow figured it out. Maybe because it was in a Coke bottle. They started running and screaming. One of them wiped out and skinned her knee. She was bawling. I think she got some piss in her mouth. George emptied the bottle onto her head."

"Oh, my fucking God!" Alex exclaimed. "Then what happened?"

"Fuck man, we had to tail it. We ran up to his apartment. Good thing his dad wasn't home. Then we watched from his balcony, crouched down so no one could spot us. Some of the girls' parents came out and asked what was going on. One of them came and knocked on George's door, but who's dumb enough to answer? The phone rang a few times, but we kept sitting on the balcony, laughing our asses off. Nothing really came of it; after a few days it was all forgotten."

"Oh God, how I love George. Such a sick fuck," Alex said.

"Yes, I think he's gotten more out of control since his mom died."

"No kidding," Alex concurred and lit another cigarette.

While Tudor was telling the story more students gathered in front of the entrance. Must have been around two hundred. Each class had its own row. They had to enter the building in

Chapter 1 The Bleeding Boredom

an ordered fashion, as a teacher pointed to each row in turn.

Tudor and Alex lingered away from the crowd, waiting to see when their classmates would enter. They stopped close to the gym doors, their usual smoking place, out of sight of their teachers, even though most of the staff knew of their unhealthy habit and even joked about it.

Tudor scanned the crowd for Edi but didn't spot him. He was usually late.

Tudor needed to copy the math homework as soon as possible. At least one or two exercises, to save face.

Turning to Alex, Tudor asked, "So what did you do today? Did you do your math homework?"

Alex released a jet of cigarette smoke through his nostrils and shook his head. "He tested me last week, remember? He won't test me again this week."

"Oh, right. So what did you do all morning?"

"Just reading. I've found some cool stuff in Cioran I wanna show you."

"Neat."

"I want to be the new Anti-Christ, that's why I study satanic thinkers," Alex said through a yellow grin.

"Christians to the lions, that's what I say," Tudor answered with a smile.

"Damn straight, brother! Did you know Cioran got a scholarship to study in Germany in the '30s, right around the time Hitler came to power? Apparently, he loved Hitler."

Tudor shook his head. He was curious about how esteem for Nazism fit with Cioran's nihilism, but didn't care enough to ask.

"When he came back from Germany, he joined Zelea Codreanu's fascist movement. You know, The Iron Guard?"

"Right," Tudor answered, hoping that Alex wouldn't start lecturing. Once he got going, he was impossible to stop. He took the last drag from his cigarette and stomped it out.

He looked again for Edi.

He spotted him this time.

Edi smiled feebly at Tudor and Alex as he slowly approached. Short and skinny, wearing his Iron Maiden t-shirt, black jeans, and white sneakers, he looked pale and exhausted under the burden of his backpack. Blue eyes magnified by thick lenses in rectangular frames peered out from under his unruly blond bangs.

As Edi closed the distance between them, Tudor asked, "Hey, man, did you do the math homework?"

"Sure, it was easy."

Tudor hated him for saying that. *Fucking nerd*, he thought to himself. Then started to ask, "Can I copy—"

"Our row is moving," Alex pointed out and crushed his cigarette.

"Shit," Tudor sputtered.

"Tudor, I'll give it to you inside," Edi tried to pacify his friend.

Tudor nodded grumpily.

Students sat two to a desk. Tudor, however, mostly sat by himself at the back of the class, with Edi and Alex just ahead. During math and physics though, Edi would strategically move next to Tudor to help him in case the teacher decided on a pop quiz. They would call Adrian, a six-foot-five giant, to sit with Alex, so that, shielded from the teacher's eyes, Tudor could cheat at will.

That was how Tudor progressed to ninth grade without doing much work.

Tudor's desk was personalized. Frequently, in moments of bitter boredom, he would write band names or draw skeleton monsters and occultist symbols on its top. A few days earlier, Tudor had found a note taped to the desk. It was from the high school student who used the same spot in the morning: "Can you please stop destroying this desk? The desk isn't yours. Other people use it. It's public property. Thanks in advance, Cornel."

Tudor had thought long and hard before adding his reply to the same slip of paper:

Chapter 1 The Bleeding Boredom

"You're <u>nothing</u> compared to ME!!!
Fuck you in advance,
ANGEL OF DEATH."

The reply made Tudor proud. It also reduced Cornel to silence.

Tudor hurried for his desk, sat down, took out his math notebook and snatched Edi's homework. He copied mechanically. Edi's writing was small and elegant; his was rushed, ugly, and barely legible.

He scrawled for a frenzied minute, completing the first two exercises. Then dropped his pen. "That must be enough for a minimum pass. God help me!"

Alex grinned. "You mean *Satan* help me!"

Tudor laughed nervously. "Whatever, I just don't want to face Mr. Stan today."

"But you never do your homework, so you never want to face him," Edi pointed out with a smirk.

Tudor shrugged. "Why should *I* do the homework when you do it for me. Just make sure you come earlier next time." Tudor delivered a solid shot to Edi's arm.

"Lazy ass," Edi murmured.

Alex turned around and set before them a page covered in a smoothly rounded, almost calligraphic script. Tudor recognized a list of quotes from Cioran. The first one read:

"Only the mediocre want to die of old age. Suffer, then, drink pleasure to its last dregs, cry or laugh, scream in despair or with joy, sing about death or love, for nothing will endure! Morality can only make life a long series of missed opportunities."

"So, we need to drink and sing in the cemetery tomorrow," Tudor concluded. "Are you coming, Edi?"

"When, after school?"

"Yep, Rude Pig will get some wine and his player."

"That sounds good!" Edi said. Then, staring at the floor, he added softly, "I'll need to make up an excuse for my dad, though."

Tudor and Alex nodded, aware of Mr. Manea's abusive

behavior.

"We'll think of something," Alex assured Edi.

Looking back at the first quote, Edi remarked, "Christian morality is stupid anyway. It's just about controlling people, making them fear God and his stupid commandments."

Alex sat on top of his desk and began playing with his pen, throwing it up in the air and catching it, like a knife. "That's right, brother. Christianity is the institution of slaves. And slaves can only lead through fear."

Edi quickly deduced the consequences of Alex's assertion. "Then their God must be a slave too. Because they're all afraid of him."

"Exactly," Alex concurred. "Slaves can only invent a weak and sick God."

Tudor couldn't agree more, but his attention was drawn to the last sentence.

Morality can only make life a long series of missed opportunities.

The idea of a failed life, a life in which you don't do what you want, disturbed him deeply. The warning implicit in Cioran's words caught like a hook in his brain, a painful question mark.

What should I do to not to miss out on life? Not to regret anything? Should I do something other than attending this dumb class? If I die tomorrow, will I regret wasting my time in school? What else is there?

The image of a helpless old man on his deathbed, regretting his life and choices, filled Tudor with dread.

"What if—"

This time he was interrupted by Mr. Stan's entrance. A gasp of horror escaped the students, but they stood and proffered the expected greeting: "Good day, sir."

"Sit down!" Mr. Stan bellowed. He placed the big, brown class roster on his desk and sat down. Mr. Stan was around sixty, bald on top, with short, grey hair on the sides. He always wore a grey suit. Cold, green eyes measured the class

Chapter 1 The Bleeding Boredom

from behind horn-rimmed glasses.

"Anyone missing today?" he asked.

Adrian, the giant fatso in the first row, stood up and looked around anxiously. Someone whispered, "Vasile."

"Gigi Vasile," Adrian said in a strangled voice and sat down.

Mr. Stan noted the absence and then started leafing through the roster. The students gasped again as a wave of terror hit them. The fact that Mr. Stan didn't close the roster meant only one thing: some of them would have to go to the board and solve problems. That torture usually lasted half an hour, after which, hopefully, Mr. Stan would start teaching new material.

The teacher flipped the pages backward from the letter "V." He scanned the names carefully with his large frog eyes. "N" for Negur and "M" for Manea were toward the middle. "Alex Antonescu" was atop the first page.

As Mr. Stan neared the middle of the book, Tudor began praying.

No God, not today, please! I swear I'll take notes this time and do my homework! I promise, God!

"Let the following student come to the board..." Mr. Stan's deep voice began.

After a few tense seconds, he decided: "Miss Alina Popovici."

The relieved class emitted a collective sigh. A skinny brown-haired girl stood up, snatched her notebook and report card, walked briskly to the front of the room and placed them on Mr. Stan's desk. Then she went to the board and grabbed a piece of chalk.

Mr. Stan stated the problem, what was given and what was to be proven. As Alina drew the required diagram, Tudor recognized the exercise he had briefly thought about that morning before he neglected his homework to watch Piggy mutilate a flock of pigeons.

Prove that the opposite sides of equal angles in a triangle

are congruent.

Alina stepped back and looked at the neatly drawn triangle.

"We draw a vertical line bisecting angle A," she announced before precisely drawing the indicated line.

Everyone copied the geometrical revelation into their notebooks. Tudor looked around with wide, incredulous eyes. Frustrated, he asked Edi, "Why the fuck should you draw that line?"

A few frowning faces turned in his direction.

Edi shushed him.

Tudor shut up and focused on Alina again. He noticed the round buttocks flexing under her red jeans as she wrote on the board. Oh, that ass wasn't bad! How come he didn't notice it before? True, she had tiny tits, but that ass looked round, springy and somehow...*proud*. It dared you to smack and bang it.

Suddenly inspired, Tudor ripped a page from his notebook and started drawing Alina naked, bent over, a muscular beast humping her. As a large phallus penetrated deep in her ass, Alina screamed in pain. Tudor titled the piece, "Breaking and Entering Through Alina's Back Door."

Tudor passed his creation to Edi, who bit his lip to stifle a laugh.

Edi patted Alex on the shoulder and handed him the drawing. Alex grinned and looked at Tudor inquiringly.

"Look at her ass. It's mighty doable," Tudor whispered.

Alex stretched his neck for a better view of Alina's behind. He nodded toward Tudor. "We should ask her whether she puts out."

"Naw, she seems uptight," Edi whispered.

"Maybe if we get her drunk..." Alex speculated.

Alex was more experienced with the ladies than his friends were. He claimed he'd lost his virginity to a slutty girl at a rock festival in Brasov. Apparently, he took her back to a hotel room and fucked her in every way, not stopping until he got bored.

Chapter 1 The Bleeding Boredom

He'd been so drunk he almost puked on her too. According to Alex's story, the hotel room belonged to Carpathian Bloodlust, one of the bands playing at the show, and the girl was one of their groupies. Alex hadn't needed a hotel room since his aunt lived in Brasov. But on that night of debauchery, he'd passed out in a hotel bed and only staggered back to his aunt's place the next day.

As the three ninth-graders were considering how to get into her pants, Alina finished the exercise and solved another one. The last one involved the Pythagorean theorem. Writing out the proof was a lengthy procedure, which left ample time for ogling and reduced the chance that Tudor would be summoned to the board.

After Alina solved the problem correctly, she answered a few theoretical questions. Her grade was nine out of ten. Mr. Stan wrote down the excellent score in the class roster and the student's report card. Smiling and blushing, Alina got her notebook and card, and went back to her desk.

To everyone's renewed horror, Mr. Stan started leafing through the roster again. Another poor soul was up for torture. This time he beckoned Livia Dumitru. Slow, shaking legs carried the girl to the front of the class. She had a vacant face and the body of a rugby player. Somehow she already resembled a middle-aged mother. Her tits sagged and her body hunched over in tired defeat.

She trudged to the teacher's desk and whispered something to Mr. Stan. The teacher directed her to the board where she went and wiped off the writing with an eraser. Then she grabbed a piece of chalk.

Addressing the class, Mr. Stan said, "Miss Dumitru says she didn't have time to do her homework because her brother got really sick and she needed to go with him to the emergency." Turning to Livia, he asked, "Is that so, miss?"

"Yes, sir," Livia answered in a low, husky voice.

Some of the students chuckled and elbowed each other.

From her posture—head down, large arms hanging limply

beside her bulky body—you could have guessed she was already resigned to her brother's tragic death.

"Well, then," Mr. Stan said, "I'll just ask you a few basic questions. What does the Pythagorean theorem tell us, Ms. Dumitru?"

Livia frowned and stared at the floor as if she knew the answer but suddenly forgot it.

After a few seconds, Mr. Stan added, "Ms. Dumitru...this theorem, Pythagoras', what type of triangle is it about?"

Livia responded by drawing a trembling line on the board, but she quickly fell back into deep reflection, hand under her double chin.

"What's that you're trying to draw, Ms. Dumitru?" Mr. Stan sadistically smiled at the rest of the class.

A chorus of laughter erupted.

Livia quickly erased the line with a sponge.

Tudor smiled feebly, trying to remember the types of triangles.

Right triangle, he thought, unsure of himself, *the one with the hypotenuse.*

Livia fixated on the floor. She knew what was happening to her wasn't right. It was the stuff of her nightmares.

Tudor joined the general laughter. He was pretty sure he knew what a triangle was.

Mr. Stan shook his head. "Silence is also an answer, Ms. Dumitru. Go back to your desk! Your grade for today is three!"

Red-faced and teary-eyed, Livia grabbed her notebook and report card and plodded back to her desk.

After she sat down, Edi asked her, "Hey Livia, that's your I.Q. score, right? Three?" He and Tudor snickered. Livia looked at them and managed to smile sadly as tears spilled down her round cheeks.

She doesn't even know when she's made fun of, Tudor thought.

Then Edi whispered to him, "These people ought to be killed! They use up our air for no good reason. And next thing

Chapter 1 The Bleeding Boredom

you know, they have a bunch of kids, each one more retarded than the last."

Tudor nodded his agreement, but he knew he wouldn't have done much better than Livia did.

As Mr. Stan finally closed the class roster, the class exhaled its relief. No more students called to the board, no more pain. The teacher stood up and began lecturing about parallelograms. Tudor tried his best to follow the lecture and take notes, but it all sounded like stupid gibberish. He started craving a smoke. When the bell rang at the end of class, Tudor asked Alex for another cigarette. Alex nodded and motioned that they should go outside. Tudor rushed to stow his math books in his pack.

That's when he heard a strange voice.

"Hey, are you the Angel of Death?"

Tudor saw an index finger pointing at a pentagram scratched on his desk. He looked up at an unfamiliar face. The stranger was taller and bigger than his classmates. He had crew-cut blonde hair and blue eyes. He looked pissed off.

"Yes," Tudor answered, rising. His mind kicked into high gear. *This is Cornel, the guy sharing my desk. He came to beat me up. He came by himself thinking the self-proclaimed "Angel of Death" must be some wimpy nerd. He came to kick my ass and teach me a lesson.*

Tudor gauged that he was almost as tall as Cornel, but skinnier. He noticed others turning their attention toward the newcomer.

Still pointing toward the desk, Cornel demanded, "Haven't I told you not to write on this? You think this is *yours*? Your parents bought it for you?"

Cornel shoved Tudor against the wall. Adrenaline surged through Tudor's body. Flight wasn't an option. He always chose to fight. He knew instinctively that Cornel would kick with his right foot. And he knew his adversary would end up on the floor. As the kick landed on his hip, Tudor snatched Cornel's ankle and, in one smooth motion, swept his assailant's left leg. It was a move Tudor had practiced over and over in his karate classes in middle school. Falling to the floor, Cornel flailed desperately for a purchase on Tudor's t-shirt that would let him pull his adversary down with him. Tudor punched him in the face. Stunned, Cornel let go of the shirt and crashed heavily to the floor.

Cornel bounced up quickly, reeling on shaky legs, and grabbed the edge of the desk to steady himself. Blood fell from his mangled nose onto its surface and the floor. Red rivulets spread over the blue inscriptions on the desk. He looked at Tudor with hateful, fiery eyes. But under that hate, Tudor detected fear, doubt, and the seed of panic.

Without waiting for his adversary to charge, Tudor jumped. He surged higher than he intended, despite his heavy boots. For a moment he floated above everyone. His peripheral vision registered his classmates' amazed faces, including Alina's gaping mouth, and the bright windows and deep green of the trees outside. He faked with his left foot and then launched his right.

The bicycle kick was meant for the opponent's stomach, but, because he had jumped too high, Tudor's boot smashed into Cornel's solar plexus.

Cornel sprawled backward, bumping his way through a group of retreating onlookers before slamming his back into a desk and then the wooden floor. He again rose quickly, but this time he could only clutch at his heaving chest as he gulped for air. He looked wildly at Tudor, panic now in full bloom.

His bleeding nose still reddened his mouth and chin.

Holding his chest in defeat, Cornel staggered backward, scanning the crowd like a paranoiac who expects strikes from all sides.

Alex, having climbed onto his desk, loomed next to Tudor, ready to pounce on the intruder. Other boys also stood by Tudor's side.

Cornel pointed a threatening but shaky finger at Tudor.

Chapter 1 The Bleeding Boredom

"I'll come back to cut your throat, you fucking retard! I'll hack you to pieces!"

Tudor lurched forward in a pretended assault.

Cornel whirled and ran from the class, slamming the door shut.

The whole altercation lasted less than a minute, but it deeply impressed the onlookers. Tudor became an instant star. He'd been relatively popular already, but now he was *The Man*. Rappers, hip-hoppers, Depeche Mode fans, classmates who would otherwise scorn him for being a metalhead, now came to pat his shoulder and tell him he was cool. Alex and Edi were bursting with pride over their friend's display of power. Even girls started watching him curiously and occasionally smiling at him. For the rest of that day, Tudor felt like he was floating inside a bubble of happiness. Everything he did and said was rad. Nothing could dampen his exhilaration.

Everyone commented on the fight, analyzing it from every angle. The consensus was that Tudor could easily have killed his opponent but nobly spared his life. The heavy-booted strike to the solar plexus bore potentially lethal force, but Tudor showed merciful restraint. Everyone agreed Cornel must be in the hospital by now.

The guys gathered around Tudor's desk suggested a variety of weapons, mainly knives and brass knuckles, that he should carry at all times. Many vowed to defend him if Cornel returned with a gang of reinforcements.

Tudor knew only a few of the boasters would stand by his side when the time came. Alex and Edi, for sure. But then again Edi didn't count in a fight.

The cowardice of idle boasters couldn't compete with his exhilaration though.

The feeling reminded him of the final game of the soccer tournament his team had won a year earlier. The stands had been full: teachers, girls, players' families. It was the perfect stage for Tudor to display his skills. He played beautifully, smoothly dribbling around the pitch as if his feet magnetized the ball. At one point, with Tudor's team on the attack, a defender headed the ball away, to the edge of the penalty area. The ball bounced high behind Tudor. He spun away from the goal and launched into the air. His heel connected perfectly and sent the ball on a screaming arc. Stunned by the acrobatics, the keeper reacted slowly, and the ball struck the crossbar and spun into the back of the net. Applause exploded from the spectators. Later, when Tudor scored from a bicycle kick, like his idol, Marco van Basten, he received a standing ovation. He elegantly jogged toward the center of the pitch and bowed to the crowd. After these displays of athleticism, Tudor's opponents regarded him with respect intermingled with envy and fear.

The game became a one-man show. An anticipatory buzz followed his every touch of the ball as crowd and defenders alike expected further stunts. In the closing minutes he gathered the ball in midfield and surged forward, chased closely by two adversaries. He saw the goal in the corner of his eye and unleashed a powerful strike with the outside of his right foot. Tudor felt like a giant controlling the entire pitch. Somehow, he was both inside and outside his body, both of average height and incredibly tall. From his lofty vantage, Tudor followed the trajectory of the ball and willed it into the top corner. Everyone, including the goalkeeper, thought the shot would veer wide, but at the last moment, it bent incredibly and found the net.

Tudor smiled at the happy memory of that magical soccer game.

He felt like a magician again, enchanting the world with his spells.

As a precaution against a possible counterattack from Cornel, Alex, Tudor and Edi stayed inside during the day's remaining breaks and only went for a smoke before English, their last class. After school, they left together, still wary of an offensive from Cornel and his gang.

It didn't happen.

Chapter 1 The Bleeding Boredom

Outside the school grounds, Alex took leave of Tudor and Edi and reminded them that their favorite radio show, Studio Rock, would air that night. Tudor irrationally feared that Cornel would jump him in the entrance hall of his apartment building. But, after saying farewell to Edi, he found the hallway empty. And, looking back, he saw no one following him inside.

He rushed up the stairs to his second floor apartment. In the living room, his parents were watching *Dallas*. Tudor glimpsed J. R.'s face on the screen. The Texan businessman took a sip of whiskey and smiled evilly.

"Hello, honey, how was your day?" Tudor's mom asked.

"Okay," Tudor muttered, shaking off his boots.

"Did you get any grades?"

"No."

"There's dinner in the kitchen. Steak and fries, your favorite."

"Okay," Tudor muttered again as he reached his bedroom. After changing, he went to have supper. Then, back in his bedroom, he closed the door and checked the jar of blood under his bed. It was still in its place, next to his porn stash. He smiled in anticipation of the blasphemous scheme planned for tomorrow. Just one more day of school left before the weekend. One month left before summer vacation. With some luck, he would pass math and be free all summer. He couldn't wait.

He put on some Pantera and sank into his armchair, hands folded behind his head.

The brutal riffs of "Mouth for War" filled the room. Tudor relived the day's events, watching them unfold like a movie, first fast and then slower, as his body began to relax.

He focused on a mental picture of Cornel. The fear in his eyes as he fell to the floor. The desperate way he grasped Tudor's t-shirt, almost ripping it. His bloody nose, the way it reddened his mouth and dripped onto the scratched desk. The blood sliding over the blue inscriptions.

An homage to Satan, Tudor thought. *Desk turned into an*

altar of sacrifice.

The steady march of the song "Walk" briefly awakened him from his reverie. Enraptured by the violent energy of the chorus, he sang along:

Re-spect, walk!/
What did you say?/
Re-spect, walk!/
Are you talking to me?/
No way punk/
Walk on home boy!

Tudor agreed with the song's message. Your inferiors should show you respect, not stab you in the back. Either respect or get lost.

Today, Tudor knew he had earned everyone's respect.

He imagined talking to Cornel.

"Get lost, you slave! You're nothing compared to me. You live because I allow it, you worm. Now, get out of my sight!"

Tudor recalled the moment when he became certain he was stronger than Cornel. He focused on the weakness in his adversary's eyes. He imagined stepping on them with the threaded sole of his boots. The rough heel flattening Cornel's nose and the defeated student accepting humiliation with perfect obedience.

Alive, yet a corpse.

Tudor rewound the tape and played the song again.

Re-spect, walk!/
Re-spect, walk!

As the powerful rhythm of the song injected into his bloodstream, Tudor entered a trance.

A wave of bright, yellow energy washed over him, and he felt himself rising. He was outside, floating high up over Main Street. He could see the rooftops of the buildings in the city.

Chapter 1 The Bleeding Boredom

The power emanating from his body lit up the town. His visual field was his killing field. When he looked down at the traffic beneath him, the cars collided with each other and swerved into the trees lining the streets. The injured people crawling from the automobile wreckage ignited and flailed wildly in their death throes. The sounds of crashes and screams and explosions drew residents out into the street. When they saw him the men fell to their knees. Women exposed themselves. Possessed by some irresistible instinct, they undressed and bent over, their wet genitals glistening in the light of the fires. A more courageous man tried to throw a stone at him, but the rock exploded like a grenade in the man's hand. Blood and pieces of meat showered the cowering wretches who survived the blast.

In a deep behemoth's voice that shook buildings with earthquake force, Tudor roared, "I dominate! Get out of my way or be destroyed. This is my dominion!"

Tudor felt so powerful, he didn't even have to act.

Willing alone realized his designs.

The crowd bowed to him even as he looked beyond them. They worshiped him because they knew, deep down, they were worthless and disgusting, and his loathing gave them meaning and purpose.

But Tudor felt like a member of a different species, with no time to waste on inferior organisms. He could neither feed on them nor fuck them. He was like the lion that disdains a tangled mass of worms.

Tudor loathed the weaklings who lived as if something mattered and wanted them gone from the face of the earth. Eradicated. The world should be freed from abominations who lived like rats trapped in the maze of the city. Driving, busily running in and out of buildings, counting money, buying and selling, jogging, dieting, raising kids and worrying about them, dutifully waiting for pensions and planning funerals. Doing the same things over and over, caught in a vicious circle of reeking monotony.

Tudor imagined stomping them, hacking them to pieces, exploding them, pissing on them, like a kid playing with dusty, broken mannequins in an abandoned warehouse.

Maybe then, in the grips of torture, they'd see how ridiculous they were.

If they still had eyes to see, that is, Tudor thought and smiled. *If I don't tear out their eyes and cum into their tired brains.*

Tudor's vision gradually receded and he felt his mind return to the confines of his physical body. He further contemplated the idea of fucking a woman's eye socket. One of her dislocated eyeballs hung down and brushed his ballsack as he thrust deeply into her head. The other eye looked up at him, begging for mercy. Her throat produced only inarticulate grunts since her broken jaw adorned her chest like a necklace. The dance of her tongue tasted the air, seeking solid ground where his violence left only absence. Tudor opened his eyes and looked at his crotch.

His rigid penis pulsated in his shorts.

He reached for his porn stash.

Chapter 2
Alex's Open Eye

Alex opened his bedroom window, lit up a cigarette, and rested his elbows on the window sill.

Tonight was Studio Rock night. The radio show would start in an hour, at ten.

He looked forward to listening to metal and learning about new releases while getting hammered. The fact that they had no math tomorrow made things even sweeter.

No Mr. Stan!

No Mr. Fucking Stan!

Alex's apartment was on the main level and he could closely follow the activity on his block. The view wasn't perfect, because of the trees in the building's yard and the chain-link fence around it. But Alex could see the Galaxy shop across the street, and its proud owner, Mr. Tache.

Mr. Tache was chatting with two guys out front, while Magda busied herself with the till inside. Short, fat, and bold, Mr. Tache wore his sunglasses. He was a poker player and, running a business, he never tired of saying, was a lot like playing poker. Sunglasses helped his bluff. His tight red Nike t-shirt barely covered the navel of his bulging belly. Left hand deep in the pocket of his tight blue jeans, Mr. Tache used his right hand to gesticulate broadly as he spoke.

Now, Alex noticed, the businessman was pointing toward his new car, a dark blue Audi parked on Alex's side of the street, right in front of the chain-link fence. The car keys hung from Tache's index finger. The West European car was something to brag about in a country where many people still drove horse-drawn carts or Russian Volgas and Ladas.

One of Tache's interlocutors, a young gypsy, crossed the street and peered inside the car. "The boss is right, it's all automatic," he shouted back over his shoulder. Tache nodded, beaming with smug pride. The gypsy crossed again and resumed listening to Tache's expostulations.

Alex hated Mr. Tache. He wanted him dead.

He remembered how the man had been a nobody before the revolution. Alex used to play with Tache's son, Florin, and had been to their apartment a few times. Alex had noticed that Florin's parents were poorer than his own. Didn't even have a color TV or record player.

After the revolution, Tache jumped on the entrepreneurial bandwagon and opened Galaxy to sell blue jeans, Coca-Cola, and the latest must-have American imports. The corrugated iron shack was a big hit. Under the influence of shows like *Dallas,* Romanians thought that under capitalism they *had* to wear blue jeans like the American ranchers. After lining up for hours, customers had to use the bushes behind the shack as a fitting room.

That's how Tache became a somebody overnight. At first, he and his wife were the only staff. When business picked up, he hired Magda, an attractive fresh high school graduate, and an older woman with retail experience. A few months later, Tache divorced his wife and shacked up with Magda in the new apartment he bought. All the men on the block looked at him with deep respect mixed with bitter envy.

Chapter 2 Alex's Open Eye

Now he was showing off his brand new car.

Alex exhaled cigarette smoke through pursed lips and spat on the ground.

He turkey fucked a new cigarette into life, smashed the filter of the old one on the window sill and tossed it outside.

He forced his mind away from the infuriating Mr. Tache

Instead, his thoughts turned to his obsession: Romania's destiny. Alex found inspiration in Romania's past: Decebal, Vlad Tepes, Stefan the Great, Corneliu Zelea Codreanu, a.k.a. "The Captain," Marshal Ion Antonescu, whose surname Alex proudly bore.

"Alex Antonescu." A name meant for the history books.

But, Alex thought, after the Second World War, Romania had deteriorated. The proud fascist leaders of the '20s and '30s, Zelea Codreanu and Horia Sima, had envisioned joining Hitler in the sacred war against the Bolshevik plague. But then, during the invasion of Russia, things went terribly wrong, especially in the battles of Moscow and Stalingrad.

Every time Alex thought about the Führer's defeat he felt like crying.

After the war, Romania was trapped in the Soviet nightmare of humiliation and degradation that culminated in the dictatorship of Nicolae Ceausescu, the butcher of his nation's soul.

In 1989 Romanians took to the streets, defying Ceausescu's regime. Many were massacred, a blood sacrifice for freedom. In the end, revolutionaries seized and killed the dictator and his horrible wife.

And what did they get in return? Alex asked himself bitterly.

They had deposed the socialist Jew only to meet his capitalist twin, the merchant Jew. Romania opened for business in the world market, and the American capitalist worm wriggled inside her.

That's how Tache had become a hero.

Trying to swallow a lump in his throat, Alex remembered

the words of his idiotic history teacher, Mr. Ion: "In capitalism, *everything* is for sale."

Alex cringed. The teacher should have been dismissed for spewing such traitorous nonsense.

Alex firmly believed that both communism and capitalism must be eradicated and Europe had to be returned to its rightful leaders: the Aryan race. Other races, whether Slavs, Gypsies, or Blacks, were to become slaves. Either that or be exterminated.

In the youth's view, Germany and the Northern Countries were waking from centuries of slumber and Romania had to join the Aryans or be destroyed in their brutal war of revenge. Alex thought of himself as the representative of the Aryans in Eastern Europe. His life's mission was to raise the racial consciousness of Romanians, to remind them of the foremost commandment from the God of nations: protect the survival of the Aryan race by enslaving or decimating the inferior races, the physically and morally ugly, the mentally ill, the handicapped, the mercantile Jews.

Unlike his classmates, Alex had definite plans for his future. He wanted to get into the Theoretical High School and to qualify for the National History Olympiad and, in senior year, the International Philosophy Olympiad. He also needed to master English and German. Then go to the University of Bucharest to study political science and form a radical right-wing political party. He wasn't sure of the name yet but "Land and Blood" tripped nicely from his tongue. Once his fascist party gained power, it would purge the nation's tired body of all foreign parasites and effect Romania's transfiguration.

Besides being a prodigy, Alex had no doubt he was a natural born leader, like his idol, Adolf Hitler. People obeyed him instinctively. Even his parents submitted to his will. They knew he was already a smoker and a drinker but never protested. The teachers loved and respected him. His classmates strove to please him. He had always felt that he radiated magnetic energy, just like the golden halo around

Chapter 2 Alex's Open Eye

the heads of saints. This meant only one thing: he was one of the chosen.

Like the Führer, Alex had a talent for oratory, a skill he wanted to cultivate during his political career. Once, when Mr. Ion had begun lecturing on Nazi Germany's war in the East, Alex, tired of the teacher's mistakes and omissions, jumped from his desk, snatched the pointer from the teacher's hands and went to the map at the head of the class. Humiliated, the young teacher sat at his desk and listened to his student. Alex lectured for a whole hour, making his classmates *see* and *feel* the battles. They listened transfixed. During that hour Alex was all-powerful. He felt as if he had hypnotized the class and they would do whatever he wanted. Kill, rape, torture. With brutal savagery.

Alex knew his best friends, Tudor and Edi, were just followers. Tudor would assume leadership from time to time but was uncomfortable doing so. He was born to follow. Alex knew of Tudor's raw power, having witnessed him destroy Cornel. But that power needed to be channeled by a true leader.

A natural ruler, Alex thought, needed to choose his acolytes carefully. If they proved faithful and competent, they were to be promoted and encouraged. If otherwise, brutally punished or mercilessly rejected. Maybe in ten years or so, Alex reflected, if they displayed enough strength and spirit of sacrifice, Tudor and Edi would lead two nests of "Land and Blood."

"Land and Blood," Alex murmured to himself, staring at the green yard outside his bedroom window.

The Blood was essential. It was about the Aryan blood pumping through Alex's veins. He was blond, with blue eyes and an elongated skull. He was already 5'7, as tall as Heinrich Himmler, Reichsführer of the SS. On his mom's side, his roots were in Brasov, a German settlement in Transylvania.

In Romanian Lit. they had learned about Mihail Sadoveanu, who claimed to hear the voices of his ancestors, unknown heroes and warriors, whispering their stories to him. Alex felt the same way. His Germanic ancestors were alive in his blood.

The language of blood transcended space and time. Alex had received the call in sixth grade. The caller was none other than Vlad Tepes, a.k.a. Dracula. It happened during summer camp at Sinaia, deep in the Carpathian Mountains. The teachers had organized a day trip to Targoviste, the medieval capital of Wallachia, the southern part of Romania. Tudor and Edi didn't want to go, being more interested in the soccer tournament at the camp. At Targoviste, they visited the Chindia Tower, the only fortification remaining from Tepes' castle. Alex and the group climbed the spiral staircase to the second floor and looked through a narrow window at the courtyard below. While the guide explained that the courtyard had been Tepes' execution grounds, Alex's head exploded.

He was rocked by a flash of light deep within his brain. Alex looked out the window again and saw the courtyard filled with impaled victims. Some dead and decayed, some still twitching like pinned frogs. He felt trapped in someone else's body, unable to control his movements.

The eyes of his host scanned his surroundings and settled on two monks. The elder of the bearded, brown-robed monks was speaking, his bushy eyebrows furrowed in anger. Alex didn't understand the words, but it sounded like Latin. Abruptly, the monk stopped talking, and his eyes rolled back in his head. Blood gushed out of his mouth, spattering his beard and chest. As his white eyes bulged in terror, the sharp tip of a bloodied stake emerged from his mouth. Alex's host shook with bombastic laughter. His visual field reddened, becoming a window deluged with a rain of blood. The laughter stopped, and a deep voice intoned a warning:

The day of judgment shall come,
My rule in blood!

Chapter 2 Alex's Open Eye

That *blood* resounded with anger and thirst, causing Alex to envision the dark prince's full, red lips under a thick mustache. He remembered how, when dining among the impaled, Vlad Tepes would chase his food with his victim's blood instead of wine.

When Alex returned to his ordinary senses, he lay on the floor, surrounded by the worried faces of the guide and the other students.

In the following months, Alex thought long and hard about his experience and read voraciously about psychic and mystic visions. It all made sense when he found Mircea Eliade's description of initiation rites in archaic societies. Around puberty, novices were sent by themselves into the wilderness, where some, the chosen ones, were contacted by the spirits of their ancestors. The spirits imparted wisdom and sacred knowledge. The more powerful novices experienced more profound visions, which sometimes shook their minds to the brink of insanity.

Since the sixth grade, Alex had regularly seen visions, usually of scenes from the history books he devoured. But school and the desolate, plain town of Tatareni didn't provide an environment for spiritual growth. He ached to escape into the wilds of the Carpathians, to find the deep roots of the Romanian nation. Now, he planned to visit his aunt in Brasov in the summer and to venture alone into the mountains for a week or so. He still needed to work out the details and find a way to hide his absence. But his mind was settled. He'd bring only bread, water, and hard liquor. He knew first-hand that alcohol facilitated entering ecstatic states by undermining the authority of the conscious mind and giving free rein to the unconscious, where the memory of the sacred lay hidden. He'd sleep in the woods, with no tent or other shelter, purifying his body and mind of the toxins of "civilization." As Eliade explained, the novice must become dead to the world. As a clean spirit craving enlightenment, Alex hoped to receive wisdom and guidance from ancient Romanian warriors and shamans, noble spirits disgusted by the degeneration of their race.

Now, with a few minutes remaining before Studio Rock, Alex thirsted for a stiff drink. He opened his bedroom door and listened. The hallway was dark and quiet. His parents must have gone to bed. The teen stepped through the darkness toward the kitchen. He flicked on the light, opened the fridge, and grabbed tomato juice and a lemon. From the cupboards, he produced an empty glass and a small pepper shaker. He placed the lemon into the empty glass.

Alex turned off the kitchen light and returned to his bedroom with the four items. He placed the ingredients on his desk and retrieved a bottle of vodka from under the bed. He filled half the glass with the liquor. Then, with a hunting knife he produced from the drawer of his desk, he cut the lemon in half and squeezed its juice into the vodka. After adding tomato juice and pepper, he took a sip.

Pleased, he drank deeply.

The liquor sent chills through his body. He released a satisfied sigh.

The Bloody Mary was his favorite drink; vodka for those who didn't want to get smashed right away.

Alex unwrapped a blank cassette, removed it from its plastic case, and inserted it into his boombox. He turned on the radio and selected the right frequency, 98.3 FM. Static ceded the airwaves to Leni's deep voice greeting the listeners. Alex pressed the *Play* and *Rec* buttons and the cassette started recording.

Alex sipped his Bloody Mary, reclined in his chair, and lit up a cigarette.

When Leni began talking about Rammstein, the German industrial metal band, Alex turned the volume to the maximum and ensured the player was recording.

The mention of his favorite band felt like an electric jolt, and the teen jumped from his chair and began pacing up and down the room.

Chapter 2 Alex's Open Eye

"Their shows are literally incendiary," Leni said. "The frontman, Till Lindemann, performs while on fire!"

Petre Malin, the co-host, added, "I bet our listeners are eager to hear about Rammstein's new album."

"Damn straight," Alex mumbled, his heart racing.

Papers rustled in the background. Then, Leni's voice: "Yes, indeed, *Sehnsucht*, their second studio album, was released last week and has already reached number one in Germany. It is selling better than their first release, *Herzeleid*, which itself was a stunning success."

"Here's the title track from the album," Malin announced. "Afterward we'll let you know how to order *Sehnsucht* through *Heavy Metal Magazine*."

Alex obsessively checked whether the tape was rolling and then struck his chest and thrust his hand outward, palm down. *Heil Hitler!*

The song started with a simple, eerie, melancholic keyboard melody. Then the musical panzer division exploded into a rhythmic frenzy. Alex banged his head wildly up and down, his blond hair lashing his face. His mind filled with black and white images of marching German soldiers accompanied by motorized divisions and *Stukas* that dominated the sky. Lindemann's deep, hypnotic voice blended into the martial music. His obsessive refrain—*Sehn-sucht/ Sehn-sucht*—was at once victorious and heartbreaking. After the chorus and the reprise of the wailing keyboard bit, the drums and guitar boomed back to life. Alex jumped onto the bed and launched himself into a flying knee. He hammered his thighs with his fists while banging his head.

When the song ended, there were beads of sweat on his forehead. Dizzied by the intensity of his musical rapture, he stumbled to his desk, sat, and emptied his glass. He pushed the bangs from his eyes and, with trembling hands, meticulously prepared another Bloody Mary. More vodka this time.

Ordering *Sehnsucht* was now Alex's first priority. Then

listening to it all day, learning the lyrics by heart, and singing along.

Buzzing from alcohol and anticipation, he took a deep drink and sat back in his chair.

Leni announced how *Sehnsucht* could be ordered by writing to *HMM*. The host also advertised new Rammstein merchandise for hardcore fans, as well as tickets for their show in Budapest. Unfortunately, the band wasn't scheduled to come to Romania. But dedicated fans could travel to Hungary for the opportunity to see their idols live. Now, after the fall of communism, Leni reminded his audience, no visa was required.

Alex considered going to Budapest for the show. He looked at the large map of Europe hanging on the wall above his desk and followed the path from Bucharest to Budapest. It led through the Carpathians. It would be a nice trip to make with Tudor and Edi, and they could stop at his aunt's place in Brasov, meet some of his metalhead friends there, and head for Budapest as a group. This was a golden opportunity to make friends with other neo-Nazis, although, as a Romanian nationalist, Alex hated Hungarians, a most inferior people. However, the youth realized bitterly, the concert was in late August, during the high school entrance exams. He couldn't miss those for anything.

Preparing another Bloody Mary, Alex thought he'd have plenty of opportunities to see Rammstein live. Maybe he could write to them, beg them to come to Bucharest. Write to them in German.

Petre Malin interrupted Alex's reverie with his top ten of black and death metal songs. The section featured brutal songs from Cannibal Corpse, Morbid Angel, Carcass, as well as the Swedish band Grave, whose song "Soulless" caught Alex's attention. Gorgoroth and Emperor represented Satanic Norwegian Black Metal.

In the middle of the Emperor song, Alex got up to flip the cassette and made a mental note to order their new album.

Chapter 2 Alex's Open Eye

As he grew more intoxicated, Alex found it increasingly difficult to keep track of all the bands and new album titles. Thankfully, he would be able to revisit the recording in the following days, when more lucid.

By the time the show ended at midnight, Alex was halfway through his vodka and seeing double. His blurred hand found the cassette with the Rammstein song and inserted it into the player.

He thumbed the *Play* button.

The quality of the recording was good.

He rewound the tape to the beginning of the song and pushed *Play* again. Now, the eerie keyboard melody impressed him more. The wailing expressed the pain of a nation. The cry of Germany, its Aryan spirit suffocated by Slavic waves of filth. The bass guitar pulsated evenly, like the heartbeat beneath the ruins of Berlin, the vital rhythm of the Nordic Man's battered soul.

The song slowly tightened its grip on Alex's mind, sending vibrations through every cell in his body. His fingers rewound the tape and pushed *Play* automatically.

Until they stopped.

Alex's body froze, like a robot that ran out of power. The song was imprinted in his brain, a code that would unlock the door to his unconscious. Alex opened the mental gate and staggered under the force of an icy gale. Clenching his teeth, he willed himself into the frozen landscape.

A blinding light exploded in his head.

His physical eyes rolled back. His mind's eye opened.

He was flying.

He was in an aircraft, piloting over snow-covered territory. Lucid and free from his physical body's intoxication, Alex looked through his host's eyes. The wind was blowing snow to powder, obscuring the land below, but during gaps in the blizzard, Alex could distinguish charred fragments of ruined houses, with only chimneys left standing. Here and there he spotted rusty skeletons of tanks, like carcasses of prehistoric giants.

Alex lifted his gaze to the horizon. Between columns of black smoke he recognized a structure: the massive Grain Elevator. The rectangular concrete building commanded the town's skyline. It stood like a decayed tooth, windows and walls smashed by artillery and *Stuka* attacks.

"I'm at Stalingrad!" he shouted in his mind.

But his enthusiasm was clouded by the sense of doom surrounding the place, its dark, heavy, suffocating ambiance. It was as if the tortured souls of the thousands of dead people coagulated into a plasma that covered the ruined city and devoured everything around it. Even the plane was unable to ascend over the clouds, seemingly trapped by the black aura of the industrial wasteland.

Fighting the gloom, Alex realized with excitement that German soldiers were on the ground below, hiding in trenches and dugouts.

"Germans, down!" he thought, trying to manipulate the hidden mechanism of his vision.

He willed himself down.

He hurtled through a tunnel of light and alit in a dugout. Despite the log-lined walls and fire crackling in the stove, the room was frozen. In flickering yellow lamplight, Alex discerned half a dozen bodies. The men were inert, and Alex was unsure whether they were alive, dying, or already dead. With scarves wrapped around their heads and their large dirty coats over their tunics, they resembled a group of old hags. Only the Nazi eagle emblem on some hats and helmets identified them as German soldiers.

Alex knew he must be inside the mind of a Nazi soldier, but his hosts' brain was devoid of thought. The young guest fought off sudden panic when he imagined getting trapped inside a soldier's dead body. But then his host moved his head and looked down at the comrade leaning against his legs. He shook him by the shoulder, sending the soldier's head lolling up and down. Alex's host rose and inspected his comrade.

Chapter 2 Alex's Open Eye

Alex saw a face disfigured by frostbite: black, lacerated nose and cheeks under sunken, vacant eyes; bloody, swollen lips twisted in a rigid grimace. A mass of lice crawled from the head of the unresponsive man onto the hand and wrist of Alex's host. The soldier shook his hand free of the parasites. At last Alex recorded a spark of brain activity: an image of winter boots. Alex's suddenly enlivened host dropped his comrade and pulled off the dead man's boots. He slowly stripped off the rags wrapping his feet. Alex looked through his host's eyes at a foot ravaged by winter. Only one crooked and black toe remained; the big one. The other piggies stayed home in the filthy rags. Or were eaten by mice. The foot reeked of rot.

The soldier's anguished scream catapulted Alex out of his mind.

Alex landed in a conference room. His new host was discussing strategy over a map spread on a large table. Hands moved in big sweeps over the chart dotted with swastika flags. The man looked up. A few Nazi generals came into view. Alex immediately recognized Friedrich Paulus, commander of the Sixth Army, and Franz Halder, Chief of the German Army General Staff.

Alex couldn't contain his excitement.

He had landed the big one. He was inside the Führer.

Afraid his joy might tear the thin fabric of his vision, Alex focused on the historical meeting unfolding before him. Paulus was explaining something, pointing at Stalingrad. Halder intervened and indicated the Caucasus. Alex felt the Führer's anger as he looked at the map and the city bearing the name of Stalin, his arch-enemy. Suddenly, ripples formed on the surface of the map, as though it had turned liquid. When he looked more carefully, Alex saw undulating snakes, their skin changing its pattern to reflect the chart below. The reptiles slithered rapidly from the Urals into eastern Russia and Poland, leaving bloody trails.

When he realized the snakes were moving toward Germany, Hitler panicked. His vision blurred and shook, stuttering like the image on a broken TV. The hands that moments before had swept grandly over the map now clenched into fists and smashed the camouflaged snakes. Blood jetted from the strikes and splattered on the paper. Red drops splashed the Führer's eyes, and he shut them reflexively. Trapped in the dark, Alex felt paralyzing venom pervade his host's body.

Afraid he'd be buried alive in Hitler's mind, Alex panicked and screamed.

He woke at his desk, drenched in sweat. For a few moments, his eyes rested on the map of Europe above the desk. He visualized the progress of the Red Army: Kyiv, Bucharest, Budapest, Vienna, Berlin.

How could this happen?

Alex broke down in tears and covered his face with his hands.

He wept convulsively, trying to catch his breath between sobs. "Fucking slaves! They were nothing! Less than nothing! The slaves of slaves! How could they beat the Führer?" he demanded through a curtain of tears and spittle.

After a while, the sobs diminished. Alex lit a cigarette, rose from the chair and sat on the edge of his bed. Dark thoughts filled his mind, the echoes of his nightmarish visions. He imagined Hitler spending the last months of the war in the *Führerbunker,* a shadow of his former self. He had a hump, Parkinson's disease, an ineradicable tremor in his left hand. His eyes were dull, and his skin had a greyish, mortuary complexion. He was nothing but a beaten dog in hiding. A scared and humiliated old dog. When he ventured outside the bunker, he looked like a ghost haunting the ruined city.

Alex clenched his teeth and his eyes teared up again when the next bitter thought came.

He knew the war was lost but couldn't understand why.

A cyanide pill and a bullet in the head wouldn't help his understanding. The old dog would die consumed by the fear that Stalin would find his body and hang it upside down in disgrace as they did with Mussolini.

Chapter 2 Alex's Open Eye

Alex started weeping again and the room blurred with his tears. "Berlin must burn!" he declared stridently. Then he took a long drag of his cigarette, clenched his left hand into a fist, and pressed the fiery tip into the pale skin of his forearm. The pain hit his numb brain, and he smelled burnt flesh.

"Burn, Berlin, burn!" he said through cigarette smoke. "You're not fit for life!"

In an agonized haze, Alex managed to crush the cigarette butt in the ashtray. Then he passed out on the bed, the darkness behind his closed eyes still lighted by flames.

A booming thunder woke him an hour later. He looked around with bloodshot, crusty eyes. He realized he had left the bedroom window open, and now rainwater wetted the curtains and the window sill. As he got out of bed, a jolt of pain from his left arm made him grimace. He closed the window, turned off the lights, and looked out into the rainy night. The neon yellow Galaxy sign warped and glimmered, refracted by the torrent. Lightning illuminated the grey apartment building across the street like artillery fire. The road was dark and deserted. The whole neighborhood slept.

Hopefully, it will swell the river and flood this fucking town.

He remembered the flood from the mid-'80s, when he was just a kid. The waters had drowned the gypsy slums in the valley, and the authorities had to build tall dikes on both sides of the Amara River. But on a night like this, the angry waters might break the dike and wash away the scum again.

A rainy night like this, Alex thought, was the perfect cover for a surprise attack. The lightning outside coincided with a flash in Alex's mind. The war wasn't over. He was a German soldier deep in enemy territory. Although Hitler was dead, he, Alex, was very much alive. And this wasn't Hitler's war; it wasn't the Great War or the Cold War. No, nothing like that! This was the primordial war between the majestic blond race and the inferior, resentful apes.

It was a spiritual war in the name of the cultural progress of humanity waged by its most evolved biological creation: the

Aryan Man.

Emboldened by the *rightness* of his sacred operation, Alex formulated his strategy in a split second. Possessed by a sense of invincibility, he disregarded all tactical obstacles.

He left his bedroom, walked to the front door, and slipped on his black high-top hiking shoes. From the hallway, he could hear his parents snoring in loud, regular unison. Back in his room, he opened his closet and grabbed a black hoodie and a black balaclava his parents had bought him when they'd gone skiing in Brasov. He also put on his pair of black gloves so he wouldn't leave any fingerprints. Together with his black sweatpants, the new ensemble would make him almost invisible against the dark night.

Then the teen grabbed his hunting knife, sheathed it, and put it in the large pocket of his hoodie. He stepped to the window and breathed a deep draft of fresh, humid air. The wet pavement glistened in the pale light of streetlamps. The paws of stray dogs on the asphalt punctuated the rain's drumbeat. *Probably on their way to the dumpster,* he thought. Another lightning strike split the horizon, but the delayed crack of thunder signaled that the storm was slowly moving away.

Alex jumped through the window into the small yard. The ground was muddy, so he shifted his weight onto his toes to avoid leaving footprints. He reached the short chain-link fence and scanned his surroundings. No one in sight. Mr. Tache's Audi was just beyond the fence, a glittering token of the triumph of slaves.

Alex wondered whether the car had an alarm system.

He squatted and fumbled for a stone. He lobbed the small rock over the fence, onto the car's hood. It ricocheted unceremoniously onto the pavement.

No alarm.

Relieved, Alex jumped the fence and crouched by the passenger door. His heart hammered in his chest, and his back was drenched by intermingled sweat and rain. After a few seconds, he brandished his knife and impaled the front tire.

Chapter 2 Alex's Open Eye

Air escaped the tire like the last exhalation of a euthanized beast, its usefulness exhausted after years under the yoke. The car slowly leaned forward. He repeated the procedure with the rear tire and then sidled to the other side. He was now visible to the street and the adjacent apartment building. Crouching in the lamplight, he impaled the two tires in quick succession and withdrew to the dark space between car and fence.

Still, no sound but the drumming of the rain. No footsteps, no movement.

Alex was soaked but ecstatic. He decided to add artistry to violence. He reversed his knife and engraved a swastika onto the hood of the car. The blade easily penetrated the dark paint. The emblem shone clearly in the Galaxy's neon light.

He sheathed his knife and put it in his pocket.

Overjoyed, he jumped back into the yard and crouched down behind a tree trunk. Still, no sound or movement, as if the constant raining lulled everyone into a deep sleep.

Alex looked at the Galaxy and the logos crowding its large front windows: *Coca-Cola, Pepsi, Levi's, Adidas.* The shelves were bursting with merchandise: on one side clothing, on the other food and drinks.

Suddenly, Alex felt the small shop was the pinnacle of perversity, the embodiment of everything he hated.

How he wished for a hand grenade! But, for now at least, smashing those windows was enough. Alex fumbled through the mud looking for a rock. He rejected one as too small for his task. Then he unearthed a stone the size of a brick and wiped away the mud adhering to its surface. Stretching his neck, he calculated the distance to the shop's window. Hefting the stone, he computed the force and trajectory of the throw. He scanned the missile's flight path for obstacles. Then, tensing all his muscles, he fired the stone high into the air. His breath caught in his lungs. A cacophony shattered the night as the Galaxy's window disintegrated into tiny shards that traced glinting arcs along their route to the shop floor. A moment of silence followed the commotion. Alex stood motionless behind the tree trunk. Although his heart pounded in his chest, he was smiling.

Shortly afterward, someone opened a window and shouted. "Who's there? I'll call the police!" the voice demanded from the building across the street. Alex saw windows light up and shadows move behind curtains. The crowns of the trees hid him from the residents of his building. He crept slowly toward his window. He grabbed the sill and dragged himself up. After he jumped back inside he carefully closed the window.

Mission accomplished!

Quietly, he stowed his gear in the closet, lay down in his bed, and folded his hands on his chest, a huge grin splitting his face.

I did it! I fucking did it! Mr. Tache will shit his pants!

Shortly afterward, Alex heard police sirens and people talking outside. Dim red and blue lights played on the rain-splashed window and on the ceiling.

Soon, Alex fell asleep, his lips curled into a smile.

There were no more nightmares.

Chapter 3
Ave Satanas!

A blind beggar greeted the four youths at the entrance to the cemetery.

"Good-evenin', sirs."

The beggar was swaying on his feet like a penguin, his head jerking from side to side with the rhythm of his body.

As the kids got closer, Tudor saw that his eyes were yellowish-white, like spoiled milk. *That's why they should wear black glasses*, he thought to himself.

George asked the beggar, "Nicule, where's your girlfriend?"

"Good-evenin', sirs," the beggar repeated mechanically. "Got some spare change?"

George stepped toward him and shouted, "Are you fucking deaf? Where's your girlfriend?"

The beggar heard this time. He stopped swaying and grinned lasciviously, displaying a set of ruined teeth.

George laughed and turned to the others, "Nicu got himself a willing pussy."

"Pussy, pussy," Nicu repeated, licking his lips.

Alex, Edi, and Tudor stared at him with incredulous disgust. Nicu was unshaven, short, and fat. He wore a winter hat with ear flaps and a long coat in the warm summer weather. He was ugly and he reeked.

Tudor stepped backward, gaining space between himself and the repulsive beggar. "Oh, my God, even this leper gets pussy and we don't."

The others laughed and resumed their stroll down the walkway that wound through the middle of the cemetery.

"Beggars make serious money, man," George said. "And Nicu has his own place."

"What place?" Edi asked.

"Near the church by our school."

"He screws his girlfriend inside the church?" Alex asked, grinning.

"How the fuck should I know?" George said. "But I don't think that would be a problem since rumor has it that Father Rusu fucks his parishioners up the ass on the altar."

The others chuckled.

"Indeed, I've also heard about that," Edi said.

"Okay, that settles it," Tudor decided. "I want to be a beggar when I grow up. And sodomize my girlfriend on the altar in a church."

"And then sacrifice her to Satan," Alex added.

"Damn straight," Tudor agreed. "As soon as I'm tired of her, I'll cut her up and offer her to the Devil and pray for fresh meat."

George frowned in thought, "I wonder what sex is like when you're blind. How do you find the hole?"

"By touch, you dumbass," Tudor said.

"But how do you know it's not the shitting hole?" George insisted.

Edi jumped in to settle the issue. "Their other senses are heightened, you know. Like their smell and touch."

"Hmm, the smell of pussy. Yum-yum!" George blurted.

Tudor slugged his shoulder. "That's not how a pig goes."

Chapter 3 Ave Satanas!

George eagerly accepted Tudor's prompt. "Oink! Oink!"

"That's more like it, Piggy!" Tudor said, smiling at his friend.

"Wasn't there a movie about a blind man smelling pussy?" Alex wondered.

"Yeah, with Al Pacino, right?" Tudor said.

"*Scent of a Woman*," Edi remembered.

Discussing the sex life of the blind occupied the four youngsters until they reached the cemetery's chapel. It was a simple structure with grey walls and a rusted tin roof. George told the others that the broken tomb was right behind it.

They followed a narrow path around the building. Tudor glanced around the cemetery and found it almost deserted. With the exception of the beggar by the entrance, the only other people were two old women attending a grave and lighting candles. It was around nine, and the sunlight faded to a pale grey.

Behind the chapel they saw the gravedigger's shed. The open door revealed picks and shovels, a pair of dirty boots, and a coil of rope hanging on the wall. The gravedigger was nowhere in sight.

"There it is!" George shouted, pointing to a tomb. He rushed ahead and, crouching next to the structure, opened its metallic green shutters. "Awesome, they didn't lock it yet!"

Edi, Tudor, and Alex approached the crypt. It looked like a small concrete bunker. Here and there the grey plaster had fallen away, exposing red bricks. A black bucket for candles stood in front. The iron grate that would typically sit behind the windows was missing.

They were free to enter.

Tudor squatted next to George and peered into the tomb. Behind them, Alex and Edi stretched their necks for a glimpse inside.

They saw a broken coffin. Interlaced skeleton hands rested on a flat chest.

Tudor felt the thrill of seeing something forbidden.

It reminded him of the time when he and George had a glimpse of a crazy woman's genitals. She had been walking on the sidewalk in front of Tudor's apartment, screaming gibberish at passersby. Tudor and George followed her out of curiosity. Suddenly, she sat down on the grass between the sidewalk and the road to rummage through her purse. Her legs were spread wide, and her dress slid down her thighs. Pretending to walk by casually, Tudor and George peeked between her legs. She wore no underwear. Tudor saw a pink slit surrounded by thick black pubic hair.

It was like real-life porn.

Tudor had felt a strange excitement mixed with guilt and apprehension.

The same feeling washed over him as he stared into the open tomb.

The dead man was wearing a dusty black suit. He looked like a forgotten marionette, gathering dust in the dark corner of an attic.

Tudor jumped into the tomb for a closer look. The stale, moldy air smelled of cement and rot. He gazed at the skull. It looked leathery and shrunken. Some patches of brown, rotten meat remained around the nose, the cheeks, and the edges of the eyeless sockets. Tufts of thin white hair clung to the head. The upper teeth were frozen in an alien grimace. The lower ones were small and decayed, like rotten corn kernels.

The corpse reminded Tudor of his paternal grandfather, Costel Negur. Costel had been an alcoholic and a heavy smoker for most of his life. Now, in his old age, he was only skin and bones. Everyone was waiting for him to bite the dust, and every breath he took was a miracle. He'd been hospitalized a few weeks earlier, and Tudor wagered that the old man's next stop would be right here in the cemetery.

Entranced by the skull, Tudor said, "I should draw this thing. It's awesome!"

Kneeling by the window, the others nodded their agreement. Smiling, Tudor put his index finger into the

Chapter 3 Ave Satanas!

skeleton's nasal cavity and started moving its head from side to side. "Hey, friend, do you want to be a model for my next work and become famous?"

George and Alex laughed, but Edi looked concerned. "Hey man, be careful! That thing might carry viruses and bacteria and whatnot."

"I'm too strong for its viruses," Tudor boasted.

Suddenly, total darkness engulfed him.

Tudor imagined the corpse biting his finger with its decayed teeth. He quickly withdrew his hand and retreated backward. He stood motionless for a few seconds, staring into the darkness and resisting the instinct to panic.

It must be George, trying to play a trick on me, Tudor thought to himself. *Or maybe they saw someone coming and shut the windows in a hurry? Maybe the gravedigger?*

Tudor's vision slowly adjusted to the darkness. A few rays of light penetrated through the holes in the metallic shutters. He heard his friends trying to bottle their laughter.

"Porky, I'm gonna beat the shit outta you!" Tudor warned, trying to sound angry.

The others couldn't resist anymore and burst into laughter.

Tudor heard George's voice. "Hey guys, listen! Someone is calling from the grave."

George flung open the shutters and pointed theatrically into the tomb. "Look everybody, it's Tudor, blowing a dead guy."

Behind George, Alex was grinning while Edi gripped his belly amid convulsions of laughter.

Tudor lifted himself out of the tomb, muttering assorted curses. Sensing the danger, George turned and sprinted. But the more athletic Tudor easily loped into range and tripped his quarry with a two-footed sliding tackle. The fat boy sprawled onto the grass and somersaulted onto his back. Tudor straddled him and slugged his chest a few times.

"Help! Help! I'm being raped," George squealed in a falsetto whose pitch oscillated with each strike to the chest.

"Shut up, Rude Pig!" Tudor shouted, abandoning his flurry of punches to seize George's throat, "How does the pig go?"

"Oink! Oink!" George uttered submissively. Tudor felt his friend's Adam's apple lurching in his throat.

"Fucking right, Piggy! Watch yourself or you'll get castrated!" Tudor stood up and returned to the others.

"You bruised me, fuckface!" George whined clutching his chest.

"What did you call me?" Tudor asked, breaking stride to turn back toward George.

"Nothing," George said.

"Damn straight, nothing, you sack of shit!"

Tudor exchanged smiles with Edi and Alex. "Porky's such a clown," he said, fishing in his backpack for a pack of cigarettes.

"To say the least," Edi added.

"You guys have a lighter?" Tudor asked.

Alex produced a lighter from his front pocket and handed it to Tudor. The three friends lit cigarettes as George rejoined the group. His knees were grass-stained from his tumble.

Exhaling a jet of smoke, Tudor pointed toward the chapel. "I think we should write on the far wall 'cause it's more visible. The other side is hidden by trees."

Alex nodded.

"I brought nothing to write with," Edi pouted. "I wanted to steal some paint but thought my dad would notice."

"Oh, I just brought a small can," Alex said. "I probably won't have enough to spare."

"Me neither," Tudor said. Then he smiled toward George. "Unless Porky can give us some of his blood. What do you say, Porky?"

George looked around with predatory eyes. "I'll get you more blood if I can find me some critters."

"No, Porky, you'll have to keep watch out front," Alex said,

Chapter 3 Ave Satanas!

indicating the walkway leading to the chapel's main entrance.

"Oh, okay," George submitted.

"It's okay guys, I can jot something with a rock," Edi said and took a drag from his cigarette.

"That's good," Alex agreed. "We'd better wait for it to get dark, though."

Tudor gazed up at the grey sky. To the west, the sunset colored the horizon in yellow and pale orange. "But then we'd have no light, man."

"I have a flashlight and candles," George said.

"Fuck that," Tudor said. Turning to Alex, he continued, "Come on, man, there's no one around, and Porky will keep watch. We'll be done in no time."

Alex scanned the area again. Their side of the cemetery was deserted. "All right, let's do it!" he assented, though he pointed a wary finger toward the far side of the graveyard. "But if someone shows up we should run that way and climb up the dike."

They all looked in the indicated direction. The yard was bordered by an old chain-link fence with gaps big enough to run through. Beyond that, there was a tall dike and then the river valley. Tudor agreed it was a good escape route.

"Okay, let's get this show on the road!" Alex said. He stomped on his cigarette butt and approached the chapel. The others followed. Looking again at the large wall, Tudor thought it made a good canvas. The plaster would be easy to write and paint on. George walked to the front of the building to keep watch. He sat down on the stairs and looked down the paved walkway, trying to appear casual.

Alex produced a can of paint and a small brush from his backpack while Tudor took out the syringe and jar of blood. Edi found a sharp rock and began engraving the surface of the wall.

By implicit agreement, Tudor took the left side of the wall, Alex the middle, and Edi wrote on the right. They looked like students working on a class project. Except no teacher had told them to write *these* messages.

After scanning the area again for witnesses, Tudor filled his syringe. The pigeon blood was thick, almost gelatinous.

He depressed the piston and a red stream spurted onto the grey wall. He wrote an "S" shaped like a lightning bolt. The liquid dripped from the edges of the letter. Tudor halted for a moment, considering whether to write "Slayer" or "Satan" or simply "SS." He saw Alex finishing a large "W."

"What are you writing?" Tudor asked.

"'Waffen-SS," Alex said. "You?"

"I'm trying to decide between 'Slayer' and 'Satan,'" Tudor said, beaming with vandalistic joy.

"Sweet," Alex said and began working on his "A." Tudor liked the sharp smell of paint better than the nauseating coppery smell of blood jelly. He settled on "Satan." It was one letter shorter than "Slayer" and more blasphemous. After all, most people in their town knew nothing about thrash metal, but they knew all about Satan. Tudor splashed an "A" onto the wall and added a "T" in the shape of an inverted cross.

When he finished his "T," he noticed that Edi was already done. He was sitting on the stairs with George, who was picking his bottled nose. He produced a booger, frowned at it, rolled it between his fingers, and flicked it into the air.

Then he dug for more.

When he squatted to fill the syringe, Tudor saw he didn't have enough blood for the last two letters. At the bottom of the jar there was only a mash of blood-soaked feathers.

"Porky!" he shouted. "I want your blood!"

George jumped to his feet and rushed to Tudor's side. "Why? Not enough?"

Tudor shook his head.

"Fuck!" George said. He turned to Edi, "Hey man, do you mind keeping watch for a bit? I gotta look for something."

"Go ahead," Edi said and lit a smoke.

Taking the almost-empty jar, George said, "I saw some stray dogs around here. Gonna go look for them."

Chapter 3 Ave Satanas!

Tudor raised an eyebrow. "Well, hurry up! Otherwise, I'll get some of your blood, fatso."

George started down the dusty path that ran between the graves. After a few strides, a dog's bark alerted him. The animal appeared from behind a short fence enclosing a forgotten grave. It must have been sleeping in a cluster of tall weeds. It was small, stocky, and short-legged. Its brown fur was matted and full of thistles.

George turned toward Tudor, grinned, and lifted the jar in salutation.

"Guys, I think you need to see this," Tudor called, barely able to contain his excitement.

After cautiously scanning their surroundings, Alex and Edi came to watch. The dog continued barking and charged George but stopped short, suddenly unsure of itself. George knelt and proffered his right hand.

"Come on, doggie, I have something for you! Yum-yum!"

The animal limped unsteadily toward George. One of its eyes seemed to be wounded. George let the dog sniff his hand.

Then he petted its head.

"Who's a good doggie?" he repeatedly asked, soothing the dog with a soft, even cadence. The dog relaxed started to wag its crooked tail.

"Oh, it's an old motherfucker," George told the others. "I think it might be fucking blind. One of his eyes is crusted over."

"Gross!" Tudor uttered.

George sat on the grass next to the dog, and the animal rolled over to expose its belly. George scratched it behind the ears, rubbed its belly, and began stroking its cock. A moment later its glistening pink penis emerged from its furry sheath.

George's friends groaned in disgust. Edi covered his eyes with his hands but peeked through the gaps between his fingers. "Fucking zoophile," Alex muttered.

Tudor grinned at them. "See? I have to put up with this crazy fuck every fucking day." Although he meant it as a complaint, he sounded proud and boastful.

Grinning with delight, George continued stroking the dog. With his other hand, he pulled a folding knife from his pocket. He opened the blade with his teeth. The dog lay on its back, panting, mouth open, eyes closed, oblivious to the sharp object. George accelerated the rhythm of the handjob as he placed, the blade against the dog's jugular. To Tudor, Piggy looked like a savage playing a strange musical instrument.

The dog tensed and ejaculated. The first load shot onto the grass. When a second load spurted, George released the dog's member and grabbed its snout. Then he cut its throat with a quick, brutal jerk. A jet of blood gushed onto the grass, covering the traces of cum. The desperate dog yelped and squirmed. George gripped the snout for a few more seconds, but when blood started flowing onto him, he tossed the dying animal aside. The dog struggled to its feet and tried to run, but its legs failed. It fell anemically to the ground, its back legs spasming as a dark puddle of blood expanded around it. George walked to the dying animal, lifted its head, and filled the jar with the blood gushing from its throat. The moribund dog wanted to bite but had no strength left. It feebly opened its jaws and moved its mouth from side to side, blindly searching its tormentor's hand.

George dropped the dog's head and returned to the others, grinning wildly.

Like Tudor, Alex and Edi worried that George had been gradually going crazy since his mom had died. But they all thought George was fun to be around and they considered new ways to exploit his shamelessness.

"There you go, Master!" George said and handed the full jar to Tudor.

Tudor patted his friend's shoulder. "Well done, Piggy!"

"Now we have a dead dog here, too. Can you guys keep watch?" Alex asked George and Edi.

George and Edi nodded and returned to sentry duty.

Alex finished writing "Waffen SS" and added "Heil Hitler!"

Chapter 3 Ave Satanas!

in smaller letters.

Tudor used the fresh blood to paint "Master" below "Satan" and crowned the message with a pentagram.

Then, in the setting sun's violet light, the four friends gathered and contemplated their work.

They laughed at the message Edi had scribbled with his rock. "Stop Stupidity! Stop Yourselves!"

Edi beamed.

"It's good, but it needs a final touch," Tudor said, fist under his chin.

"It's an homage to Satan and the Führer," Alex added thoughtfully.

"Right, so we better sacrifice something to them," Tudor suggested and pointed to the dead dog lying in the middle of the dusty path.

Alex grasped the idea. "So, should we hang it somehow?"

Tudor rubbed his short mohawk. Then an image popped into his head. "We should crucify it. You know...like a parody of Jesus."

A yellow smile spread across Alex's face. "That's wicked!"

Tudor immediately turned to George. "Hey man, can you bring a wooden cross and the dog? We're gonna crucify it!"

"Yes, Master," George said and walked away to search the graves for the requested cross. When he reached the dog's carcass, he hefted it by the tail, spun around, and flung it toward his friends. It dropped with a thud near Tudor's legs. Disgusted, Tudor kicked it away.

"So, what do we crucify it with?" Edi asked.

"A hammer and nails would be good," Tudor said.

"Or a rope. Or maybe wires," Alex chipped in.

"There was a coil of rope in the gravedigger's shed," Edi remembered.

When George returned with a sturdy wooden cross, they sent him to retrieve some rope from the shed. Tudor grabbed the cross and placed it against the desecrated wall of the chapel.

George soon returned with a length of rope of about one meter. "Will this be enough?" he asked.

Alex and Tudor nodded. Edi's booted foot flipped the dog onto its back. "I don't think we can tie it by the front legs; they'd snap."

"So what?" Tudor asked.

"Then the cross would tip over. You want it to stand up, right?"

Tudor frowned and looked at the mangled carcass. "Piggy, can you spread its front legs?" he asked. George dutifully squatted and splayed the dog's front limbs. They opened wide, but not wide enough. Tudor saw that Edi was right; applying the necessary force would break one of the dog's shoulder joints. He was vaguely reminded of chicken wings. "Okay," he said, "maybe we can tie it upside down, by the back legs?"

Alex grinned. "That would make the sacrilege even greater. An inverted Jesus."

"Who's actually a stray dog," Tudor said and smiled.

"Still," Edi insisted, "we'll need to secure the body too. Otherwise, it's gonna fall sideways."

"Do you think we'll need more rope?" George asked.

Edi looked at the length of rope in George's hand and nodded. "Yes, get another piece of that length!"

When George came back with the second piece of rope, he lifted the dog onto the cross and asked the others to hold its hind legs in place. Tudor and Alex each held a leg while George cut the rope in half and lashed the limbs to the cross's horizontal beam. Tudor could feel the tiny bones in the dog's ankle. They seemed very fragile. With the last piece of rope, George secured the animal's midsection to the vertical post. The front legs jutted stiffly. The gaping throat was a black hole.

The dog's weight held the cross in place.

They stood back and admired their work. Tudor thought it a twisted message, a beautiful and sinister picture. The dog's splayed legs lent a touch of obscenity. Remembering

Chapter 3 Ave Satanas!

that Jesus had been pierced by a spear, Tudor decided on a final touch. He asked George for his pocket knife. He thrust the blade deep into the dog's abdomen and jerked his arm downward, tearing a jagged hole in the crucified beast. Dark intestines forced their way outward and slithered down the dog's chest like a mass of large worms. The kids recoiled from the stench of escaping viscera. They covered their noses and stepped back from the grisly scene.

"This will scare the shit out of these idiots when they see it in broad daylight," Tudor said.

The others nodded.

"Hey guys, let's move away from here, in case someone shows up," Alex suggested. Gesturing toward the far side of the cemetery, he indicated that they seek the cover of the trees at the back of the yard.

Tudor smashed the empty jar against the desecrated wall, shouldered his backpack, and followed the others. A murder of crows perched on the chain-link fence. When the four kids approached, they cawed and withdrew to the nearby power lines.

Alex followed a path toward a cluster of pine trees. Fallen needles blanketed the grave markers and the ground.

On their right, one grave was marked by the bust of a young girl instead of the customary cross. She had short hair and a gentle, pretty face.

George stopped and patted her head. "She seems mighty doable."

"I think I heard of this one," Edi said. "She poisoned herself because her lover dumped her."

The funeral stone showed that Violeta Nicolae had died at nineteen. Her overdramatic epitaph read:

I flew up toward the sky,
a girl, a bird, a spirit;
I flew up toward a world
with no time or boundaries.

An accompanying inscription read, "Your parents and brother will never forget you."

George smirked. "She flew up toward my balls."

Tudor frowned and asked, "She poisoned herself?"

George and Edi nodded.

"That's strange," Tudor continued, "I thought suicides weren't buried in the city cemetery."

"That sounds right," Alex concurred. "It's against God to commit suicide."

"Oh, I bet she sucked her way into it," George said. "These pretty babes always get their way."

"How can she suck if she's dead?" Edi wondered.

George shrugged. "Well, her mouth is still there, isn't it?"

"That's gross, man! And who would put his shaft in a dead girl's mouth?" Edi pressed.

George cocked an eyebrow. "I would. Shit, I'd probably do her right now."

They all chuckled.

"George has a point, though," Alex claimed. "Suppose the cemetery keeper or the priest is open for business and her parents want a Christian burial to make sure her soul gets into heaven. They can offer the body to the priest."

"But isn't screwing the dead unchristian?" Edi asked.

"Maybe... But *loving* the dead is very Christian," Alex answered with a grin.

Laughing, they headed toward a tomb surrounded by pines.

Tudor noticed metal handles on the sides of the concrete lid. Excited, he ran and grabbed one of them.

"Hey guys, help me move this thing!"

George grabbed the handles on the opposite side. As Tudor pulled, George pushed. The heavy lid shifted and ground its way across the tomb's concrete base. They peered inside through the triangular opening. The fading light outlined a coffin at the bottom of the deep cavernous vault.

Chapter 3 Ave Satanas!

Looking at the others with wide eyes, Tudor said, "Oh man, we should throw someone down there and leave them for days. Just for fun."

"Like who?" Alex asked.

"Maybe stupid Livia Dumitru," Edi suggested.

"Who's that?" George asked.

"Oh, just a retard in our class," Tudor said.

They all glanced inside the vault thoughtfully.

"You mean let her die in there?" George asked.

Edi grinned. "Well, she's already dead."

"Born dead," Tudor added.

"Brain-dead," Edi put in.

"No use to mankind," Alex contributed.

"Maybe we can put a stray dog in there with her," George suggested.

The others chuckled. "Right on," Tudor said. "We can ask her to have sex with the dog in exchange for her release. And then she'll give birth to a hybrid."

Alex laughed. "I guess I was wrong. Her only use is being experimented upon."

"Our guinea pig," Tudor said.

Edi shook his head in disgust. "The way she looks, no normal male would fuck her, anyway."

Tudor smirked. "The dog would probably have a hard time, too."

"Ugly *and* dumb," Edi said. "You guys remember in geography class when she said that winds are caused by gods blowing?"

"Oh man," Alex cringed. "She's a retarded, fat, hairy lump. She's like the cow from that *Cow and Chicken* cartoon."

They all laughed at the succession of insults.

After peering into the tomb for a few more seconds, Tudor and George pulled the lid back into place. Then George reached into his backpack and produced a two-liter plastic bottle of white wine.

The others welcomed the sight with cheers.

Tudor and Edi sat on the tomb while Alex rested on one knee on the ground.

George passed the bottle to Alex. "Go ahead! Pop its cherry!"

Alex accepted the bottle, removed the cap, and gulped deeply. His throat pulsated rhythmically as he swallowed. After a few throatfuls, he wiped his mouth with the back of his hand. "Oh, that hits the spot," he said and passed the bottle to Tudor.

Tudor took a healthy gulp and passed the drink to Edi. As Edi took a swig, George dug a flashlight from his backpack and placed it on the ground.

"You came well prepared, Porky. Good job!" Tudor said.

"Damn straight. I brought some candles too, for the satanic ritual." George produced half a dozen long, skinny candles and walked toward one of the grave lanterns on the side of the nearest marble cross. He opened the small, hinged door, set the candle in the holder and lit it. Tudor gazed at the flickering light. It brought the surrounding darkness to life. Looking out over the tops of the buildings across the street from the cemetery, he saw the first stars dotting the night sky.

George lit a few more grave lanterns and then rejoined the others. Candlelight and the flashlight's beam bathed them in a soft, warm glow.

After taking his first swig of wine, George asked, "So what are you guys going to do if Cornel comes after you again...with his gang?"

Tudor had told George about the fight with Cornel, but they hadn't had time to discuss its possibly dire consequences because it was Tudor's mom's day off and he needed to pretend to do his homework.

Nonetheless, George's question had occupied Tudor since Cornel had threatened him the day before. "That's true," Tudor began. "They might come to beat us up. After all, they're older and think we're just a bunch of wimps. But they don't know *us*. If they jump us and beat us up, we're going to chase them

Chapter 3 Ave Satanas!

down. But not to beat them. No, sir! Fuck that! We'll seek and *destroy*!"

Alex laughed and struck his knee with his fist. "Yeah, we'll kill 'em all."

"Make them jump in the fire," Edi said and smiled.

George gave them a puzzled look.

Alex smirked at him. "You should listen to more Metallica, Piggy."

"I am," George said defensively, "but I don't understand—"

"Okay, okay, let me finish!" Tudor said and raised his hands to quiet the others. "Let's say he attacks us next week. After that, I'm going to lay low for a while and find out stuff about him. Where he lives and shit like that. Then I'm gonna wait for him one night, maybe even a year later, when he'll barely remember me. He'll come from a nightclub or something stupid like that, and I'll be right there in the lobby of his building. A hunting knife or ninja sword in my hand... Or a fucking hammer..."

"Or an axe," Alex suggested.

"That's right."

"Or a chainsaw," George said.

"That would make too much noise," Tudor said. "The neighbors might show up. But, anyway, I'd be like, 'Remember me, you piece of shit?' and then I'd hack him to pieces, pop his eyeballs out, and fuck his skull."

Tudor hacked at the air with his hands.

Alex nodded and said, "We'll *all* hunt them down, brother. We'll get them one by one. This is *our* war against the scum... But we need some fucking weapons."

George fished the folded knife out of his pocket and threw it to Tudor, who cupped his hands to catch it. "For starters, I give you my blade, bro. My dad got it from America when he visited my uncle there last year. It's a Buck hunting knife."

Tudor opened the blade with his fingers. It was sticky with blood from cutting the stray dog's belly but still looked very sharp. "Wow, thanks, man!"

"You're welcome. Be careful when you close it. It might cut your finger off."

Tudor folded the blade carefully, and it clicked shut. "Wow, look at that!" Tudor exclaimed. The others eyed the weapon curiously.

Tudor opened the knife again and handed it to Alex, who grasped the black handle and tested the blade with his thumb. "I have a large hunting knife at home. But this one is better 'cause you can carry it around in your pocket."

The others nodded.

Alex snapped the knife shut and threw it to Edi.

George took a self-satisfied swig of wine and said, "My old man also has a couple of shotguns and a rifle. Brought them from America, too. And I have access to them and to the ammunition."

"Wicked," Tudor uttered, slapping his knee in excitement.

Taking the bottle from George, Alex said, "Rifles are cool. You can shoot people from rooftops. Kill them one by one like rabbits." Alex raised the bottle, tilted his head back, and took a big gulp of wine. Then he passed the bottle to Tudor.

"You know, we can also build bombs and other explosives. I saw a documentary about it. It's really easy. And then we can blow up entire buildings," Edi said.

"Awesome," the others exclaimed in unison.

In the ensuing brief silence, Tudor contemplated the possibility with dreamy eyes. Blowing up entire buildings. Demolishing everything like an earthquake and then taking pot-shots at the people crawling from under the rubble, like rats from a burning landfill.

After taking a big drink, Tudor realized he was getting tipsy. And it was good. Suddenly, the present moment dilated, and the world became full, warm, and welcoming. The air was rich with sweet smells: lilac, pine, raw earth. Objects seemed to lose their solidity, becoming malleable, pulsing to the rhythm of his mind, and easily bending to his desires. Transfigured, the cemetery was their playground, their toy store, their own

Chapter 3 Ave Satanas!

world to explore, try out, use and abuse.

Tudor passed the bottle to Edi and smiled. Edi returned a soft smile. His sparkling eyes showed he was also getting drunk.

Alex interrupted the silence. "I want to blow up that fucking store in front of my place. The Galaxy. You know, Mr. Tache's store? It drives me crazy."

Then Alex told them about the acts of vandalism he'd committed the night before; how he'd slashed the tires of Tache's new Audi and smashed the front window of his store.

"Sweet!" "Awesome!" the others exclaimed in unison.

Alex explained that he didn't want his neighbors to suspect him and report him to the police. That's why he planned to stop dressing like a neo-Nazi until the whole thing blew over. Stretching the front of his t-shirt, he said, "I'm just wearing this white Burzum shirt today. Who the fuck knows about Burzum?"

Edi grinned and said, "You should wear a Vanilla Ice or Ace of Base shirt. Then no one would suspect a thing."

Alex shook his head. "I'd rather die! If you see me in one of those just shoot me on the spot. But, anyway, I don't want to advertise my Satanism in this town full of retards."

Then, looking at Alex and Tudor, Edi asked gravely, "Hey, guys, I meant to ask you about that... I've been thinking a lot about it... Like, how come you're Satanists? I mean, if God doesn't exist, how come Satan does?"

Alex looked inquiringly at Tudor, who needed more time to think, and so signaled his friend to proceed.

Alex said, "Well, brother, different people mean different things by Satanism. From what I've read, LaVey, you know, the guy who wrote *The Satanic Bible*, says that Satan is more powerful than God. Satan symbolizes our animal instincts. And LaVey says...okay...so man has an animal side and an angelic side. But, when we look at society, it's obvious that the animal side is stronger. I mean, everybody wants to fuck, kill, and cheat others, right? Even priests and shit, they are so hypocritical, you know? They are only after your money..."

They all nodded their agreement with that point.

Edi added, "You know what they say: do as the priest preaches, not as he does."

Taking Edi's remark as his cue, George made a circle of the thumb and forefinger of his left hand and penetrated it with the index finger of his right. He moaned as he moved the finger in and out of the circle.

Edi and Alex laughed, but Tudor only smiled thoughtfully. Yellow light briefly flicked across his face as he lit a cigarette. He'd seen in Edi's direct and simple question a problem that had been haunting him as well. Although he sensed that Edi just wanted to imitate him and Alex and become a Satanist himself, Tudor thought that the question of how Satan could exist without God deserved serious discussion. After all, it went to the heart of what separated *them* from the herd. An answer slowly formed in his mind. It was an answer he already knew deep down but it only surfaced because of Edi's probing. It was strange that he could think so many things unknowingly and that he would realize what he thought only when talking to his friends.

Pleased with his idea about Satanism, Tudor turned his attention back to the conversation.

"...LaVey says we should stop worshiping God, like a bunch of hypocrites, and worship Satan instead. We shouldn't feel bad when we sin, but be proud of it. Like Cioran said, 'Drink pleasure to its last dregs.'"

To demonstrate, Alex took a few big gulps of wine. The bottle was almost empty now. He passed it to Tudor, who polished it off and threw it onto a nearby grave.

"Father Rusu's parishioners know everything about drinking pleasure," George said. "Apparently, he likes ass to mouth."

Alex smirked. "That's crazy cause homosexual sex is forbidden in the Bible. Father Rusu is on a highway to hell."

Edi nodded and said, "I also watched a documentary about

Chapter 3 Ave Satanas!

the Catholic Church. They were talking about the Vatican and how rich and powerful the Pope is."

They all agreed that was fucked.

George picked his nose deeply and asked, "But if Satan wins then we all go to Hell, and there's no one left in Heaven?"

Alex shrugged. "Fuck, I'm not even sure I believe in Hell."

Edi and Tudor shook their heads too. "There's no Hell, that's just stupid."

"Anyway," Alex said adjusting his hair behind his ears, "about Satanism, what I wanted to say was that, personally...I don't believe in LaVey's version. I mean that Satanism is for animals and retards like Piggy here."

Alex patted George on the back, and George obliged his insulter, "Oink! Oink! Me tarded."

Alex smiled and continued, "Even Pamela Anderson can be a Satanist if she enjoys sucking doorknobs and is proud of it. But that's stupid, right? So...the story of Satan is that he was one of God's angels, and he rebelled because he didn't want to be a slave. He wanted to be a master. And if you look at history, you know, the great leaders are like Satan. They rule and do whatever the fuck they want. Society listens to them, and not the other way around."

Alex looked at them with intense, wide eyes, trying to gauge their understanding.

A frown formed on Edi's face as he stared at the ground. In a small voice he asked, "So, do you think Satan and God are real or not?"

"Hmm," Alex uttered thoughtfully, stroking his chin. "I think of Satan more as a symbol of rebellion, but he could also be real. Like, his spirit animates great warriors like Genghis Khan, Attila the Hun, Vlad the Impaler, or Hitler... But then... Yes, you're right. God has to exist too."

Alex stopped for a few seconds and frowned deeply, unhappy with his conclusion. He resumed in an uncertain tone, "So, maybe there are, you know, two powers that struggle for supremacy over the universe. The God of slaves and scum and the Satan of masters." His eyes began to sparkle with this new insight, and he continued more confidently, "And the Aryan race fights in the name of Lucifer while the dark races, the slaves, the sick, and the handicapped fight in the name of their weak, blind God."

Alex's last remarks were Tudor's cue.

"Exactly," he said, "I feel like we, Satanists, are a different species. Satanism, for me, is living in the moment and seeing it for what it is." Tudor swept his right hand in a wide arc, including the entirety of his surroundings in the *moment* he claimed to see clearly. "You see all these retards lighting candles and leaving them at the graves, and you think, 'What the fuck? Those people are dead and buried. Rotting in the ground. They don't give a shit.' But the living treat the dead as if they were still around in spirit. They even talk to them and stuff."

Tudor stopped, took a drag of his cigarette, and exhaled the smoke through his nostrils.

"Like my disgusting mother," he continued, "when my grandpa died she wasted a whole year of her life with funeral customs and giving charity to the poor and crap like that. When people came for the vigil, she gave them food and water, and she also left food and water on the window sill. You know why? So her dad wouldn't go hungry or thirsty on the other side."

The others laughed and Tudor smiled, pleased with his audience's favorable reaction.

"And do you notice how people throw change at street corners when they're going to bury the dead? Apparently, that's money the dead person can use on the other side to buy protection from the evil one."

"Oh, my God, that's so stupid!" Edi exclaimed.

"Fuck yeah! But my point is that these people don't see the world as it is. They are weak like Alex said. And we Satanists are strong. We don't lie to ourselves. I mean, being dead is being dead, and being alive means living your fucking life. In

Chapter 3 Ave Satanas!

the moment! You know, as Cioran said, don't let your life pass you by because of some stupid obligations that society places on you."

"*Carpe diem!*" Alex said.

"Carpay what?" Tudor asked.

"*Carpe diem.* It means to live in the moment."

"Right on," Tudor nodded.

Edi said, "This also reminds me of what Dave Mustaine says in a song: 'Don't ask what you can do for your country! Ask what your country can do for you!'"

"Who says that again?" Tudor asked.

"Dave Mustaine from Megadeth."

Alex looked Tudor straight in the eye and said, "That is such an important lesson, brother." The compliment made Tudor's heart soar, but he tried to stay cool and conceal his pleasure. Alex continued, "I strongly believe we are chosen. You know, the chosen few."

Alex stopped and looked at George, who was idly scratching himself. "Maybe not so much Porky..."

The others laughed, and George playfully walloped Alex's shoulder.

"But, you know, the rest of us brothers, we have a mission!"

Tudor found himself thinking that there was something about Alex. He felt more inspired, more alive when around his friend. As if Alex radiated an energy they all could feed on. Tudor wondered if Alex felt the same around him.

Well, why else would he hang out with us? he thought. *He must like us too.*

The great thing was, with Alex around, you never knew what was going to happen. He never did anything very extreme, but his presence electrified those around him. As a result, as a group, they'd end up doing all kinds of crazy stuff they never would have thought about individually.

That was Alex. He was the firestarter.

"So what's our mission?" Edi asked Alex.

Alex took a deep drag from his cigarette and seemed to collect his thoughts.

"I wanna tell you about something I read that got me thinking. It's a theory advanced by an Austrian occultist who influenced Hitler. To be honest, I don't fully understand it, and it goes against everything we know about Christianity. But anyway, the view is that God...or Satan, or what have you, created these majestic creatures, like dinosaurs with wings. And they had psychic powers like telepathy and seeing the future. But then these gigantic angels started having sex with a species of apes..."

George chuckled. "Dinosaurs screwing apes. That's rich!"

"Shut your hole, Porky," Tudor warned.

"I know this sounds strange, but bear with me, brothers. Okay, so humans were created as a result of illicit sex between these two species. That's the story of Adam and Eve from the Bible. And the snake... You know, that's why they were thrown out of Paradise. But now, there are two kinds of humans: the Aryans and the Blacks. The Aryans still have the powers of the primordial giants, but they're unaware of it. On the other hand, the pygmies, or the dark races, like Gypsies, Blacks, Arabs and so on, are more like apes. They have no spiritual powers, and they want to destroy the ones who are so gifted. Also, their eyes are brown like shit, because they like anal sex."

George chuckled but, remembering Tudor's warning, bottled up his laughter.

Edi asked, "How about the Chinese?"

"Oh, the yellow race?" Alex rubbed his chin. "I think they must also be the result of interbreeding between Aryans and some type of reptile, because of their elongated eyes. But their eyes and hair are black, so they must be a dark species after all. 'Cause, you know, Aryans have blue eyes, the color of the sky. And that's because in the primordial times they were able to fly."

"Oh, my God, sometimes I feel like I'm able to fly," Tudor

Chapter 3 Ave Satanas!

interjected.

"Right, that power is within you from your Aryan ancestors and God...or Satan, or whatever you want to call our maker. But because our forefathers copulated with apes, your powers now lie dormant."

"So, you guys think I'm an ape?" George asked, pouting.

"No, you're a pig," Edi said and grinned.

"How does the pig go?" Tudor asked, smiling.

George continued to pout.

Alex patted George on the shoulder. "Listen up, George. You are very important to us. You are our helper. As long as you know your place, you can hang out with us, brother."

"That's all right," George said, eyes downcast. "I want to help you guys."

"That's good," Alex said. "You're a soldier in our army, man."

George nodded and mumbled, "That's cool."

Returning to his summary of occultist racialism, Alex asked, "So, you know who had special spiritual powers?"

The others shook their heads.

"Our friend Jesus," Alex said, delighting in the shock of the others.

"Oh, so you think Jesus was an Aryan too?" Tudor asked, puzzled.

"That's what this occultist says. Like, the crucifixion scene in the Bible is just Jesus being sodomized by apelings. And it is well known that he had supernatural powers like spiritual healing and performing other miracles."

"Walking on water," Edi added.

Alex nodded. "But, you know, to make a long story short, our mission is to unite with the other members of the Aryan race and annihilate or enslave the black races. Then, over time, our psychic powers will awaken, and we'll dominate the world."

After a few seconds of thoughtful silence, Edi said, "I always thought that Jesus was...some kind of *alien*."

"Sure," Alex agreed, "it's totally possible that the primeval giants were aliens. Like, they were able to fly, and their bodies radiated light and energy."

Edi frowned, trying to wrap his mind around Alex's ideas. "So, aliens were sexually corrupted by stupid apes?"

"That's right."

"It's funny; I was just thinking about this a few minutes ago," Tudor said. "There's so much energy when we're together. It's like we become more powerful as a group."

They all nodded at that.

"It may be," Alex speculated, "that we were connected in past lives, like members of the same species. And if we stay united, we'll become more and more powerful as our past rises up inside us. We'll probably gain psychic powers too, as long as we avoid the subhuman hordes."

"Do you think we'll grow horns and spikes like dinosaurs?" Tudor asked. "*That* would be awesome!"

"It's entirely possible," Alex answered. "You know, your blood carries the entire history of the species. So, the potential is there. We just need to focus and achieve contact with our ancestors."

"Fucking right!" Tudor exclaimed and slapped his knee. "I want a horn like a rhino," he said, banging his fist on his forehead. "And some large fucking wings," he added and flapped his arms, imitating a bird in flight.

Edi smirked. "Did you know that birds actually come from dinosaurs?"

The others gaped at him. "Really?" Tudor asked.

"Yep. So, you and Porky, when you guys killed those pigeons, you killed your own species."

"Fuck, I had no idea," Tudor said, brushing his mohawk.

"And crows too?" George asked. "They also come from dinos?"

Edi nodded and smiled.

"Weird...Crows are black and their eyes are black, although they fly..." George pointed out.

Chapter 3 Ave Satanas!

"Fuck, I hate all birds and insects, they're gross" Tudor uttered. "I like majestic animals like lions or rhinos."

"Eagles are majestic," Alex countered. "They're a symbol of the Nazi Party."

"That's true," Tudor conceded half-heartedly.

"But, going back to Edi's point," Alex continued, "I'd say crows and pigeons and other crappy birds like that are degenerate dinosaurs with no psychic powers left. Us humans, especially Aryans, *we* inherited those powers. And also, you know, this is sacred, occult knowledge, and modern science is profane."

"I see," Edi mumbled, avoiding a direct argument. "Like we say Gypsies are crows because they're so black and stupid."

"Exactly!" Alex exclaimed, happily realizing that Edi is starting to buy into his racist ideology.

"So, what you guys are saying," George said, grinning, "is that my great-grandfather screwed your great-grandmother in the ass?"

"Can it, Porky!" Tudor said.

But there was no putting his perverse showmanship back in the can now that George was again the center of attention. "You guys is all stupid. Only me is smart," he declared, drooling on his chin. Then he sucked some of the saliva back and asked, "Do you guys know the one about the drooling retard?"

The others shook their heads, smiling with anticipation.

"Ok, so this retard stays in his room, drooling and being all like, '*Argh!*'" George picked up the flashlight and held it under his chin to illuminate his contorted face. He let a rope of saliva drip from the corner of his mouth.

The others laughed.

"All of a sudden someone knocks at the door. The retard's eyes widen in alarm, and he goes, 'Who there?' And the person at the door says, 'It's me, open up!' And then the retard, his eyes bulging in wonder, goes 'ME?!!??'"

The others chortled, and the weight of their philosophical

discussion lifted from their shoulders.

Gleefully carried along by the momentum of his performance, George asked, "Do you know the one about the faraway king?"

The audience shook their heads.

"Oh, so there's this king, and he wakes up one morning, opens his windows and looks outside. His kingdom stretches as far as the eye can see. There are gardens, fortresses, wooded hills, and so on. And then the king stretches and yawns and goes, 'Oh, I'm so far away.'"

The audience exchanged puzzled looks.

"What the hell? It makes no sense," Edi said.

"What kinda stupid joke is that, Porky?" Tudor asked.

"Oh, c'mon, it's funny right?"

"Not really," Alex said.

"You're fucked-up, man," Tudor added.

"Not as fucked up as your mom, though," George retorted. "She still picks up cucumbers with her ass?"

"What?" Tudor asked, looking at Edi and Alex for help.

"What do you mean 'what?' Your mom's a slut. Everybody knows that. Can't you see how much makeup she wears?"

Tudor considered retaliating with a remark about George's mom but remembered she was dead. "Whatever, man. I don't give a shit about my mom."

George looked like he was going to say something, but then changed his mind and stared at the ground.

Alex stood up and stretched his legs. "Time for some music guys. Let's make some fucking noise. There's too much silence in this place."

Tudor rose and did a bicycle kick toward George. "Wake up, motherfuck; I ain't got no time to waste."

George looked confused.

"That's Altar, Porky. Have you heard of them?" Tudor asked.

"No, but I know who kicks ass on the altar."

"Oh, yeah, Father Rusu. We know that," Tudor said.

Chapter 3 Ave Satanas!

"Ok, so I vote for Altar and Slayer. What other music did you guys bring?" Alex inquired.

"I brought Pantera," Tudor answered, reaching for his backpack.

"Iron Maiden," Edi said.

"Faggy," Tudor whispered.

Edi turned to him and frowned. "Pantera is faggy."

"How is Pantera faggy? They're the very opposite! They're all about power and domination. Hence the title of the album, *Vulgar Display of Power*."

"Yeah, but I read somewhere that they like to suck each other off before going on stage."

"No, you misunderstood. It's the vocalist from Iron Maiden who gives them head. That's how he hits them high notes...'cause he likes to gurgle cum every night."

Edi fumed but couldn't devise an adequate retort.

"No offense, Edi," Alex intervened, "but Bruce Dickinson is kinda gayish."

Sensing he was losing the argument, Edi frowned and mumbled, "You guys just don't know good music."

"Okay," Alex said, raising his voice above the dispute, "so we have Pantera, Iron Maiden...George, did you bring anything?"

"Michael Jackson for me, please! I thought *Thriller* was good for a party in the cemetery." George stood up, danced like the zombies in the video, and sang in falsetto, '*Cause this is thriller,/ thriller night.*'"

Tudor slugged him in the shoulder. "Shut it, Porky!"

"Talk about gay..." Alex said, rolling his eyes.

"You can't hit me, I got the player," George whined.

"Okay, I'm sorry. Now let's get this show on the road!" Tudor said, and pointed to George's backpack, which contained the ghetto blaster.

George obediently crouched and removed the cassette player. Alex took it from him and placed it on the concrete tomb where Tudor and Edi had been sitting. Tudor and Edi set their tapes beside the player.

"Okay, let's get it going," Alex said. "Let's start with everyone's favorite, Altar's 'Stop the Silence.'" Alex turned on the player and pressed the eject button. The tape compartment door opened like a mechanical mouth. Alex fed it the tape and pushed it shut. Then he rewound to the beginning of the side.

A voice full of anger and gravel resonated in the empty cemetery.

Edi, Alex, and Tudor shouted along.

Hey suckers,/
What's this fucking silence in this place?/
Wake up, motherfuck!/
I ain't got no time to waste./
Come on...now!

A guitar riff alternated the gritty thumps of a powerful engine with cacophonous squeals. Thunderous drums beat along with the electric chugging. The screaming voice repeated its imperatives, and the young rockers sang along.

Do what you want to do!/
Go where you want to go!/
See what you want to see!/
Fuck what you want to fuck!

Then the chorus:

Stop the silence!/
Silence is death.

When the chorus repeated, Tudor shouted the first line, and the others screamed the refrain.

After the song ended, Edi said, "That was great. We should form a fucking band, guys."

"I do vocals," Tudor said hoarsely. "And bass, like Tom

Chapter 3 Ave Satanas!

Araya."

"I'm lead guitar and backing vocals," Edi said.

As he replaced the Altar tape with Pantera, Alex said, "I'm rhythm guitar and keyboards...and backing vocals."

"Porky, you wanna play drums?" Tudor asked.

"Hell, yeah," George said. "I'll play negro, African drums —"

A powerful guitar riff interrupted George. The four friends started thrashing around to the rhythm of the song. They banged their heads, strummed air guitars, jumped into karate kicks, and shoved each other, transforming the graveyard into a mosh pit. Alex banged his head so hard that Tudor half-expected it to fly off his shoulders. Alex then leaped on top of the tomb and surged into a flying knee. Edi pulled a wooden cross out of the earth and used it like a guitar. George vibrated as if he were being electrocuted, his hair slapping his eyes. Private rituals of musical enjoyment burst unabashed into the public world in a frenzy of aggression, violence, and metal.

Since he didn't have long hair like the others, Tudor didn't bang his head, but he made up for it with an onslaught of Van Damme-style karate kicks. He side kicked a marble cross, focusing his power into his heel. After the third kick, the cross tumbled over and shattered on the ground.

The others cheered.

As Phil Anselmo began to repeat the chorus—*Re-spect, walk!/ Re-spect, walk!*—Tudor turned toward the others and raised his hand in a Nazi salute. He beat his chest to the rhythm of the first two syllables and thrust his arm skyward on *walk*.

His friends responded accordingly, deeply aware of the significance of the gesture.

As Iron Maiden's "Fear of the Dark" started, Edi jumped onto the tomb, next to the player. Wooden guitar in hand, he began swaying like Slash and then kicked his right leg back and forth while hopping forward in imitation of Angus Young's duck walk. George played the drums, beating on a grave marker with two sticks, while Alex belted out high-pitched vocals. To show his disdain for Iron Maiden and assert the superiority of death metal, Tudor grunted out a guttural vocal line.

None of the previous songs matched the absolute aggression of Slayer's "Angel of Death."

Auschwitz, the meaning of pain,/
The way that I want you to die.

The rockers screamed along with Tom Araya and let the furious guitar riffs pull them into a maniacal rapture. Suddenly burning with irrepressible rage, Tudor jumped over the small fence of a well-tended nearby grave. He let fly a savage barrage of kicks, decapitating roses and tulips and creating a storm of stems and petals. As he ravaged the flowers, Tudor screamed, "He's fucking dead and buried! Can't you see he's gone for good, you stupid piece of shit?" When he finished thrashing, the garden looked like a tornado's wake.

As a wild guitar solo began, Tudor, in the grip of inspiration, conferred with George. They disappeared down the walkway, into the darkness. Engrossed in their dance, Alex and Edi didn't notice their departure.

Tudor and George returned to the broken tomb. The pale moonlight shrouded the funeral stones in silver.

Tudor asked, "So can you help me carry this corpse?"

"Sure...if you want," George said uncertainly. "Where will we take it?"

"Back to the others," Tudor said. "Come on, it will be fun!"

When they reached the tomb, Tudor opened the metallic doors and jumped inside. George followed. In almost total darkness, they grabbed the broken coffin lid and threw it on the floor.

"You hold that end!" Tudor ordered.

The two friends laboriously dragged the coffin to the window and, straining to the limits of their strength, succeeded

Chapter 3 Ave Satanas!

in shoving the vessel out into the night air. Lifting again, they trundled their cargo down the dark trail.

When they saw their friends returning, Alex and Edi stopped dancing and stared wide-eyed. Alex reached over and stopped the music. Overjoyed by his friends' shocked faces, Tudor told George to throw the remains on the ground.

They upended the coffin, and the corpse tumbled out like a large black bag of bones. They dropped the empty coffin onto the grass. Tudor kicked at the sack and it moved like a broken mannequin. Taking the cue, the others began kicking savagely at the corpse till it separated into a pile of disembodied parts. The skull broke off of the spine and rolled on the grass like a soccer ball. Tudor kicked it into the grassy area illuminated by candlelight. The head ricocheted off of a marble cross with a crack and rolled back along the ground. Alex started dribbling but was body checked by George, who assumed control of the makeshift ball. Laughing, Alex tripped George from behind, and the chubby kid sprawled onto the grass for the second time that evening. Tudor imperiously won control of the ball and ran away from the group with Alex and Edi in hot pursuit. The skull's unpredictable movements added to the fun of the spontaneous game.

In the throes of their newfound sport, the four teens didn't hear the rocks ricocheting off of crosses and tombs.

Winded but still laughing, Tudor protected the skull with his body while George tried to kick it free from Tudor's control. Alex and Edi were resting, hands on their knees, breathing heavily. Suddenly, Tudor heard George scream in pain. Worried that he had injured his friend by mistake, he turned around to see George doubled over in agony, hands covering his face. "*Ahhh!*" he moaned.

The others straightened their bodies and looked around.

Then they heard the sound of rocks pelting their position.

Someone shouted from the darkness near the chapel. "Get outta here, you hooligans! Or I'll call the police!"

"Run!" Alex commanded as he rushed to grab his

backpack and the player. The others snatched their packs and sprinted after him toward the edge of the cemetery. They escaped through a gap in the chain-link fence and hurried to the top of the dike. They stopped to catch their breath and looked back toward the graveyard, but no one seemed to have followed them.

Alex approached George. "Are you okay, bro?"

"Yes, I just have a bump on my forehead," George said, smiling and rubbing a newly-formed lump.

Tudor shouted toward the dark cemetery, "You can come with the police and suck our cocks, you dumb piece of shit."

Turning to the others, he asked, "Hey, how about going to jump him right now? It's probably just the caretaker. It would be four against one."

Tudor brandished his pocket knife.

The blade flashed in the moonlight.

Alex rubbed his chin. "Not now, man. Not yet. We had our fun for tonight, but next time we'll blow this place up."

"Amen to that." Tudor said, placated by the promise of future violence.

Nodding, Alex declared, "We'll eradicate it in the name of Satan."

Chapter 4
Midday Mutilation

"My dad didn't give me any money. He hates this music, thinks it's stupid." Edi sulked. Because of lack of funds, he hadn't been able to order tapes through *Heavy Metal Magazine*, as Alex and Tudor did.

Tudor grinned. "I didn't even ask for money. Just took it!"

"And they didn't find out?" Edi asked.

"No, because I steal a bit at a time. My dad puts his money on the bookshelf in his study before he takes his afternoon nap. I grab only small bills and change, but I do it every day. That's how I have money for beer and music." Tudor took a swig of his beer as if to demonstrate.

"Awesome!" Alex and Edi exclaimed.

"And he never knows?" Alex asked.

"Not a clue."

"I try to pocket some change when they send me grocery shopping but they always ask for the receipt. They'd probably catch me if I stole even a dime," Edi confessed.

"That sucks," Tudor said.

Alex shook his head in disgust and swallowed a throatful of beer. "Jesus, to think that they were like us when they were young. Like, my dad used to listen to Pink Floyd and Scorpions. He thought he was a rebel fighting the system. And your dad used to be in a rock band, right Edi?"

"Yeah, both him and my mom. My dad was lead guitar and my mom played the drums. I can't understand how they became so toxic. Maybe Ceausescu and his communism destroyed their minds."

Alex nodded. "Totally! They had to get married and form a beautiful communist family. And work together for a triumphant future."

"Except now Ceausescu is dead and buried. So they should stop it already," Tudor interjected.

"Well, at a certain age it's difficult to change your habits and mentality," Alex pointed out. "The old generation, they still have the communist views they were indoctrinated with. They just have to be annihilated by the youth. No way around it!"

Alex puffed a cigarette into life and exhaled the smoke through his nostrils. Tudor and Edi took another drink of beer. The bottles of their second-round were almost empty.

The three friends were celebrating the beginning of summer vacation. School had ended on Thursday. Now, on Friday, their classmates were attending a dance party at the school, but the rockers didn't bother going. It was lame, with teachers and even some parents around to spoil the fun. They needed to go somewhere they could get drunk and rowdy without interference. Outside the confines of the school. Outside the confines of the town. They chose a restaurant on the western edge of the city, where Main Street became the highway to Bucharest. Behind the pub, the dike and the river valley beckoned like an unsupervised playground. The dike would take them all the way to the cemetery and, further still, to the landfill. To their drunken minds, these locations promised rich sources of fun and destruction.

Chapter 4 Midday Mutilation

The day was nearly perfect, perhaps only slightly too hot. Although it was early June, the sun hammered the town with an intensity normally reserved for July or August. A soft, lazy breeze rustled the leaves of the poplars surrounding the patio. The tall trees mercifully shielded the boys.

Tudor stood up and reached for the wallet in his left front pocket. "I'll get the next round."

Alex checked his pack of cigarettes. There was only one left. "Would you mind buying some smokes too?"

"No. What kind do you want?"

"Well, this is the cheapest brand: Bulgarian Tobacco. The cheapest ones that are more decent than the poisonous Romanian smokes."

"At least they have filters," Edi added.

"Fuck cheap, man!" Tudor said, opening his wallet. Inspecting the bills inside, he said, "This is the end of fucking school party. We need to treat ourselves!"

"Whatever you say, bro," Alex said, grinning.

Tudor walked into the restaurant. The barmaid, a stocky middle-aged woman, was solving a crossword at the bar. She looked at Tudor with a mixture of boredom and aggression. Tudor asked for three more bottles of Ursus and checked the prices on the cigarette packs. He chose long Kents. While the barmaid was prying off the beer caps and counting his change, Tudor remembered a recent incident involving his parents and decided to share it with his friends.

Tudor put the change in his wallet, grabbed the beers and the Kents, and stepped back onto the patio. The beer was cold and fresh. He noticed other customers at the far end of the terrace: two men and a woman eating lunch.

Tudor placed the new bottles and smokes on the table.

"Kents! Wow! That's fancy, bro!" Alex exclaimed.

"That's because we're cool, man. We deserve the best," Tudor said, smiling.

"I've never smoked Kents!" Edi said.

"Go ahead and have one then," Tudor suggested.

Edi opened the pack and pulled out a long cigarette. He sparked it, inhaled a long drag, and leaned back in his chair. "Oh, so relaxing! It feels so good being rich and carefree!"

"Isn't this what hookers smoke?" Alex asked.

"No, man," Tudor answered, "these are for rich people, like doctors and lawyers. You know, when you go to the doctor you need to give them a pack of Kents. Otherwise they treat you like shit."

"Yes, Kents and expensive coffee," Edi agreed and exhaled a thick jet of smoke.

"Well, some hookers are rich too," Alex insisted.

"Why would you prostitute yourself if you had money?" Edi wondered.

"Never heard of luxury hookers, my friend? They are filthy rich but still enjoy cock. As long as that cock has a deep wallet attached to it."

Edi and Tudor exchanged smirks. "You seem to know a lot about prostitutes, Alex. How come? Is your mom one?" Edi asked.

Alex flashed his yellow tooth smile. "She likes to suck on Kents, that's for sure."

They all laughed and took a swig of the fresh, cold beers.

Tudor said, "Hey guys, I have a good one for you." He leaned forward in his chair, elbows on the table. "A few days ago I was on the couch in the living room, watching soccer. My parents came in and sat in their armchairs." Tudor jabbed the table at various points with his index finger, creating a map of the scene. "They kept talking about stupid stuff like paying bills and people at work and shit like that. Their constant chatter was getting on my nerves, and Steaua was losing 'cause they're Steaua, and they suck. And all of a sudden I looked at them, at how they were sitting there like a pair of losers, content with their petty lives, like pieces of furniture gathering dust."

Tudor stopped for a large swallow of beer. Half-smiling, his friends waited for him to continue.

Chapter 4 Midday Mutilation

He belched out the gaseous content of his drink.

"Sorry!" he muttered in a tiny voice and wiped his mouth with the back of his hand.

"Oh, you fucking pig, that stinks. What did you have for lunch?" Alex said, waving his hand in front of his face.

"Oh, just some roadkill, cats and such," Tudor said, grinning. "Anyway, back to the story. Where was I? Oh, yeah, my stupid parents...So, anyway, I stared at them for like five minutes and then asked, 'What did you achieve in this life?'"

Edi chuckled.

Alex slapped his knee with delight. "Point blank. Bullet to the head."

Goaded on by his audience, Tudor continued, "They just looked at me dumbfounded, mouths hanging open. My mom's bovine eyes were bulging, but she couldn't say anything. After a while, my dad said 'We had you, Tudor.'"

They all laughed at this.

"Wow, I thought. This was their claim to fame." Tudor's eyes teared up from laughter. "They had a kid. That's something to brag about. Anyone could do it. Although, not anyone could have *me*, but you see my point." Tudor nervously plucked at his Napalm Death shirt. The black shirt clung to his skin, held in place by a sweaty paste. "But they didn't do anything new or revolutionary like Hitler or some other historical figures. Didn't even try." Content with his judgment, Tudor took a smoke from the pack, lit it, and sank into his chair.

"Even animals can procreate. It's just biology," Edi concurred, adjusting his glasses, which tended to slip down his slick nose. Then he stabbed out his cigarette in the full ashtray.

Stroking his chin, Alex said, "The problem with our parents is that they do what society tells them to, and our society is lazy. Romanians have always been lazy. They always fought to defend themselves, rather than to attack and conquer. With the exception of a few great warriors and charismatic leaders, like Vlad Tepes, Stefan the Great, and Codreanu, who most definitely carried Aryan blood, Romanians have always been victims and slaves. A nation with no history. What Romanians need is total war. The struggle for survival would unleash their power."

Alex stopped to sip his beer and light his first Kent. He pushed his hair out of his eyes and continued, "Did you guys know that during the two world wars Europe achieved its greatest technological progress? Think about it! If you know that the Nazis will attack you with their Panzers and Luftwaffe and torture and enslave you, you fucking create better weapons to defend yourself, right? And this arms race is progress, you know? The problem with Romanians right now is that there is no one to shake them, to make them come to their senses and either die or become better. You're really alive only when at war."

Tudor and Edi listened attentively. As his brain computed his friend's remarks about war, Tudor gazed at the peaceful surroundings. A family of four was eating lunch at a nearby table. Tudor surmised the family, already clad in swimsuits, was headed for the seaside, probably coming from Bucharest. The Black Sea resorts were only two hours away. At another table, the two men and the woman had finished their lunch and were smoking and sipping coffee. Tudor made eye contact with one of the men and quickly looked away. The cooks at a nearby tavern were grilling ground meat and serving it with mustard and fries. The smell was inviting, but Tudor had already eaten lunch. A long queue awaited stretched away from the pumps at the gas station across the street. Impatient honks intermittently punctuated the afternoon.

More people going on vacation, Tudor thought. *Going to relax on the beach, charge their batteries, so they can survive another year at the office. Doing the same things every year, over and over, until they die.*

Tudor lit a cigarette from the old one and extinguished the butt in the overflowing ashtray. Chain-smoking was a new habit.

Chapter 4 Midday Mutilation

The trio sat in silence for a few moments, drinking and smoking. Tudor flicked his ashes onto the ground and spat. The glob of saliva arced through the air and landed on a tree trunk. George had taught him how to spit through clenched teeth. Now that his smoking somehow made the saliva heavier and easier to direct, the liquid projectile wouldn't fall apart in midair. Gladdened by his improving proficiency, Tudor mused that he could hit targets even ten feet away.

He saw the man who had made eye contact with him walking their way. He must have been in his forties, slim build, with short dark hair.

When the man reached their table, he said, "Good afternoon, boys! I see you're enjoying the beautiful day."

The boys nodded half-heartedly, irritated by the intrusion.

"May I ask you a quick question? If you answer sincerely, I'll buy you another round of beer?"

"Sure, why not?" Alex said.

"Fantastic! Now, do you guys see the woman over there, sitting next to my friend?"

The kids looked in that direction and nodded. The woman was thirtyish, plump, with long curly dark hair.

"Now, in your honest opinion, is she fuckable? I mean, if you saw her on the street would you think, 'Oh, I need to nail this bitch'?"

The boys eyed the woman more thoroughly. She was no sex bomb. Her face was okay but not beautiful by any means. Her boobs were medium-sized and her ass seemed a bit large, covering the entire surface of the chair. Although she was sitting, you could guess her legs were short and thick.

Tudor broke the awkward silence, saving the three boys from deepening embarrassment. "I'd do her if you got me another beer!"

They all laughed, including the older man. Tudor noticed a mouth full of cavities when the man tilted his head back and bellowed heartily.

"You guys are a riot! I love you so much!" the man

exclaimed, wiping joyful tears from his eyes. "Now, let me tell you a secret." The man leaned over, put his hands on the table, and whispered, "You know, pussy's basically all the same. I mean, Marga here, she's not hot or anything. But when you fuck her, you feel the same as when you fuck a supermodel. Because the vagina is the same, you know, the inside of the pussy. It really makes no difference."

The man stopped talking and looked deep into their eyes, to make sure they understood.

"So, my advice to you, don't say 'no' to the uglies or the fatties! Just fuck 'em, 'cause they need love too. That's why God Almighty put them on this earth. And it all feels the same. But then, of course, if a sexy one shows interest, fuck her too. That said, you'll see that, in the end, pussy's all the same. You follow me, boys?"

They managed a round of embarrassed nods. Although the man was funny, his presence made them uneasy.

"Good!" The man straightened up and ruffled Edi's curly blond hair. Acting out a nervous tic, Edi immediately pushed his curls back behind his ears. "Now, let me buy you a round, my friends. What do you drink? Ursus? It's coming. Anything else you need?"

Alex and Edi shook their heads. Relieved that the man was about to leave, Tudor hazarded a joke. "Can you get the ugly to blow us?"

The man laughed again, exposing his cavities. "I'll see what I can do. But, first, a round of beer for my new comrades."

He disappeared into the pub. The kids smiled at each other. "What a creep!" Alex said and polished off his beer.

"A creep with benefits," Tudor noted.

The man came back and put three fresh, cold beers on the table. Then, patting Tudor's shoulder, he said, "Thanks for your help, lads. Now, I'm going back to my ugly pussy. Y'all have a good day!"

He patted Tudor's shoulder one more time and left.

Tudor took a swig of one of the new bottles and then

Chapter 4 Midday Mutilation

looked at his friends, "What the fuck were we talking about?"

"Oh, Alex was saying that Romanians need total war," Edi said.

"Oh, yeah."

"I actually agree with Alex," Edi said, nervously adjusting his glasses, "and I think we can start a war right here in our town. I told you that I did some research on how to make nitroglycerine and artisanal bombs. Let's just say it's feasible. I can trick our old chemistry teacher into using the lab since she already thinks I'm a science wiz. And then we can blow places up. Instigate terror!"

"Awesome! I'd like to blow up Queen," Tudor said, smirking. All three of them were disgusted by the habits of the young people in their small town. Recently, Queen, a new nightclub near downtown, became the place to go. Every Saturday night, the girls did their best to look like cheap sluts and went to Queen to get drunk and dance mindlessly. Guys followed them, hoping a piece of ass would come their way. Then, the following week at school, everyone babbled about how wild and crazy it got at Queen, how so-and-so ended up dancing topless on a table and so-and-so had his cock sucked by a total stranger in a hotel room or the nearby woods.

"Oh, Jesus," Edi exclaimed, "I overheard Gaby and Alina talking about it during recess. Alina was like, 'Oh, when I go to Queen I try to smile and be happy. Like, I force myself to have fun, you know, sis? Fake it till you make it.'" Edi started batting his eyes and impersonating Alina's high-pitched, whiny voice. "'I ought to have a good time at Queen every Saturday night. Dancing and partying, I mean, that's what being a girl is about, right?'"

"And I ought to drain as many Gypsy doorknobs as possible," Tudor added.

Alex grimaced. "Oh, shit, this reminds me. A cousin of mine got gangbanged by Gypsies after going to Queen one night."

"You mean raped?" Tudor asked.

"No, I think she was just too drunk to say no. But anyway, now she's diseased."

"Oh, shit!"

"Yeah, if I were in her place, I'd blow my brains out. She's fucking infested meat."

"You can say that again, bro. I can't think of anything worse that could happen to a girl," Edi concurred.

"And you know the crazy part?" Alex asked.

"What?" Edi and Tudor wondered in unison.

"She said she liked it. She had multiple orgasms and shit. Apparently, she ripped her clothes off and bit herself while she climaxed repeatedly."

"Oh, gross! What a skank!" Tudor recoiled in disgust.

"You should put her out of her misery, Alex. If my sister did that, I'd fucking kill her," Edi said.

Tudor took another drink of beer. He was getting tipsy. Warmth spread through his body. His mind slowly drifted away from the conversation. He couldn't believe that only yesterday Mr. Stan had computed their final grades (he had barely passed with a 6), and now the school year was officially over. Tudor was already in vacation mode, hanging out with his best friends and planning acts of violence and extremism.

Shit will go down this summer, he said to himself. *Worthless people will either die or be scarred for life.*

Speaking loudly, as if he had suddenly remembered something important, Alex interrupted Tudor's daydreaming. "Hey brothers, remember how a few weeks ago we talked about burning down one of the churches?"

"Yes, Father Rusu's church," Tudor confirmed, suddenly excited.

"That's right. Apparently this is a trend in Norway right now. The Satanists in Norway set churches on fire."

Tudor frowned. "What?"

"Yes, I read about it in *Heavy Metal Magazine*. They want to obliterate Christianity in Norway."

Tudor felt a pang of envy. The idea that there were other,

Chapter 4 Midday Mutilation

more extreme Satanists in the world deeply unsettled him. "Oh, man, we should do it too then. As soon as possible!" he said through clenched teeth.

"Sure, but we also need to keep quiet about it. You know, Varg Vikernes from Burzum bragged about burning down churches and killing people and they threw him in jail for like twenty years."

"So what? Now everyone thinks he's cool," Tudor said.

"The awesome thing is that he's still recording music. Apparently, they let him use his guitar and keyboard, and he's releasing albums from prison."

Alex and Tudor were embroiled in a musical arms race, a competition to discover and listen to the most brutal music. Tudor liked Cannibal Corpse, Napalm Death, and Mortician, but now it sounded like Alex had discovered an even more extreme sound: Norwegian Black Metal.

Tudor decided to order some black metal albums as soon as possible.

"It's cool that they let him create music while behind bars," Edi agreed.

Alex frowned. "Yes, but my point is just that when we start burning down and blowing up places, we should keep quiet about it."

"But then no one will know how extreme we are," Tudor pleaded, his tone aggressive and whiny.

"Maybe we can be like a terrorist group. We need to think of a name...and then we can assume responsibility for the attacks...and say we're Satanists," Edi suggested.

"That's good; I like that," Tudor agreed and took a swig of beer.

"We can be like... The Angels of Death," Edi put in.

"Yes, I love that. Or SS—Tatareni," Tudor added.

Alex nodded his agreement and rubbed his chin. "First things first, though. I think we should get in touch with these guys from Norway. Even if Varg is in jail, many of his followers are still active. He probably guides them from behind bars.

They are very extreme. We should network and coordinate with them. Like, at the beginning they posed as Satanists, but now they worship pagan gods like Odin. You know, the god of war. They say their music brought Odin back to life. And this is interesting because it's well known that World War II was caused by Odin rising again in Germany, especially in the German youth. It's Odin who guided and inspired Hitler!"

Alex sat back in his chair and talked rapidly, his mouth like a machine gun emptying one magazine after another. His blond hair fell into his eyes, but he didn't bother pushing it away. He held his cigarette in his outstretched right hand. Tudor's gaze wandered from that hand up the robust white arm, where there remained the still whiter scars of the inscriptions Alex had cut with his razor.

Slayer. SS. Satan Master.

Listening to their cherished friend express his deepest thoughts and hopes, his most foundational motives, triggered mixed emotions in Tudor and Edi. They were grateful for Alex's friendship. But they were also scared of letting him down, of disappointing him. Having such a charismatic friend, with such talents and such a strong personality, was cause for pride but also a heavy burden.

Tudor found himself wondering whether people like Alex ever felt lonely and disappointed in their peers. That kind of loneliness, Tudor thought, must be a hundred times heavier than that of ordinary people.

I'd die for Alex, Tudor found himself thinking. *I'd be happy to do it. No one will fuck with this guy, not when I'm around.*

Tudor bit his tongue, fighting back tears. Then he focused again on Alex's words.

"Guys, I'll let you in on a secret. But make sure you don't talk about this to others, because noninitiates don't understand." Behind the curtain of blond hair, Alex frowned deeply, his intensely focused eyes hunting for a good way to communicate. To his friends' surprise, his voice wavered slightly when he resumed speaking. "I've been in contact with

Chapter 4 Midday Mutilation

the spiritual world of our ancestors and gods. They chose me. They want to guide me on a secret path by showing me visions. A few days ago they showed me something that rocked me to the core. I spent days trying to understand it, but now I think I know what it meant."

Tudor and Edi listened to Alex like zealots before a prophet.

"I was having some coffee while reading this book about Odin, and suddenly I felt dizzy and light-headed. I lay down on my bed and closed my eyes for a moment. When I opened them again, I was on a battlefield. My bedroom was replaced by a field of butchered corpses. I felt this terrible pain in my chest. When I touched my breast to inspect it, my hand came away red with blood. I looked at the horizon and saw the Wild Hunt, Odin's army of the dead. Then I felt my body rising toward the galloping horses, as if attracted by a magnet. Next thing I knew, I was back in my bedroom, lying on my bed. But here's the crazy part..." Alex's voice slowly dwindled, and he leaned forward as if to safeguard the secrecy of his revelation. Tudor and Edi also leaned forward, stretching their necks.

"I was still bleeding from that wound."

Alex lifted his black Negura Bunget shirt to reveal a jagged, purplish scar that stretched horizontally across his chest, just below the collarbone. I had to go to the doctor to get stitches. I told them I fell on a shard of a broken bottle while playing basketball. It was crazy. But I'm sure it was made by a spear or something. You know, in battle."

Tudor and Edi stared at the newly-stitched wound, dumbfounded. It reminded Tudor of one of his drawings: the warrior pierced from within, stabbed by a small soldier hidden inside his skull. Like in a fortress. Was this wound self-inflicted? Was Alex crazy? Delusional? Tudor didn't believe that. He believed Alex's story.

At least he *wanted* to believe it.

Alex leaned over the table again and folded his hands. He looked deeply into Tudor's and Edi's eyes and spoke in a solemn, secretive voice.

"I think Odin rises in us as we speak. Right here, right now!"

Goosebumps scurried up Tudor's spine.

Alex went on. "Odin pushes us to declare war on the weak and feeble. The Aryan race is under attack by the apeling hordes, the degenerate mongoloids. It's time to take a stand and fight back!"

Tudor and Edi nodded as if hypnotized.

"Think about it, my friends! Stand back and think for a moment! Why else would we have these hostile thoughts all of a sudden? This time last year, Tudor was captain of the soccer team and was considering becoming a professional player. Edi and I were studying to go to the Olympiad, Edi in physics and me in history. Remember, Edi, we were shooting for the nationals? And now, one year later, we're planning to blow this fucking town to pieces. What changed?"

Alex's voice had grown hoarse from his extended oration, and he soothed his throat with a large swig of beer.

"And do you guys have dreams?" he asked. "Dreams of mayhem and destruction, in which you kill and kill and destroy everything as if possessed?"

Tudor nodded. "I fucking do, man. I have very violent fucked-up thoughts and dreams. Even strangers on the street, they irritate me. I obsess about pushing their eyes deep into their skulls with my thumbs and stomping on their heads..."

"Exactly. These obsessive thoughts come from your Aryan blood. It's kinda like your blood feels the danger in your surroundings and pushes you to fight. It's basically the survival instinct of our warrior species."

Tudor nodded. Alex's explanations made a lot of sense to him.

"And another thing," Alex carried on, "my dream was about how, if you died in battle but had fought courageously, Odin would take you to Valhalla, which is his kingdom of warriors. And then you would continue to train for the final

Chapter 4 Midday Mutilation

battle against the apelings, a perverted race of giants and mutants. The final war, that's Ragnarok or Armageddon. So, my point is that even if you die—let's say a Gypsy or Jew manages to kill you—you still have a chance at getting your revenge during Ragnarok. So, basically, dying...it's nothing to be afraid of, you know?"

Tudor's brain hungrily absorbed Alex's mythological picture. The god of war sounded so much cooler than the old, lame Christian God. He wanted to be one of the chosen ones and go to Valhalla, just as last year he had wanted to make the local soccer team.

Satanists in Norway, Odin, the god of war, burning down churches, killing in the name of a superior race, these were like magical words that dissipated the fog of a dull, meaningless existence. Alex's revelations infused Tudor with a new sense of purpose.

Contemplating these intriguing new ideas, he took another drink of beer.

While Tudor immediately accepted Alex's claims, Edi couldn't dispel his skepticism. Picking at one of the zits on his forehead, he ventured a question. "But if Odin is the Norse god of war, what does he have to do with Romania?"

Tudor hated Edi a bit for that awful question. It seemed weak and in bad taste. However, instead of ridiculing the questioner, he decided to listen to the answer.

"That's a fair question, comrade," Alex began. "I thought a lot about it myself. Like I said, Romanians are mostly cowardly, lazy, and stupid. But there were a few Aryan leaders in our history. You know, like Himmler said that Genghis Khan must have had untainted blood because he was so brutal and courageous. But, you know, Mongolia isn't a nation of history. It's even worse than Romania. Anyway, what convinced me that we have an Aryan destiny was the Iron Guard and its leaders. Especially Zelea Codreanu and Horia Sima. And also how Romania, led by Marshal Antonescu, fought alongside Germany in World War II. But I'm not going into details. I could go on for hours. I could teach an entire fucking class on it."

Tudor and Edi nodded and laughed. They knew this was Alex's favorite subject, and they had heard it all before. But now, in the context of the discussion about Norse gods, the familiar story gained new meaning.

Alex took a drink of beer and continued.

"There were tensions between Antonescu and the Iron Guard. The Legionnaires had massacred Jews during the pogroms with no method or plan and ended up hurting the Romanian economy, which was owned by the fucking Yids. Hitler needed a strong ally in Romania; he was after our oil, you see, and he agreed with Antonescu that the blind butchery of Yiddish scum should stop. So, after his meeting with Hitler in Berlin, in mid-January 1941, Antonescu came back and began replacing key Legionnaire ministers with his own men. In response, the Legionnaires' rebellion ensued. The end of January 1941. In Bucharest and other centers like Iasi. During those days, I swear to you, Bucharest was in the grip of Odin. Three or four days of maximum fucking brutality. Like, in a slaughterhouse near Bucharest, the Legionnaires impaled dozens of Jews on hooks. Hung them like cattle, their entrails hanging out. Some corpses bore the inscription 'Kosher Meat.'"

"What's 'kosher'?" Edi asked.

"Oh, it's the Jewish word for good quality food."

Tudor and Edi smiled.

"How many Jews did the Legionnaires kill?" Tudor inquired.

"It's not clear, but maybe a thousand during the Bucharest pogrom and like ten thousand in the Iasi pogrom," Alex answered.

"Wow," Tudor exclaimed, trying to imagine the scale of the violence.

Alex finished off his beer, burped, and smiled. "But, yeah, back to Edi's question... I'm just saying that about fifty years

Chapter 4 Midday Mutilation

ago, Odin rose in Bucharest for a few nights of terror. Berlin, Rome, Madrid, Budapest, Iasi were all in the grips of the Nordic god. We are now thirty miles from Bucharest and Odin is rising again here. I'm sure there's more Romanian youth who feel the same way we do, but they just don't know what's going on. We need to recruit them and organize ourselves. You know, like Zelea Codreanu did with the Iron Guard and The Legion of the Archangel Michael."

Edi agreed, his feeble skepticism squashed.

Tudor drained his bottle of beer. "I need to take a leak."

"Me too. Should we ditch this place?" Edi asked.

"Sure, but not before we get some hard liquor," Alex said. They stood up and Tudor pocketed the pack of *Kents*. They headed to the restaurant entrance. For a second, Tudor wobbled on his inebriated legs, and his shoulder crashed into a tree trunk as he tried to leave the patio. But he soon regained his balance. Edi also struggled to walk straight. While they stumbled toward the washroom, Alex bought a 750ml vodka bottle.

They exited the restaurant, rounded the corner, and climbed onto the dike. Alex passed the bottle to Tudor. "Hold on, I need to take a leak too." He descended to the riverside and expelled a thick, yellow stream of urine. He sighed with relief and contentment. When he finished, Alex walked back up to his friends.

Tudor lit a smoke and looked at the river. It was swollen and broader than usual. Its surface shimmered in the sunlight, making him squint. Shielding his eyes with his hand, he saw the thick forest covering the other bank. A willow's branches touched the murky water.

On his side of the river, in the distance, Tudor could see the cemetery's multitude of tiny white crosses and the landfill's grey mounds of garbage.

Tudor took a drink of vodka and cringed as the liquid burned his throat. Then he passed the bottle to Alex. After swallowing a large mouthful, Alex grimaced and shivered. He passed the bottle to Edi and said, "Maybe we should get some water; this fucker burns."

"It's okay, man; it's not going to kill us," Tudor reassured him, smiling.

"It will," Edi said huskily after taking a drink. His face was contorted in disgust, as if he had just bit into a lemon.

"Our bodies will get dehydrated," Alex insisted.

Tudor grinned. "Fuck our bodies!"

As proof of his bodily disregard, Tudor took a big gulp. Unconvinced, Alex said he'll get a bottle of water and headed back to the restaurant.

"Pussy!" Tudor yelled and passed the bottle to Edi.

Looking at the murky stream again, Tudor inhaled the sweet, thick aromas of wild grass and flowing water. He remembered swimming in the river as a kid, during summer vacations. He used to roam the area on the opposite side with other kids, in search of fun and adventure. Sometimes, when they were lucky enough to have binoculars, they would spy on the girls sunbathing topless on the sandy beaches, or on couples who thought the seclusion of the riverside would allow for unobserved sex in broad daylight.

Now, Tudor realized, he wasn't a kid anymore. This summer was serious. As soldiers of Odin, they were on a mission to disrupt and destroy.

It will be a different kind of summer, Tudor thought, *but just as magical and full of adventure as the previous ones.*

Alex returned with a two-liter bottle of water. He handed it to Edi, who was complaining of a burning throat.

Tudor felt grateful for his two friends. But he also realized they weren't exactly an army. "I think we need to recruit more rebels into our ranks," he told them.

After a moment's thought, Alex said, "We have a good core of people. Trust is the most important thing. Us and George, you know, we all trust each other."

Tudor and Edi agreed.

"So, whenever we recruit, we need the newcomer to pass

Chapter 4 Midday Mutilation

some tests to gain our trust," Alex continued.

"We'll have to ask them to do some crazy shit and put their asses on the line, to prove their commitment," Tudor added.

"I've noticed a few young metalheads around town. And there was a guy in the seventh grade I saw in the schoolyard once. He was wearing a Pantera shirt. Maybe we can approach them." Edi said.

Tudor shook his head. "No, man, *they'll* approach us. When we make a name for ourselves, they'll know we're extreme, and they'll come to us."

Alex nodded. "The first thing we need to do is find a place to use as headquarters. Like an abandoned house that we can clean up. Maybe a basement or someone's apartment. Then we'll invite potential recruits over for drinks and, if they pass the tests, we'll initiate them."

"Wow, that's a great idea," Tudor said, bursting with enthusiasm. "I know a few abandoned houses near my grandma's place, by the train station. George's apartment came with a large storage unit, in the building's basement, but his dad barely uses it."

Alex raised the vodka bottle in salutation. "That's awesome; we should check it out! Cheers!" He took another swallow of liquor and chased away the burn with a gulp of water.

Edi felt the need to contribute, "We can also use my house when my parents are away."

"Sure," Alex said. "But that's only a temporary location; we need a permanent one."

"Yes, a place of our own, Edi. Where we can paint the walls black and have skulls and swastikas and shit like that. Can we do that at your house?"

"Not really," Edi smiled. "Unless you want to give my dad a heart attack."

"Oh, that wouldn't be so bad," Tudor grinned. "Then we'd have full access to your mom and sister."

"Oh, my God, you sound like George, the Rude Pig. Stop hanging out with that slob," Alex commented.

Tudor grinned. "George is my muse."

"Also, Tudor," Edi said, "I didn't know you wanted my mom."

"Oh, but she's fuckable."

Edi grimaced. "You're sicker than George, man." He punched Tudor lightly in the chest.

"But Ioana, your sister, she's still available, right?" Alex asked, a yellow grin splitting his face.

"She's a stupid turd; you guys can do whatever you want to her," Edi said, clearly embarrassed by the subject.

Alex lifted the vodka and the water and squinted at the two bottles in the bright sunlight.

"Brothers, do you want to get really drunk really fast?"

Tudor and Edi nodded.

"Okay," Alex continued, smiling, "let's pretend there's water in *both* of these bottles. You know? Like, tell yourself it's water when you're drinking vodka...sorry, *water*."

"Can you show us an example?" Tudor asked.

"Okay, in this bottle we have normal water. And it's soooo fucking hot outside, and I'm very thirsty." Alex lifted the vodka to his lips, inverted the bottle, and swallowed. The liquid gurgled as his throat pulsed once, twice, three times. He passed the bottle to Tudor and then drank a generous mouthful of real water.

Not wanting to be outperformed, Tudor looked at the vodka and told himself it was water. He lifted the bottle skyward and said, "Thank you, Odin, for this fresh, crystal clear water on this hot summer day!" Steeled by his invocation, he brought the consecrated vessel to his lips and chugged. Then he passed the bottle to Edi. It was more than half-empty.

Edi did the same as his friends. The bottles were quickly emptying.

As he watched Edi drink, Tudor felt the wave of alcohol hit his brain. The impact staggered him, and he nearly lost his

Chapter 4 Midday Mutilation

footing. He noticed Alex's blue eyes were shot through with innumerable tiny veins.

"Go with it, bro," Alex said, giving him a yellow and reassuring smile.

Tudor grinned drunkenly. He felt all-powerful, light, and joyful. The world around him came to life. The grass became more intensely green. The sun was brighter. His powers of perception increased, and he thought he could see into the core of reality, if only he focused hard enough.

He walked down the dirt path atop the dike, raised his hands to the sky and began singing, *"In my dominion/ Blood will always rain."*

Edi and Alex followed behind him and joined in the song: *"I damn your soul/ to everlasting pain."*

Edi put a new spin on the lyrics: *"In Odin's dominion/ Blood will always rain."*

They repeated the chorus many times as they followed the path to the cemetery. The river valley was on their right. On their left, they passed a milk plant and a few houses. When a vast greenhouse came into view, Tudor felt the surge of inspiration. The glass roof glistening in the sunshine begged to be broken. He hefted a rock, ran ahead of the others, and shouted the opening lines of their favorite song:

"Hey, suckers,/ what's that fuckin' silence in this place?/ Wake up, motherfuck/ I ain't got no time to waste!"

He let the rock fly, lobbing it high into the air. A moment later, the report of shattering glass pierced the afternoon silence.

"Stop the silence!/ Silence is death!" they shouted and ran down the path.

Since Tudor's violence had summoned no outraged gardeners or botanists, the friends slowed after about fifty yards and resumed walking casually and singing.

Further down on their left, an abandoned service station appeared. Tudor remembered that he used to come here to fill his bike tires or patch a punctured tube. The business had moved to a new location, and now the small garage and its yard stood neglected.

"Come on, guys, let's make some fucking noise!" Tudor shouted, running down the side of the dike. Only, it felt more like gliding. He could barely feel his feet, and only a miracle prevented him from stumbling and sprawling into a drunken heap.

He stepped through a hole in a fence and onto the forsaken property. Weeds grew unchecked between tall poplars. Here and there lay discarded car parts. A rusted car with no wheels sat atop stacked bricks.

Running up from behind Tudor, Alex jumped onto the car and stomped on its hood. He raised the vodka bottle and proclaimed prophetically, "We are the bringers of destruction and pure blood. We will burn slave blood!"

Then he took a big swallow.

Tudor found a large stone on the ground, wound up, and hurled it at one of the windows of the forlorn building. The projectile missed its mark and pinged off of the tin roof.

Edi's stone didn't miss.

The sound of shattering glass erupted into the languid midday air.

A startled flock of crows took flight from one of the trees. Tudor heard a high-pitched cawing coming from somewhere on the ground nearby. He stumbled in the direction of the call. A crow hopped away from him on the grass, dragging a broken wing. It tried to conceal itself in a cluster of weeds. Tudor launched a rock at the bird and hit its wounded side. The frightened animal hopped further into the thicket. The youth armed himself with another stone and approached the bird. The crow started cawing louder, caught in a rising panic. Tudor flattened a cluster of weeds with his boot, uncovering the bird's pitiful refuge. He noticed its black eyes and thin pink tongue and the blood staining its feathers. The animal's terrified stare, animated by the blind will to survive at all cost, seemed irreducibly alien. A hideous organism shaped

Chapter 4 Midday Mutilation

by the accidents of nature, following rudimentary, absolute commands. *Live! Go on living no matter what! Struggle! Struggle! Feed to live! Hide from danger!* Tudor thought he could hear the hoarse voice of Mother Nature, that old hag, behind the injured bird's desperate calls. The voice spoke through a throat gargling shards of glass. Its cadence was a rhythm of colors: green, red, black. Green of the grass, red of the blood, black of the crow. The colors intermingled into the heartbeat of life, forming the grammar of everything. Mother Nature, the mad, sadistic witch. A witch with razor-sharp teeth.

Tudor suddenly felt afraid and repulsed. He wanted to look away from the disturbing vision. The stone seemed heavy in his hand, and he let it drop.

He spat on the crow and walked away.

"Too bad George isn't here," he mumbled. "He'd have smashed your ugly head."

He walked back toward the others, intending to suggest that they explore the ruined building and break more stuff.

Alex and Edi were taking target practice with the remaining windows. Alex launched a rock, but it thudded off of the wooden frame of the last intact pane of glass. Suddenly a hole appeared, the pane disintegrated into multiple glinting shards. Edi's stone. The hail of glass loudly splashed onto the floor.

"Good aim, four eyes," Tudor said.

Edi smiled.

That's when someone yelled at them.

"Hey, you! What in God's name are you doing?" an adult's voice demanded.

They whirled to face the sound. Twenty yards to their right, a man's voice bellowed commandingly from behind a grapevine, "Stop! Stop right there! Just wait right there; I'm coming for you!"

The kids panicked and sprinted back toward the levee. Tudor jumped the fence while Alex and Edi crouched and squeezed through a hole. Having regained the dike, they turned and hurled curses at the stranger. "Hey, you fucking scum! Why don't you drop dead, you retarded old fart?"

Tudor grabbed a rock and hurled it full force toward the grapevine. It disappeared noiselessly into the foliage.

Didn't break anything, Tudor thought. *Or maybe it broke his head.*

"Let's haul ass!" Alex shouted and ran down the path in the direction of the cemetery. The others followed. After a short sprint, they slowed to their normal pace but looked back from time to time, in case the man had given chase.

But no one was following them.

They descended on the right side of the dike toward one of their favorite places: a cluster of poplars by the waterside. About a month earlier, during the May Day celebrations, they had gotten really wasted here, and Edi ended up puking on a girl. A group of girls had been picnicking nearby and had flirted with the boys, but nothing came of it after the vomiting incident. Now, on a workday, the area was deserted. The boys found a shady patch and sat on a group of large, grey boulders to pass around the remaining vodka. The river had overflowed its bed, flooding the grassy shore, and water rippled only a few yards away from the grove.

Tudor took a drink and scanned the water's surface. "Oh, my God, the river is so fucking swollen!" He pointed with the bottle to an area a few yards away. "We used to swim right there and jump from the cement platform between those rocks, but now it's all underwater."

Alex and Edi looked at the spot. Another group of boulders was now almost entirely submerged, their tips jutting out of the water.

Edi gazed upstream. "Look, tree limbs floating."

"Once I saw a dead sheep floating. And a cow or horse, I wasn't sure," Tudor said.

Alex took a drink and said, "I imagine they try to drink from the river, fall in and get caught in the current."

Chapter 4 Midday Mutilation

Tudor grinned. "Either that or they get raped and strangled by farmers and thrown into the river."

"How do you rape a sheep?" Edi asked.

"What do you mean?" Tudor smiled. "It's obvious: you have sex with it against its will."

"A sheep doesn't have a will," Edi claimed.

"Of course it does. The will to *not* get raped by farmers."

Alex chuckled. "It's okay, Edi, Tudor is just pulling your leg."

Edi looked puzzled. Tudor and Alex laughed.

Scanning the thick forest on the opposite bank, Tudor had an idea. "Hey, guys, I know that forest pretty well. George and I used to roam those woods a few years back. I'm pretty sure there's an abandoned ranger's cabin in a clearing nearby. We can turn it into our headquarters."

"A center for raping sheep?" Edi asked, unable to let go of the issue.

"We can rape real women," Tudor said. "But if you're fixated on sheep then go for it."

Alex drank and said, "Yes, that might work, except that it's too far from the city. We need a place in town, but we can use the cabin in the forest for other purposes. Like rape and torture. 'Cause there's no one around to hear the screams, you know?"

"Yes, our own private Auschwitz," Edi said.

"I'll drink to that," Tudor said. "The Auschwitz of the Romanian plain." Tudor took a swig. There was only one finger of vodka left. He emptied the water bottle and threw it into the river. "We can get more water at the cemetery."

The others nodded.

"A private Auschwitz does sound good," Alex concurred. Then, after a few moments of thoughtful silence, he asked, "Have you guys heard of the forest of the impaled? The most horrific sight in the history of torture?"

Tudor shook his head.

"I've heard of the forest of the hanged," Edi said.

"Oh, that's just Rebreanu's fiction, brother. I'm talking about historical reality here," Alex replied professorially. "In the summer of 1462, Mehmed the Conqueror invaded Wallachia from the south. He crossed the Danube with a huge fucking army. As many soldiers as there are leaves and blades of grass, like the poet says."

For dramatic effect, Alex waved his hand toward the forest across the river.

"What poet?" Edi ventured.

"Our national poet, you ignoramus. Mihail Eminescu." Alex pronounced the name with pride. "The Turks probably passed through this very land, because Vlad Tepes, a.k.a. Dracula, had abandoned the fortress of Bucharest and retreated to the foothills of the Carpathians.

"He burned the crops and poisoned the wells and everything so the Turks would starve. Also, he would attack them at night, when they least expected, slaughter the Asian scum and take prisoners. Then, just outside Targoviste, Mehmed came upon a nightmarish site: the forest of the impaled. A mile-long semi-circle of stakes. More than twenty thousand Turks, some impaled, others crucified, were decomposing in the summer heat. Ravens nested in their fucking skulls and disemboweled stomachs."

Alex's story sparked Tudor's alcohol-soaked imagination. Gazing at the crowns of the trees on the other side of the river, Tudor fantasized that they concealed a jungle of the dead and dying. People impaled on branches like worms on fishhooks. Others nailed through the head and neck, dangling limply from tree trunks. Severed limbs and bleeding stumps. Many hanging upside-down from branches, wriggling like bats unable to spread their wings. Birds nesting in ruined eye sockets, mutilated mouths, and shattered ribcages.

And then, Tudor thought, fall would come, and the trees would shed their leaves to reveal a new Holocaust.

To make the dark vision stick, Tudor made a few mental notes. *Summer: green leaves, red blood. Fall: yellow leaves,*

Chapter 4 Midday Mutilation

brown blood, black crows.

Another note: *Paint while drunk; vodka inspires.*

Back in reality, Tudor focused again on Alex's eulogy for Vlad Dracula.

"...as a kid he learned from the Turks impalement was a tool not only of death but also of torture. But then he took it to the next level. Anyway, Mehmed retreated, tail between his legs, and was probably scarred for life. He— "

"Someone's coming!" Edi interrupted, pointing toward the dike. His voice trembled with a panicked urgency.

Alex and Tudor turned their heads in that direction. A man on a bicycle was furiously pedaling toward them atop the levee.

"Maybe it's that guy from earlier," Edi mumbled.

To Tudor, the brief encounter with the man seemed to have happened days ago and was all but forgotten. He didn't believe it was the same adult they had cursed until the cyclist rolled down the slope of the levee and pedaled straight toward them.

Panic surged through the three kids, but its power to effect action was disrupted by their drunkenness. Rather than bolting, they retreated only a few steps toward the water and tried to look casual. In the corner of his eye, Tudor saw the man dismount from his bike and prop it against a tree.

Tudor turned and looked at him.

He was old, short, and skinny. A ring of neatly combed grey hair clung to the sides of his head beneath a gleaming bald crown. His thick glasses magnified his black eyes, lending them an insectile cast. He wore grey pants and brown sandals, and his unbuttoned white polo shirt revealed tufts of silver chest hair. He lacked a neck, and walked hunched over. His disproportionately long arms hung limply at his sides, knuckles forward, hands cupped like the shovel on an industrial excavator. He strongly reminded Tudor of a chimpanzee.

The elderly man stopped a few yards short of the kids and

interrogated them in a voice driven into the upper register by indignation. "What were you hooligans doing back there?" His insect eyes bored into them. "Throwing stones at that shop? Is it your shop? Is it your parents' shop?"

"It's abandoned," Edi mumbled, staring at the ground.

"So what? That means you can destroy it?" the man demanded, his voice growing into a shout. "Don't you boys have anything better to do than smash windows and curse at people? Is that what they teach you in school?"

The kids didn't answer. They tried to assume an air of guilty shame by staring at the ground.

Singling out Edi, the man asked, "What is your name, blond boy?"

"Eduard," Edi murmured.

"Is that so? Do you happen to be Mr. Manea's son?"

Edi gasped. "Yes, I am."

"Well, I happen to know your dad, kid. Ask him if he knows Mr. Oprea, Mr. Ilie Oprea from Tatareni's Agricultural Cooperative. That's me." The man was clearly pleased to hold the inimitable leverage of knowing a guilty boy's father. "I retired a few years ago but he must still remember me. So, Eduard, my dear boy, what if I told your dad about all this? About how you've been drinking vodka?" the man asked, pointing to the almost-empty bottle in Alex's hand.

Alex tried to hide the liquor behind his back, but it was too late.

"It's all about freedom nowadays!" Mr. Oprea continued, building to a crescendo of self-righteousness. "We killed Ceausescu, and now we're free! Well, let me tell you this: it was better under communism. You boys would be working the land..."

Tudor stopped listening. He didn't like where this was going. He saw the pain written on Alex's face. Alex, being humiliated and lectured to by an idiot. Usually, in these situations, they would just look guilty, and the adult would content himself with a firm scolding and a few moral lessons.

Chapter 4 Midday Mutilation

But Tudor sensed that Mr. Oprea was just getting started.

He was afraid the old man might decide to escort them to Mr. Manea's house. That would trigger a series of unfortunate events since Mr. Manea would feel obligated to call Alex's and Tudor's parents. This outcome seemed all the more probable since Mr. Manea's house was not far from the cemetery. Something similar had happened to Tudor before. Once, he and George got caught stealing plastic tubing for their blowpipe games from a construction site. The game consisted of making paper bullet-shaped projectiles, inserting them in the tubes and blowing them at the members of the opposing team. George's and Tudor's addition to the game was that they put pins at the top of their projectiles. Two workers apprehended them, however, and took them to their parents. George got a good whipping from his dad, and Tudor was grounded for a week.

Tudor didn't want that humiliation again.

He felt his anger rising.

Looking at the screeching Mr. Oprea, standing there and repeating his empty platitudes, Tudor found the absurdity of the situation more and more unbearable. Here they were, the glorious servants of Odin, taking crap from Mr. Oprea. A nobody. An old fart. A shit-for-brains peasant. A trained ape who had been working the land all his life.

Mr. Oprea from the Agricultural Cooperative, he had bragged.

A sorry fucking slave. The lowest of the low.

Tudor noticed a mole on Mr. Oprea's lip, bulging there like a piece of excrement waiting to be licked and swallowed. He intuited that the hideous old man was lecturing them because no grown-up would ever take his bullshit seriously.

Suddenly, Tudor decided to take a stand and end this nonsense.

How could they take the whole town by storm if they let themselves be pushed around by a frail, senile senior citizen?

Tudor's anger turned to rage.

He felt it rise and flood his mind like a mighty wave.

The wave submerged his vision into a bloody tide and transformed Mr. Oprea from an aggressor into a target, a victim.

Before unleashing his attack, Tudor vaguely imagined the part from *Terminator* where Arnold's robot vision shows various commands flickering on his inner screen. Or was it *Universal Soldier*? He wasn't sure.

But he was certain of the content of the flickering red command. It said: *Target: Mr. Oprea/ Useless Old Fuck. Assessment: Terminate!*

Tudor stepped toward the elderly man.

A vision of his pocket knife flashed into his mind, but he decided this was a job for his boots. His heavy, black boots. A grin spread across Tudor's face as he anticipated his friends' reaction.

When he saw the big kid approaching him, Mr. Oprea stopped talking and frowned.

Tudor noticed the man was much smaller than him, an unworthy adversary.

He feinted with his left leg, luring the man into an instinctive attempt to parry the blow.

"Too slow," Tudor whispered.

He jumped into a bicycle kick and landed a booted toe in the center of the old man's chest. Mr. Oprea fell backward, the air driven from his lungs. Tudor maintained the offensive, swearing through clenched teeth.

"You fucking stupid peasant, you worthless piece of shit. Do you even know who we are, you scum?"

Mr. Oprea scrambled on his hands and legs like a crab. He stared at the dangerous youth through lenses knocked askew, his eyes panicked and puzzled. His mouth worked but produced nothing meaningful. The needle of his fight or flight compass immediately pointed to "Flight." He turned, pulled himself to his feet, and ran. Tudor took two quick steps in pursuit and savagely kicked the fleeing man's ankle. Mr. Oprea

Chapter 4 Midday Mutilation

stumbled over his own tangled legs and fell to the ground in a whimpering heap. Relentless, Tudor booted his prone foe's ribcage. Bones cracked. Gasping in pain, the man rolled over on the grass, trying to reach the water. Tudor kicked his hip in mid-roll, and the injured elder tumbled all the way into the stream. He screamed when the jagged submerged rocks pierced his back. For a second he disappeared under the brown, frothy stream. Tudor found the man's glasses and tossed them into the water. They broke the surface with a plop.

The old man thrashed about in the river, beating his limbs in a desperate bid for breath, and finally regained his footing in waist-deep water. Under his right arm, the white of his waterlogged shirt slowly reddened. In a frenzy of bloodlust, Tudor seized the man's bike by the handles and rolled it toward the river. At the edge of the water, he lifted the bike by its frame and heaved it at the wounded and reeling man. Mr. Oprea took a twenty-six-inch wheel to the face and fell back into the current he had tried so desperately to escape. Alex joined the attack as the beleaguered man tried once more to get to his feet. He took a running start, whipped the vodka bottle toward the enemy, and scored a direct hit to the chest. The last of the vodka spilled into the air and glinted for a second in the afternoon sun. The old man's search for solid ground beat the water into a white froth. For a moment, it looked like he was trying to fend off his bike which, like a weird metallic sea monster, wanted to drown him.

When he finally found his footing again, he stood submerged to the chest. Violent teenagers, injury, and, now that he was further from the shore, a strong current, numbered among the old man's foes. He was outnumbered, surrounded, and fighting a losing battle.

"...kill you...kill you...stupid..." Mr. Oprea sputtered, spittle flying from his lips. With trembling hands, he wiped the water from his eyes and looked toward his tormentors. Tudor realized his victim could barely see without his glasses. The boys must have resembled three dark spots moving against a green backdrop.

The sight of the near-blind old man threatening to kill them filled Tudor with disgust and drove him to new heights of fury. Frantic, he scanned the ground around him. He located a stone and bent to grab it. When he couldn't separate it from the earth, he fell to his knees and clawed the dirt with furious intensity, until at last he could wield this new weapon. It filled his hand like a softball. He wound up, kicked his leg, and pitched it at his target with all his might. At first, it looked like the pitch would sail wide of its mark, but, in an instinctive attempt to avoid the blow, the myopic old man ducked and put his head directly in the projectile's path. The rock struck with a wet thud. A red bud bloomed on the man's forehead. Blood trickled into his left eye, down his cheek, and onto his chest. Stunned, Mr. Oprea stopped cursing and went limp. The current bore him quickly away.

A devilish grin on his face, Tudor turned back toward his friends. They were looking at the scene with incredulous eyes.

"Let's see if he drowns!" Tudor said and jogged along the grassy bank to stay abreast of Mr. Oprea and satisfy his morbid curiosity. Alex and Edi followed closely. Dressed in their black t-shirts, the kids looked like wolves intently stalking their prey.

The injured man's bald head shimmered in the sunlight whenever it momentarily surfaced. When he finally succeeded in orienting himself, he broke into an awkward dog paddle and then a gimpy forward crawl. He was aiming for the opposite bank, but the current was too powerful and the distance too long for his diminished strength. Then, reaching the middle of the stream, the man suddenly reverted to dog paddling, and looking over his shoulder in a terror-stricken attempt to monitor his tormentors' pursuit. Exhausted, Mr. Oprea paddled aimlessly, barely keeping his head above water.

Afraid someone would spoil their fun, Tudor momentarily turned his attention from his prey and scanned the

Chapter 4 Midday Mutilation

surrounding valley.

There was no one.

The kids started running to keep up with the swift current. Downstream, the river narrowed and bent to the left around a sliver of beach. Fortunately, it was free of swimmers and sunbathers, despite the heat.

It would be more populated on the weekend, Tudor thought. *Good thing it's only Friday afternoon.*

The current carried the beaten man toward the edge of the beach. He feebly grasped at the reeds on the bank and pulled himself out of the water. Tudor ran down a treacherous slope toward the victim, his friends in tow. They approached Mr. Oprea. A high bank upstream from the beach shielded the scene from potential witnesses on the kids' side of the river. The other side was forested, deserted.

The trio silently observed the battered man.

He lay face down in the reeds, his feet still submerged in water. He was breathing in shallow, ragged gasps. His pants had been pulled down during his ordeal, and a hairy crack and the upper third of his white buttocks were exposed beneath his darkly tanned back.

Alex broke the silence. "What the hell do we do now?"

Tudor shrugged.

"We can end up in a juvenile home for this, you know?" Alex pressed.

Tudor stared at the man without answering.

"He knows my dad," Edi reminded them in a whisper.

Tudor walked toward the injured man. Alex grabbed his shoulder in a half-hearted attempt to restrain his friend. "No, man, wait! Let's talk about this!"

Tudor shook himself free of Alex's hand, closed the distance, and stood over the immobilized old man.

He pointed at the wretched body lying face down amidst the reeds. "You mean *this* guy? Make *us* go to juvenile home and ruin *our* lives?" When he said "us," Tudor pointed his index finger at his chest. "This scum ruin *our* lives?" he repeated, expelling a stream of spittle in his indignation, green eyes wide in wonder.

Then he lifted his heavily booted right foot and stomped on the man's head. The blow forced the victim's face deep into the mud. The second blow was more focused. Tudor concentrated all his power in his heel and brought it down squarely in the middle of the man's head. The third blow came with a crack. A skinny red snake of blood slithered out of the man's head and down over his shoulder.

For a second, Tudor stood motionless and stared at the gushing wound. Then he stomped, again and again, shouting curses to the staccato rhythm of his violence. "Die you fucking scum! You mo-ther-fuck-ing no-bo-dy! You re-tard-ed disease!"

He finished by jumping into the air and landing with both feet squarely on the man's spinal column. Bones cracked.

Walking back to the others with a huge grin splitting his face, Tudor impersonated Arnold Schwarzenegger poorly. "This man has been terminated!"

Alex and Edi looked at him with confused and angry eyes.

"How does that solve anything?" Alex demanded furiously.

"Solve what?" Tudor replied, annoyed by his friends' lack of enthusiasm.

"You just killed somebody, you crazy idiot!"

"I killed nobody," Tudor said and smiled, delighting in his pun.

Alex turned to Edi.

"Shit, we need to make sure no one sees this. Can you go and check, Edi, please?"

Edi ran up the steep embankment, hurriedly looked around, and scrambled back. "There's no one!"

"Okay, that's good. Now we need to get rid of the body," Alex said, composing himself and reasserting his leadership of the group.

For a few moments, they gazed at the mangled man.

"It's not yet a body," Edi said faintly. "He still breathes."

Chapter 4 Midday Mutilation

"Oh, shit! Oh, my fucking God!" Tudor exclaimed. It was true; though the movement was barely perceptible, the man's lacerated back still rose and fell.

Deeply annoyed, Tudor fished his knife out of his pocket and flicked it open. "Time for absolute termination," he announced, approaching the victim. Fighting his revulsion, he grabbed Mr. Oprea's shoulder and flipped him onto his back. Oprea's face was a mask of mud. A mixture of dirt, sand, and plant matter caked his eyes and partially filled his open mouth, which was paralyzed in a silent scream. Tudor crouched, placed a hand on the victim's dirty chest, and buried the blade deep into his throat. Then he severed the jugular with a brutal jerk of his arm. Tudor flinched and staggered backward as warm blood sprayed his face and chest. He stared at the dying man with both disgust and fascination. After the initial expulsion, Oprea's throat began to pour forth a measure of lifeblood with each beat of the man's expiring heart. The gradually ebbing fountain painted the man's chest red and streamed down the sides of his body and into the water.

"Shit, I need to wash off this blood," Tudor voiced his sudden realization. He removed his drenched shirt, wiped his face with it, and dropped it on the ground.

Edi and Alex were transfixed. They stared at the corpse, mouths agape.

Tudor knelt at the waterside and sluiced away the gore on his face and neck. Then he submerged the black shirt and scrubbed the blood out of it.

"Killing is hard fucking work," Tudor said, wiping water and sweat from his brow with the back of his hand.

Alex frowned, trying to detach his attention from the grisly spectacle and think clearly. "Tudor, my man, we still need to dispose of the body," he forced out through clenched teeth.

"Why can't we just throw it into the river?" Edi asked.

Alex shook his head. "Once he gets discovered they'll see he was murdered, man. What the hell?"

Tudor tossed his wet but mostly bloodless shirt onto the grass and looked at the dead man, hands on his hips. "Maybe we can eat him. No body, no crime," he suggested, directing a wicked smile at his friends.

Alex looked at him with furious eyes. For a moment, Tudor expected a punch to the face. It felt weird to imagine fighting Alex. He would surely retaliate but might hold back a bit. He wouldn't want to hurt his friend. But he couldn't afford to appear weak, either.

Alex clenched his hands into tight fists. "Hey, Tudor, you crazy fuck, do you realize we can go to jail for this? We need to think and be smart about it!"

Tudor smirked. "So what, man? We had our fun!"

"But if we're reckless and stupid we'll rot in jail like Varg Vikernes. Is that what you want? And for what? For killing a stupid peasant?"

Tudor thought Alex's fretting was grossly disproportionate to the gravity of the problem. Suddenly, Tudor's cool friend became a ridiculous coward. Alex failed to see the main point: that they had fun. They stood up to the scum, and the afternoon was a great bout of alcohol-induced violence and destruction. Nothing else really mattered.

Both Alex and Edi missed the whole point.

Deep down, on an almost unconscious level, Tudor tasted bitter disappointment. But he didn't like what he saw on his friends' faces. Besides anger, Alex's bloodshot eyes expressed panic, and terror was creeping into his usually calm voice. Edi seemed to be in shock. Although he spoke normally, he seemed detached from reality, looking into the distance as if hypnotized.

Tudor hated seeing his friends like this. He didn't want them to worry and fret because of his actions. Gazing at the scene of his carnage (Oprea *must* be dead by now, he thought), Tudor decided it was his responsibility to dispose of the corpse. He had to do it for the sake of his buddies.

Impelled by this new sense of duty, Tudor focused on the

Chapter 4 Midday Mutilation

problem at hand.

He remembered his grandmother scolding him for leaving a mess after finishing his chores.

Always clean up after yourself, she used to say. *Put everything back in its proper place, you lazy boy. Only then is the job done.*

Once the fun part of the work was over, like chopping wood, say, he needed to neatly pile the wood, sweep the area, and return the axe to its place in the shed.

That's what I need to do, Tudor reasoned. *Clean up my mess to keep my friends happy.*

"How about taking him to the landfill?" Edi suggested. "We can stay by the riverside, and one of us can go ahead to scout for people."

Alex shook his head. "I don't know, my friend. Dead bodies are really heavy. I mean, if we had a sack and a wheelbarrow, maybe..."

Having resolved his inner struggle, Tudor joined his friends' deliberation. "I'm pretty sure there's a sheepfold between us and the landfill. Someone will spot us. And they have dogs."

"Fuck that! I hate dogs," Alex said, putting Edi's idea to rest.

After a few moments, Alex pointed toward the narrow beach. "Maybe we can bury him there."

"No, someone would discover him soon," Edi cautioned. "People sunbathe there. It would stink."

"Right," Alex acceded, nervously pushing the hair out of his eyes.

Tudor, at last, broke in with a suggestion of his own. "What if we chop up the body and bury different parts in different places. Like, we bury the legs on the beach, we take the head to the landfill, and we hide the torso in a bush or something."

"That's too much fucking work," Alex said. "And can you imagine how many traces of blood we'd leave behind?"

Tudor accepted his friend's point. Cutting off the limbs

would be hard work. Especially when he had only a knife and not a chainsaw. He lit a cigarette and offered the pack to Alex and then to Edi. He noticed Edi's fingers trembling.

These guys are scared, he told himself. *Fuck, I don't want to see them like this. Focus! Focus!* he commanded himself. The mangled body was like a piece of dirt to be swept under a rug. Only they lacked one large enough. Tudor thought of another plan. "Maybe we can tie a boulder to—"

"That works better in lakes; in rivers, the body will probably float back up," Edi interrupted.

"But it might be days or weeks till then," Tudor insisted.

"Still, there's no boulders around. And no rope," Alex indicated, expelling smoke through his nostrils.

Tudor remembered the caretaker's shed. "We can find rope in the cemetery. Like when we hanged that dog."

Alex and Edi nodded. "Still no boulder, though," Alex repeated. "And it would take too long anyway. We need something quick, something we can pull off before someone sees us."

An idea flashed in Tudor's mind. "Oh, I know. I can cut him up and take out his lungs and heart and entrails. I know how to do it; I watched my grandfather butcher pigs. Then we can put stones in his ribcage. There's a bunch of rocks around. That ought to keep him at the bottom, right?"

"Maybe, it depends..." Edi mumbled uncertainly.

"Too long, too messy," was Alex's verdict.

After a moment's thought, Alex added, "You know what? Let's take him to the other side of the river and hide the body in the forest somewhere. Who's gonna know?"

They all gazed at the forest across the water. Tudor and Edi could think of no objections.

The more they reflected, the better the plan sounded. While their side of the river was a popular destination for day-trippers, especially on weekends, the other side was virtually deserted. During the May Day celebrations everyone in town would picnic in the woods, set up a stage for music and plays

Chapter 4 Midday Mutilation

in a large clearing, and try to enjoy the outdoors. But it was already June. There wouldn't be another May Day till next year. Even then, Tudor thought, people probably wouldn't venture deep into the dense forest. The bridge over the river was a mile downstream, and the clearing where they would set up the stage wasn't far from the bridge. No one would have any reason to come this far upstream.

"I think that's a great idea," Tudor said.

Edi nodded his agreement.

"Okay, let's get to it" Alex commanded, flicking his cigarette butt into the water. "Edi, you don't swim, right?"

"Sorry, I don't know how."

"That's fine. You can stay here and clean up all the traces of blood."

"Okay," Edi agreed in a small voice, but he looked at the thick blood with fearful disgust.

"Good. Let's do it." Alex pulled off his shirt. Tudor noticed his white skin. Alex had lots of padding but wasn't fat, just robust and strong.

Tudor urgently untied his boots, slipped them off, and peeled off his socks. He piled the soggy clothes on the grass next to his shirt. Then removed his shorts and threw them onto the pile. He left his underwear on, as did Alex.

Tudor waded into the cool, chest-high water. He seized the body by the right ankle and pulled it into the stream. The corpse trailed fresh blood. The mud-caked face disappeared underwater for a second and then resurfaced, its wetness glinting in the sunlight.

"Great job, Tudor!" Alex encouraged his friend before he jumped into the water and grabbed Mr. Oprea's other ankle. "See you soon, Edi. Make sure you clean all that mess. Please and thank you, my friend," Alex shouted over his shoulder.

Gazing at the dead man's foot, Tudor noticed that Mr. Oprea had lost his sandals in his struggle with the river. His bare feet were small, bony, and covered with corns. The toes were crooked, and fungi grew in place of a missing nail. Tudor fought his curiosity to inspect the body as he waded across the river.

He's just garbage we need to dispose of, he told himself. *Nothing. A scumbag.*

In a way Tudor was happy he didn't have to dismember the body; taking the man's pants down and cutting through the hip joint next to his crotch, while glimpsing tufts of grey pubic hair around a fossilized cock barely covered by a pair of soiled underwear, might have been too gross. On the other hand, having two legs to use as clubs and play with would have been fun. Also, desecrating the peasant's body by turning it into a legless, defaced mannequin might have been worthwhile, except there would be no audience appreciating Tudor's art. Especially with his two friends chickening out.

The strong current forced Alex and Tudor off course with each step, and they trudged diagonally toward the opposite shore and dog-pedaled when water would get over their heads.

"I'll climb out and grab him," Tudor said once they reached the other side. "Hold on for a second."

Tudor lifted himself out of the water, turned, crouched, and grabbed the ankle Alex was holding. Alex released his grip and ducked underwater to let the body float over him to the shore. Alex resurfaced a moment later and joined Tudor on the shore. He grabbed one of Mr. Oprea's hands and helped Tudor pull the body out of the stream.

The exhausted teens rested for a minute, doubled over, hands on their knees, and tried to catch their breath.

Alex pushed his wet hair out of his eyes and looked back at the opposite bank. Edi was crouching by the waterside, seemingly laboring to conceal the traces of the crime.

Turning toward the steep, grassy bank behind him, Alex said, "Okay, let's get this over with!"

They began dragging Mr. Oprea up the embankment. The body was as heavy as a large sack of sand. Now and again their feet slipped in the muddy, weedy soil. They began to sweat profusely under the unrelenting sun, and their breath

Chapter 4 Midday Mutilation

came in ragged pants. Sweat trickled down Tudor's face, and his attempt to wipe it away with his sweat-slicked forearm only forced it into his eyes.

"That's the vodka we had earlier," Alex huffed.

"Fuck yeah, you were right: this is fucking heavy."

Tudor imagined the body was a sack of corn he needed to carry into the mill for his grandmother. He focused every ounce of energy on completing the task. He shut his burning eyes against the torrent of sweat. Low branches lashed his arms and legs. Nettles stung his bare soles, but he ignored the pain and trudged blindly up the incline.

Alex sensed the intensity of Tudor's labors and renewed his own efforts. Finally, with a last desperate heave, they managed to pull the body to the top of the bank. Letting its legs drop into the high weeds, the kids again doubled over in a search for breath.

"Get down!" Alex whispered suddenly.

Tudor imitated Alex and lay down among the tall weeds and saplings.

"A cart on the dike," Alex pointed out.

Through the branches, Tudor saw two horses pulling a cart atop the levee across the river. A cloud of dust rose in their wake. The cart was filled with sacks. Headed for the mill by the stadium, Tudor thought. Fortunately, the driver didn't stop or look their way.

Hidden by the steep bank, Edi continued his cleanup, unaware of the passerby.

When the cart disappeared from sight, the boys quit their concealment.

"Good thing they didn't pass by earlier," Alex said.

"Yes, we lucked out," Tudor agreed.

"Okay, let's put this scumbag to rest and get it over with!" Alex scanned the thick forest and underbrush around them. "Let's find a good hiding spot!" he said and walked into the dense trees. Tudor followed. Twigs and dead leaves crunched under their bare feet. Tudor spotted a large bush ten yards to their left and pointed it out to Alex.

"That should do it," Alex agreed.

They dragged the body over the green and brown forest carpet. Mr. Oprea's once-white shirt was completely red. Only one of the crumpled and torn shirt's buttons remained fastened. Blood oozed from the hole in his neck. His eyes, mouth and nose were still plugged with mud.

Tudor knelt next to the shrub and opened its panoply like a set of curtains. He crawled inside. Insects scurried up and down his skin, but he tried to ignore them. Alex dragged the body to the opening, and Tudor pulled it inside. The plant's maw gradually devoured the corpse.

Alex said, "Wait here just a second, I'll bring some weeds and twigs to cover him."

"Okay."

Alex uprooted nearby plants until he had accumulated a bushel of leaves and grass. He handed them to Tudor, who tossed them over the body. The corpse was soon concealed by both weeds and the crown of the bush.

Tudor crawled out, and the two friends circled the green tomb, inspecting it from every angle. The body was not visible.

"Maybe animals will drag him out?" Alex worried.

"So what, man? It will be a long time from now. He will be fucking decomposed. How will they relate it to us?"

Alex nodded, but Tudor could see his friend's lingering unease.

"Okay, let's go back and make sure we get rid of all the evidence."

In order to avoid fighting the current, they walked upstream before wading into the water. Then, when they crossed the river, the current bore them along a diagonal course to their destination. The crisp and helpful water offered a welcome reprieve from their strenuous labors.

Back on dry ground, Alex closely inspected Edi's job. He was pleased to find no traces of blood.

"I uprooted some of the stained weeds and threw them in

Chapter 4 Midday Mutilation

the water." Edi explained.

"Very good," Alex approved.

Alex and Tudor lit cigarettes and waited for the sun to dry their skin.

After a moment's quiet reflection Alex said, "We need to split up. No one should see us together."

Edi and Tudor nodded.

"We should leave one by one. Edi, you go first! We still need to get dressed and stuff."

"Okay," Edi mumbled.

"And we need an alibi, just in case," Alex claimed.

"Alibi?" Tudor asked, confused.

"You know, a story about where we were today when the crime was committed. And we need to stick to the story no matter what." He looked deeply into his friends' eyes and Tudor saw fear and panic once more.

Alex rubbed his chin and stared at the ground. "Okay, let's think. If we hadn't come to the river, what else would we have done?"

Edi and Tudor frowned in thought.

Tudor said, "My parents are out of town today. So we can say we were at my place."

"That's good," Alex said. "And what were we doing?"

"But wait," Edi uttered in a panic-stricken tone, "people already saw us at the pub."

"Right, okay, we admit to going to the pub, and then we say we went to Tudor's place."

"Yes, let's say we watched a movie or concert or something on my VCR."

"That's good. You have that Kreator concert right?"

"Uh-huh."

"Okay, that settles it," Alex decreed. "This is what we did: we had a beer at the pub and then went to Tudor's place and watched the Kreator concert."

Edi and Tudor agreed.

"Good. Now, Edi, go up the dike, and when you get to

the cemetery, wave at us if there's no one around. If you see someone, keep going and try to hide. Remember: we weren't at the river today."

Edi nodded.

Alex put a hand on Edi's shoulder and stared intensely into his eyes, as if trying to hypnotize him. He spoke slowly, "Nothing unusual happened today. It was an ordinary day. We had *one* beer and then went to Tudor's place to watch a show. Nothing more, nothing less. You understand, buddy?"

"Yes, nothing happened," Edi mumbled, staring at his feet.

"Don't look down like that! That shows you're lying. Look at me!"

Edi raised his head and met Alex's gaze. "It's okay, man; I get it. Nothing happened. I won't say anything."

"Attaboy!" Alex said, patting his shoulder.

Tudor watched his friends with a mixture of amusement and repulsion. *These guys are scared shitless. They're ready to shit their pants when all we did was kill a nobody.* He bit his lower lip to stifle laughter.

"See you guys," Edi said, waving goodbye. He turned and climbed up the embankment.

Alex took a last drag of his cigarette and flicked it into the water. Tudor did the same. "If he spills the beans, we're fucked."

"Don't worry too much about it, man. If we get discovered I'll take all the blame."

Alex looked at him as if trying to gauge his reliability. Tudor returned an unflinching stare. Alex looked away and began dressing. As he pulled on his shorts, he said, "But we were accomplices nonetheless. We didn't try to stop you or anything."

After slipping into his shorts, Tudor sat down to pull on his boots. "Be cool, man. You worry too much. As you said, nothing happened today. Nobody died." Tudor smirked again at his little joke.

Chapter 4 Midday Mutilation

After donning their footwear, the two started climbing the steep bank. Alex put his shirt on, but Tudor carried his sopping shirt over his shoulder. Tudor felt uncomfortable wearing shorts over his still-wet underwear. It felt as though he had pissed himself. He considered throwing his jockeys away, but then remembered the sensation of the zipper on his crotch and that dissuaded him.

I need to shower once I get home, he told himself.

Having reached the top of the bank, they saw Edi walking down the levee's dusty path in the distance. When he neared the cemetery, Edi turned around and waved. In the late afternoon sunshine, his smile appeared stiff, his face caught in a grimace.

Odin Rising by Axl Barnes

Chapter 5
The Storm of Bones

The closer Edi got to his house the more anxious he felt. Although he'd felt sober when saying goodbye to his friends, he was beginning to feel drunk again, as if fear and anxiety had activated the alcohol in his blood.

It was late afternoon, and people were returning from work. Cars passed him on the narrow street but seemed far away. Usually, after drinking and smoking with his friends, Edi would stop at a convenience store close to his place and buy gum to freshen his breath. Now, trapped in the dizzying carousel of his thoughts, that concern seemed distant and irrelevant.

The events of the afternoon played over and over in his mind, as he reminded himself repeatedly not to tell.

Say nothing about the killing, Alex had ordered. *Nothing happened.*

But *something* had happened. When someone's blood starts flying, that's something, isn't it? Edi remembered Tudor throwing the stone at Mr. Oprea's head and then cutting his jugular. The splatter of blood added to the surreal character of the whole afternoon.

Something happened, all right. An innocent man got killed.

Edi couldn't believe it. He half-expected to wake up at any second, to emerge from this nightmare.

Recalling Tudor's crazy suggestions for dealing with the body amplified the sensation.

Eat him?

Break him into pieces?

Disembowel him and place stones in the abdomen?

Where was he coming up with that stuff? Probably the death metal albums he listened to or the crazy horror movies he watched.

Before today, Edi had thought that Tudor acted crazy just to impress Alex, but now he thought there might actually be something deeply wrong with Tudor, something missing upstairs or, like George, a few screws loose.

But Tudor and Alex were Edi's best friends. Without them, his life would be a never-ending cycle of school and homework. He didn't want to spill the beans and cause them trouble.

"I'm not going to say a word," Edi muttered to himself. Thinking of his authoritative father, he added through clenched teeth, "He can't beat it out of me."

But dread swept over Edi as he saw his dad's car in the driveway. Mr. Manea had evidently come home early to work on one of his pet projects: tearing down the backyard fence. In cut-off jeans and a dirty green t-shirt, he was pushing a wheelbarrow full of the weather-beaten old boards to the back of the house, where they would sit in a neat stack until becoming firewood on the family's next camping trip.

Heart pounding, Edi ducked quickly behind a car and waited for his dad to round the corner to the back of the house. Then he dashed up the steps to the front door, opened it and stepped inside.

"Edi, is that you?" his mom called from the kitchen.

Chapter 5 The Storm of Bones

"Yes," Edi answered hoarsely, struggling to untie his shoes with trembling fingers.

"Can you come help us with supper?"

"Yes, just a second." Edi barely managed to force the words out before running to the bathroom upstairs. He washed his hands and face and checked his reflection for blood spots on his skin or clothes. He peeled off his *Iron Maiden* t-shirt and inspected it closely. He found nothing but thought it safest to change his clothes, so he went to his bedroom, opened a drawer of his dresser, stuffed his t-shirt in and grabbed a white undershirt and a clean pair of shorts.

Back in the bathroom, he gazed at his face in the mirror. His eyes were bloodshot, terrified, distant. While brushing his teeth he considered going straight to bed, but that would make his parents suspicious.

"Try to act normal," he told himself. But the memory of the mangled dead man surfaced in his mind, and he winced. He saw his own face twitch in the mirror and half-expected the word "murderer" to appear on his forehead in red letters.

He headed for the kitchen.

The room felt like an oven. The windows were open, but no breeze came through. Only flies. They were everywhere, squirming on the tiled walls, on the table, buzzing through the air, probably attracted by whatever was cooking in the oven. Mrs. Manea was doing dishes while Edi's sister, Ioana, was cutting vegetables.

"Peel and cut the potatoes!" his mom ordered, pointing to a bowl full of potatoes on the table.

"Okay," Edi murmured and sat down across the table from his sister. He grabbed a knife and swatted away a group of flies.

"Where have you been all day?" Edi's mom asked over her shoulder.

"I was at Tudor's place with Alex," Edi answered quickly.

"Doing what?" his mom probed.

"Oh, we just watched a concert on VHS," Edi repeated

mechanically what Alex had instructed him.

"You know you guys can also watch here," Ioana jumped into the conversation.

Edi looked into the pale blue eyes on his sister's acne-riddled face and felt a familiar pang of irritation. He knew she had a big crush on both Tudor and Alex—and on any healthy male who would give her some attention. He noticed she was wearing only a skimpy white top with no bra. He could see the crease between her large, saggy boobs with their pink nipples that jutted against the fabric of her top. The breasts jiggled to the rhythm of her vegetable cutting. Edi didn't feel the usual sexual arousal but only nausea and disgust at his sex-starved sister.

His mom continued her string of annoying questions. "Edi, why didn't you do the dishes?"

"I thought it was Ioana's turn," Edi said, perhaps too defensively.

"I did them yesterday, stupid," Ioana snapped.

"Oh, I'm sorry," Edi mumbled, trying to keep his fear in check.

Now, in a sweet, pouty voice Ioana asked, "So, do you guys still wanna form a band?"

"Maybe, what's it to you?" Edi said.

"Oh, you know, you can always come here to practice. In the basement or garage or wherever you want."

"Yes, sure, we'll see," Edi answered, trying to remain non-committal.

Edi found it weird, being able to carry these banal conversations as if nothing had happened. He felt as if he were occupying two places at the same time—the ordinary world of routine and banality, and underneath it a world of terror and violence.

How can they not notice there's something wrong with me, he wondered. *Something deeply wrong. Something broken.*

A nagging feeling told him someone would see sooner or later, that he'd give himself away somehow. It was just a

Chapter 5 The Storm of Bones

matter of time, like a game of hide-and-seek.

To Edi's relief, his sister and mom started gossiping about some girls in Ioana's class. He tried to focus on peeling the potatoes, but heat and anxiety were making him perspire, and sweat was dripping into his eyes. He wiped them a few times with the back of his hand and swatted at the annoying flies. Many of them were running frantically across the flower-patterned table cloth, and some were tasting the potato peels with their tubular mouths. Others were cleaning their eyes with their front legs.

House flies spread disease and germs, Edi remembered. Maybe they came from the dump or some nearby outhouse, and now they were covered with parasites, and they were spreading them on Edi's and his family's food. Granted, the carved potatoes would be fried, but there were also flies crawling on the salad Ioana was working on.

The thought revolted him, and he had half a mind to tell his mom about it.

Edi pictured a mass of flies moving around Mr. Oprea's frozen face and laying eggs in the orifices of his already decaying body. *We did this to him; now he's maggot food.*

The morbid thought made him heave. Bile invaded his mouth, but he immediately choked it back down. But then he thought maybe it was a ball of squirming maggots that he had swallowed.

This image pushed Edi over the edge, his stomach heaved again, and he frantically got to his feet, meaning to vomit in the sink. At the periphery of his vision, he saw Ioana's eyes widen. His mom turned around from the counter, but she seemed suddenly far away. He couldn't hold it any longer. He doubled over, and the puke spurted out in a yellow-brown torrent and splashed onto the linoleum floor. The two women gaped at Edi, mouths hanging open.

His face had turned a livid, blotchy red, and his body still heaved with nausea. His vision blurred, and for a moment he thought he was going to pass out. He closed his eyes, fought for breath and waited for his stomach to settle. He gagged as one final heave croaked out of his mouth, but this time nothing came out.

When he opened his eyes again, Ioana was no longer in the room.

"Sorry," he muttered, looking at the yellow-brown mess in disbelief. *Oh, this is not good. I gave myself away.*

His father came into the kitchen, Ioana close behind him.

"Eduard, what's going on here?"

The harsh, commanding voice felt like a chain-saw rending Edi's back. He immediately stood upright and said, "Nothing, I just feel sick...because of the heat."

"He said he was with Tudor and Alex at Tudor's place," his mom informed his father, hands on her hips.

"All right, let me handle this!" Mr. Manea said and stepped closer to Edi. Instinctively, Edi looked down and saw his dad's sandals stop inches away from the reeking puddle of vomit.

"Have you been *drinking?*" The word was pronounced as if it were the greatest sin. The question sent shivers down Edi's spine.

Edi managed a weak "no," and briefly looked up at his dad. But when he saw his father's frown and the anger in those ruthless black eyes he went back to studying the floor.

Don't look down or he'll know you're lying, Alex's voice shouted in Edi's head.

Oh, fuck! I can't! I can't! Edi screamed internally.

Mr. Manea leaned over toward his son's face.

"Breathe!" he commanded.

Edi exhaled weakly into his dad's face. The nose sniffed hungrily and the man's face contorted.

"Vodka! They had vodka at least," Mr. Manea said, turning toward his wife.

Edi's mom gasped and held her chest. Although Ioana was slightly worried and shocked, her lips curled into a sadistic grin.

Mr. Manea grabbed Edi's right ear and twisted it, hard.

Chapter 5 The Storm of Bones

"You feel this?"

Edi wanted to pass out. The pain was there, but it was far away, on the other side of an expanding abyss of dread and humiliation. "Yes," he heard himself whisper.

Turning back to his wife and daughter, Mr. Manea gave his diagnosis: "He's smashed." Then he clouted Edi brutally with an open palm. Edi's glasses flew from his face and landed with a click on the kitchen floor. The boy's cheek reddened and his eyes brimmed with tears.

"Look at me!" Mr. Manea commanded.

Edi gazed up tentatively, just in time to see his father spit. Edi instinctively closed his eyes but felt the spray on every inch of his face. His squeezed his eyes shut, and fresh tears ran down his cheeks.

"He said he was with Alex and Tudor," his mom repeated.

"Alex and Tudor," Mr. Manea uttered through clenched teeth. "Did *they* ask you to drink?"

Another slap prompted Edi to answer "no."

"If *they* jumped off a bridge, would *you* jump too, like a dumb sheep?"

"No," Edi said, bawling without restraint now, his face red and contorted.

"Whose idea was it to drink alcohol?"

Edi shrugged. "I don't remember."

To his wife, Mr. Manea said, "Can you go and phone Tudor's parents? We'll get to the bottom of this."

Mrs. Manea nodded and left the room.

Edi was now in full panic mode. He didn't want to get his friends in trouble.

Fuck, they'll think I told everything!

Mr. Manea resumed his interrogation without missing a beat. "So, what did you have to drink, dumb ape?"

Edi felt his dad wouldn't relent until he found out everything. And Mr. Manea always knew when Edi was lying or hiding something. He was like a mind-reader. There was nowhere to hide from him. Nowhere to hide from those black, angry, inquisitive eyes that seemed to stare directly into Edi's trembling soul.

But Tudor's eyes were there too. And Alex's.

Nothing happened, Alex had said.

The full force of those pairs of eyes bore into Edi's psyche, commanding him, pushing him in different directions. A vortex of panic engulfed him. He saw his dad and the kitchen as if they were on a theatre screen gradually diminishing in the darkness of the cinema. Mr. Manea's voice was farther and farther away.

Abruptly the movie ended, severed as if by a scissor-wielding projectionist.

Edi collapsed onto the kitchen floor.

"Look, the drunk ape can't even stand up!" Mr. Manea said and kicked Edi in the ribs.

But Edi didn't feel any pain.

Blessed unconsciousness temporarily stopped the nightmare of reality.

* * * * *

Edi woke up when his dad turned on the bedroom light.

Staring at his son, Mr. Manea walked to the foot of the bed.

"Eduard, wake up, we have a guest!"

Edi sat up in bed and rubbed his eyes.

His father pointed toward the open door.

A faint swooshing sound drifted in from the hallway. A legless man shambled into the room, walking on his hands like a chimp, dragging his maimed lower body across the floor. The bleeding stumps of his legs left a red trail on the grey carpet. His shirt and underwear were sopping with muddy slime. His face was a mask of mud, with spots of skin visible here and there. His blank eyes stared without seeming to see.

The apparition filled Edi with icy dread. He instantly recognized the glittering bald dome of Mr. Oprea's head. He

Chapter 5 The Storm of Bones

knew he was responsible for the man's mutilation. But he didn't remember exactly how.

"Do you know this man, Eduard?" his dad asked gravely.

Edi nodded feebly.

"Yes or no?"

"Yes."

"Yes, what?"

"Yes, sir."

"Good. Now, what's the man's name?"

"Mr. Ilie Oprea, sir, from the Tatareni Agricultural Cooperative."

"That's right. Mr. Oprea has a complaint to make." Edi's dad turned toward the disfigured man. "Go ahead, Mr. Oprea, state your complaint."

The man's mouth started moving, but mud and murky water came in place of words and dribbled on his chest. A small jet of blood spurted from the hole in his neck. His throat produced an inarticulate gargle.

Mr. Manea listened attentively and nodded as if he understood. He turned his gaze back to Edi.

"Sorry, I didn't get that," Edi said.

Mr. Manea smashed his fist against the dresser. "He said you stole his legs. You and your stupid friends. And he wants them back. Now, where did you hide them?"

Edi suddenly remembered. "In the cemetery, in one of the graves," he said quickly.

"Well, now you'll have to go and give them back to Mr. Oprea. They're *his* legs. How many times do I have to tell you that stealing people's legs is wrong?"

Mr. Manea produced a ball of twine from his pocket. It had a massive needle stuck into it. He tossed the ball onto Edi's bed. "Use this to sew his legs back on."

I don't know how! Edi thought in panic. But he knew better than to say it out loud. *Mom will do it for me. Or Ioana,* he reassured himself.

Next, Edi found himself driving Mr. Oprea to the cemetery

in a wheelbarrow. It was cloudy, and the street was deserted. The bumps in the sidewalk made Mr. Oprea shake. He kept moaning as if in pain. Then he began humming. Edi didn't recognize the song coming from the tattered throat. But Mr. Oprea hummed louder and louder and, to Edi's disgust, he reached under his dirty underwear and began stroking himself to the rhythm of the private music.

Edi looked ahead, trying to ignore the old pervert. He pushed Mr. Oprea through the open gates of the cemetery and down the main alleyway that led to the chapel. When he reached the chapel, he turned down a dusty path between the graves. A cluster of pines hid the concrete tomb where they'd tossed the old man's legs.

It was Tudor who did it, Edi seemed to recall. George, Alex, and Edi only helped him move the lid. Tudor also performed the amputation, using a rusted axe he'd found in the gravedigger's shed. Edi tried to repress the dizzying memory and focus on the task at hand: retrieving the man's legs and sewing them back onto his body.

When Edi put the wheelbarrow down, Mr. Oprea stopped stroking himself, but the head of his erect penis bulged from his fist. The annoying humming also ended abruptly. The man just lay there, frozen, gazing up toward the treetops.

Edi stepped toward the tomb, grabbed a handle of the cover and tried to move it. He pulled as hard as he could, but the lid wouldn't budge.

Wiping the sweat from his brow, Edi looked around meaning to ask for help.

There was no one.

It's a weekday, he told himself. *Everyone's at work.*

His gaze turned to Mr. Oprea. Even without his legs, the old man could offer some help. His arms, after all, were long and muscular.

"Hey, Mr. Oprea, can you please give me a hand moving this lid?"

No answer came. The man didn't even lift his head.

Chapter 5 The Storm of Bones

As he looked at the unresponsive man, Edi was engulfed by a sense of doom.

What if he's dead? He is in really rough shape. It's a fucking miracle he survived Tudor's torture in the first place, given how much blood he'd lost.

Edi approached the body on rubbery legs.

The crippled man lay motionless. His chest was flat and still. His eyes were open but now all white and empty. His fist was still curled around his cock but seemed paralyzed, and the penis had retreated inside it like a turtle into its shell.

Edi bent over close to the man's face, trying to catch a sign of breathing.

There was none; the nostrils and the slightly open mouth seemed frozen.

God, my dad will think I killed him. Edi felt the icy hands of panic squeeze his heart. Suddenly, *he* felt unable to breathe.

He'll beat the shit out of me and lock me down in the basement. For weeks and months. Down there in the darkness.

Frantically, Edi grabbed the man's shoulders and began shaking him.

"Wake up! Wake up!" he screamed.

The old man's head shook limply from side to side, chunks of dried mud falling from his waxy face. A brown iris surfaced through the milky haze in the left eye, and Edi stopped shaking, expecting a sign of consciousness. The iris moved downwards through the red-threaded white and ended at the bottom of the eye as if Mr. Oprea had glimpsed something strange on his own body.

Edi had the fleeting sensation that he was holding a large, hideous doll; something invented for deranged children.

Then it seemed Mr. Oprea's mouth opened wider as if he meant to say something. Did he also inhale a bit? Edi noted the man's mouth was filled with mud. Maybe that obstructed his breathing and made him unable to speak?

Swallowing his disgust for a moment, Edi began removing the dirt from the man's mouth with trembling fingers.

He wanted the man to speak.

Speaking meant being alive.

In his rush, Edi pulled out a tooth. It detached easily from the gum as if it had no root. A white worm wriggled out of the dark hole the tooth had left and began probing the surrounding skin curiously. Edi cringed and bitter bile invaded his throat. He closed his eyes and fought to swallow it back. Then he looked at the pieces of mud on his fingers and saw they were crawling with worms. He shook his hands hard and wiped them on his jeans.

Backing away in repulsion, he inspected his hands closely, gripped by dreadful certainty that the worms had managed to burrow under his skin. *They feed on your flesh,* he told himself. *Then they multiply and infest your body.*

Despite his fear, his hands appeared normal and free of maggots.

Racked by cold shivers, Edi sat down on the tomb and tried to think. *What's the point of getting Mr. Oprea's legs if he's already dead? Will dad insist on my sewing them back on before the funeral, so the old fart goes before God in one piece? That would suck!*

Edi smiled bitterly. *Stupid Christians with their stupid ideas about the afterlife.*

The wind picked up, and Edi felt the first drops of rain on his skin. He saw a large leaden cloud looming over the roofs of the apartment buildings and moving toward the cemetery.

Edi decided to take cover with Mr. Oprea in the chapel or the gravedigger's shed. He jumped up and trotted toward the wheelbarrow.

But he was stopped dead in his tracks. The wheelbarrow stood empty. The mutilated man was gone.

"What the hell?" Edi muttered.

He was right here seconds ago, as dead as a doornail. And I heard nothing.

Edi felt cursed, a magnet of misfortune..

Now his dad would think Edi *killed* Mr. Oprea and got rid

Chapter 5 The Storm of Bones

of his body.

Feeling hopeless, Edi scanned the deserted graveyard and shouted Mr. Oprea's name. But he knew deep down it was in vain.

The man was gone, vanished.

Today, the world was against him.

The wind picked up again. The nervous wails of wooden crosses accompanied the rusty, rhythmic moans of metallic shutters. Funeral wreaths flapped like broken wings. The branches of the trees lining the alley quivered in the wind.

Edi felt like the gusts of winds were directed at him, were meant to terrify *him*. They were the souls of the restless dead who were seeking their revenge on the living.

The wheelbarrow was blown onto its side and the wind rifled through Edi's clothes and hair.

He ran for the shelter of the chapel as fast as he could.

The clouds opened, releasing a torrent. In a few seconds, Edi was drenched to the skin. Through the curtain of rain, he glimpsed the chapel. But it had no door or windows. Behind it, the shed was also without a door. They both looked like impenetrable cubes of grey concrete.

He stopped running and gaped at the two foreboding structures, rain splashing his face.

He was horrified but somehow knew this would happen. That he wouldn't be able to find shelter. That the whole universe turned its back to him.

The surrounding tombs, too, had turned against him. All the shutters were padlocked, and he knew somehow that even if he broke the locks, the screens would just reveal a grey wall. No entrance allowed.

Edi was engulfed by loneliness and despair, and hot tears mingled with the cold drops of rain on his cheeks.

A sudden gust of wind knocked Edi off his feet. As he tried to stand the wind slammed him into a marble cross and lifted him high into the air. He felt like a marionette at the mercy of a mad puppeteer. Through the gaps in his windblown hair he caught glimpses of the river and the forest beyond. The woods rocked like a green, stormy sea.

The dead man! he screamed internally. *That's where we killed him!*

As if knowing his fear, the wind carried him toward the dike and the river. The turbid water was coursing furiously.

I'm gonna drown! I can't swim!

At the last moment, he saw a set of power lines and hoped he could grab hold of them. It looked like a dozen crows were perched on the wires. But when he got closer, Edi saw they weren't perching but hanging. Someone had hung dead crows from the power lines. And there weren't only crows but also cats and dogs. All hanging there, wet, and ravaged by the wind.

This must be Tudor's doing, Edi thought. *Tudor and his retarded friend George.*

Desperately, Edi tried to grab one of the lines, careful not to touch any rotten bodies. He caught one of the slick wires, close to where a small, brown mongrel dangled, its filthy fur matted and wet. Disemboweled, its ropy intestines blowing in the wind, the dog looked like a twisted kite. Edi tried to fight his revulsion and held on for dear life, hoping that the storm would abate. It was now blowing so hard he was parallel to the ground, pointing like a weather vane. The significant drop horrified him, as did the wooden crosses, funeral wreaths, bits of broken coffins, and other debris forming dangerous projectiles all around him. Edi glimpsed the chain-link fence bordering the graveyard and saw that, like a fishnet, it was catching human remains unburied by the fierce gusts. Bones, skulls, and bodies still held together by rotted, dusty clothes were pressing against the fence, longing for the exhilaration of boundless flight.

Edi squeezed his eyes shut in panic.

To his amazement, he heard a growl coming from the dog that hung beside him as if his clenching the cable had somehow jolted the animal back to life. The dog began barking

Chapter 5 The Storm of Bones

and shaking wildly, looking at Edi with eyes glistening with rage. The cur was foaming at the mouth, drops of spittle flying from his snout. Like a lunatic trapezist, the dog began swinging and twisting in the wind, his snapping teeth reaching closer and closer to Edi's left hand. He stared at the savage creature with unbelieving eyes.

Its guts are hanging out in the air. How is it still alive?

A gust of wind pushed the frenzied dog closer to Edi and the cur bit savagely into his forearm. Teeth tore through Edi's skin and sinew, not stopping until they hit bone. Panicked, Edi wrenched his bleeding arm free of the beast's maw, and his right hand released its hold of the cable a moment later. He was back in the wind's violent grip. *I'm infected now for sure,* Edi thought desperately, as the wind jolted him up and down like a torturous rollercoaster. He felt as if he would puke.

The wind carried him high up over the Amara before it suddenly stopped. Screaming vainly, Edi plunged into the deep water. Submerged and unable to feel the bottom with his feet, his survival instinct kicked in, and he began thrashing frantically toward the surface. Once his head was above water, he began to dog-paddle, the only style of swimming he'd ever tried. Bitter water entered his mouth and blurred his vision. He pumped his hands and legs harder and managed to stay on the surface. He was in the middle of the river and didn't know which shore he should aim for.

To his shock he saw his dad on the tall bank, on the side with the cemetery, waving at him, encouraging him. Edi couldn't see clearly through the sheets of rain, but it was his dad all right, dressed in his cut-off jeans and green t-shirt, which now looked black in the downpour.

"Come! Come!" Mr. Manea seemed to say, his shouts silenced by the wind and rain.

The sight of his dad gave Edi another boost of energy and, for a moment, he thought he was making progress against the strong current. His dad was now running on the shore to keep up, still waving his hands.

But suddenly Edi sensed that his advance had stopped despite his constant effort. He felt heavier as if his weight had doubled instantly. Looking down, he saw someone's head close to his chest. It was Mr. Oprea's bald dome. It looked like he wanted to pull Edi down. The man's long, muscular arms were tight around Edi's waist. Edi hit the head with his right fist, and in retaliation, the man began ferociously biting at his chest with his toothless, ruined mouth. That empty mouth biting at his skin and slobbering on his nipples deeply unnerved Edi. He struggled to pull his attacker's head away from his chest. But Edi couldn't budge the old man, who seemed to have joined himself to Edi's body like a deformed Siamese twin.

Edi was horrified to see that Mr. Oprea's lips and cheeks were now sewn to his own skin. The stitching was a bloody zigzag of rough twine, entirely haphazard but, Edi feared, wholly unbreakable. He used both hands in a desperate effort to rip the man's face off him. But his legs didn't pedal hard enough to keep him afloat, and Mr. Oprea kept pulling downward. Blood oozed from the stitches, surrounding Edi and his foe in a crimson froth. As he screamed in pain Edi was dragged into the depths of the river. A rancid mixture of blood and bitter water flooded his lungs.

His attacker squeezed tighter and tighter like a snake coiling around Edi's body.

Edi's head broke the surface one more time, snatching one last breath. And then it sank, first the face, then the long, blond hair. He tried to scream again, but only bubbles came out in the blurry water. His last thought was about the maggots. Mr. Oprea's maggots crawling into his own body and befouling it.

At last merciful darkness covered Edi's agony.

Chapter 6
The Enemy Inside

Tudor was drifting off to sleep when the phone rang. He heard his dad answer. Shortly after came a knock on his door.

Edi let the cat out of the bag, Tudor thought with disappointment.

"Yes, come in," he said out loud.

His parents entered the room and turned on the light.

They looked at him with worried, fearful eyes. Tudor moved his blanket aside and sat up on the edge of the bed.

His dad said, "Tudor, Edi's mom just called."

Surprise, surprise!

"So?" Tudor murmured.

"Were Alex and Edi here today?" his dad inquired.

"Uh-huh."

"And did you drink alcohol?"

The big question. Tudor felt a giant relief that it wasn't "Did you kill someone?"

"Yes, just one beer," he mumbled, looking at the floor and

trying to appear guilty and ashamed.

His mom gasped and grabbed the golden crucifix hanging between her ample breasts. "Did you hear that, Claudiu?"

"Yes, dear," his dad said, furrowing his thick unibrow.

Mrs. Negur stepped toward her son. "Tudor, if you already drink alcohol at fifteen, what are you gonna do when you're eighteen? *Drugs*?" When she pronounced the evil word her eyes bulged as if threatening to jump out of their sockets.

Tudor shook his head. "No, of course not."

"Where did you get the beer?" his dad probed.

"We went to a pu...restaurant to have lunch."

"Whose idea was it to order beer?"

"Alex's," Tudor answered quickly. He knew his parents thought highly of Alex Antonescu. It was well-known he was a promising, brilliant student.

Mr. and Mrs. Negur paused their interrogation and looked at each other, puzzled. Tudor studied them with a smirk. His mom was wearing her pink nightgown, which hugged the rolls of fat around her hips and belly. A low hum emanated from the slimming belt that massaged the blubber around her waist. The gown's cut revealed the tops of her large, sagging breasts.

With her round face and droopy cheeks, Mrs. Negur looked like an exhausted and overgrown baby, a frightened infant who cries too much, as if destined to taste all the bitter flavors of sadness. Without her makeup, the brown bags under her large black eyes were clearly visible. Her dark, short hair reinforced her infantile appearance.

Mr. Negur was wearing black slippers, baggy sweatpants, and a grey t-shirt. He seemed to wear the same clothes every day, and they stunk. Tudor hated that odor, which made him think of boiled cum mixed with sweat.

They probably don't have time to do laundry with their parents being sick and all.

Tudor tried not to gag.

Mr. and Mrs. Negur debated whether to call Alex's parents

Chapter 6 The Enemy Inside

but decided against it. Edi's parents had probably already called the Antonescus, whom the Negurs didn't really know well.

Turning his attention back to his son, Mr. Negur asked, "And you only had one beer? Are you sure about that?"

"Yes, I swear to God we only had one," Tudor said and looked straight into his father's eyes, smelling victory. "I didn't even like it; it was bitter and gross." Then, staring at the floor, Tudor added in what he hoped was a pitiable voice, "I'm really sorry. It won't happen again." He bit his lower lip to suppress a smile.

Mrs. Negur opened her mouth to say something but her husband silenced her with a raised hand. It was time for his lecture.

He grabbed the chair from Tudor's desk, turned it toward his son and sat down. He adjusted his rectangular glasses and began his somber entreaty. "Tudor, your mom and I are going through some difficult times. As you well know, my dad and Angela's mom, your granddad and granny, are sick in the hospital, and it's our duty to take care of them just like they took care of us when we were little."

Tudor imagined his parents' gigantic ugly heads on baby bodies and bit his lip again, afraid he would burst into giggles. He forced away the thought and studied his dad's gestures. Mr. Negur's hands groped the air as if he were checking out an invisible stack of books. The hands were pale, sweaty, and fat.

Stupid bookworm, Tudor thought, *never had a man's job in his life.*

Tudor knew he could now overpower his dad. He was taller and stronger. While Tudor had built a lean, muscular body during his years playing soccer and practicing karate, his dad had acquired a hunched back and sizeable gut from sitting at his desk all day, reading, checking books out, and writing book cards. Tudor thought his dad was aware of his growing weakness, deep down, but was too much of a coward to face up to it. Mr. Negur was no longer the head of the household, but he desperately clung to that role, still dispensing his little lectures as if Tudor were a hapless kid. Tudor meant to teach his dad a lesson of his own, but now wasn't the right time.

Mr. Negur continued, oblivious to the disdain in Tudor's eyes. "Now, we don't want you creating trouble for us, okay? Your responsibility now is to study and do well in school."

"I understand," Tudor managed, hoping this farce would end soon.

"Good. That's good," Mr. Negur said and nervously adjusted his glasses again. "But right now, on this summer vacation, you need to prepare to go to high school. You remember when the entrance exams are?"

"Late August," Tudor mumbled.

"Math, History, and Romanian Lit, is that right?"

"Yes."

"And I believe you want to get into the Theoretical High School, do you not?"

Tudor shrugged. "I guess."

Only the Theoretical High School gave you the license to go to university and end up with a high-paying job. The other two high schools produced tradesmen and farmers. Tudor couldn't imagine himself being any of those things. He couldn't even begin taking those options seriously. The notion of working and making a living was distant, alien, and ultimately irrelevant.

Mr. Negur continued in a funereal tone. "Tomorrow and Sunday we have to go to Bucharest again. Your grandma's condition is critical; she might not make it."

Mrs. Negur's face twisted in pain and she began sobbing quietly.

Mr. Negur held his wife's hand and looked like he was about to cry, too. "So please stay home," he said. "We'll call you in case your granny wants to see you one last time."

Tudor nodded.

Mr. Negur resumed his stern tone. "But you're not allowed to have friends over. You should start preparing for your

Chapter 6 The Enemy Inside

exams. After all, you want to go to university and do something with your life, don't you? Make a name for yourself?"

That's a new one. Make a name for yourself. Who cares? Tudor felt like puking.

This guy is lucky I already had my fun today. Otherwise, I'd carve my name into his forehead with my fucking blade. Jesus, what a bad joke this idiot is!

"Sure," Tudor mumbled, staring at the floor.

Tudor's mom ceased weeping to join the lecture. "Tudor, my dear boy, we don't mean you can't have fun. Like asking a girl out for ice cream and Pepsi. Going with her for a stroll in the park downtown. But only after you start preparing for your exams. And you'll feel a lot better when you know you've done your work. You'll see!"

Tudor gazed into his mom's red-rimmed eyes and nodded as if he understood perfectly.

"But no alcohol," Claudiu Negur repeated. "It's too dangerous for your age."

"Edi's mom said Edi got sick," Mrs. Negur chipped in.

"Edi's a wimp. He's always sick," Tudor blurted.

"But that's not the point, Tudor! Alcohol affects both your body and your mind," Mr. Negur claimed, pointing to his temple.

"And your heart and soul," Mrs. Negur added quickly. "Just like porn and...touching yourself. They dirty your soul. And then how will you stand in front of our Lord Jesus on Judgment Day?"

Tudor shrugged, feeling a bit embarrassed. Things were awkward enough before his mom brought masturbation into the picture. He despised everything his mom had said about Jesus the Bastard but was in no mood to express his commitment to Satanism. And there was no point denying that he masturbated almost every day, sometimes more than once. Even if she hadn't caught him in the act several times, she would have figured it out from doing his laundry; she knew about those crispy towels, and the stains on his underwear, and the bedsheets that looked like old maps.

Mr. Negur also decided to evade the issue of masturbation but agreed with his wife on the matter of the cleanliness of the soul. He stood up and shook his finger at Tudor. "Your mom and I will think of an appropriate punishment to make sure you don't poison yourself again."

"No, sir, it won't happen again," Tudor promised, hoping the insertion of *sir* would please his dad and make him go away already.

"That's good of you to say, but we'll have to make sure of that, won't we?"

Tudor nodded, trying to control his rising anger.

Get the fuck out of my room right now! Or watch me explode!

"Okay, you go to bed now. But make sure you hit those books first thing in the morning."

"Sure, I'll hit 'em hard!"

"I'll make breakfast for you tomorrow. There's also lots of food in the fridge you can have for lunch, dear," Mrs. Negur added in a sweet voice.

"Okay."

His parents wished him goodnight, turned off the light, and finally left the room.

Tudor lay down in bed and sighed deeply.

Although he was glad Edi hadn't spilled the beans about the murder yet, Tudor was pissed at his parents. Couldn't they see he didn't care about anything they said? How could they be so blind and stupid?

Make a name for yourself, his dad had advised.

Tudor remembered the expression with disgust. The idiots were probably thinking of something like "Doctor Tudor Negur" or "Professor Tudor Negur," when "Serial Killer, Rapist, and Arsonist Tudor Negur" was closer to the truth.

Tudor smiled at his own joke.

But serial killers only got caught after murdering *lots* of people. Hence the name "*serial* killer." Tudor's count was only one. He hoped he'd get away with this first killing and move on.

Chapter 6 The Enemy Inside

Now that the phone had stopped ringing, the threat of being caught immediately had passed. Edi was probably asleep by now and unable to spill the beans at least until morning.

Tudor looked out the window. It was already dark. The cloak of night covered the town and their crime. He was almost certain he'd get away with murder. There were no witnesses—nobody saw them on the dike or on their way back to town—and no motive. And Alex had drilled it into Edi's head not to say anything. So far so good on that count.

Tudor also intuited that no one really cared about Mr. Oprea. Maybe a dog would die of starvation and a broken heart, but no humans would miss him. He was a forgettable character.

A nobody.

It would suck to go to a juvenile home for such a minor infraction. Tudor needed to make sure that wouldn't happen. He needed to commit more serious crimes.

This summer.

As soon as possible.

Carpe Diem.

And maybe juvie isn't that bad. As long as you get fed and have a roof over your head. You don't have to go to school and do homework and all that jazz. You have a chance to meet extreme, like-minded people. In a way, Tudor thought, *it would be like summer camp.* Thoughts of summer, of hiking on narrow, shadowy trails up wooded mountains, hiking and singing, lulled Tudor to sleep.

* * * * *

Tudor slept in. He woke around ten to a bedroom full of sunshine. But a brief shadow crossed his face as he remembered the crime—the slaughter of Mr. Oprea, the bleeding old man convulsing in the mud, his moldy toenails, his green tomb.

Tudor frowned and listened. The house was quiet. His

parents had probably left for Bucharest. The phone wasn't ringing, which meant Edi had managed to guard their secret. He got out of bed and looked out the window. There were no policemen or police cars in sight.

"Keep rotting motherfucker, soon your remains would become useless to the cops," Tudor whispered to himself.

Tudor left his bedroom and inspected his apartment to make sure no one was home. As promised, his mom had put his breakfast on the kitchen table. That was a good sign. Nothing outrageous had broken her routine. Tudor ate his meal and then watched an episode of *Scooby-Doo* on the Cartoon Network. He remembered how he had once tried to masturbate to Daphne, the hot one of the bunch. He hadn't been able to finish, probably because she was just a cartoon. Her voice, at least, was real, but it was hard work to jack off solely to a voice.

Out on the balcony, Tudor lit up a smoke. It was a beautiful Saturday, and the street was lively with people going shopping or just out for a stroll. Tudor was surely not about to ruin this perfect summer day by studying, or by staying indoors at all. In any case, the police would find him more easily if he just stayed home. If they figured out he'd killed Mr. Oprea, it would be better to be out and about so he could monitor any police activity from a distance.

He considered calling George but decided against it. If he met George he'd have to brag about the crime, and George would insist on seeing the body.

I might as well go and confess to the police. Tudor smiled to himself.

No, George would have to wait.

The same with Alex. His paranoid friend would argue they should lay low and not hang out for a while.

Tudor figured he'd have to have some fun by himself today, which was okay. As an only child, he'd learned to enjoy his own company.

As he took a drag of his cigarette, he remembered that

Chapter 6 The Enemy Inside

the cinema downtown played American movies on weekend afternoons. Sometimes they featured horror and sci-fi movies. While he still enjoyed a Jean Claude Van Damme or Chuck Norris flick now and again, Tudor's tastes had gradually changed in the last few years, shifting definitively toward horror.

Tudor took one last drag, flicked the cigarette butt off the balcony onto the street below, and decided to head downtown to see what was playing.

Back in his bedroom, he put on some music and began to get dressed. The blistering assault of Cannibal Corpse's *The Bleeding* filled the room. He sang along to his new favorite track, "Stripped, Raped, and Strangled."

She was so beautiful,/
I had to kill her.

He quickly checked his Napalm Death shirt for bloodstains, found none, and threw it in the laundry basket. Then he fished around his drawer for a clean shirt and pulled out a Slayer one. The black shorts he had worn the day before looked clean enough.

He decided to follow Cannibal Corpse with Grave's "Soulless," placed the switchblade in his front pocket and began doing karate kicks and banging his head to the ripsaw guitars.

In my dominion,/
Blood will always rain,/
I damn your soul,/
To everlasting pain.

He remembered they had sung this very song yesterday before the murder. Did they damn Mr. Oprea's soul to everlasting pain? Did the scum even have a soul? Wasn't the soul of garbage yet another piece of garbage? Garbage in, garbage out.

Tudor recalled his mom saying that if someone didn't get a proper Christian burial, his soul would be condemned to wander aimlessly between this world and the next.

Smirking, Tudor imagined Mr. Oprea's decayed soul slithering like a bloated worm across the forest floor and getting ripped apart by wolves and birds of prey.

After pulling on his boots and lacing them up, Tudor stopped the music and stuffed his wallet, cigarettes, and house key into his pockets. He was almost out of Kents. He grabbed some money off his dad's bookshelf for the movie ticket and cigarettes.

Tudor stepped onto the sidewalk and headed for the town center, hands in his pockets. Large chestnuts shaded the path, their deep green foliage partly hiding the ugliness of the bland, grey, four-story apartment buildings on each side of Main Street.

Tudor inhaled the sweet aromas of the colorful flower beds between the sidewalk and the street. On this sunny day, Tudor thought, the town looked almost livable.

Suddenly energized, Tudor started whistling and smiling. People smiled back at him.

Idiots, they think I'm one of them. Fucking morons.

"Hi Tudor," tweeted a girl's voice.

Tudor recognized Alina, one of the fuckable girls in his class. She and her mom were smiling at him as they walked past.

"Hi there," he managed as he took in the girl's body. She wore red short shorts and a white top. Her coltish legs were long and slender, and her wide hips swayed enchantingly. Tudor couldn't resist another glance and turned his head to ogle her ass. It was round and tight, with buttocks flexing with each step. Tudor imagined caressing the smooth, firm mounds, and then had to look away, the powerful image making him tear up with desire.

"Fuck you and your mom both," he said through clenched

Chapter 6 The Enemy Inside

teeth.

Looking ahead, Tudor saw a less attractive individual. His elderly neighbor, Mr. Schmidt, was struggling with three full bags of groceries from the farmer's market. Carrots, potatoes, and eggplants stuck out ready to fall on the sidewalk. The man's pale face was a frozen grimace. Watery blue eyes identified Tudor, and the retired teacher seemed prepared to ask for the youngster's helpful hand. But Tudor stared down at the sidewalk, quickened his pace, and gave the feeble man a wide berth. He couldn't care less about the old fart he and George liked making fun off.

If carrying those heavy bags gave the walking relic a coronary, that was fine by him.

Farther ahead, Tudor stopped at a convenience store to buy cigarettes. Nicu, the blind beggar who had greeted them at the entrance to the cemetery, was now panhandling in front of the store. This time he had company. A legless Gypsy sitting in a wheelchair next to him was playing the accordion, and a morbidly fat man was sprawled on a small chair in front of a beaten-up scale that charged five lei for measuring your weight.

Having bought a new pack of smokes, Tudor resumed his walk. He spotted Ruxandra through the crowd of pedestrians. The town's greatest beauty. She was admiring a skimpy dress on a mannequin in the window of a retail store. Tudor was intrigued she was in the company of a short, bald guy.

God, don't tell me that's her boyfriend.

Rumor had it she had given syphilis to half the men in town and ruined as many marriages. Diseased or not, Tudor thought, she was stunning. Her dark curly hair was caught high in a ponytail, a few strands falling along the sides of her forehead and high cheekbones. Her eyes were large, green, and intense. A small elegant nose and full lips were the final touches on a face that reminded Tudor of a Greek goddess. She was tall and curvy. She wore high heels and a very short flowery skirt that showcased her long, slender legs and gently hugged an ass that was thick yet firm. Her low-cut white top revealed the tops of perky, full breasts. She was braless, and her nipples protruded under the soft fabric. Her skirt hung low around the gentle slopes of her wide hips, baring a taut midriff.

Tudor instinctively slowed and casually stopped at Ruxandra's side, slightly behind her, pretending to check out something in the display window as well. He tried to peek at her side-boob and cleavage out the corner of his eye. He could see the soft hair down on her lower back and the very top of her panties. He was painfully close.

That perfect, springy rump was happiness. And it was within reach.

Go ahead, grab her butt, a voice in his head demanded. *She'll probably like it.*

Tudor fought the powerful impulse. This wasn't the right place. He'd just make a fool of himself in public. Not that he cared what people thought—it just wasn't worth it. He didn't want just a brief squeeze; he wanted Ruxandra all to himself for hours, or even days, on end. Plus, her minion might decide to prove himself and defend his mistress. Males are territorial like that, Tudor reflected. I just need to find *my own* territory. Do a bit of planning and strategy.

Tudor sighed and left the side of the goddess, quietly singing the lyrics of his new favorite song, "*She was so beautiful,/ I had to kill her!*"

Farther down on the left, Tudor stopped in front of the music store. The black bass guitar he dreamed about was still in the display window. He, Alex, Edi, and George had formed a band called Epitaph. Tudor handled the vocals because he could scream better than the others, do both high-pitched and guttural vocals. Edi knew how to chug and shred on his electric guitar, and Alex was good on keyboards. That left George playing drums.

But now, admiring the showcased bass, Tudor wondered whether he could manage both bass and vocals like Tom

Chapter 6 The Enemy Inside

Araya from Slayer. And he was fascinated by the dirty sound a low tuned bass could make, like in Napalm Death or Cannibal Corpse. A hellish, earthy vibration that, in Tudor's mind, would one day raise the dead from their graves and make them feed on the living.

The price tags said the guitar and a basic amp were almost one thousand lei. Tudor would either have to save money all summer or ask his parents explicitly. Maybe they could buy it for his upcoming birthday.

Or he could just *command* them to do it.

As he left the music store, Tudor remembered Epitaph also needed a place to practice. George's and Edi's basements were good options. The former was better because it was isolated and there were fewer distractions. At Edi's place, Edi's mom would insist on serving them cookies and whatnot, and Ioana would be all over them like a sow in heat.

Now that they'd shared the experience of eradicating scum like Mr. Oprea, Tudor mused, their creative power would be unleashed. They'd be more confident and original.

Just like the previous day in the river valley, Tudor was overwhelmed by happiness and joy. This was going to be, by far, the best summer of his life. He'd do stuff he couldn't even have imagined in previous years.

He didn't know exactly how things would turn out, but that made everything more exciting.

That unpredictability was part of the magic of summer.

Tudor walked past the terrace of the pub and nightclub Queen. The place was already full of people either having breakfast and coffee or a cold beer to kick-start the day.

At the four-way intersection marking the center of downtown, Tudor crossed Main Street and then Traian Street. To his amusement, a pack of stray dogs traversed Main Street on the zebra crossing, following the pedestrians, probably having learned from grievous errors.

Once at the movie theatre, he checked out the day's featured films. *Texas Chainsaw Massacre* and *The Thing* were playing in the afternoon. Two horror movies, Tudor noted with delight. Intrigued by the posters and the synopses he decided to go.

But the movies wouldn't start until two. Tudor gazed at the big clock in the park across the street. It was a quarter to twelve.

He had two hours to kill.

He sat down on the stairs in front of the theatre and lit a smoke.

He remembered telling Alex and Edi about an abandoned house near his grandma's place, by the train station. The house would make a good meeting place for their gang, a spot where they could party at night and plan their destruction of the town, away from the prying eyes of adults. He decided to check it out and see if he could find a way in.

Tudor planned to walk to the train station, cross the tracks, and take a closer look at the abandoned house. Then, if he still had some time to kill, he'd stop at the soccer stadium. FC Tatareni usually played on Saturday afternoons.

Pleased with his plan, Tudor re-crossed Main Street and walked alongside the downtown park to the red brick train station. Like the cemetery and the river valley, the area around the train station was a usual hangout for Tudor and his friends.

Last summer, his grandmother had asked him to get rid of her cat. She said it was too old and lazy and wouldn't catch mice anymore. She handed him the cat in a grain sack and told him to toss it into someone's back yard, as far away as possible. Tudor knew the animal vaguely; it was grey and fat and would sometimes rub against his feet while he ate, purring and mooching.

George and Tudor had just gotten back from a soccer game and had stopped at Tudor's grandma's place to eat watermelon and pick apples. They knew the cat squirming and moaning in the sack promised relief from their late-afternoon boredom—but how?

Chapter 6 The Enemy Inside

Tudor remembered with a smile how he and George had come up with the idea of tying the bag to the railroad tracks. They followed the tracks out into the field where no one could see them, secured the brown sack on the iron rails with two lengths of twine, and hid behind a stand of tall weeds. As the train appeared on the horizon, the rails began to vibrate. The bag started jumping. Instinctively, the cat thrashed around in desperation. But it probably knew, deep down, that this was a new beast charging toward it, not something its cat ancestors had to worry about.

As the metallic rumbling and whistling got closer, the cat's thrashing mounted to a paroxysm, and Tudor was worried for a second that it would free itself from the sack.

But it was too late.

The wheels of the train instantly sliced the cat to pieces, taking all nine of its lives.

Both Tudor and George thought they heard a final, frenzied hiss before the cat got smashed. But it must have been their imagination, the relentless chugging of the train being too loud.

Tudor contemplated the memory with joy.

It's time to try that on people, he thought as he picked up his pace down Traian Street.

It occurred to him again that terminating Mr. Oprea wasn't really something to brag about. But the killing was a significant step toward more meaningful slaughter like murdering young people in the prime of their lives. Raping and butchering young, sexy girls full of energy and hopes and dreams.

"She was so beautiful, I had to kill her," Tudor repeated his new mantra.

Tudor was engulfed anew by a wave of euphoria. He felt like he had stumbled upon a treasure by accident, like Ali Baba in the famous story. By stabbing Mr. Oprea, he had carved out new territory, a land of doing whatever he felt like. The world was no longer a cage in which he had to suffer, go to school, and do what he was told. No, it was a dreamland of doing whatever the fuck he wanted.

Just be smart about it, plan carefully and don't get caught, Tudor told himself, heeding Alex's advice.

He couldn't wait to share his revelations with Alex. But Alex might want to kill only certain people, like Gypsies and the handicapped. And he might not be that excited about rape. Who knew? But George would be thrilled. Yes, Porky would gladly help him out.

Tudor dropped out of his pleasant reverie when he noticed the train station was crawling with Gypsies. Men were hawking jewelry or their underage daughters. Women in long, colorful skirts, puffy-sleeve blouses, and headscarves were eager to read palms or sell sunflower seeds or Turbo chewing gum.

Tudor liked sunflower seeds but he'd stopped buying from Gypsies when he'd heard the women pissed on them to make them saltier. He'd also stopped collecting the Turbo gum wrappers featuring the newest, fastest cars. George, on the other hand, was still enchanted by them.

What is it with trains stations and Gypsies? Tudor wondered vaguely, rounding the corner of the red brick structure.

Even the trains are filled with the scum. With their shouts and smells and shifty, feral eyes.

Eyes the color of shit, as Alex was fond of saying.

Tudor walked over the tracks at the designated crossing. Four tracks were in use, with most trains taking passengers to Bucharest or in the opposite direction, to the beach resorts on the Black Sea. A fifth track, rusted from disuse and half-hidden by tall weeds, held a desolate old locomotive with a single car still attached. The car's peeling blue paint revealed the rust underneath.

Curious, Tudor approached the decrepit vehicle. Gravel crunched under his boots as he stepped around the empty bottles and paper bags littering the space between the tracks. He opened one of the doors of the car and climbed in. The

Chapter 6 The Enemy Inside

place stunk like a public toilet. Dried pieces of excrement dotted the floor. The seats were covered with dust, and some of the grimy windows were broken.

The place was no good for rape, Tudor thought. The windows were too large, and the people on the platform, as well as anyone just passing by, could see inside. Even at night, the beam of a flashlight would be easy to spot, and the windows were too big to cover.

He jumped out of the car and climbed inside the locomotive. It was much narrower than the car, with space for only two seats in front of the broken-down control panel. The windows were smaller and higher up, offering less visibility from outside and easier to cover.

If we block the door from inside and cover the windows, we can easily bring a girl here.

Tudor lit a cigarette and began pacing up and down in a small space bounded by the seats at one end and a small, grimy toilet at the other, imagining an abduction and rape scene.

It's night, and he follows a sexy girl. She stands on the platform waiting for the train. He comes from behind and hits her over the head with a hammer, hard enough to knock her out but not hard enough to kill her. He drags her to the locomotive, hoists her inside, ties her up, gags and blindfolds her, and then fucks her into oblivion.

"Raped before and after death, stripped, naked, tortured," Tudor sang quietly and took a deep drag of the cigarette.

Then do whatever you want with her, till you get bored.

Tudor thought the plan would be easy to enact, especially since he could count on George's full-hearted help.

Would they have to kill the victim right away? What if someone found her? Tudor worked out the logistics of his plot.

Maybe we could just hide her in the toilet. Maybe tie her to the toilet bowl in case she needed to use it. Though if we don't feed her there won't be anything to come out the other end.

Except maybe cum.

Tudor chuckled to himself.

Stroking his chin, he estimated that the victim would probably be in good shape for a few days, maybe a week. Once she died, they could put her clothes back on, place her body on the tracks and watch it get splattered.

That would be a perfect crime. The police would probably think it was suicide. What else could they suspect based on the mangled body parts scattered around? They'd probably be too lazy even to put them back together, let alone to study them carefully.

Pleased with having found such a promising crime site, Tudor jumped out of the locomotive and resumed his walk to the far side of the tracks. Once he reached the road, he tossed the cigarette butt onto the pavement and stepped on it. The houses of the residential neighborhood stretching in front of him had escaped Ceausescu's urbanization project. The dictator's execution had come just in time to save them. Most of the homes were concealed by trees and grapevines. The abandoned house Tudor wanted to check out was on the same street as his grandma's house. Tudor walked down the back alley and entered the back yard of the decrepit structure through a hole in the broken fence. There were a few fruit trees on the overgrown lawn. Stepping on the tall, springy weeds, he plucked a green apricot from a hanging branch. He took a bite and savored the bitter taste.

The area was quiet, just a few dogs barking in the distance and the faraway rumbling and whistling of trains. Tudor inspected the back of the two-story house. A wild grapevine slithered up the wall, framing the sagging porch. The cement plaster was broken in places, revealing the layer of brick underneath. Two grimy windows stared down from the upper floor like empty eye-sockets. The attic window above was a smaller third eye.

Tudor climbed the wooden stairs of the porch, opened the door and stepped inside. A padlock and chain secured the door to the kitchen. He cupped his hands around his eyes and

Chapter 6 The Enemy Inside

peeked inside. The room was empty except for an old potbellied fridge in one corner. A faded floral pattern sprawled across the once-white tiles over the rusty sink. A cupboard door hung crookedly from a single hinge, revealing bare shelves inside.

Tudor stepped down from the porch and rounded the corner of the house. A tall fence and stand of trees hid him from neighbors and passersby. On the side of the house was a black French double-door also secured with a chain and padlock. Tudor looked up and noticed a window on top of the door. He lifted his left foot onto the chain, grabbed the window ledge with his left hand, jumped, and struck the bottom of the window frame with the heel of his palm, all in one swift motion. The window inched open with a crunch. Just enough for Tudor to see it wasn't locked from the inside.

The window was large enough to allow easy entry into the house, even for a lardass like George.

Peeking through a small pane of the French double-door, Tudor saw a large living room and a stairwell leading to the second floor. Like the kitchen, the living room was mostly empty. There was a large fireplace, a beaten-up brown couch, and a chair with one leg missing, some papers scattered over the seat, and more paper was strewn across the wooden floor. A broken oval mirror hung on the wall above the couch, and the grey flowery wallpaper was peeling off in places to reveal the decayed plaster underneath.

Tudor was curious about the upstairs bedrooms and the attic but decided to leave them for later, when he'd return with George, Edi, and Alex. For now, he was pleased to have found easy access to the house. The place was perfect for getting together to party and organize satanic rituals at night, with candles and pentagrams and an altar of sacrifice. They could also bring girls here and persuade them to offer their bodies and souls to the Horned Adversary.

Tudor continued to muse about uses for the forsaken house as he made his way back to the alley. A few houses down, he entered his grandma's back yard, grabbed a green apple from the tree, and drank water from the pump. He sat on a bench and began eating the fruit. As Tudor studied the peaceful one-story house between bites of his apple, it suddenly occurred to him that it too would make a cool place for debauchery.

Fuck me! How did I not see that till now? It's so obvious.

Suddenly, he was no longer indifferent to the old hag's fate.

He wanted her dead.

The sooner, the better.

Then he could have the house to himself. Homes in this area were a tough sell; that's why some of them laid abandoned. In any case, Tudor knew his mom would never dispose of her parents' house, where she had grown up. She cared too much for the old dump and was probably afraid the ghosts of her family would haunt her if she abandoned their home full of cherished memories.

No, she won't sell. She'll treasure the fucking ruin.

Tudor thought he'd be able to tell his parents he needed a quiet place to study for the summer, and then come here with his friends and trash the damn place. But he could do it *right now*, while the old bag was in the hospital. "Hell Yeah!" Tudor exclaimed to himself. "*Carpe diem!* No time like the present!" He couldn't wait to tell George and Alex about it.

Who would know? Who would suspect? No nosy neighbors would ask questions about his being here. It was his folks' property, after all. Some rooms in the house were barely used. And the attic, no one ever set foot in the attic. At night this place would be a perfect hideout for their gang.

Tudor tossed the apple core onto the grass and lit a smoke.

He knew the key to the house was right under the tablecloth on the patio table. And the door to the attic was not even locked. Access to the house was easy. Everything was set.

Thrilled by his ideas, Tudor savored the last of his cigarette, flicked away the butt, drank some more water, and

Chapter 6 The Enemy Inside

left his grandma's place. He made his way back to the railroad tracks and followed them toward the soccer stadium. His boots ground the gravel beneath. To his left, a few poplar trees were scattered around a vast, weedy field, at the far end of which stood the concrete cylinders of several grain silos. Next to the silos, Tudor recognized the yellow buildings of the tobacco factory. The old factory had a haunted-insane-asylum vibe to it. Its windows glistened in the sunlight and some appeared broken. It was surrounded by a tall concrete wall topped with barbed wire. Many such enterprises, Tudor knew, had been either privatized or left to rot after the revolution.

Sudden, savage barking interrupted Tudor's daydreaming. A pack of stray dogs was running toward him through the tall grass of the field. Tudor must have infringed upon their territory. He crouched down and grabbed a few larger rocks out of the gravel. Then he resumed his walk, a bit faster this time, tracking the dogs out the corner of his eye. When one of the feral mongrels got close enough, Tudor stopped, whirled around, and let the first stone fly. It hit the animal's rib cage with a muffled thud, and the dog yelped and stopped in its tracks. Tudor threw another rock toward the other strays, and they all stopped ten yards away from him and continued their fierce barking. The lead dog, a powerfully muscled yellow cur, had mismatched eyes, one brown and the other blue. Each frenzied bark lifted the beast's front paws off the ground in a spasm of feral rage.

That must be the Alpha of the group. The one with the crazy eyes.

Tudor turned and walked away slowly, knowing the dogs just wanted him gone and wouldn't risk attacking such dangerous prey. He remembered Alex telling him and Edi how crazy Russians in WW2 would tie dynamite to dogs and make them run into the German trenches at Stalingrad. That was a great idea, Tudor thought. Training dogs to run into populated areas, like a farmer's market or a night club or a soccer game, and then tying explosives to them. They'd go unnoticed since stray dogs were so common in their town. And then *BOOM!* The whole crowd ripped to pieces in one second.

Another perfect crime, Tudor thought, excitement accelerating his pace. How would anyone know who did it?

As the dogs' barking subsided behind Tudor, the soccer stadium came into view on the right side of the tracks. He'd guessed right; a game was on. He could hear the chanting crowd and see the large white and blue flags waved by the fans of the home team. He crossed the railroad tracks and Main Street and made his way toward the arena. Through a hole between the concrete slabs of the fence, he saw the scoreboard showed it was the middle of the second half. The home team was leading one to zero. No point in buying a ticket this late. Instead, Tudor clambered up the fence and sat on the edge of the top slab, feet dangling, elbows on his knees.

The stadium was full. The fans of FC Tatareni were packed into the bleachers behind the far goal. They were waving their flags and banners, jumping and chanting. Most of the other spectators were sitting on benches, eating sunflower seeds and hurling insults toward the visiting players. Others, like Tudor, followed the game from the top of the surrounding fence or perched on the branches of nearby poplar trees.

Tudor's attention was quickly grabbed by the game he used to love. The home team was now defending, hoping to preserve their slim advantage and secure the three points. The attacking team's passing was predictable, and they seemed to be running out of ideas. When they finally managed a cross into the box, their striker attempted a bicycle kick but connected with a defender's head instead of the ball. The defender threw himself theatrically to the ground, hoping to milk some time off the clock.

Tudor remembered how many times he'd tried bicycle kicks and failed. He'd been obsessed with imitating Marco van Basten, the AC Milan striker, the best player in the world. Tudor's errant kicks had injured many innocent kids from his neighborhood, including George, who'd once been knocked

Chapter 6 The Enemy Inside

unconscious after Tudor's boot left his face a bloody mess.

After the striker was penalized with a yellow card, the home team took their free-kick but lost the ball in midfield. The visiting team resumed their unimaginative offensive, committing everyone to the attack. However, a reckless pass gave away the ball and triggered a counterattack. Number ten from FC Tatareni managed a flurry of dribbles through midfield and threaded a wicked pass to the striker, who had just a single defender in front of him. The attacker faked right and went left, leaving his opponent flat-footed and gaining a clear path to the goal. From just outside the box he unleashed a violent strike. The goaltender jumped but must have known he was beaten. The ball struck the crossbar and bounced downward to bulge the net. The crowd exploded in cheers for the goal scorer.

Tudor jumped down from the fence. There was nothing else to see; the victory was sealed.

The beautiful goal reminded him how much he'd enjoyed playing in the midfield, intercepting the adversaries' passes and crisply distributing the ball to the strikers. Those counterattacking situations had been his favorite. He loved the wild chases that occurred in the spaces vacated by defenders. Those tense yet exhilarating moments all players on the field knew would decide the game. The make-it-or-break-it seconds.

For a tall player like himself, with long, robust legs, Tudor had amazing ball-control skills. Usually, small, bow-legged players, like most South Americans, had the best dribbling technique. However, Marco van Basten showed you could be tall *and* have amazing control. That's why he was the best soccer player ever, because he was the most complete: he had an outstanding aerial game, passing, dribbling, shooting, and scoring.

Reflecting on the beautiful game, Tudor made his way back to the movie theatre. The clock in the central park across Main Street showed 1:30. Still, half an hour left to kill. Tudor crossed the street, sat on a bench in the park, and lit up a cigarette. The day had turned hot. Some kids were splashing around in the water fountain in the middle of the park. On other benches, older people were feeding pigeons or playing board games in the shade of oak trees. Further down, girls were playing hopscotch or drawing on the grey walkway with colored chalk. To his left, in the distance, the farmer's market was still crawling with people, some carrying their loaded bags through the park while eating ice cream or fruit and drinking soda.

Tudor watched them disdainfully, taking deep drags from his cigarette.

He felt an ant scurry across his forearm, found it, and squashed it between his fingers. He noticed a small ant mound under his bench. Bending over, he touched the fiery tip of his cigarette to the top of the nest and watched panic spread among the hundreds of insects, boredom and revulsion intermingling on his face.

He crushed a few ants with his boot, but the others continued their frenzied running around, oblivious to their dead and dying comrades.

Just like people of this town are oblivious to Mr. Oprea's death.

Like the injured crow he'd wanted to kill the day before, insects were programmed only to feed and reproduce.

Tudor leaned back on the bench and stroked his chin in thought. He imagined that from high up, like from a helicopter, the town itself would look like an ant mound. The boxy buildings would seem like small ashen structures, while the green forests and fields would be nothing but grass. The people coming and going, nothing but a chaos of black moving dots.

The only difference is that people also feed on the future, on hopes, goals and projects.

They gorge upon tomorrow.

They chew and rip at the bright future like a cat on a dead

Chapter 6 The Enemy Inside

mouse.

"Can't they see how pathetic and disgusting they are? How can they fail to see the obvious?" Tudor murmured to himself.

What repulsed Tudor most was the urgency of their movements, the lack of hesitation. The instinctive relentlessness of rushing in and out of buildings, of driving around, of smiling and chatting, dancing, fucking, celebrating, buying and selling.

And then dying, leaving without a trace.

Tudor sensed that the fear of death pulsated under the surface of keeping busy.

It was the hidden engine driving these hideous insects. Fear of starvation, freezing, violence, extreme loneliness. Ancestral terror of horse-riding Tatar invaders, barbarian hordes raping, pillaging, and burning their sordid settlement to the ground. The maddening anguish of being swallowed by absolute darkness. The dread of nameless monsters going bump in the night.

Supreme Anxiety was the secret name of their God, hidden yet omnipresent, trembling yet omnipotent.

The human species: the cataclysmic result of the primordial fear shackling the organic dominion, the decrepit apex of eons of infested meat mutation, the mushroom cloud of ruination growing in the tremors of the first cell.

Just like insectile drones, Tudor thought, the people around him surrendered to a funeral march of empty gestures and mechanical movements. They resigned themselves to being just another pair of bovine eyes in the herd.

Tatareni, the world capital of anguish, the Mecca of stillborns.

But primal fear is irrepressible, Tudor mused. It grows in the shadows and bleeds into their nightmares. A reeking venom mummifying them, making them more insectile and grotesque.

Tudor swore he'd never be one of them, never slavishly

devote himself to their meaningless drudgery. Rather than drive cars, he would slash their tires and set them on fire. Rather than run up the stairs of a building, he would sit on them, smoke, and plan its demolition.

Always disrupt, instigate, make the sheep afraid. Mock them, burn them, stone them!

Bring death right into their faces so they can't avoid it anymore. Unearth corpses and hang them from balconies, by lampposts, or lay them on benches in the park. Decorate their homes with human remains and infuse them with the pungent smell of decay. So the scum has nowhere to run, nowhere to hide, no sanctuary. Suicidal rats trapped in a maze.

Suddenly seized by inspiration, Tudor counted the change he had left and ran to buy a small notebook and a pen from the stationery store at the edge of the park.

Back on his bench, he chewed the cap of his pen while trying to collect his thoughts.

"But how do you want the world to be? What should people do?" an imaginary opponent challenged him.

Tudor jotted down his answer:

"I want a world in which each person creates his own personal madness. Each individual does something different. People come up with different languages, different screams, different dances, different songs. They torture, murder, rape. Only, in that world, there are no words that could describe their actions. The old language would be shed like old skin. Only poetry would remain. Playing the violin would be no different from cutting your wrists. Fucking, disemboweling, and skating on someone's guts spread on the asphalt would be part of only one action. Even the words 'the same' and 'different' will no longer exist. In the emerging full, unbound chaos, everything will invade and morph into everything else. And this collective insanity would produce an atonal symphony of agony and ecstasy which would create earthquakes and send destructive waves throughout the dying cosmos."

Tudor read the description of his utopia over and over,

Chapter 6 The Enemy Inside

a bit saddened that the actual world fell short of his intense, orgasmic ideal.

But that's okay. It's okay that the world isn't yet as it should be.

The fact that most people chose to be nobodies, primitive animals, was an opportunity for him. The gap between him and the rest of society was a warm, wet orifice where he could stuff himself, push and push and ejaculate. It was his playground, the white canvas awaiting his brush.

The next thought flashed in his mind with the force of a revelation. His heart lurched; his fingers tightened on his pen.

That's what it meant to be a Satanist, a warrior, a soldier of Odin. It meant raping and abusing the world with no mercy or regrets. Ripping apart the world's insides with your cock and your knife, thrusting deep, until it screams and squeals, and then penetrating deeper into the silence of rot.

"Satanism is necrophilia," Tudor jotted down with a trembling hand. "Screwing the creation of a dying God. Fucking while grinning."

The Satanist is a necrophiliac, a drunk, horny surgeon conducting an erotic autopsy in broad daylight on a table in the farmer's market; a Jack the Ripper who shakes off the cover of darkness and exposes himself to elderly God-fearing women on hot summer days, before dissecting them.

The force of the twisted vision brought tears to Tudor's eyes. He underlined the last two sentences over and over. He looked forward to sharing his insight with Alex. Hell, even George might understand it. The message was simple, true, and to the point.

Happy and reinvigorated by his philosophical conclusions, Tudor stood up and stuffed his notebook into his back pocket. He strode back to the movie theatre, purchased a ticket, and entered the auditorium just in time to see the image of a corpse wired to a monument in the dusty cemetery of rural Newt, Texas. The film's macabre action immediately absorbed Tudor's attention. Leatherface chasing his victims with a chainsaw to cook them for dinner made him laugh hysterically. The sadistic idiot reminded him of George. Tudor's unhinged friend could well become the Leatherface of Tatareni. The next feature, *The Thing*, was as somber and sinister as a dark winter day in a mountainous wilderness. Through wide eyes, Tudor's hungry brain absorbed all the grisly special effects: the invading alien seizing human and animal bodies and using them for mindless destruction, necks stretching unnaturally, severed heads growing spider legs and scurrying around and hiding in corners, tentacles shooting from mangled torsos and limbs, infected blood splashing from ripped flesh and infiltrating a new, unaware host.

The movies scared, disgusted, and inspired Tudor.

On his way back home, his mind swarmed with violent images demanding to be drawn. But when his apartment building came into view, Tudor remembered killing Mr. Oprea and felt a jolt of panic. For the last few hours, as his mind had explored distant celluloid worlds, he had totally forgotten about the bloody events of the previous day.—

Maybe the police are looking for me. Maybe Edi told on us.

But there were no police cars parked on the street, and no one looking for him from his apartment's balcony.

Slowly, he made his way into the building, ready to bolt the moment he saw a cop. As he climbed the stairs, he took the key and the folding knife out of his front pocket.

He opened the door and quietly entered the apartment.

From the foyer he saw the TV was on, signaling that his parents must be in the living room.

Suddenly, the screen went dark and Tudor heard whispers and movement. Icy claws squeezed his heart. He held the knife more tightly.

His parents appeared in the living room doorway. They looked serious and gloomy as they walked toward him.

"Where have you been Tudor?" his dad asked.

"I went to the movies."

"With Alex?" Mr. Negur demanded.

"What kind of movie? Porn?" his mom inquired, always

Chapter 6 The Enemy Inside

expecting the worst.

"No, it was an action movie, actually. Action, sci-fi," Tudor said. He put the knife back in his pocket, crouched down, and began untying his boots. He was relieved. His parents wouldn't be asking these stupid questions if they knew about the killing.

But there was still a lot of tension in the air he didn't care for.

What the fuck do these idiots want from me?

He finished taking off his boots, stood up straight, and looked at them.

Mrs. Negur opened her mouth to ask something, but her husband quieted her by raising his right hand. "Tudor," the man began, "remember what we talked about last night, about how you need to start studying?"

Tudor nodded, shifting his weight uncomfortably from one leg to the other.

"So, did you study today?" Mr. Negur asked, adjusting his glasses nervously.

Tudor sighed with frustration. "It *is* the weekend. Maybe I'll start on Monday."

Mr. Negur furrowed his unibrow. "So, you didn't do *any* math today?" he asked, his voice trembling with anger.

"Fuck no!" Tudor barked, losing his patience. "I'm on vacation, remember?"

His mom gasped at the dirty word and pressed her hand to her ruined mouth as if the oath had come from there.

Mr. Negur tried to maintain control of the situation and sound authoritative. He folded his pale arms across his chest. "Well, mister, we'll have you know that you can't become somebody in this world without math."

Here they go again with the making-a-name-for-yourself *bullshit.*

"Everyone knows math," his mom added.

"Engineers, scientists, economists," Mr. Negur counted the groups on his fingers.

His parents defied him to reply to their argument.

"Whatever," Tudor spat.

Then, as if remembering something important, he asked, "So, how's grandma doing?"

Mr. Negur frowned in anger and frustration. "Don't you try to change the subject, boy. And for the record, she's not doing well. She might pass away any minute now. We have to go there again tomorrow."

Mrs. Negur started sobbing quietly, covering her droopy face with her hands.

"So, what do you want from me?" Tudor demanded.

Trying to ignore his son's disrespectful tone, Mr. Negur adopted a soothing voice, accompanied by conciliatory hand movements. "Your mom and I came home today, fully expecting to find you studying. When we found no signs of you hitting the books, we decided we must take drastic action to guide you back to the right path, toward the light."

Tudor didn't like where this was going and listened apprehensively, his anger rising.

"Tudor, your mom and I feel that this music you listen to is not a good influence."

"It's satanic, dark music," Mrs. Negur added, her red-rimmed brown eyes wide again.

Tudor smirked at them. "What other music should a Satanist listen to?"

His parents gaped at him, his mom's eyes ready to pop out of her head. To Tudor, she looked like a cow at the slaughterhouse, facing death after two hammer strikes to the head.

Mr. Negur tried to ignore Tudor's remark and resumed his argument, calm and solemn. "So, from now on, as punishment for drinking alcohol and smoking and not doing your schoolwork, we decided to take away your audio cassettes —"

"What?" Tudor shouted.

Frantic, he ran into his room. He opened the top desk drawer where his tapes should have been.

Chapter 6 The Enemy Inside

He gasped.

The drawer stood empty, except for the skeletons he had drawn with a marker on the bottom panel ages ago.

That bare drawer must have been the saddest thing Tudor had ever seen. Suddenly, he felt hollow and disoriented.

For a moment, that emptiness made him see red.

"Where are they?" he asked through clenched teeth.

His parents were now in the doorway of his bedroom.

"We put them away—" his dad began.

Tudor shot him a savage look. "I want them back!" he yelled.

"When you start studying—"

"I want them *right now!*" Tudor shouted and smashed his fist against the top of his desk.

Framed by the bedroom door, his parents stared at Tudor puzzled and terrified. His mom gripped her crucifix necklace.

Tudor sensed their fear.

I'll cut them up! I swear I'll hack them to pieces and have them for dinner. Texas Chainsaw Massacre-style!

He stared his parents down, nostrils flaring, fists clenched, ready to take out his blade. The only sound in the tense silence was a pencil rolling off the desk and falling to the floor. The mask of a lazy but obedient kid had fallen away, and deep hatred showed nakedly on Tudor's face.

The tension proved too much for Mr. Negur. He caved in. "All right, all right! We'll give you the tapes back if you promise you're gonna start studying." The man's words were steeped in fear.

Mrs. Negur mumbled something in the rhythm of prayer. "You've started down a dangerous path, Tudor. The Devil is full of deceit and comes in many forms—"

"Tapes, here, now!" Tudor yelled again, pointing at the empty drawer.

His dad hurried into his office. His mom waited, her head bowed, still muttering something about the Devil's grip on Tudor's soul.

Mr. Negur returned to the threshold of Tudor's bedroom and handed his son a white plastic bag filled with three dozen audio cassettes.

"We're doing this for your own good. You're too young to understand, but you'll thank us later."

"I doubt it," Tudor spat. He snatched the bag and fished out a random tape. It happened to be Pantera's *Far Beyond Driven*. He extended his right arm and showed it to them like a sacred talisman meant to ward off spirits and vampires. He swallowed his anger and uttered his threat in a low, steady voice: "If you touch my tapes again, you're both dead!"

His parents gazed at him stunned, mouths agape. His dad tried to laugh but managed only a shrill and trembling cackle.

Tudor slammed his door in their confused faces.

Then, with trembling hands, he placed the tapes back in his drawer. Out of spite he put on Pantera's album, rewound to the first track, "Strength Beyond Strength," and played it at maximum volume.

If they come back, I'll have to use the knife on them. No way around it; they're asking for it.

As Pantera's abrasive roar flooded his room and spilled into the rest of the apartment, Tudor took out his folding knife, small notebook, and smokes, and arrayed them on his desk.

Then he sat down, grabbed a blank sheet of paper, and began drawing. He drew his parents in the grips of dying agony: butchered, dismembered, and disemboweled, their mangled bodies tossed away by the side of a dumpster, partially buried by refuse. Crows pecking at their bulging, panicked eyes. Mouths opened in silent screams, maggots burrowing into their tongues and gums. Stray dogs ripping and chewing at their entrails. Decrepit vagrants spitting and pissing and defecating on their skeletal faces.

Feverishly, Tudor filled several pages with his hellish sketches.

At last Tudor's rage began to drain out of his body, through his hand, into the drawings. He turned the music

Chapter 6 The Enemy Inside

down, hoping his parents had learned their lesson.

Later on, he went to the kitchen to eat dinner. He was aware of his parents following his movements from the living room. The meal, spaghetti and meatballs, was waiting for him on the table, as usual.

While eating, Tudor realized that although his parents were scared of him, their fear did nothing to disturb their sedated routine. He was certain they were still watching their favorite shows—*Dallas,* in particular—drinking their cognac while eating peanuts and gossiping about who did what in their stupid small town.

Fear doesn't go away; it bleeds into your nightmares, spreading like a stupefying venom.

After dinner, Tudor drew more of the ghastly images that had permeated his psyche since the afternoon and listened to music before going to bed. He placed his knife under his pillow, just in case. His parents were going to Bucharest tomorrow. Maybe the old hag would finally die so he could have her house to himself. Regardless, he had another free day in front of him. A long, sunny summer day. Who knew what crazy shit he and his gang would end up doing?

First things first, Tudor reminded himself. *In the morning, touch base with Alex and plan the next attack. Then call George, in case we need his help.*

Then, Tudor thought of the small toilet in the abandoned locomotive. Ruxandra was sitting there, helpless and naked. Her eyes begging, tears streaking down the duct tape covering her mouth. Her hands were tied up at her back, allowing a perfect view of her full breasts, which jiggled to the rhythm of her sobs.

Then, Ruxandra changed into Alina, his doable classmate. More innocent than Ruxandra, probably a virgin.

Tudor approached the terrified girl and placed the blade of his knife to her throat. "If you scream, you die," he said.

When he removed the duct tape, she didn't scream but went on crying and begging for mercy in quiet whispers. Her submissiveness made him hard.

In the grips of the erotic vision, Tudor grabbed a towel and pulled down his shorts.

He closed his eyes just in time to see her lips wrap around his engorged member. Those virgin lips that probably never kissed a boy were now encircling his shaft. Warm and wet, they tentatively moved up and down his cock, her timid eyes looking up at him, pleading for him to spare her life. Tudor dropped his knife, grabbed her head with both hands, and pushed it down hard. She choked and gagged and slobbered but didn't resist. He released himself deep into the welcoming throat.

Tudor tossed the soiled towel on the floor and pulled up his shorts.

A bit later, sleep engulfed him.

He woke in the middle of the night, went to the bathroom to urinate, and returned to his bed. Sleep escaped him. His mind replayed the events of the day, and the behavior of his parents alarmed him.

He decided to teach them a more explicit and radical lesson and put them in their place once and for all.

Who the fuck do they think they are, taking away my music, my life basically, and ordering me around?

A wave of now-familiar anger swelled inside Tudor. He knew other parents ordered their kids around and disciplined them. But that was because other kids were spineless weaklings who deserved to die anyway.

Tudor, on the other hand, was a Satanist, a member of a different, vastly superior species.

He worshiped Satan, while their gods were sick and dying.

And the fact that his parents were older and more experienced didn't mean squat in Tudor's books. There were plenty of stupid old people out there. And sometimes, younger people, like Alex for instance, were much smarter than elderly ones. That's why Alex's parents let him do whatever he wanted.

That settled it for Tudor: his parents had to be more like

Chapter 6 The Enemy Inside

Alex's: quiet, submissive, out of his way.

He had to make them understand that as soon as possible. Tonight.

Carpe diem. No time like the present.

They must already be asleep, Tudor thought. Probably a shallow sleep, given his earlier display of aggression. "They sleep like rabbits with one eye open," Tudor muttered, grinning in the dark. He jumped out of bed and grabbed his switchblade from under the pillow, and tucked it into the front pocket of his shorts.

But maybe the small knife wasn't emphatic enough. He needed to teach his parents a lesson they wouldn't forget. And people don't forget what shocks them and makes them suffer. He could use a chainsaw and go all retarded butcher on them like the freak from *Texas Chainsaw Massacre*. Cut them up while wearing a dead-skin mask and squealing like a pig. The image of his parents freaking out doubled Tudor over with mad laughter.

When he settled down and caught his breath, he realized they didn't have a chainsaw, and the tool would be too noisy for an apartment building like his, especially in the dead quiet of the night. Crafting a mask, dead-skin or otherwise, was too much work. But a hammer, Tudor decided, would be an excellent addition to his arsenal. He needed to break some bones, maybe his dad's hand, as a sign of the leadership change. He could also drive nails into different parts of their bodies, just for kicks, to see what would happen.

Tudor would be the new Alpha of the household.

Too bad that new status wouldn't come with any good pussy, only his mom's spoiled muff.

Tudor wrinkled his nose at the thought.

I'll leave her to my dad, too old for me.

He went out on the balcony, opened the old wooden chest that held his dad's tools, and grabbed a hammer.

The night was quiet. A soft breeze caressed his skin. Dog paws clicked on the sidewalk.

Back inside the apartment, Tudor swung the hammer a few times through the air, enjoying the heft of it, its bone-crushing force.

Then he sat down on the couch in the living room and reconsidered his actions. He wanted to start by knocking his dad out with a hammer blow. His mom presented no danger. She was too fat and slow to do anything other than cry the whole time and pray to Jesus.

But he didn't want to kill his dad yet. Just knock him out, tie him up, and wait for him to regain consciousness and negotiate the conditions of the leadership change.

First, he would demand to be left alone. No more school or homework. He'd probably drop out of high school altogether; he'd already wasted too much time with the fucking thing.

Second, he wanted his grandma's house.

What if they say "No"?

Well, in that case, I'd have to kill them. And go to juvie with bragging rights. After all, what's cooler than killing your parents in cold blood?

But Tudor didn't want to go to juvie just yet. He needed to find a way to dispose of the bodies and then run away. A frown knitted his eyebrows while considering the issue. He could probably cut them into pieces with a handsaw, fill up a few trash bags, and take them to the dumpster. Time was not a factor as in the case of Mr. Oprea, who had barely escaped being hacked to pieces because of Alex's panic. He could also go all Texas redneck cannibal and separate the meat from the bones with a knife and fry it. No one would miss them on Sunday, except possibly his hospitalized grandma, but she was probably either unconscious or spaced out on drugs and most likely didn't know what day of the week it was. George would be happy to help him deal with the bodies and find a place to stay for a while. He could possibly deposit most of his stuff—tapes, posters, books, some clothes—in George's basement. On Monday Tudor could hit the road with the cooked remains of his parents in his backpack, and other

Chapter 6 The Enemy Inside

foods and beverages.

Another worrying possibility popped in his mind.

What if the parents say they agree but then *go to the police? What if they deceive me?*

Tudor lay down on the couch and thought deeply about the distressing possibility. He didn't think it was very likely since he knew his parents loved him dearly and he was an only child. Still, it was hard to predict their behavior once their lives were at risk. After all, these rudimentary organisms were programmed to prolong their own lives at any cost, which might include dooming their progeny. Focusing on the worst-case scenario, Tudor visualized the policemen coming to arrest and handcuff him. He saw himself pull out the knife.

Then the cop pulled out his gun.

"Fuck!" he shouted in frustration. "You don't go with a knife to a gunfight!"

But part of the answer was there, in the mental image. He needed a gun.

A flash burst in his mind.

George had bragged repeatedly that his dad had an arsenal of rifles and pistols. Armed with those Tudor could kill the policeman or even more than one. And then become a living legend. Killing a pig was even more extreme than killing your own folks.

But in the meantime, until he got in touch with George and got a hold of the firearms, Tudor thought it would be prudent to hide out for a while after revealing the new commandments to his parents. He'd follow them from a distance, see if they tried to reach out to the authorities.

A new idea struck him: he could go live in the abandoned house by his grandma's place for a few days. Steal some food from home, bring his tapes and player, and make that forsaken house his retreat.

No one knew about that spot. He'd only return home to check on his parents at night, when his folks would least expect him. And once he got his hands on the guns, he wouldn't have to worry about a thing.

Above all, it was imperative that he get in touch with George on Sunday. His twisted yet reliable friend had an essential role to play, no matter how things turned out.

Pleased with his plan, Tudor stood up, went back to the balcony, and reopened the tool chest. After a brief search in the dark, he grabbed the large bowl of twine laying at the bottom. With his knife, he cut a long string to tie up his dad's hands. The twine was thin but strong. If his dad tried to escape it would cut into his skin and the pain would make him give up.

Back in the apartment, Tudor made his way through the darkness to the hallway and his parents' bedroom.

As usual, the door was closed.

Knife and thread in his front pockets, hammer in his right hand, Tudor stood in front of the door, head hanging low, eyes closed, going over the moves in his mind.

His mom slept on the side of the bed closer to the door. He'd have to walk slowly to the far side, hoping they didn't wake up before he reached his dad.

Besides his accelerated heartbeat, Tudor could hear his parents snoring in unison and his mom grinding her ruined teeth.

It sounded like claws on a blackboard.

She must be having a nightmare. Maybe about me, coming to kill them.

Tudor smiled at the thought.

But his smile turned into a grimace when he heard a long fart coming from the bedroom. It was drawn-out, high-pitched, like air escaping from a balloon.

Tudor felt suddenly disgusted like he could taste the acrid gas.

All fight left him.

He took a step back from the bedroom door.

These people are like sacks of decayed meat. Why even touch them? It's like touching garbage dipped in wax.

Chapter 6 The Enemy Inside

And I was just thinking of eating them.
Tudor gagged.

An unexpected dread began to rise along with Tudor's revulsion. He was assaulted by an irrational fear of what was behind that door. Not fear of his parents, but of something that had swallowed them during the night, without their even knowing. He thought of their nightmares dripping like thick oil from their heads. Their frustrations, their sicknesses, their ugliness seeping through their pillows and mattress, leaking onto the floor under the bed and coalescing into a pulsating, reeking creature. A hairy, black, misshapen abomination with a rudimentary mind ordering it to feed and grow. His parents were floating in the black slime, and the moment he opened the door the creature would shoot a tentacle into his mouth, and he'd instantly be paralyzed and infected. Then he'd become its food.

"Fuck it!" Tudor mumbled and hurried back to his bedroom, quickly shutting the door behind him. He placed the hammer and rope under his bed and the knife under his pillow.

He definitely needed to call Alex tomorrow to see what his friend thought of the plan to subjugate Mr. and Mrs. Negur. In the meantime, Tudor reflected on the misfortune of owning slaves that disgusted you. That's what the Egyptian pharaohs must have felt when dealing with sweaty black Africans.

The best option at this point, Tudor thought, was to move into his grandma's house and pray she'd bite the dust. Then he'd have his mom come to cook, clean, and do laundry, preferably when he was out. *I can put duty sheets on the fridge every week, and my parents can follow them. I won't even have to see them.* Contemplating the logistics of this arrangement, Tudor fell asleep again.

His sleep was troubled. As he twisted and turned, his eyes began moving frantically under his eyelids, and a deep groan issued from his throat. He started grinding his teeth.

Odin Rising by Axl Barnes

* * * * *

Tudor lit another cigarette and decided to go home. He'd been waiting for Alex and Edi on a bench in the park downtown, but his friends hadn't shown up.

The large clock showed it was close to midnight. Pale lamplight spilled onto the concrete paths, the grass, and the trees.

Tudor took a deep drag and exhaled jets of smoke from his nostrils. They were supposed to go to the abandoned house tonight, but maybe Alex and Edi hadn't been able to sneak out as they'd planned. Frustrated, Tudor took a few more puffs and flicked the smoke onto the concrete path. He stood up, stepped on the butt, and headed home. He left the park and waited briefly to cross Traian Street. The light was red and didn't seem to want to change, so he crossed the empty street.

All cars slept on the curbs.

Tudor was surprised to see that the Queen nightclub was closed. No lineup outside, no loud music and shouting, no multicolored disco lights dancing in the windows. The place was usually crawling with people at this hour.

That's weird. Maybe it's closed for renovations.

Looking up at the four-story apartment buildings lining Main Street, Tudor saw no lights. The windows were silent, gaping black maws. He noticed the sidewalks were also dark and deserted.

Everyone's asleep already. Resting before a workday?

Tudor frowned as he wasn't sure what day of the week it was. It must be a Sunday; even God rests on Sundays, he thought to himself.

As he stopped to light a cigarette, he heard a voice call to him from behind. "Watch out boy! Don't step on the graves!"

Tudor whirled around but saw no one. It had been a woman's voice. Sounded like his mom. She used to repeat this warning every time they visited the cemetery and Tudor, always curious, wandered off the path and trod on someone's

Chapter 6 The Enemy Inside

weed-choked plot. It brought bad luck, she'd say.

But the center of town was devoid of people. Carefully, Tudor scanned the park, the streets and the sidewalks on both sides of the street. Nobody, not a soul. He recalled he'd seen a few people earlier, on another bench in the park. As he scrutinized the memory, though, he realized those people had no distinctive features. Were they male or female? Young or old? Gypsies or white? Tudor couldn't say. In his mind, they looked like a group of whispering shadows.

I was deep in thought, so I didn't pay much attention to them. Tudor tried to explain away the featureless apparitions, but a peculiar doubt lingered.

Tudor resumed walking. The only noise was his boots slapping the sidewalk. In the clothing store, the faceless mannequins were dimly lit by pale bulbs. Tudor stopped briefly and looked inside. The murky light spilled onto the displays of shoes, jewelry, and cosmetics. The store seemed frozen in time, its contents trapped and fossilized like insects in amber. The world behind the large window was a mere arm's length away, yet it seemed distant, untouchable, a rigid and orderly configuration, an inviolable monument to uniformity.

Frowning, Tudor took a deep drag from his cigarette. The town was giving him a strange vibe. He no longer believed that people were resting in their homes but that the town had somehow, unbeknownst to him, become *unlivable*, unfit to support human life, like Chernobyl in the aftermath of the nuclear disaster. As if sensing his growing unease, the voice spoke again: "They all left because of the earthquake. God found out what they were doing and punished them."

Tudor's frown deepened. The voice sounded like someone talking on the phone, only the handset was buried deep in his brain so he couldn't hang up. He angrily flicked the smoke away and pounded his temple with his right fist, as if his head were a broken radio.

Mom, or whoever you are, just shut the fuck up!

The voice continued, unperturbed. "God knew that they

hid their fetuses and their stillborns in their drawers and inside the walls. That's why this town is slowly dying, and its dwellings will be swallowed up by the earth. For, you see, Tudor my dear boy, if you put a stillborn in a wall, the wall crumbles, but if you cement someone alive, then the building will stand. That's how our Lord wills it."

Tudor turned and studied the grey apartment building across the street. Indeed, its geometry was imperfect. The balconies and windows were not aligned, and deep cracks zigzagged down the walls. To his left, one section of the building seemed to have sunk; its main floor and a good part of the second floor were underground. As it stood, you could jump directly onto the balconies of the second floor. The colossal movement had heaved one side of the building inward, into a violent collision with the largely intact right half, and the crush of concrete on concrete left a large mound of rubble that spilled into the sidewalk. Some of the cars parked on that side of the street had broken windshields and dented hoods.

The ruin filled Tudor with dread.

So no one lives here anymore?

"No, they all left after the earthquake. Many people died on that night. Jumping from the balconies and splattering on the pavement or the hoods of cars. And the survivors left because they knew the town was cursed."

Tudor knew some of the kids from that building; he used to play soccer with them. He wondered whether they were still alive. It seemed strange that although he wasn't friends with those boys anymore, the fact that they were gone left him feeling hollow and forsaken. Those kids and their families were familiar faces, neighbors, part of the decor of his day-to-day life. Their abrupt disappearance disoriented Tudor. He kept his eyes on the ground and let his legs carry him home along his habitual route, and he was relieved when he saw the living room light on in his apartment. His family's section of the building seemed unaffected by the quake. Maybe his parents would be able to explain what had happened.

Chapter 6 The Enemy Inside

I hope we're not the only family left in this damned town.

The voice inside his head had stopped, but a ferocious chorus of growling dogs suddenly punctured the ensuing silence. A pack of strays clustered near the entrance to Tudor's building. They were feeding on something. When he got closer, Tudor saw that their meal was none other than his elderly neighbor, Mr. Schmidt, the old guy he and George had always made fun of. The dogs were chewing the old man's insides, their jowls slapping hungrily.

Tudor walked by quickly but managed to catch another glimpse of the body. The old teacher was dressed in a black suit and black shoes. His open midsection revealed garbage instead of inner organs. The dogs were rummaging through milk jugs, potato peels, apple cores, empty soup cans, and an assortment of leftover bones.

The dead man's eyes were staring vacantly at the night sky.

One of the dogs turned to Tudor, bared his teeth and growled. Even in the murky yellow light, Tudor saw it had eyes of different colors, one black and one shining light blue.

Seized by fear, Tudor ran up the stairs to the lobby, whipped the door open, and pulled it closed behind him as fast as possible. Through the window he saw the dog watching him with its strange eyes, waiting.

Tudor navigated the darkness of the stairwell and reached his apartment on the second floor. Once inside, he was glad to see his parents were watching TV and everything seemed normal. He entered the living room and collapsed on the couch. On TV was a documentary about spiders. A black widow was dancing around a fly caught in its web, wrapping it in a silk cocoon. The commentator explained in a monotone that the spider injected venom into its prey to liquefy its internal organs for easy consumption.

Tudor couldn't focus on the show as his mind kept returning to the dead man getting eaten by dogs just outside their balcony, and to the ruination of the city. Should they maybe call an ambulance or the firefighters? Maybe there were survivors still trapped underground?

Tudor turned toward his parents, getting ready to tell them what was happening outside. They were sitting in their armchairs, facing each other over the end table with the rotary phone on it.

"I have to pay the electricity bill tomorrow," Mr. Negur said. "What are we gonna have for dinner?"

"Chicken soup and cabbage rolls," Mrs. Negur answered.

"Yum-yum! That's good."

"I could make fish soup instead, but I know we sometimes choke on those damn bones," Tudor's mom added.

Mr. Negur nodded. "Those bones are a nuisance. If you're not careful they could kill you, you know?"

"Tell me about it," the wife said.

There was a pause and Tudor got ready to speak, but his dad broke the silence first. "Tomorrow I have to pay the electricity bill. What's on your agenda?"

"Doing some laundry and cooking. I'm thinking chicken soup and cabbage rolls."

"Oh, and another thing," Tudor's dad said, "I have to pick up a prescription for my dad."

"That reminds me," Mrs. Negur said, "I need to stop at the pharmacy for glycerin suppositories. I'm constipated again."

The conversation halted again.

Tudor started, "Hey, there's a guy—"

They didn't seem to hear. His dad repeated, "Tomorrow I gotta p-pay the elec-tri-ci-ty bill."

His speech was slurred.

Tudor frowned.

His mom tried to say something, but mud and brackish water came out instead of words. It soiled her chin and fell between her breasts, staining her necklace and pink gown. Oblivious, she continued moving her jaw in a purely mechanical effort to communicate. She produced only a gargle as more mud and water poured out.

Chapter 6 The Enemy Inside

Then she stopped moving her mouth and looked at her husband as if expecting an answer.

Mr. Negur tried to speak but gagged and choked on his own brown vomit. Mud came out of his mouth in sinewy strands, like meat from a grinder.

Tudor was reminded of little babies burping out their food.

His dad slowly moved his hand to his chest and neck to wipe up the mess. A thick jet of blood gushed from his throat as if he had inadvertently opened a faucet attached to his jugular.

Tudor jumped up from the couch, took his knife out and released its blade, sensing danger, although his fear had no precise cause.

The sound of choking gargles and spilling blood permeated the room, a tense pall that threatened to overwhelm Tudor.

Wide-eyed, Tudor looked at the white rotary phone on the table between his parents and thought of calling an ambulance.

But what should I tell them? He took a tentative step toward his parents.

As blood sprayed from his throat, Mr. Negur was jolted by spasms. Then, all at once, he went still and sagged in the armchair, his shirt and pants drenched in gore. His eyes were now milky white, vacant, like those of the blind, his irises all gone. Tudor's mom's eyes had suffered the same odd transformation. Like tears, a milky liquid dribbled down his parents' cheeks and mixed with the dirt on their chins. The viscous white liquid reminded Tudor of semen, and he could bet it tasted salty.

The strident yowl of violins exploded in the room and made him jump. The sound, which made Tudor envision a demented kid sawing the strings with a serrated knife, was coming from the TV.

Tudor whirled around and saw that the documentary had been replaced by a black-and-white movie. The grainy picture showed a tomb in a cemetery. The lid of the grave moved as if pushed by invisible hands. Two bare white legs slithered out like worms and jumped onto the grass. They moved in sync like the legs of an expert rower. The feet shot out, took hold of the ground, and the knees flexed up. In spite of the mechanical urgency of their movement, their progress was snail-like.

The music stopped. The brief ensuing silence was crushed by the familiar voice booming in Tudor's head, "It's coming for you!"

Dazed, Tudor turned back to face his mother. Her blank eyes were staring right at him. He realized with a mixture of disgust and morbid curiosity that the voice in his head was nothing but the expression of her maternal instinct to defend her progeny. It was a sort of mental umbilical cord, and now, even dead or dying, she struggled to warn and protect him. With the last power she had over her ruined body, Tudor's mom lifted her right hand and clutched the gold crucifix.

Tudor knew he was in mortal danger. He felt it in his guts, the nauseating sense of impending doom.

His mom's voice continued in his head, now in the rhythm of panicked prayer. "When the Devil calls you, don't answer! It comes in many forms. If Satan finds you, he'll take you to the house with no windows and no doors. To the rotting place, where it feeds!"

His mom's bulging blank eyes expressed the certainty of the agony to come.

No windows, no doors. The rotting place.

Tudor knew without needing to check that the living room window was gone, along with the balcony door. A new wall stood in their place, identical to the wall on his side. The same white and green flowery wallpaper, the same oval mirror.

Panic hit him with renewed force when he realized his apartment must be sinking underground, just like the building across the street where the first two floors had disappeared into the earth.

His mom's warning echoed in his head.

Chapter 6 The Enemy Inside

This cursed town will be swallowed by the earth. That's how God wills it.

Tudor thought of running, but there was no point. There were no more windows, no more doors leading out of the apartment. He was trapped in a cube plunging deep into the ground. He felt his vision flutter and blur as waves of panic rushed over him. His apartment was now a cage, an inescapable prison. He stood in the middle of the living room, suffocated by fear, his mouth dry, his throat tight, his shallow breaths coming faster and faster.

"TU-DOR!" a voice gargled from the hallway.

Tudor didn't answer, so his mom shrieked in his mind.

Tudor knew the Devil was calling and would come even if he didn't answer. Like any beast, it would be attracted by the smell of fear, and now fear exuded from every cell in Tudor's body.

Someone pushed open the living room door.

As he expected, the dead man, Mr. Oprea, lurched into the room. He pulled his legless torso forward with his arms, "walking" on his knuckles like a crippled chimp. His face was covered in dried mud, and his mouth was filled with dirt. His bloodshot eyes seemed to look in opposite directions and move independently, like the eyes of a chameleon. The tatters of a blood-soaked shirt clung to his hairy chest. Soiled underwear still covered his crotch. Blood gushed from the red muscles around the ragged edges of protruding femurs that seemed to have been broken apart by brute force, and seeped into the rug underneath.

The sight of the legless freak dissipated some of Tudor's fear.

He tightened the hold on his knife. The weapon gave him some courage, as it was the only thing he could count on in a universe that seemed to crumble around him. He'd killed Mr. Oprea before, and he could do it again, especially now that his opponent had no legs and was basically a slow, disabled zombie. As adrenaline burst inside him and broke his temporary paralysis, Tudor thought maybe he'd be able to escape the prison of his apartment after all. Even if there were no doors and windows, he could break a hole through the walls or ceiling or crawl up through the ventilation system, find the stairwell, and climb all the way up to the roof.

Tudor got ready to kick down the abomination and hack it to pieces. But Mr. Oprea didn't charge; instead, he stopped a few feet short of Tudor and lifted his right hand to point at Tudor's legs. The dead man's throat produced a wordless burble as blood leaked from the hole in his neck.

Tudor looked down at his own legs and shrieked, eyes wide in terror.

His long, athletic legs were gone, replaced by a pair of short, gnarled limbs. Tudor knew instinctively they were Mr. Oprea's ruined legs and the dead man wanted them back. His vision blurred again as his mind reeled, struggling to get a hold of the new horror. He always counted on his fit body when stepping on a soccer field or into a fight, and his footwork and kicks were his most reliable weapons. But now when he needed them most, they were gone. He had only these stiff limbs, with rotten nails, wormy toes, and knotty varicose veins crawling up atrophied muscles. The skin was wrinkled and pale, almost translucent. And now the ruined legs were moving, guided by a twisted mind of their own, seemingly wanting to wrestle and trip each other. Tudor was briefly reminded of victims that had head injuries who try to learn to walk again, or short, bowlegged soccer players who dribble too much and end up tripping over their own stumpy feet.

Tudor's outer screams were accompanied by his mom's shouts inside the dome of his skull. "Cut them off! Cut them off! They're infected."

Frantic, Tudor lifted the edge of his shorts and saw that the rotten legs were sewn onto his own stumps with twine. It looked like a rushed, rudimentary job. Fighting to keep his balance like a performer walking on stilts for the first time, he

Chapter 6 The Enemy Inside

began cutting the threads with his knife.

But he wasn't fast enough. He sensed the infection spreading through his body as if his blood were slowly turning to lead. As his strength drained, cutting the threads became harder and harder.

Something bit his finger.

A black beak protruded from the hole his knife had opened. A crow's head appeared from inside his mangled right thigh. Two black, beady eyes looked at him and blinked. The beak pecked again at his hand.

In his leg, Tudor felt the ruffling of feathers, as if his muscles and bones had turned into a restless, angry flock of birds. A black wing poked out of the hole in the stitching. It stretched like a hand fan and began fluttering.

A cacophony of shrieks filled the room and Tudor's mind.

He lost all control. As the new apparition refueled his survival instinct, he began stabbing the crow in a mindless frenzy. Blood and dark feathers flew from his mangled leg. He lost his balance and fell backward, slamming his back into the hard floor. But he kept stabbing savagely at the bird and the infected limb.

Soon the rotten right leg came off, and the bird lay motionless on the floor in a puddle of blood, rent meat, and feathers. Tudor gazed at his bleeding stump with unbelieving eyes.

There was no respite. A sharp pain speared his abdomen.

With a trembling, bloody hand, he lifted his shirt. His belly looked like skin stretched over a nest of hungry birds. A dozen beaks were pecking it from below. A smaller crow managed to crawl out through a hole it had ripped in the skin and hop down to the floor. Then it began flying madly around the room, elated by the newfound freedom outside the cage of flesh.

As all fight left him, Tudor witnessed the disintegration of his body, paralyzed and helpless.

They're within me. I'm infected. I'm about to die.

Even his mom's screams had now turned into a mumbled prayer, a lullaby.

The beating of his heart became the beating of dark wings. He thrust his knife at his stomach and his chest without conviction, acting out a mechanical reflex. He stabbed and screamed until his raw throat issued only a feeble rasp.

Slowly, his cries became squawks as a crow squirmed out of his wide-open mouth. For a split second, the dying teen looked down and saw the small black head covered in his blood and saliva. In the background, his parents' dead eyes followed the flock of black birds birthed by their son. Mr. Oprea clutched the leg Tudor had cut off to his chest, like a knotty log. He grinned at Tudor, a purple tongue slithering across his ruined teeth. *He wants his other leg,* Tudor thought with disgust. *And will probably rip the stitching with his jagged, decayed teeth.*

Defeated, Tudor squeezed his eyes shut, and his thoughts ran down the deep, twisted roots of his screams. His mind begged for silence, but the roots were black, bleeding, and endless.

They choked him like snakes.

* * * * *

Tudor woke up at ten, still in the grips of the nightmare. Wet with sweat, the blanket clung to his chest. Bright sunlight filled the room but couldn't dissipate the force of his dark visions. The disturbing dream pulsed like a severed artery, flooding his mind with bloodstained visions.

He grabbed the knife from under his pillow, opened the blade and inspected it, half-expecting to find traces of blood. Then he lifted his right leg and touched his thigh and knee and calf and ankle, trying to make sure it was all in one piece. He made a kicking motion to see if the leg functioned properly. His abdomen also seemed intact, although covered in a film of sweat. He put the knife in his front pocket, folded his arms

Chapter 6 The Enemy Inside

under his head and stared at the ceiling, thinking.

He lay like that for an hour, as if paralyzed, letting the morbid vision recede and free his body and mind. He'd have to write down some of the images from the dream, but, for now, he just wanted to get rid of the deep feeling of dread.

The apartment was quiet. His parents must have left for Bucharest again.

Tudor remembered last night, how he'd been too grossed out to attack them and teach them a lesson.

He also recalled he had to talk to Alex and George.

With George about his dad's guns.

Set in motion by the thought of carrying a firearm, Tudor got out of bed and sat down at his desk, where he briefly jotted down the central images of his nightmare.

Then he went to the washroom to take a leak and a quick shower.

In the kitchen, he found his breakfast on the table as usual. While he ate, he decided to call Alex first and then George. A sunny day like this was good for deciding on their headquarters and planning future attacks on the small town.

Just before noon, Tudor sat down in one of the armchairs by the phone and repeated in his mind. "Good afternoon, Mrs. Antonescu, Tudor here. May I please speak to Alex?"

He grabbed the handset, waited for the tone and dialed Alex's number.

Someone picked up after the second ring.

"Hello!" It was Alex's voice.

Tudor was relieved. "Hey man, it's Tudor."

"Hey, is something up? Did the cops—"

"No, no cops, man. I told you no one would find out." Was Alex still worried about the killing? Tudor could sense panic behind his friend's words. To Tudor, the murder felt like ancient history. "Edi spilled the beans about us drinking, though," Tudor continued, sounding almost cheerful.

"I know. His parents called, but my folks don't really care. I hope Edi keeps quiet about the other stuff, though. Did your folks give you trouble?"

"Oh man, they pissed me off so much. I was about to kill them last night," Tudor boasted.

There was a moment of silence at Alex's end.

"Why?" Alex finally asked in a cold, distant tone.

"Well, the freaks took away my tapes. They said they'd keep them till I started studying for those stupid exams. So I said, 'Give them back or I'll fucking scalp you!' And so they did. You should have seen them. They almost shit themselves."

"Tudor, my brother, I think your parents are right. You *should* start studying."

"Why, so I can make a name for myself?" Tudor tried to laugh but the sound was forced and unconvincing.

"Obviously," Alex retorted immediately. "And make sure you get into a good high school and go to university. You know, make something of yourself."

Tudor didn't care much for Alex's advice or tone. He tried to joke. "Sorry, am I speaking to Mr. Negur? I thought I was talking to Alex Antonescu, the cool guy from our school."

Alex huffed with annoyance. "You can joke all you want, bro, but the joke's on you. Fact is, you're not prepared for those exams, and you think you could cheat. I hate to break it to you, but that's *not* gonna happen. We'll be seated in alphabetical order, so you, Edi, and I won't even be in the same classroom. These are *national* exams, remember? You'll probably be surrounded by students you don't even know, kids from other schools. And you'll *fail.* You'll end up in the shitty Industrial High School or, even worse, the Agricultural High School, surrounded by peasants, Gypsies, and other scum. You'll end up being some drunken, greasy plumber who beats his wife and kids when his favorite soccer team loses."

Now it was Tudor's turn to be quiet. He listened to Alex's rant dumbfounded. At first, he thought his friend was joking, but Alex sounded too damned serious. Worse, he seemed pissed off at Tudor.

Trying to sound sarcastic but unable to keep his voice

Chapter 6 The Enemy Inside

from trembling with anger, Tudor asked, "So now what, you're gonna study all summer to get into the Theoretical High School with flying colors?"

"If you must know, I'll go visit my aunt in Brasov for the rest of the summer. I'll definitely prepare for the exams, which I suggest you do, too, but I'm also going on a spiritual journey in the Carpathians."

Tudor felt a lump in his throat. He was speechless. He couldn't even begin to express his outrage, frustration, and sense of betrayal. "What the hell?" he managed to ask. "I thought you were going to stay here, and we'd take this fucking town by storm. Isn't that what we agreed upon, you know, what Odin wants us to do?"

"I changed my mind," Alex said abruptly. "I don't want to hang out with troglodytes who commit reckless crimes which can jeopardize my superior destiny."

"But we can do more planning and be more methodical..." Tudor said faintly.

"Well, feel free to do that with George and Edi. I have other plans now."

Tudor sighed deeply. "Man, I can't believe this. A few days ago you said we should blow up the Theoretical High School and now you're aching to go there and study like all those losers."

"What?" Alex went. "I don't remember saying that. I must have been drunk."

After another awkward moment of silence, Tudor spoke with bitter resignation. "So what happens after that?"

"After what?"

"After you go to university and become a big politician. What next?"

"Well, then I'm gonna implement my policies as Hitler did."

"Uh-huh, kill all Jews and Gypsies. And then what?"

"What do you think, Tudor? Naturally, I'm gonna unite Romania with the other Aryan nations of Europe."

"And then you die," Tudor added bluntly.

"So what if I die?" Alex pressed.

"What? Are you planning to come back?" Tudor asked, sensing he was losing the handle on his argument.

"I already told you I believe in the afterlife. I'm regularly in contact with the spirits of our ancestors."

"Okay," Tudor assented. "So you reincarnate and come back. And then what?"

"What the fuck is your point?" Alex barked.

Incited by Alex's dismissiveness, Tudor jumped furiously from his armchair and unleashed an avalanche of criticism. "My point is that you always wait for something to *happen in the future*. But it won't. What, are you gonna become a dinosaur with telepathic powers roaming the earth, as you told us in the cemetery? And then what? Who gives a shit? Even psychic dinosaurs suffer from boredom; don't you get that? Can't you see it's all stupid, all these projects... Whatever you want to do, you can do *right now, this summer. Carpe diem*, man! Isn't that what you said? Whatever is worth doing, we can do right now. There's no point in waiting. No time like the present, bro. It really doesn't matter anyway.-But if you wait, then you're like *them*. And Hitler, he was weak. Not extreme enough. Not a real Satanist."

Tudor heard Alex laugh at him, and it was the most horrible sound, a frozen ice pick driven into his spine. The humiliation made him go rigid.

"Tudor, my friend, you're not making any sense. You've read a few pages of Cioran, and now you keep saying that nothing matters." Alex laughed heartedly. "What you're saying is so stupid and self-defeating I can't even begin to argue with it. Why don't you pick up a book and learn how to argue and speak properly? Anyway, just so you know, once the Aryan race rules the earth, it will bring about a period of spiritual revival. Our race will evolve to new heights of consciousness. Things we can't even imagine now. Next to the Aryan man, you'll be nothing but a slave, an apeling. Unless you join our

Chapter 6 The Enemy Inside

ranks and educate yourself."

"Fuck education!" Tudor shouted, clutching the receiver so hard his knuckles were white. Barely controlling his fury, he managed to say, "You're all fake, Alex, you fucking poser. You're not a real Satanist. Do you think these bands we listen to care about going to university and shit like that? Like those Satanists from Norway, they don't give a fuck about school, man. That's not what being extreme is about, you dumb whore. You're just another sheep, and you deserve to die!"

Alex hung up, leaving the dial tone pulsing in Tudor's ear. Tudor slammed the handset down into the cradle and smashed his fist against the wall. "Alex, you fucking piece of shit! You fucking coward! So help me Satan, I'll fucking kill you! I'll teach you a lesson in pain!"

Tudor pretended to floor his adversary with a haymaker and then straddled his grounded opponent. He took out his pocket knife, unfolded its blade, pinned his invisible opponent's head with his left hand, and slashed his jugular with his right. Then he made some squealing, gargling noises. "That's right, squeal like a pig, you worthless sack of shit! Squeal! Squeal!" Tudor stabbed and stabbed at his imaginary opponent, hot tears running down his cheeks.

When his furry finally dissipated, he collapsed onto the floor and sobbed for some time, letting out his frustration and sense of betrayal. When done crying Tudor lay on his back, right hand with the knife resting on his chest, blood dripping from his knuckles, eyes staring at the ceiling. He contemplated his revenge.

He lay there on the living room floor for about an hour, motionless as a corpse in a coffin. Only his eyes moved as he assessed different courses of action in the theatre of his mind. When he, at last, reached a satisfying conclusion, he went to the bathroom, washed his hands and face and flushed the snot from his nose.

Back in the living room, he picked up the handset and dialed a number. "Hey, George, what the fuck are you doing, pig-man? Jacking off? Can you come by? I need to talk to you; it's important."

Chapter 7
The Wild Hunt

Carrying a heavy backpack, Alex made his way up the winding mountain road. The blazing afternoon sun prompted him to take off his black hoodie and knot it around his waist. On his right, the narrow Arges river trickled over stones, shimmering in the sunlight. On his left, the other side of the not-so-busy road was a thick, tall wall of pine trees and shrubs that hid the mountain beyond.

Around the next curve, Alex saw a weathered, rusty sign pointed to a trail leading into the forest. "Cetatea Poenari," the sign read. Poenari was the real Dracula Castle, not the Bran Castle, the big tourist attraction. Vlad had only spent one day at Bran. On the other hand, he himself had ordered the building of Poenari Castle, for his own strategic purposes, and he retreated within its thick walls during crucial times in Wallachia's history.

Besides military purposes, however, Alex was convinced that a significant factor in Vlad's decision of the location was that this area of the Carpathians was the spiritual center of his ancestors: the great Hyperboreans, the Nordic Aryan people who came down from the Arctic and turned the majestic mountains into their sacred center.

These wooded summits were spiritually charged. Alex could sense their energy as he stepped inside the coolness of the forest. Suddenly he felt calm and serene, like a believer upon entering his church.

Slowly, as he walked up the narrow trail, he felt the troubling experiences of the last few weeks loosen their grip on his soul.

Alex had decided to leave Tatareni, shortly after they had killed the pigmy, Mr. Oprea. The annual Brasov Extreme Metal Fest offered the perfect excuse for his parents. Once at his aunt's place he was able to relax a bit and reflect on what happened. The reckless killing made him feel confused and vulnerable. He wasn't sure Edi or Tudor wouldn't talk about it. Edi because he was scared and Tudor because he needed to brag.

But Alex couldn't allow himself to get caught, at least not for such a minor crime. Hitler himself had gone to jail, but for trying to overthrow the German Jewish-controlled Government, not for murdering a senile Mr. Shit for Brains.

Alex had carefully considered the causes of the unfortunate situation while reading through Codreanu's *The Nest Leader's Manual*. "The Captain" organized the legionary movement as a system of cooperating nests, around ten members each, with strict duties, rules and a clear hierarchy. The main reason for the difficulties faced by the Tatareni's newly formed nest was lack of discipline, caused mainly by heavy drinking in public. Thus, from now on, only him, Alex, the leader of the movement, would be allowed to drink alcohol, as a shaman and spiritual leader, to establish contact with the wise supernatural beings guiding the Aryan crusade. The celebration of victories would take place privately, preferably at a residence deep in the mountains, something similar to Berghof, Hitler's "Eagle Nest." Anyone who endangered and compromised the group by

Chapter 7 The Wild Hunt

reckless, public drinking and violence would be immediately excluded. An application of this rule would result in Tudor's dismissal from the Tatareni nest.

Alex still couldn't believe that Tudor had the nerve to challenge his authority during their phone conversation. All Alex wanted was to help the ape evolve by offering priceless advice. Tough love.

Even psychic dinosaurs suffer from boredom, Tudor spat back.

You're not a real Satanist, he accused.

Alex thought that only inferior, degenerated organisms suffered from boredom. The world opened like a beautiful nymph to a strong mind and will. It submitted and offered terrific thrills. But Tudor was just a meathead, a stranger to the spiritual light of Lucifer.

Just an ignorant thug.

Dumb *and* arrogant, like only the *really* stupid are.

The self-deceived fuck thought that he was part of the elite, of the chosen ones.

Alex smiled bitterly.

Maybe a thousand reincarnations down the road, Tudor would get a glimmer of magical power.

Not likely, though.

But the phone conversation also made Alex uneasy. Which was another reason he left Tatareni in a hurry. Alex was weary that Tudor would chase him down to teach him a lesson in the only language he knew, that of fists and kicks. Tudor needed to prove to himself, in his small and twisted mind, that *he* was the more dangerous and extreme of the two.

Alex wished he could overpower the brute but knew his athletic opponent had an edge. Also, the very thought of seeing and striking the aborted ape filled him with dread and revulsion. Thus, what he needed to do was arm himself and find some new followers. Bigger and stronger than Tudor.

At the Brasov Extreme Music Fest, Alex had met many like-minded people. To his relief, he didn't see Tudor in the crowd. In all probability, the brain-dead thug didn't have enough money to make it to the event. As usual, Alex managed to mingle with the band members and join them for after-show drinks. He had an especially deep and illuminating conversation with the drummer of Negura Bunget, a portly, bearded fellow who called himself Zalmoxis' Disciple. True to the aesthetics of Norwegian Black Metal, the musician was wearing corpsepaint, which was now smudged after the intense show, but still lent him a fierce, outlandish look. The artist confirmed Alex's intuition about the Aryan descent of Vlad Tepes. Speaking softly, wisely, while twisting the locks of his beard, Zalmoxis' Disciple revealed that the ancient Dacians, the most heroic of the Thracians, were Aryans who settled in the plateau of Transylvania, surrounded by the Carpathians. They descended from up north during the last Ice Age. Those who stayed behind became known as Vikings. That's what explains the similarities between their mythology and that of the Dacians. The members of this superior race were warrior priests with enormous magico-religious powers. Some decided to migrate South to Egypt, some east to Tibet, and others yet West to the ancient German lands. The ones who moved south became the ruling elite of Egyptian Pharaohs, and they psychically coerced the indigenous population into slavery and building the great pyramids.

The sage's words sparked to life something Alex already knew deep down, in his blood. Every time he'd read about these great heroes, his blood would whisper: *This is you Alex. This is your race, this is your home.* The sacred knowledge encrypted in his genes was more certain than any other, although it was mostly implicit in the language of dreams and music, it was more profound than anything ever spoken.

Extreme music festivals were great grounds for recruiting members into his fascist party, Land and Blood. Those youngsters, Alex thought, especially those listening to black metal, responded to an imperative coming from deep within their minds, a call toward dark forests and high mountains;

Chapter 7 The Wild Hunt

Odin's call to arms. They probably had dreams of swastikas and other runes, without the slightest idea of what they meant. Their blood screamed its right to self-preservation from the deep caves of their collective unconscious. If you gave them guns, Alex mused, they would immediately start shooting the non-Aryans, no warning shots.

Such devastating psychic power needed to be brought to life and channeled properly by a leader like him.

The youth walked vigorously up the narrow trail, which now became steeper. Thick, tangled roots formed a helpful stairway. Watching his step, Alex continued his reflection. He recalled that the turnout for this year's festival was much higher than last year's. The thing was growing. There were people from all over Romania and Eastern-Europe. Alex couldn't help but wonder what brought them together? Why did this dark, sinister music appeal to them? Many fans came from the vast Wallachian plains, from Bucharest, or the shores of the Black Sea. These kids knew, instinctively, that they were spiritually lost, that they've been lied to and brainwashed by corrupt politicians. They craved something today's society couldn't offer. And that had to do with the vast urbanization projects, with deforestation and the destruction of a rural, traditional way of life. A forest is something that hides, a forest is a mystery, the unknown. Tear it down, and nothing is hidden. But where there's no mystery, there's no revelation.

So teens followed the magnetic attraction of the sacred. This is why the festival looked more and more like a religious cult and coming to it, more like a pilgrimage.

Definitely, Alex decided, all the initiation rituals for the new recruits will take place deep in the Carpathian mountains. In the wild, like the warrior initiations in archaic societies, the novices would be left on their own to struggle for survival and find their spiritual path.

And, as Nietzsche said, you can determine the value of a person by how much solitude they can endure. For little people, solitude was tough and dreary. They were completely void on the inside, empty vessels meant for being used by others. For Alex, on the other hand, solitude was the only space in which he could regain his psychic vision, focus, and determination.

It was the fire that forged his iron will.

The ruined Poenari Castle, at the heart of the Carpathian wilderness, was the perfect place for him to meditate over these issues, under the spiritual guidance of his ancestors. Alex hoped he'd re-establish a channel of communication with Vlad the Impaler and the former prince would become his tutelary spirit and show him the way.

He was also convinced that isolation increased one's magical power. Every time, after periods of hermitting in the past, he'd found that people were quicker to obey him, as if a sixth sense told them of his inner strength.

That's why, Alex thought, great rulers would live in the mountains, in eagle's nests or caves, and the minions of the plains would come to them, just like Germans were going on pilgrimage to Berghof. And this is how Zalmoxis and other warrior-priests used to rule Dacia, ancient Romania, long before the arrival of the Christian plague.

Energized by his thoughts and the cold interior of the woods, Alex fished a sturdy branch from the forest floor and began striking the trunks of trees at regular intervals, to keep wildlife away. From previous trips, Alex knew there were many large carnivores in these woods. You needed to be on guard for wolves and black or brown bears as well as wild boars or lynxes.

Legend had it that Vlad Tepes used to hunt in these areas bare-handed, rumble with the beasts, kill them and use their claws or tusks as trophies.

Alex wasn't yet at that level of warrior initiation. He carried a large hunter's knife in a sheath fastened to his belt, both for wild beasts and aggressive humans he might encounter.

Moreover, Alex thought, large meat-eaters weren't likely

Chapter 7 The Wild Hunt

to come his way because he carried no food whatsoever. Only water and vodka, two plastic bottles each. And, in a side pocket of his pack, he stashed some weed Helga had given him. And lots of smokes.

All of these substances were meant to facilitate entering an ecstatic trance.

But Alex was sure that psychic visions would come to him anyway, even without the help of narcotics. The deep mountain forest was already making his soul flutter, like a bird of prey ready to spread its wings. The area was definitely spiritually and emotionally charged.

The steep, arduous climb began to take its toll, and soon Alex found himself huffing and puffing, beads of sweat popping on his forehead. When the path became gentle again, he stopped to catch his breath. Hands on his hips, Alex inhaled the earthy smell of the pine forest. He figured he was half-way to the castle, so he decided on a smoke break.

Through a gap in the trees to his right, he caught a glimpse of some beautiful scenery and walked toward it, leaving the main trail. His hiking shoes crushed the dead leaves and cones with a crunching sound. Alarmed, a squirrel climbed up a tree and gave a shrill call, soon answered by its mates. As Alex trudged through the underbrush, his legs got scratched, and he had to duck under the lower branches of trees. Soon, he reached the edge of an abrupt drop. He was surprised to see a few dark clouds suffocating the sun since earlier on it was shining from a clear blue sky. But the weather in the mountains was unpredictable. Shadowed by the clouds, the view was still beautiful. The river was nothing more than a silver line in the valley below, running in parallel with the twisting, dusty road. In the distance, upstream, there was a village which appeared like a set of red and white Lego pieces spread around the river, the dome of the towering church still bright in the pale sunlight. Dark green pines covered the mountain on the other side, with a few clearings here and there. In one of them, a flock of sheep was grazing the lush grass. The shepherd wasn't in sight, but his dogs were circling the herd.

Alex sat down on a boulder by the edge of the precipice. He fished his smokes from the side-pocket of his pack, lit up and turned his attention to the neighboring mountain.

He hoped there were no shepherd camps around the old castle. He was in no mood to fight off dogs or make small talk with peasants. The distant ancestors of these shepherds might have been wise warriors, but now their minds were clouded with alcohol and you couldn't make out what they said because of their missing teeth.

Alex unzipped his pack and took out a bottle of vodka and one of water. He took a gulp of hard liquor and then extinguished the burn. As his stomach rumbled, he took a deep drag from his cigarette. Last food he had was a sandwich in the Brasov train station that morning. He'd lied to his aunt and said that he was going with Helga to the medieval festival at Sighisoara, so she packed some food for him. After finishing his sandwich, he threw the rest of the provisions to the garbage.

This was the first day of fasting, of spiritual detoxification. First out of seven.

After a moment's reflection, Alex decided it wasn't probable that there were shepherds' huts around the fortress. These backward local people were very superstitious. They thought the castle was cursed and Vlad was a *strigoi* or vampire protecting a golden treasure that he'd supposedly amassed during his reign. Alex was convinced that was a gross misunderstanding on the part of the common folk. These legends usually carried an esoteric meaning, which was lost on the literal-minded degenerates. The gold that lay hidden in the fortress was the alchemist's gold, the philosopher's stone. Vlad was part of the golden Aryan race, a people who worshipped the sun.

But these deep-seated superstitions, Alex hoped, were enough to keep locals away from him and the silence necessary

Chapter 7 The Wild Hunt

for his initiation.

Another big swig of vodka. The alcohol shot right to Alex's head, making him feel warm and light. A fallen birch tree lay to his left. Its exposed tangled roots still clutched large chunks of dirt. Its top stuck out over the cliff, leaves blown by wind gusts. It looked like the storm had meant to knock the tree over the edge but ran out of steam at the last moment. The sight reminded Alex of a fertility ritual performed by the Druids. They would dig a tree out of the ground and bury it upside down, with its branches in the earth, and the roots up toward the sky. This way the vital spirit of the tree would infuse the land and secure its fertility.

Gusts of wind continued to stir the crowns of the trees around him but Alex was calm, he felt now one with nature. The wind was nothing but whispers from the past, revealing the ancient secrets of this mystical land. Looking up at the leaden, towering clouds, he recalled that the ancient Dacians would shoot arrows at them. This ritual puzzled him for a moment. Even if they were sun-worshipers, they still must have welcomed the clouds as a sign of rain and good harvest.

There must be a deeper explanation, Alex thought, stroking his chin.

The truth was revealed to him in a flash. The arrow was a shamanic symbol of the flight toward the gods. The flight of the shaman's soul or astral body. Dacians were known for killing the messengers they wanted to send to their God, Zalmoxis, by throwing them into spears. So, they must have believed in the human soul.

Another image broke the surface of his mind. Witnesses of the events said that during the Bucharest pogrom, legionaries went all mad. A young man, in a frenzy of joy, emptied his machine gun at passers-by in downtown Bucharest, tears running down his cheeks. And the church bells were tolled for every dying legionary. Because, in those wild days when Bucharest was in the grip of Odin, death was celebrated in the streets. The dead would go to Valhalla and prepare for

Ragnarok.

Just give them guns and they'll start shooting the scum.

Alex thought the young, mad hero must have been happy to revenge Codreanu's death as well as join Codreanu in the phantom national army, the army of those who spilled their blood for Romania.

"Codreanu," Alex whispered, sitting on his boulder, staring at the thick forest on the other side of the valley.

"Co-drea-nu," he repeated. *Codru* meant "deep forest." Codreanu was the son of forested mountains, of the storms on snow-covered peaks, of the lakes and rivers. Even in death, he was still the Captain.

The army of dead, unknown heroes was here in these mountains, waiting for a battle call. Alex thought he could catch glimpses of them, if he focused hard enough, moving under the thick foliage. A force pushing at the edges of this world. Their machine guns were loaded, their bows pulled back, their swords drawn.

Alex stepped down from the boulder and sat on the grass at the edge of the cliff. He straightened his back and crossed his legs, in a yogi's lotus position. He breathed deeply, in and out, rhythmically.

Heil Odin! Heil Zalmoxis!
Heed my call!
Your army is here, ready for battle.
These mountain peaks and deep forests
hide the berserkers of this land.
You lead them wise Odin, Zalmoxis,
Through me! Through me!

Alex felt his soul tense, spread its wings, and get ready to fly toward the clouds. He imagined it cutting the air like an arrow, high up over the gorge below, and then feeding itself off of the energy of the floating mass, growing darker, more menacing, lightning and thundering with the power of his

Chapter 7 The Wild Hunt

thought.

His soul was now a restless eagle ready to soar.

A few cold drops of rain splashed his forehead and nose. At first, he managed to ignore them. But then the skies opened, and the downpour broke his concentration. Alex gave a crooked smile. That was ok, he thought while standing up, it wasn't the right time for a journey out of the body anyway. The proper time was twilight. And by then he'd be at Dracula's Castle. He put on his hoodie, placed the bottles back in his pack and shrugged into it. Walking stick in his right hand, he stepped again into the cover of the woods. The thick foliage stopped some of the force of the sudden downpour. Alex turned toward the valley again. Sheets of rain covered the dark green like a white veil while the sheep continued their grazing unperturbed. The youth backtracked to the trail and continued his climb at a brisk pace. The leaden clouds made the forest much darker, and the thunder and lightning above sparked a wave of primitive fear. He instinctively touched the handle of his knife.

Soon, the trees thinned out, and Alex saw the castle. The ruined fortress was perched on the summit of a stony ridge. Its red layers of brick looked like rusted blood. Through the windblown rain, Alex could recognize the three round towers that were still standing connected by a high curtain wall. The fourth one, Alex knew, had been destroyed by an earthquake. One of the remaining towers still had a conical shingled roof.

That should do for shelter, Alex thought to himself, barely able to contain his excitement, heart hammering in his chest.

He was finally here, at Vlad's eagle nest, following the prince's summoning. He'd dreamed of this moment for so long.

Alex tossed his stick to one side and stepped out of the forest. Trying to ignore the heavy rain, he looked down through the opening of his hood, careful not to slip on the wet rocks forming the spine of the ridge. The pelting rain soon made his hoodie feel like body armor.

On top of the wall at the entrance to the castle was a large

Romanian flag, blue, yellow and red, blowing in the wind. In this forsaken, secluded spot, its fluttering sound made Alex think of the wing of a dying pterosaur.

Once inside the courtyard, Alex looked around to make sure no one was there. The fortress appeared completely abandoned. Pleased, Alex rushed toward the roofed structure and entered it through a decayed wooden door. The tower stood empty, desolate. A faint light seeped through a group of arrow slits and an arched window which was higher up, overlooking the courtyard. To the right, the remains of a spiral staircase climbed toward the door which led to the battlements. The wooden floor separating the two levels of the tower was gone, and, gazing up, Alex could see a few crows perched on the window and the beams of the roof.

Alex removed his pack and sat down on the stone floor to catch his breath. He took off his wet hoodie and lay it down. He was drenched to the skin. A fire would dry his clothes and keep him warm overnight. But the rain had to stop first so that he could go gather some deadwood from around the fortress.

Vodka would keep him warm for now. Bottle in his hand, Alex climbed the cracked stairs and looked through the arched doorway. It led to a walkway with crenellations on the side. The rain was now only a drizzle, the bruised thunderheads rolling away in the distance.

Sitting inside the archway, Alex waited for the rain to die down. Soon, a few sun rays made the wet stone of the battlements shine. The air was rich with the earthy smell of pine. Alex stepped out on the walkway and took in the spectacular view. To the south, the dark clouds hovered over the rolling foothills of the Carpathians. Beyond that, there was the vast Wallachian plain, spread all the way to the river Danube. Turning around, Alex could see the snow-capped peaks of the Fagaras Mountains reach above the wispy clouds. To the right of the massive range lay the Bucegi Mountains, with the most sacred site in the Carpathians, the mountain

Chapter 7 The Wild Hunt

peak Omu. On the vast plateau on top of that mountain, there was a sculpture of a giant human head, an ancient temple of a spiritual and ceremonial significance comparable to that of the Egyptian Pyramids and the Sphinx.

Alex moved his gaze to the clearing on top of the mountain across the gorge. That must have been the place from which the Turks bombarded the fortress in 1462. He imagined the Turkish Janissaries busy manning the cannons and small artillery bombards. The Janissaries, with their stupid tall hats, daggers thrust into their brass belts, and curved swords hanging on their side. The image of their ridiculous baggy red pants and pointy shoes made Alex smile sadly.

Circus clowns, he thought.

Trained apelings to be displayed at the zoo or tour with a circus.

Legend had it that Vlad had escaped at the last moment before the Turkish attack and used a secret passageway which went from the well in the courtyard down a system of caves all the way to the Arges River. Alex intuited that Vlad hadn't run because he was unsure whether he could defeat the Turks. But instead, he must have been worried about the pigmies desecrating these pristine, energetic heights with their toxic presence. The prince wanted them to go back to their dwellings in the desert, away from sacred mountains they couldn't understand.

Then it occurred to Alex that Janissaries were slaves from other areas under Ottoman control. So they weren't necessarily brown. Not all of them, at least. But still, brainwashed, enslaved foreigners. What a disgusting sight, slaves ruling over their natural masters. Vlad himself, Alex recalled, alongside his brother Radu, grew up around the Sultan, Radu becoming Mehmed's minion. Moreover, it was at the Sultan's court that Vlad had learned the grisly technique of impalement, which would make him famous and was added to his name.

As the next thought formed in Alex's mind, his heart sunk.

Had Vlad been raped by the Turks when he was just a boy?

That would explain his obsession with impaling them, as a way of getting his revenge.

The teen looked down, angry and disgusted. He thought he would probably find out what happened directly from Vlad, sooner or later. That is if the prince became his master and tutelary spirit.

But it was obvious, killing all Turks was the only option if you were raped by one. Either that or suicide. In that way, Vlad was a sodomized martyr like Jesus, but he couldn't sit around and wait for the kingdom of heaven. He needed vengeance in this life.

The humiliation must have been eating Vlad like cancer.

Alex took a deep swig of vodka and tried to push away the repulsive thought. Warmth spread through his body and he noticed his shorts and shirt were beginning to dry up in the gentle wind. He turned and scanned the courtyard below searching for a well. He found none, but the sight revealed precisely what was wrong with contemporary Romania. Multicolored wildflowers, lichens, moss, shrubs, and small trees grew around the abandoned yard. From the bushes close to the wall, lizards scurried up looking for the warmth of the sun. The criminal neglect of the authorities was obvious. Instead of restoring and protecting the castle, Romanians left it in the care of Mother Nature. Giving up on their history, and thus on their identity and their will.

To Alex's mind, not only did the castle have to be restored and preserved but there should have been yearly ceremonies involving torture and the public execution of the scum of society: Gypsies, lazy and corrupt politicians, greedy capitalists, beggars, prostitutes, and so on. Just like in Vlad's time. Only such bloody festivities would properly honor the Impaler's memory and his legacy.

Alex's mind went down the beaten pathway of his grandiose obsessions. If Romanians didn't show an iron will

Chapter 7 The Wild Hunt

to keep the body of their nation strong and healthy, then who would want them as allies? No strong countries would. And then Romanians would reclaim their place in the universal subhistory of slave peoples.

But if they revived the memory of the Impaler and resumed his policy of terror against the parasites infesting the nation's body, then other countries would become attracted to Romania, just like an eligible woman becomes attracted to a healthy, aggressive male.

And then Romanians would have a chance to move upwards on the evolutionary scale and fulfill the Aryan potential latent within their genes. Together with other proud Europeans, they would focus on saving their race by implementing eugenics programs on a large scale. Gradually, they would become better and better than other peoples. They would be bred up while the other races, devoid of noble blood, will regress to the status of apes. Then, the inferior races will gladly sell themselves into slavery. There would be no war, because of the enormous gap of psychic and intellectual powers separating the two races, who by then would look like different species. The Aryans could use their innate bioelectric energy to strike their foes like lightning. One kind would naturally rule while the other would instinctively obey. All slaves would be sterilized though, and, eventually, with the progress of science, they'd be created in labs, and designed to submit. Maybe created with no sex organs so the Aryans wouldn't be tempted to fall from grace again.

That had been Hitler's problem, Alex thought. He rushed into things. He thought that the Aryans would become superior overnight, after centuries of decadence. Also, his fraudulent doctor kept him high on cocaine, distorting the Führer's perception of reality. But, Alex knew, one single generation couldn't wash away the sins of thousands of corrupt ancestors. For a methodical, astute warrior, Hitler was too reckless, too impatient.

Alex promised himself not to make the same mistakes. If

within his lifetime, the Aryans wouldn't rise above the other races, he would gladly take his place in Valhalla and follow their progress from above. Or reincarnate as another Nordic crusader.

Waking up from his deep reflection, Alex noted the sky took on a reddish hue in the west, the sun touching the mountain peaks. He needed deadwood for the fire. Back in the tower, Alex placed the vodka bottle on the floor and emptied the contents of his pack. From the front pocket, he produced his walkman, together with a Negura Bunget tape, their new album *Sala Molska*. He meant to fill up his pack with wood. Out in the courtyard, he walked toward its center and looked again for the remnants of the well where the secret passageway may have been. There was nothing.

He descended in the wooded area surrounding the ridge of the castle and gathered logs, kindling, and some dry leaves and pinecones. He broke a few skinny logs on his knee to fit them in his pack. Backpack filled, he took an armload of thicker logs and made his way back to the fortress.

The air was gray with sunset, and the structure was still, in deep slumber.

Inside the tower, Alex cleared the moss off the floor with his feet and placed down the bigger logs. Then he formed a small pile of dry leaves, cones, and small twigs. He lit it with his lighter and waited for the fire to catch. A skinny wisp of smoke floated from the mound. Once the flame got larger, he added some kindling and then a few thin logs. Crackling, the fire spread and began licking at the side of the wood.

Pleased, Alex rubbed his hands on his shorts and then placed his hoodie closer to the heat to dry up. He sat down and had a drink of vodka. Gradually, the tower filled up with smoke, like an Indian tepee, the perfect setting for an ecstatic journey. Alex grabbed his walkman, put the earphones in, inserted the new tape and pressed play. It didn't feel like the music broke the silence of the sacred place, but instead, made the mystery at the heart of that darkness vibrate.

Chapter 7 The Wild Hunt

Wooded mountains had secrets which they whispered only to the chosen ones, those who could shoot lighted arrows into the pulsating center of the night.

The music was the almost forgotten runic language of these dark, forested mountains. Alex was happy to note, from the first song, that Negura Bunget turned to a more atmospheric type of black metal, as opposed to the over-aggressive, poorly produced debut album. *Sala Molska,* Alex remembered from his conversation with the drummer, was the sacred place where Dacian knights went after dying in battle; the Valhalla of ancient Romanian mythology.

Alex was deeply moved by the traditional musical instruments the band had organically incorporated into their sound. He recognized the alpine horn and the pan flute. The first track, "Bad Wind Through the Valley of Hell," created a cold, pagan atmosphere. In the background, you could hear burning fires and the howling of winds and wolves, sounds which fit eerily with Alex's medieval surroundings.

The youngster stared into the hypnotic blaze, his heart beaming with content. Then he grabbed his cigarette pack from the floor and took out one of the joints Helga had rolled up for him. He lit it and inhaled deeply, holding the smoke in his chest for a few heartbeats.

The next song was called "The Shaman's Roar," and it lived up to its name. Shrieked vocals accompanied ascending guitar riffs. The drums sounded like a mad sculptor hitting the trunks of trees in a frenzy. This fast, aggressive tempo was counterbalanced by a sublime flute melody which moved Alex almost to tears. In the background, there was another sound like a bullroarer or the deep bellow of an ox.

Alex remembered that, during initiation, master shamans whirled a bullroarer which was supposed to be the sound of a monster coming to eat the novices. And then they gestated in the monster's belly and were finally disgorged. Ritual death followed by rebirth, the key pattern to any initiation ritual.

In the grips of inspiration, Alex took a deep hit from the

joint and stubbed it out on the stone floor. Then he folded his legs into the lotus position and rested his hands on his knees with his palms up.

He took a deep abdominal breath in and exhaled slowly. He imagined himself in the belly of the primordial monster, the womb of Mother Nature. His tower was the womb of a ferocious beast perched on top of the mountain.

Deep breath in. Slow breath out.

The walls pulsated in the rhythm of Alex's breathing, shimmering in the heat of the crackling fire. He began whispering a personal incantation, partially improvised under the spell of the moment.

I am the first Aryan man,
I am this mountain, the center of the Earth.
This castle and I are one.
It's mortar, bricks, and stones are my skin, muscles, and bones,
The clouds and fog around its walls are my thoughts.

I grow taller and taller toward the sky,
like an acrobat I jump and plant my roots into the deep blue of the firmament,
and push my branches deep into the earth,
wild green into the land of the shadows.

I am everything, the center,
The sky, earth, and sea spread within me like fire,
I breathe the air of dreamtime.

Gradually, as his breath settled in the rhythm of the chant, Alex felt lighter and lighter. When he opened his eyes, he wasn't surprised to see that the fire was no longer in front of him, but down below. He was floating up, through the smoke, to the window above. Looking up, he moved his hands through the air as if swimming, the command of his will

Chapter 7 The Wild Hunt

flowing like an electric current through his ectoplasm body.

He grabbed the edges of the window and rested in the opening. Outside, the first stars shone in the dark blue sky. They seemed close enough to touch.

Moving his gaze to the darkened courtyard below, Alex gasped in fear. In the center of the yard, where he had looked for a well about an hour ago, there was now a horseman in a black cloak. Although his face was hidden by his lowered hood, he seemed to look straight at Alex.

A familiar voice spoke clearly in his head:

The time of judgment has come,
my rule in blood.

Alex was ready to answer the call when someone attacked him from behind. The words died in his throat as he found himself locked in a triangle choke. Frantically, he tried to pull at the muscular arm pressing his air pipe and push his chin underneath it.

An astral fight is a lot like a physical fight, the theoretical part of Alex's mind noticed, while the other part screamed. *Which makes sense since the astral body is a double of the physical body.*

Ruthlessly, the unknown attacker dragged him back into the tower. Only this time, Alex knew with the intuitive certainty one gets in nightmares, it wasn't a tower but a deep well. A long-forgotten well.

Alex attempted to scream but only managed a high-pitched croak. At his back, he heard his attacker snicker mischievously. Panicked, the youth tried to bite at the hand that seemed as hard as stone. As if guessing his intention his tormentor dug his biceps deeper under Alex's chin. Next, Alex was immersed in ice-cold water. He kicked and flailed frantically.

After a few seconds of pure, blinding terror, he woke up and retched a mouthful of water into the fire. Heart pounding hard, he jumped to his feet and looked around the room wild-eyed. The thick smoke stung his eyes, obstructing his vision. Quickly, he took out the hunter knife and retreated slowly toward the wall, expecting to get jumped at any moment, from any angle.

The glow of the fire didn't reveal anyone. Looking up, Alex saw no monster ready to pounce from the window.

Carefully, Alex walked along the wall, opened the door, and stepped outside. The dark courtyard appeared empty, no trace of a cloaked horseman. He took in some deep breaths of fresh air, still holding tightly to his knife, trying to calm down.

Maybe it was just a dream, he told himself. *Weed can make you paranoid like that.*

Except it hadn't felt like a dream. There had been a continuity of consciousness through it.

Maybe a lucid dream?

Indeed, he had experienced many lucid dreams in the past. But they were very different from out-of-body experiences. Lucid dreams took place in a dreamscape where you suddenly become conscious of yourself, but out-of-body experiences occurred in your actual surroundings, and they were always more forceful and vivid.

And what about the water in my mouth that almost extinguished the fire?

Deep inside, Alex was certain his experience had been more than a dream.

A wolf's howling pierced the night, sending a chill down Alex's spine. Pure panic stripped his surroundings of all their previous warmth and romantic beauty. He was in the middle of nowhere, at the mercy of forces beyond his comprehension. The closest human settlement was more than a mile away, and he wouldn't make that trip at night. It was a full moon and wolves were howling, and he wouldn't have been surprised if a pack, smelling his fear, raced toward him from the entrance to the courtyard.

Still clutching his knife, Alex returned inside the tower.

Chapter 7 The Wild Hunt

He saw no one in the yellow glow of the embers. He sat down in front of the shimmering ashes, knife still at the ready. The answer to his questions formed clearly in his mind: he'd been the victim of a psychic attack. Maybe there was some truth to the belief this castle was haunted. But his astral tormentor hadn't been Vlad Dracula. The dark Prince was the cloaked horseman. No doubt about it.

But then who attacked me? Alex wondered, rubbing his chin.

Did Dracula know about the attacker? Were they working together? Were they enemies?

But you knew all that, he said to himself, trying to regain his composure. *You knew what you were getting yourself into. Initiation means facing your deepest fears. You just have to stay focused.*

Focused, he repeated as he made a cut through the muscles of his left forearm with the knife. Blood trickled from the wound and dripped onto the stone floor.

The sharp pain brought the world into clear focus. The feeling was familiar, now part of Alex's identity and will.

Looking at the blood, he tensed his arm's muscles and inhaled deeply.

"I'm too strong. Nothing can break me! I may bend but never break," he whispered to himself. "Never, not by a long shot."

Considering the incident again, he thought his tormentor might have been the spirit of Mr. Oprea looking for his revenge.

But Alex dismissed that idea immediately. First, he hadn't killed Mr. Oprea, Tudor did. So, the ghost of the old man would rather haunt Tudor. Second, although spirits could travel through space easily, they were known to linger around familiar places for a long time after death. So, Mr. Oprea was probably wandering around his house, still trying to tend his vegetable garden or something dull like that.

Plus, his tormentor's intentional and calculated cruelty, not to mention his brute physical strength, seemed far beyond anything Mr. Oprea could achieve.

Frowning, Alex recalled the sensation of being suffocated and the evil snicker of his attacker.

He was right there, following with delight the pain he inflicted.

So, it probably was one of the mischievous spirits still haunting the castle.

Alex remembered one of the most grisly stories surrounding the fortress of Poenari. In order to get his revenge for the many injustices the boyars committed against him, Vlad had forced them to build this castle. The noblemen worked like slaves, side by side with their wives and children. Legend had it that they had worked till their expensive clothes fell off. Many of them, exhausted and dizzy from hunger, had fallen to their death from the top of the ridge into the gorge below. The ones who survived the ordeal were impaled on stakes around the castle, together with their families.

Alex thought maybe these tortured spirits still haunted the castle. Or perhaps the negative energy released by their gruesome deaths still blew around the deserted place like a ghostly whirlwind.

The memory of another horrific story surfaced into Alex's shaken mind, amplifying his dread. Legend had it that Vlad's wife had been driven insane by the voices of the dead coming from the stone walls or from the river valley below. Especially the cries of phantom children calling for their missing parents. Finally, to make their calls stop, and also because she didn't want to be molested by the invading Turks, Vlad's wife had jumped to her death from one of the castle's windows.

Reflecting on the incident, Alex thought she probably got astrally raped by the phantoms of the tormented boyars.

Which was probably what almost happened to him too.

Curious, Alex listened for ghostly voices and whispers coming from the walls of the tower, but could only hear the crackling of the dying fire.

Alex's next idea helped him make better sense of his

Chapter 7 The Wild Hunt

agonizing experience. Shamanic initiations, he remembered, involve both an ascent to the sky and a descent into the underworld. The shaman's astral body reaches the world of shadows and the dead by descending into a well or a cave. Both these spiritual territories, the above and the below, were part of the shaman's ecstatic itinerary.

And no one said that finding your way through this multidimensional labyrinth would be easy and painless.

If it was easy, then everyone could do it, Alex reminded himself.

All spiritual masters emphasized that the novice had to pass through many ordeals, and only the stronger ones were successful.

"Okay, so stop being a coward!" Alex whispered to himself, clutching his knife in his fist. "There's nothing to be afraid of. You get killed only to be resurrected on a superior plane of existence. You suffer only for the better. All agony is for the better."

Alex breathed deeply, trying to calm down and stay focused.

As the fire was dying, the room turned cold. Alex continued his abdominal breathing in an attempt to generate magical heat from within. He'd read somewhere that experienced Indian shamans were able to immerse themselves with their robes on in ice-cold waters in the middle of winter and then come out and dry up the wet clothes with heat produced by their bodies. Shamans were, after all, also called masters of heat and fire.

He felt his inner fire spark to life, gradually warming and relaxing his body.

His stomach rumbled angrily. This time the hunger was intense, vicious. Weed made you ravenous like that, Alex remembered. He felt so famished he could eat leaves and the bark off of trees.

But he continued his breathing and meditation. Hunger was just a feeling of his body, but a strong spirit could control the flesh he was attached to. The body couldn't dominate the spirit. Slowly, Alex's heart rate went down, and his eyelids felt heavier and heavier. He curled up on the hoodie lying on the floor and let his stream of consciousness disappear into the dark sea of sleep.

Hitler was right there at the castle, giving a speech. He sat on top of the battlements, exactly where Alex was the day before. He was facing the court, which was now full of people. Looking at him, Alex noticed something strange. The Führer and his immediate surroundings were all in black-and-white as if he wasn't really there, but just a movie projection. However, the details of the picture, like the crenellations of the walls, fit perfectly into the multicolored reality of the fortress. A group of people stood in front of Hitler, looking up at him from the ground, chanting and applauding. However, most of the audience was casually sitting down on the grass, smiling and chatting as if they were out for a picnic. Some were smoking and passing bottles to each other, eating sandwiches or cookies, paying almost no attention to the speech. Alex joined the group in the front and listened. He got soon carried away by the urgency of Hitler's message and his electrifying delivery. The Jewish plague, the subhuman Russians, they were all threatening to wipe Aryans off the face of the earth.

Alex looked back at the people who were just chilling on the grass. They all seemed lethargic, like a herd of satiated sheep going about their domestic lives without care. He meant to scream at them, to attack them.

That's when he recognized George and Tudor in the laid-back crowd. Like the others, they were sitting on the grass, drinking beer, laughing.

Alex ran toward them. "Guys, we need to join the Führer! What the fuck are you doing?"

Tudor and George looked at each other and back to Alex. They shrugged in unison.

"Chill man," Tudor said, "this is only a historical re-enactment. It's not really happening."

Chapter 7 The Wild Hunt

Both George and Tudor smirked at Alex.

"But that *is* Hitler," Alex repeated and pointed to the frenzied speaker.

George and Tudor stood up and flanked their friend. Tudor put his arm around Alex's shoulder. "Man, we need to show you something cool, but don't tell anybody!"

The three kids moved toward one of the stone walls circling the courtyard. Tudor pointed to the weed-covered base of the wall. George crouched down, pushed the weeds aside and removed two large cubical stones. Alex leaned over to look. He saw a girl's pale ass and legs. They were tensing and relaxing as if she were sobbing. Alex noted she wore high-heeled red shoes that were one size too large, the left one ready to slide off. Pleased, Tudor nodded at George, and the chubby kid placed the two stones back, covering the girl and her cries.

Tudor grinned at Alex. "We're gonna fuck her later! Once everyone's gone home. Are you in?"

Alex's frustration was about to explode. He was getting ready to scream that it didn't matter, that Hitler was right there calling them to arms.

In an instant, the dream dissipated and Alex woke up on the hard stone floor. Pale morning light spilled through the windows and arrow slits. The fire was a small heap of ash. Alex's back hurt, and he needed to urinate. The hunger was still there, sucking his energy. He lit a smoke and tried to forget both the starvation and the bad dream.

This was the second day of fasting. Second out of seven.

Cigarette in the corner of his mouth, he made his way out of the tower and pissed on the ground. The courtyard was still quiet, deserted, and the warm morning sun dispelled the terrors of the night before. Bird tweets and a woodpecker's drumming came from the surrounding forest. Back inside, Alex began thinking of the day ahead. He had to wait until dusk for the next out-of-body attempt. So he needed other projects. Thinking, he took a deep drag off his cigarette, puffed out a cloud of smoke, unsheathed his knife, and started playing with it.

The rule about fasting wasn't absolutely binding. During the ritual of initiation, the novice had to live like a wild animal. Particularly like a wolf. And what do wolves do all day? They hunt. Thus, Alex figured, he could hit two birds with one stone: feed himself *and* also achieve the spiritual transformation into a wolf.

Some small prey would be good, like a bird or a squirrel, but you needed a bow and arrows for that. He had to go down to the river too, to fill up his water bottles, so he could try to catch some fish there, maybe use his backpack as a trap.

Thinking of the river reminded him of the herd of sheep he'd seen the day before, a prey that befitted a wolf. It was something he could use his knife on. Plus, a sheep, or even a lamb, provided more nutrition than a tiny squirrel.

But you'll have to deal with the shepherd and his dogs for that.

It might work to stealthily follow the herd, patiently wait for one sheep to isolate itself and attack it before anyone noticed, break its legs and cut its throat. This reminded Alex of another rule of the initiation period: you can do whatever you want, as long as no one sees you. You are a predator, a wild beast. You are also dead, as far as the members of your community are concerned. And that's what predators and the dead have in common; they hide and wait to strike.

Alex recalled the tiny village he saw further upstream. That could be a good day trip. Just snoop around, scavenge for food. Many of those farmers had chicken and pigs in their backyards, and sometimes livestock was left alone to roam the streets. Alex wouldn't have been surprised if he found a lone cow grazing in a ditch by the side of the road. He could stab it, cut off some good chunks of meat, stuff them in his backpack, and hightail it.

That would be enough meat for a week. The teen found himself drooling as he thought of the roasted beef he could cook right there in the tower.

Chapter 7 The Wild Hunt

All in all, it was a challenge, and Alex always welcomed one. Be a wolf, hunt like a wolf, without mercy or fear.

Pleased with his plan for the day, Alex stood up and placed two empty water-bottles and his hoodie in his backpack. He would leave the vodka and the walk-man in the tower. He sheathed his knife and shrugged into his pack.

He pocketed his smokes and lighter and left the tower.

The sun was shining brightly by now, and the forest below the castle was alive with the flutter of birds and their calls. Alex found a dirt trail and walked in the direction of the village, leaving the summit of the castle behind. Soon, he began whistling. Confident in his sense of direction, he decided to take a short-cut through the underbrush maybe thus he could spot some larger prey that usually kept away from the trails. After pushing away branches and trudging through small bushes, Alex came upon a clearing. On the other side of it, he spotted a group of deer, grazing peacefully, snowy tails sticking up in the air.

Alex bit his lip and unsheathed his knife. He removed his backpack, dropped it on the ground, and crouched down. Hoping the tall grass would give him enough cover, he started moving slowly toward the prey. He knew he couldn't chase them but aimed to get close enough to throw his knife at one. The injury would weaken it, and he could follow the resulting blood-trail.

Stealthily, he made his way to the middle of the clearing, focusing on the group, mentally trying to make them stay put. He also tried to suggest to himself that he was invisible.

I'm not here, nothing dangerous here. Keep on feeding!

The deer, three of them that he could see, were still grazing, lifting their heads from time to time, alert, rotating their ears.

A horn bellowed, ripping the quiet of the forest.

Quickly, the deer ran to the left, swiftly disappearing in the cover of trees. Instinctively, Alex stood out meaning to give chase and score a lucky hit.

But what he saw next gave him pause. From the other end of the clearing a group of five horsemen were galloping straight toward him. His reflex was to run and hide, as he wasn't supposed to be seen by other humans. Too late though. The horsemen already spotted him and were closing in.

Alex's heart sunk as he recognized Tudor and George in the lead.

"Oh, fuck, this can't be good," he murmured as his blood turned to ice.

What are these idiots doing here? he wondered uneasily, remembering the ruthless way he insulted Tudor in their last conversation.

And there was something else that made his insides knot. Something to do with the dream he had last night, which he could remember only vaguely.

Alex's bafflement increased as he noted the cloaked horseman he saw last night in the courtyard ride along with his friends. The one he thought was Vlad Dracula. Bestride a black stallion, his face was covered even in daylight.

Besides these three figures, there were two strangers that seemed to be part of a medieval fair. One wore a white, conical janissaries hat while the other had a mask helmet on.

Alex looked at his friends and smiled instinctively. They grinned back at him, stopped their horses and dismounted.

"Good to see you, man," Tudor greeted, approaching Alex. As they shook hands he added, "We've been looking everywhere for you."

"How did you find me here?" Alex managed, trying to keep the growing anxiety out of his voice.

Tudor was quick to reply. "Well, you told me you're going to your aunt in Brasov, remember? And we decided to pay you a visit. It's really boring in the city without you, man. Isn't that right Porky?"

Tudor turned to George and winked at him complacently.

A grin split George's round face and his eyes sparkled. "Fuck yeah, nothing to do all day...except masturbate. One

Chapter 7 The Wild Hunt

day, I jacked off like five times..."

Tudor raised his hand. "Can it, Porky! Too much information."

"But how did you know I was *here*?" Alex repeated.

"Your aunt told us," Tudor said simply. Suddenly, looking at Alex, the smile died on his face and he frowned, "Why? Aren't you glad to see us?"

Alex was confused. He was sure he'd lied to his aunt and told her he went to Sighisoara, but a part of him wanted to believe Tudor.

"Sure, I am," Alex said. "Actually, I expected you to come to the Brasov Extreme Fest but haven't seen you there."

"Oh, we were there," George pointed out. "That's where we bought these cool tees."

George sported a Cannibal Corpse *The Bleeding* t-shirt while Tudor wore Pantera's *Vulgar Display of Power*. With growing disgust Alex noticed that George was growing his hair long, his bangs now getting into his eyes, in a pathetic attempt to look like a legit metalhead.

"We were too busy having fun with this slutty metal chick and forgot all about you," Tudor added. "But then, yesterday we went to your aunt's house, and she told us of this historical play they put on at the Poenari Castle. And we thought, 'Alex's wouldn't miss this for the world.' Right, Porky?"

George nodded, looked at the ground and bit his lip to suppress giggles.

Now, Alex knew for sure they were bullshiting him. The castle was all abandoned, and he hadn't told his aunt of any events going on there.

But why would they lie like that?

Ignoring the frown on Alex's face, Tudor turned and pointed to their companions still on horseback. "On our journey here we met these actors who have parts in the historical play. This is Vlad the Impaler and two Ottoman Turks."

Alex gazed at the so-called actors. Only one of them looked their part: the one dressed like a Janissary, sitting at Alex's left.

"That is Hakan," Tudor said, following Alex's look.

Hakan was brown, either Gypsy or a real Turk, big and stocky, with a severe face, sporting a handlebar mustache and a unibrow. Under a narrow, creased forehead, his eyes were close together, small and hateful. The cut-off sleeves of his shirt revealed big, muscular arms covered in tattoos. Alex noted the star and crescent moon, a symbol of the Ottomans. The shirt was tucked into red, baggy shalvary. His knee-high boots were also red, pointed up in front. One large dagger was tucked in the sash around his waist.

"This is Serkan," Tudor said, pointing to Hakan's companion. Serkan was tall and skinny, and the only part of his outfit connected to the Dark Ages was his conical helmet which came with a mask covering his face. It reminded Alex of the beak-shaped masks doctors wore during the Black Plague. Serkan didn't bother lifting his visor once he was introduced, so Alex had no idea what he looked like. Mail hung from the brim of the helmet to his shoulders and chest. Pointed pieces of armor covered his elbows and knees. At his back, Alex could see the top of a crossbow.

Other than this, and in contradiction with his role, Serkan wore a grey t-shirt, faded blue jeans and white sneakers.

Tudor finished the introductions. "And this is the one and only Vlad Dracula a.k.a Vlad the Impaler." Alex was surprised to see the cloaked horseman take down his hood and hiss at him, displaying a pair of plastic fangs. This unfortunate incarnation of Vlad the Impaler was a long-haired metalhead, about their age, with no facial hair and a forehead full of zits. Like a vampire, he was dressed all in black. He stared at Alex with black eyes encircled with black eyeliner, as if trying to hypnotize him.

"I vant to suck your blood," Fake Vlad said. Then he tilted his head and drank from an almost empty vodka bottle.

Alex couldn't control his sarcasm. "I thought vampires couldn't stand the light of day."

Chapter 7 The Wild Hunt

Tudor and George snickered.

"We're just having fun, man," Tudor explained.

"So, what's the play about?" asked Alex, playing for time to assess the situation and figure out his next move. It was clear to him that he'd been ambushed and Tudor and his crew would reveal their true intentions soon enough.

"Oh, we're going to the castle, and there's a bunch of diseased whores in there and...first, the two Turks fuck'em and then the women get impaled by George and then Vlad feasts on their blood."

The others nodded as if this was indeed the gist of the play.

"The spoiled blood?" Alex inquired.

"Well, he *is* a vampire," George said. "That's how they quench their thirst."

The fact that he was the butt of a cruel joke was now clear to Alex. But he couldn't understand why George and Tudor would go to such great lengths to deceive him. A part of his mind intuited the truth, but another side of him preferred not to know. The sensed truth was ugly and dark and filled him with dread.

A wave of fear and apprehension washed over Alex when he looked at the fake clownish smiles spread over his friends' faces. And their piercing, cold eyes, measuring his every move. There was definitely something odd about this encounter, weird like something from a dream, but Alex was sure if he pinched himself, he'd feel pain.

Tudor stepped toward him and struck his shoulder playfully. "Alex, my friend, we also came all this way to show you something crazy. You know those Turbo chewing gums with images of fancy cars and stuff? George and I have bought some last week from a Gypsy woman. When we unwrapped them we found no pics of cars, but shots of Adolf Hitler."

On cue, George fished a bundle of small, shiny papers from his pocket and showed them to Alex. Feigning curiosity, Alex looked at the images on the gum wrappers. Instead of colorful photos of flashy cars, these were poor quality, grainy, black-and-white pictures of someone resembling Hitler.

"Isn't that something?" Tudor asked eagerly, getting close to Alex to have a look.

"It's bizarre," Alex murmured.

"Check out this one!" Tudor pointed to one picture and snickered.

The picture showed a nude blonde woman squatting over and pissing on the chest of a naked man. The man looked transfixed at the woman's genitals. He resembled Hitler, but also Charlie Chaplin or some other random dark-haired man with a toothbrush mustache. Alex recalled pictures depicting Hitler's fake dead body on front pages of newspapers right after the Russians have pounded the Reichstag into submission.

"These are all fake," Alex said curtly, handing the pictures back to George. "Hitler never posed naked."

Tudor retorted immediately, "That's what everyone thought. But these shots were found in the photography collection of Eva Braun's employer, who only died last year."

"That's right," George added. "They say that this is early in their relationship when Hitler got the first taste of her urine and liked it more than he liked beer." He licked his lips to emphasize his point.

Alex was stunned. Anger swelled up inside him. He couldn't bear being contradicted, especially when it came to Adolf Hitler. This conversation was absurd, and he didn't want to engage in an argument regarding the Führer with these two troglodytes who probably haven't read a book between them in their entire lives.

"So, what's your point?" Alex spat through clenched teeth.

Tudor tilted his head back and barked laughter. Then he said loudly for everyone to hear, "Isn't it obvious? This clearly shows Hitler wasn't extreme. He wasn't a Satanist."

George was quick to throw more fuel onto the fire of Alex's anger.

"Even Goebbels said that Hitler was a softie when it came

Chapter 7 The Wild Hunt

to women. He couldn't get it up."

George made some masturbation gestures to his mates' delight. Fake Vlad took off his fangs and raised his left hand, showing his pinky. He declared in a nasally voice, "Historians agree that Hitler had a minuscule penis, smaller even than my pinky. Even if he got it up, there wasn't much he could do with it."

"Ha-ha!" George uttered. "Where did you hear that?"

"Animal Planet," Fake Vlad said.

Tudor raised his eyebrows, "*Animal* Planet?"

Fake Vlad shrugged, "Or maybe Discovery. I don't remember."

Everyone followed the conversation with amusement, except Alex who was pale with anger, his wild eyes tracking each speaker, desperate for a target. Finally, he decided on George, "What do you know about Goebbels, lardass?"

George ignored him and turned to Tudor and the others. "And real Satanists piss on women and treat them like shit. What kind of Satanist submits to a blonde airhead?"

Tudor nodded his approval. "Damn straight! You can't be an airhead's asswipe and consider yourself extreme!"

Alex couldn't stand being ignored by a nobody. Hands clenched into fists, he turned to Tudor, rolling his eyes in disgust. "What the fuck are you talking about, you retard?" he shouted. "He exterminated millions of Jews and other scum."

"That's not extreme!" Tudor yelled back, giving Alex a death stare that finally acknowledged his existence. "That's only a project, don't you get it? How stupid are you?"

Alex felt both relieved and terrified at Tudor's revealed rage. He was glad that the bullshit games have stopped, but now that Tudor's wrath was undisguised Alex became more aware that he'd be the loser of a physical fight. Trying to sound firm, he managed to ask again, "What the hell are you talking about, you pathetic idiot?"

Tudor took a few steps back as if in retreat and fished his folded knife out of the pocket of his cut-off jeans.

Everyone's attention turned to him, and he spoke to all of them. "You want to see something extreme? Something really mind-blowing? Watch and learn!"

He opened the knife and the blade flashed in the sunlight. Next, Tudor pointed its tip close to his left eye. Both his eyes looked at the sharp, shiny object and for a moment he appeared cross-eyed. Then he stabbed the blade deep into his eye socket and twisted it.

Everyone gasped in shock.

In spite of himself, Alex stepped toward Tudor moved by a basic instinct to help.

Tudor raised his left hand for him to stop.

Blood and eye-jelly jetted out of the fresh wound, reddening Tudor's clenched fist. It dripped onto his still smiling lips. Instead of agony, it appeared that the self-mutilation gave Tudor great pleasure. His remaining eye was fixed upon Alex, carefully observing the shock and puzzlement of his friend. Quickly, Tudor extracted his blade, and a torrent of blood gushed out, splashing his cheek and chest and drenching the front of his Pantera t-shirt.

Everyone gaped at Tudor, mouths hanging open. Even Serkan lifted the visor of his helmet for a better look. It seemed to Alex that Tudor was performing some kind of magic trick, keeping his audience spellbound. The sight of Tudor's blood diminished Alex's aggression toward his friend, leaving room for shock and awe.

Casually, Tudor folded his knife and put it back in his pocket. Then his head started pulsating, rippling as if the solid bones of his face liquefied. His red grin was still discernible in the quivering mass of his face. He lifted his hands and started pressing on his temple and his cheek around the bleeding socket.

In a low, gargled voice, he said, "I have this giant zit on my face, and I feel it's finally ready to pop."

"Gross!" Fake Vlad exclaimed while the Turks averted their eyes. Hakan spat on the ground. George's eyes instead

Chapter 7 The Wild Hunt

sparked with sadistic fascination.

Tudor's head contracted and relaxed like a giant muscle, as he kept on pressing the area around his eyehole. The skin became loose like the lips of a wet, warm vagina. Gradually, the hole expanded as something pushed from inside. Blood was now replaced by a viscous discharge that might have been pus or sperm. Alex couldn't tell. He only knew that the substance reeked like rotten eggs. Soon, the head of a bird popped out, all covered in goo. The beak opened and let out a gargled croak. Then a wing appeared and stretched out over Tudor's changing face, briefly covering his staring right eye.

The bird squirmed and cawed and finally managed to push itself out of the leathery eggshell. It fell on the ground, jumped up, and shook the white goo off its feathers. Then it hopped away into the tall grass, struggling to fly.

Gradually, Tudor's face turned back to its proper form, his eye socket still empty, red, and raw.

Looking at him, Alex felt like he was part of some sci-fi movie with state of the art special effects. Back to normal, real and solid, Tudor stepped toward his opponent.

"Your turn," he said, pointing to the hunting knife tucked in Alex's belt. "I see you have some self-cut marks so you should be good at this." Loudly, he added, "Show us what you've got!"

Alex gazed down at his left arm covered in scars from previous self-mutilation rituals. Last night's self-inflicted wound was crusted with dry blood. But these little cuts paled in comparison to Tudor's grisly display. Was he to stab through his muscles and tendons and scrape his own flesh from the bone? And what would that prove since he had no magical powers like Tudor seemed to, and would probably just bleed to death? Could it be that maybe if he focused his mind deeply enough, he'd be able to control his body in the way his rival did? Alex frowned at his opponent in fear and disbelief. The others measured him with mean and curious eyes.

Alex unsheathed his knife and gazed at its long blade.

He wants me to kill myself, he thought anxiously, suddenly unable to think or breathe, his mouth as dry as the Sahara. Heart hammering in his chest, he gazed back at Tudor. The remaining green eye stared back at him, seemingly wider, bulging out of its socket, devoid of all mercy, daring him.

Why doesn't he pass out or scream in pain? Alex wondered idly.

They want me to commit suicide right here and now, just for show, like a circus freak.

He looked around at George and the rogue actors. They were all waiting in a growing, oppressive silence. Fake Vlad's vodka bottle now stood almost empty, glistening in the sun.

Alex made his decision in an instant.

As fast as he could, he charged Tudor and plunged his hunting knife into his chest. Tudor didn't try to defend himself, taking the stab with a smirk on his face. Alex released the handle of the weapon and dashed toward the edge of the clearing. He heard Tudor's mocking laughter behind him and the sound of hooves hitting the ground. The tall grass impeded his run. The vodka bottle hit the ground on his side with a soft thump, and an arrow whistled close to his ear and struck a tree in front of him.

It's as if they expected it, Alex thought desperately.

Just as he prepared to jump into the line of the trees, a rope fell around his neck. As he reached to get it off, the noose was pulled taut, his neck snapped, and he landed hard on his back. His windpipe obstructed, Alex gasped for air as he tried to get back on his feet. Harshly, the rope was pulled again and, this time, Alex fell on his face in the rough grass. In his fall, he managed to catch a glimpse of his tormentor: Hakan, the orangutan.

The beefed-up Turk caught Alex with a pole-lasso, the type nomads used to seize cattle or wild predators. The thought of being treated like an animal enraged Alex as he tried to pull at the rod and force it out of Hakan's hands, but the Turk yanked it more strongly, and Alex went sprawling for the third

Chapter 7 The Wild Hunt

time.

Coarse laughter came from the others as a lump rose in his throat.

He bit his lip and tried to hold back burning tears.

Next, Hakan tied his end of the rod to the horn of his saddle and spurred his horse back to the group. The rope bit into Alex's neck again as he was dragged through the grass. Fighting the immediate danger of suffocation made him forget about the tears brimming in his eyes. Twigs and cones scratched his back through the soft fabric of his t-shirt, but the pain seemed distant compared to the primal need for oxygen.

Hakan continued his merciless progress. Once beside the others in the center of the clearing, he dismounted and released the rope just as Alex felt he was going to pass out.

Tudor ordered, "Tie up his hands!"

Desperate to fill his lungs with air, Alex didn't have the energy to resist. Strong, expert hands turned him facedown, grabbed his wrists and pinned his arms behind his back. His limp hands were tied with rope. The knot was tight, secure, cutting into his skin.

The same brutal hands grabbed him by the hair and dragged him in front of Tudor. Alex squirmed and swore at his attacker but to no avail. Hakan pushed him to the ground, and Alex tried desperately to get to his feet.

"Sit down, don't move! Or Serkan will pierce your skull and Hakan will slit your throat" Tudor warned.

Alex shot a wild look at Serkan. The crossbow was engaged, an arrow pointing straight to his head. He also remembered Hakan's dagger and imagined the Turk now stood ready to use it. Slowly, resigned, Alex sat down on his butt, legs spread in front of him, head hanging down.

He clenched his teeth and tried again to fight back tears but soon felt their warmth spread on his cheeks, as his face crumpled.

"Running away like a scared rabbit," Tudor said, leaning

toward Alex. "And here I was, thinking you were a warrior."

A wave of scornful cackles broke on Alex's head. He looked up at Tudor through a blurry veil. Half of Tudor's face was a gaping red wound and the hunter knife still stuck out of his chest. Now, a long chain dangled from Tudor's right hand. It had spikes on both ends.

"And now crying like a baby, 'Ma! Ma!, the bullies beat me up!'" Tudor resumed his mockery in a high-pitched voice. Then, in a serious tone, he added, "Alex, my friend, I knew you'd try to run like a coward, so I came prepared. This chain will hold you in place, both mentally and physically. Because, you see, I need to teach you a lesson. And I don't like it when students don't pay attention."

With an outburst that surprised him too, Alex spat back, "There's nothing you can teach me, you dim-witted freak! You know nothing! Haven't read a book in your entire life, except the ABC's, and probably haven't even finished that."

Alex forced himself to laugh but only managed a hiccup sound.

At first, Tudor only snickered, but then he laughed louder and louder. Shaking, he doubled over, holding his stomach, still ignoring the knife protruding from his chest. To Alex, the howls sounded hysterical and lunatic.

Trying to control himself between giggles, Tudor managed, "You think...just because you stay in your little room and read your crappy history books, that you know what's what? Believe this, you disgusting bookworm: no books can teach you what I'm about to."

Tudor nodded at Hakan. Next, Alex felt the meaty right arm of the heavyset Turk around his neck, locking him in a triangle choke. Suddenly, he remembered the assault he had suffered during his out-of-body experience the night before. The torturing arms were the same. The attacker must have been the same.

Hakan, the sodomite apeling.

Alex wasn't able to consider the implications of this

Chapter 7 The Wild Hunt

conclusion as he caught a whiff of Hakan's sweaty armpits and the nauseating stench brought fresh tears into his bulging eyes.

Through the watery veil, Alex saw George approach him with a spike of the chain in one hand and a hammer in the other. Tudor must have left the dirty work to his handyman. George's small porcine eyes were inquisitive and eager. A clown's grin split his round face. He placed the tip of the spike on top of Alex's head. Alex squeezed his eyes shut, struggled, and tried to shake his head, but Hakan's grasp was firm, ironlike. Under a layer of fat, his muscles seemed chiseled in concrete. Alex was beginning to asphyxiate again when George managed to hammer the first blow. The dome of his skull shook and cracked with a sickening sound. The second blow drove the spike down, punching through the soft matter of the brain.

Alex expected to pass out because of the extreme, unbearable pain, and the inevitable inner bleeding and swelling of the brain. He hoped he would pass out. But throughout his ordeal, his stream of consciousness kept flowing undisturbed, strictly registering his agony.

George yanked at the spike, sending another shockwave through the victim's head. The point was firmly rooted in Alex's skull. Pleased, George stepped away and handed the chain back to Tudor.

Alex felt Hakan's hands release his neck. He inhaled deeply but sensed that reality was slowly slipping away as if he was sliding down a dark tunnel, the world nothing but a diminishing image.

Finally, I'm passing out, Alex thought with a sense of relief.

"No, you're not!" Alex shouted, and he pulled the chain forcefully. Pain exploded, and Alex heard his cranium crack again. His surroundings came back into sharp focus.

"You're not allowed to pass out, my friend, or you fail the class. Is that what you want? I thought you were a top student, the teacher's pet."

Another wave of cackling laughter. Alex looked down, keeping silent.

What the fuck is happening to me? How do I escape this? The question nagged at him with renewed urgency, amplifying his sense of helplessness.

"There is no escape!" Tudor yelled, showing Alex again that he could somehow read his thoughts. "Until you pass my class, that is...You want to pass, right?"

Stubborn silence from Alex.

Tudor jerked the chain. Pain exploded, this time accompanied by dizziness and vertigo.

"Speak when you're spoken to, you fucking slave! Yes or no?" Tudor ordered.

"Yes," Alex mumbled.

"Fuckin' right. So, do you, my learned friend, think that a slave can also be a Satanist and a true warrior?"

Alex shook his head.

"Good, now we're getting somewhere. You're not a complete waste of skin. A slave is just that, a tool for others to use, but a Satanist is a rebel, a leader and a teacher. Kinda like you wanted to be, right?"

Tudor was pacing up and down now in front of his agonizing interlocutor, no longer caring whether Alex responded or not. He was counting the loops in the chain, like a priest his prayer beads. Deep in thought, he finally noticed the hunting knife jutting out of his chest and pulled it out casually and tossed it on the ground.

"Okay, so far so good. But now the question is: why is a slave like a tool? The way I see it, a slave is someone who takes orders and doesn't make decisions himself."

Alex nodded to avoid another brutal jerk of the chain.

"Good," Tudor said, folding his hands around his bloody chest and resuming his professorial pacing. "Now, let's take your body, for instance. Your legs." Tudor stopped and kicked at Alex's right leg. "Did *you* decide how to use them? To walk around as opposed to...I don't know, fuck or play the flute

Chapter 7 The Wild Hunt

or...sing?"

George and the others chuckled and murmured something between them.

"How can you—" Alex began.

"Yes or no?" Tudor shouted and pulled at the chain.

"*Ahh!*" Alex groaned in pain, a fresh line of blood now trickling down his forehead and his cheek. "No! No, I didn't!" he promptly conceded.

From his side, Alex heard George address the Turks and Fake Vlad, "It's in one of our pictures if you guys want to see. Eva Brawn is fucked by a war veteran with his leg stump. Maybe Hitler thought that the juices of her blonde vagina would make the leg grow back."

Another round of rough laughter. Alex looked at Tudor and saw a sparkle in the green of his right eye. Another morbid idea? Something about the leg stump?

Then the flash was gone, and Tudor resumed his argument.

"So, Alex, you're surely smart enough to see that the same goes for *all* organs that make up your body. You had no say in how they work. You just followed what your biological ancestors did before you... You followed right into their footsteps, like a dumb sheep."

Tudor suddenly charged Alex and lashed him with the chain over his head and back. Alex instinctively hunched his shoulders and cowered his upper body but the chain slapped his face, and soon he tasted a salty mix of tears and blood.

Tudor retreated just as fast as he had charged. The others greeted the violence, appreciating the unusual spectacle Tudor offered. "Good! Good! Good! Yes! Yes! Yes! You sack of spoiled meat," Tudor hissed under his breath. As if nothing happened, he immediately continued his lecture and playing with the chain. "Now that we reached the conclusion that you're nothing but a disgusting slave, we need to make sure it's imprinted into your body *and* mind."

Tudor bent over and looked Alex straight into his eyes.

"You're nothing but a worthless slave!!" Then he shouted "SLAVE! SLAVE!!"

Saliva splashed Alex's skin. To his horror, Alex glimpsed into the gaping hole where Tudor's eye used to be and saw pairs of beady, black eyes staring back at him as if nestlings resided in Tudor's orbit.

Ropes of saliva and blood flew from Tudor's mouth as he yelled his insulting conclusion again.

"You're just a stupid peasant, born to be used and abused."

Alex shut his eyes tightly.

Now, there was only one certainty in his mind: *there will be more pain.* More blood and more screaming and there was nothing he could do about it. He was trapped in a limbo where agony and humiliation were the only reality, and the cage walls were quickly closing in. Should he embrace the suffering like a martyr? Like the Captain preached?

With detachment and resignation, Alex opened his eyes and saw Tudor walk to his horse, open a brown leather saddle bag and take out a meat cleaver.

Tudor showed his victim the hatchet. "I inherited this from my grandfather, the butcher."

Cleaver in one hand and chain in the other, Tudor approached Alex. The sight of the new instrument of torture shattered Alex's Zen-like attitude, and he instinctively struggled to get on his feet.

Tudor kicked his victim in the chest, sending him back to the ground. "Stop crawling like a disgusting worm! I'm doing you a favor. Pain is the best teaching tool. I'll brand SLAVE on your brain like Negros were branded back in the day, or like cattle, so you always remember who you are!" Gazing at the others, he ordered, "Hakan, George, can you secure his right leg? It's memorization time!"

Hakan's strong arms locked Alex's head again, but the victim kept kicking up with his feet, and George had a hard time pinning down his right leg.

Chapter 7 The Wild Hunt

"Serkan!" Tudor called.

The skinny Turk dismounted his horse, stepped in front of Alex, and suddenly jumped in between his legs, hitting Alex in the chest with his pointy elbow cup. Then he pressed the metal against Alex's ribcage, cutting through fabric and skin. Alex screamed in pain, and the fight left him for a brief moment. This was enough for George and Serkan to hold Alex's right leg to the ground. Alex desperately kicked Serkan's back with his left knee, but it was like hitting a brick wall.

Tudor watched the brawl with sadistic fascination. Then he moved to Alex's right, sat down on his knees, lifted the cleaver over his head and swung it down forcefully.

Alex shrieked when the axe was still in the air. The blade cracked his bone with a sickening sound. After a second, a strange chill shot through his body and then bright red pain exploded like lava from a volcano. The wave of agony drowned him and his screams. He prayed for the relief of unconsciousness. But his awareness was still there, stubbornly absorbing and magnifying the pain like a watchful, restless eye.

Tudor frowned at the bleeding cleaver. "Fuck, I forgot to sharpen this. It's so rusty and blunt."

Alex couldn't see his leg, except in his mind's eye. The femur was smashed just above the knee cap, but not yet cut. Muscles and tendons laid exposed, blood leaking from ripped veins in the dusty grass.

The tormentor raised the hatchet and hit again. This time the blade cut through the bone and bit into the earth below. Lava erupted in Alex's mind, burning his screams. Next, Tudor stood up, holding Alex's leg as a trophy. He gripped it by the ankle and waved it like a bat, blood still dripping from its top. Hakan released Alex's neck, and George and Serkan let go of him and raised to their feet.

Over his victim's tortured shrieks, Tudor shouted, "Don't worry, Alex. If you stick your stump in a blonde's vagina, it's bound to grow back. Isn't that what Hitler said?

The others laughed mechanically as they gazed down at their mutilated victim greedily absorbing the grisly sight.

Alex couldn't help but examine his chopped-up member in disbelief. Below the cut of his black shorts, blood gushed out of his stump like water from a broken pipe.

Raising his eyes to Tudor's trophy, Alex felt dizzy and nauseated. He noted his dark, low-cut hiking boot and black sock, the puffs of blonde hair growing on his shin, his chubby yet muscular calf.

Only they're not mine *anymore. That leg is no longer* mine.

The thought pushed Alex on the verge of madness. In the vertigo produced by examining a body part that was no longer his and was now being used as a baseball bat, he felt his mind slip away from him.

Wide-eyed, Alex gazed down at his stump, desperate to find a new center of gravity, a new fixed point of reference in a once stable world suddenly turned into a furious vortex. The jet of blood now diminished into a slower flow. He stared at it for a few moments, still unable to fully believe it.

What the fuck is this? Why don't I pass out? He screamed inside his head. *I'm losing so much fucking blood? How can I still fucking think with no blood going to my brain?*

A voice from the more theoretical part of his mind added: *This must be a morbid vision, a really bad trip, like some drug users experience. Maybe the weed Helga gave me was bad, or it was something stronger. Stupid bitch fucked me up.*

But Alex couldn't get himself to believe that, no matter how hard he tried. The grisly events of this unfortunate day had the solidity and vivacity of anything real. They lacked the fragility of a lucid dream or the blatant incoherence of a hallucination. They were firm, heavy, and brutal.

They were as inescapable as metal bars in a prison cell.

And this was, on an almost unconscious level, what scared Alex the most. The fact that this morbid vision wouldn't go away like a bad dream, no matter how intense. And that the more he stayed in this prison, the harder it will be to recover.

Chapter 7 The Wild Hunt

This nightmare would cripple him for life, physically *and* mentally.

Tudor pulled at the chain, alerting Alex out of his thoughts. "Wake up, slave!"

A big grin on his injured face, Tudor was now playing with Alex's leg pretending it was a phallus. He swayed his hips back and forth and poked its gory tip at Alex's face, dotting it with red. Alex closed his eyes and tried to avoid the hits with no success.

"Look! I cum blood! Oh, no!" Tudor jested.

George and the others bellowed and made lurid remarks.

"Choke her, Tudor!"

"Slap that cunt."

"Fuck her in the head."

Abruptly, Tudor began clubbing Alex viciously with the leg, just as he'd previously lashed him with the chain. Two, three, four, five strikes in rapid succession. Wet, meaty thuds filled the air as the hard knee cap hammered and bruised Alex's back. The victim cowered under the blows, dropping his head between his shoulders.

Then, as fast as he started, Tudor stopped, tossed the leg into the grass and rubbed the blood off his right hand on his cut-off jeans.

Just as the strikes ended, Alex felt his body start shaking uncontrollably.

Oh, fuck, now what? Am I gonna shit my pants? he wondered bitterly, as he felt hot urine flow between his legs. He bit his lip in frustration for not being able to stop the pissing and trembling. Vaguely, he remembered shell-shocked soldiers from the Great War who couldn't stop spasming every time they heard air attack sirens. He wanted to laugh and cry at the same time.

Oh shit, I'm broken! Pulverized! Damaged goods!

Seeing his victim flop like a fish out of water threw Tudor and his companions into another fit of laughter. After it passed, Tudor turned to the others and pointed to Alex.

"Alright guys, you may be wondering why we stopped here to demolish this expired piece of meat when we could have gone to the castle and have some fun with more attractive and willing cunts."

Still grinning, the others nodded.

"But what made me angry," Tudor began, pressing his right hand on his chest, "is that this trembling coward—who fancies himself a soldier of Odin, the great god of war— this sack of shaking, spoiled meat, thinks he's better than us," Tudor emphasized his last word by moving his arm in an arch, pointing to his crew. "And you know why?" He touched the center of his forehead. "Because he has a third eye and only people of the master race have it. That eye catapults his wormy spirit out of the body and makes him see everything far and wide. Stuff that we, dumb apes that we are, can't see! But let's take a closer look at this magical eye! You guys wanna see it?"

"Damn straight," George said and the others approved.

Tudor turned to Alex, who was still shaking like an epileptic, his teary eyes staring at the sky. Not expecting his victim to understand, Tudor announced, "George will perform this invasive surgery on you, Alex. Sorry but we have no anesthesia, so we'll have to proceed in Dr. Mengele's fashion."

Catching Tudor's gist, George sang some lyrics of Slayer's "Angel of Death": *"Inferior, no use to mankind / Strapped down, screaming out to die."*

Next, Alex felt Hakan's now-familiar arms push up his upper body and locking his head. In a blur, he saw George approach him, carrying a hammer and a spike. Vertigo accompanied his sensation of *déjà vu*. This time, the tip of the spike touched the area right above the bridge of his nose. Alex squeezed his eyes shut. The first blow cracked the bone, the second one pierced through it. Then George ripped the skin and removed a piece of the skull. George's fingers crudely ripping through his brain-tissues made Alex cry out in agony. But the screams seemed distant whereas the stubby fingers

Chapter 7 The Wild Hunt

were so near, tearing at his most intimate self. The sensation made Alex sick. He gagged and wanted to throw up, but his jaw was locked tight by Hakan. The cold, rational part of his mind recalled a philosopher's idea that the pineal gland was the seat of the soul. Carelessly, George was ripping apart that subtle ectoplasm with the eagerness of a gold digger. Finally, George managed to extract something. Alex instinctively opened his eyes, but his vision was immediately painted red.

Through blood and the dazzling sunlight, Alex glimpsed the wriggling body of a small animal.

Hakan's arms released his head, and Alex let himself flop to the ground, his body still shaken by less intense tremors.

He squeezed his eyes shut and prayed for death.

"Look at that!" Tudor said as George put the extracted organ on the ground. Curious, his companions came closer to look at the oddity. Even Fake Vlad dismounted to inspect the critter.

It looked like a grey lizard.

Its body and tail were covered by pointed spines and its normal eyes, on the sides of its head, were crusted over. Instead, it had a large, elongated eye on its back, half-closed, staring lazily at the sky. The eye's vivid green was cut by a black vertical slit. The reptile was about eight inches long, and it moved slowly, like a newborn exploring the alien environment outside the womb of Alex's cranium.

Tudor tossed his end of the chain on the ground and picked up a small stick. Tied up and mangled, Alex wasn't able to run anywhere. Tudor crouched down and poked at the eye. Probed, the organ became alert, opening all the way.

All of Alex's tormentors gathered around the bizarre creature now, studying it with an interest mixed with repulsion.

When George prodded at the eye with his own stick, the black pupil moved slowly toward him. Then George touched it again, this time pressing harder on the gelatinous globe. Jets of red ink spurted from the corners of the eye-ball. They all gasped in surprise.

"What the hell is that?" Tudor asked with dread and fascination.

"Blood," George said and wrinkled his nose, "and it stinks."

The others spread out waving their hands around their noses.

"Gross!" Tudor exclaimed, pinching his nose. Quickly, he crushed the anomaly under his boot with a crunching sound. Then he kicked the dead body toward Alex as if it were a deflated soccer ball, rushed and struck his damaged opponent in the ribs. Alex groaned but didn't move much; his blood-covered eyes absently staring at the clear blue sky.

George fetched the lizard's broken body and threw it on Alex's chest. The others snickered. Looking down at his demolished enemy, Tudor said, "Having a third eye is as special as having a third nipple. You don't go around bragging about it, but try your best to fucking hide it, man. Or have it surgically removed. So, you see, we actually did you a favor. Now you can live like a normal person."

George laughed out loud. "Like a normal and completely handicapped person that is!"

They all howled looking at the broken, inert body, pleased with a job well done.

Alex could still hear them, but they seemed far away. He was now in a semi-catatonic state, not even sure he had a mind or a self. The crude lobotomy administered by George, opened up a cognitive void, and the darkness made his self shrink into a point, craving non-existence. He knew he was still there, in a clearing on the forested mountain, surrounded by sadistic demons, but he didn't care anymore. He was cold, frozen, dead, just a sack of meat and bones.

In addition, on a deep, almost unconscious level, Alex calculated that if he freezes and plays dead, Tudor and the others would get bored. After all, they had said whores were waiting for them at the castle. A vulgar play was on the

Chapter 7 The Wild Hunt

agenda. That should be more entertaining than playing with dead or dying things."

In support of that, Alex noted that Tudor had stopped pulling the chain, probably increasingly disgusted by Alex's mangled face and body. His work here was done, his lecture finished, his adversary broken to pieces and demolished forever.

Tudor's next question confirmed Alex's expectation.

"So, you guys say there's some women of low morals waiting for our judgment at the castle?"

"Yes, sir," Hakan confirmed, "We've gathered all the dirtiest scum from nearby villages. They're all tied up and ready to go."

Tudor nodded, "Let's proceed then, and exert out brutal punishment."

Then, gazing at Alex with contempt, Tudor added, "I don't think this empty husk will go anywhere unless he could slither like a snake. But I'll chain him to the ground just in case. Maybe we can have more fun with him later on when he comes to his senses."

Alex heard the hammer strikes as Tudor drove the spike at his end of the chain deep into the ground.

A moment later, a hard object fell on his chest. Then, Tudor whispered in his ear, "I'll leave you the hunting knife, bro. After all, a Viking is to die with his weapon in his hand if he is to join Odin in Valhalla." Tudor bit on his lower lip to stifle chuckles. "No doubt, he'll be aching to have you on his side after such a heroic display... Anyway, I'll leave you with something to think about, if your broken nugget is capable of any more thought that is. Consider it a homework assignment if you like. So, in your educated opinion, did Hitler go to Valhalla? I mean, did he gloriously die in battle?"

Tudor roared laughter as he stepped away. Then, Alex heard hooves hitting the ground nearby, horses neighing, and then trotting away.

In a few moments, the clearing was silent once again,

except for the chirping of birds and the buzzing of bugs.

Alex felt relieved to be alone, but had no idea what to do next. He opened his eyes and scanned his surroundings through a curtain of coagulating blood. His vision was red and blurry. He tried to wipe his face against a cluster of weeds. It was tough doing it with no hands, like a dog. The rope tying his hands was as tight as at the beginning.

His first instinct was to hide. The line of trees was about thirty yards away. But getting there meant pulling out the stake from the ground. And that was a hard job with your hands tied.

To his puzzlement, Alex noticed that his thinking was flowing normally, in spite of the abuse his brain has taken. The simple fact that he was still conscious was abnormal. But then again, abnormality seemed to be the theme of the day.

His knife was now on the ground, beside the foul-smelling lizard that had somehow inhabited his brain. Alex turned on one side and pushed his body with his good leg so he could grab the knife. With trembling hands, he began the arduous process of cutting the rope. His wrists felt stiff, as well as his face and neck.

In his rush, he slashed his skin and dropped the knife a few times. Finally, he managed to cut through the rope and free his bleeding hands. Only they didn't feel free, but heavy, as if made of concrete. Slowly, he grabbed the spike in his head with both hands and pulled it out. It came out with a gruesome gurgling sound, like something you would hear from a congested drain. More blood oozed on his face, but this time he could wipe it with the back of his hand.

Gazing at the dense trees, Alex started to crawl through the rough grass. It was like plowing through sludge. Despite his efforts, the forest seemed impossibly distant, as his body felt like a hollow shell slowly filled with lead. Gasping and out of breath, Alex stopped moving and dropped his head in the grass. He realized that he wanted to hide inside the forest not because he thought he could escape—Tudor and the others

Chapter 7 The Wild Hunt

would easily track him down—but because he was ashamed. Ashamed of being seen like this. Beaten and broken. In the forest, he'd be invisible to others and, consequently, to himself. This reminded him of Mr. Oprea, how he and Tudor had hidden him under a bush in the forest by the riverbank. It seemed like it happened a lifetime ago.

Another memory resurfaced, an image of his mom's cat, Tom. Usually fat and feisty, when it stopped eating they knew it was a goner. Many old cats suffer kidney problems, the vet had explained. Alex's mom had tried everything, but Tom was losing weight at an alarming rate, and one of its eyes seemed to be always covered in pus. It would sleep a lot, in the dark corners of the house. Especially in the closet, or in boxes in the storage room. Curled up in the dark, waiting to die. One day, Alex brought it its favorite treats and shook the box. He wasn't expecting Tom to come running, but he was shocked by the sight of the cat nonetheless. It walked like a poorly programmed robot, trembling legs no longer sure where the ground was, eyes and brain instructing a vague sense of direction. Its fur was all shaggy, from all the dark corners it'd slept in, a sign that it was no longer able to groom itself or it no longer cared. The cat banged its head on the wall a few times before finding its way to Alex, and then lethargically scratched its front nails on the floor in a parody of his usual enthusiasm for treats.

Alex had crouched down for a closer look and what he saw sent a cold shiver through him.

Both of Tom's eyes were now crusted over with pus. The cat was practically blind, and it reeked of excrement and death.

Trembling, Alex went to the phone and called his mom.

They had put Tom to sleep later on that day.

The memory brought fresh, hot tears to Alex's eyes.

He was now like Tom the cat, just trying to hide away and die in peace, dreaming of the merciful euthanization. Alex sobbed for a long time, shaking and hiccupping, taking deep breaths that shouldn't have existed. Then he fell into a shallow sleep, his mind swinging over his body like a Jack-in-a-box clown on its spring.

For an hour or so, Alex kept jerking and blubbering in his sleep. Then he was rudely awakened by something pecking at his stump. His eyes went wide. A large, fat raven stared at him with black, hungry eyes, a thin rope of flesh hanging from its beak. Alex screamed and kicked at the bird with his uninjured leg; it then hopped away and spread its wings, meaning to take flight. But it didn't, the danger wasn't grave enough. The raven began cawing, probably alerting others to the prospect of a hefty meal. It seemed willing to wait till its pray was completely immobilized.

Up in the sky, Alex saw more ravens circling in a funeral dance. Plus, he imagined that the smell of spilled blood would soon attract wolves and other carnivores. Cringing, he remembered how in the morning he thought he was the wolf, the archetypal hunter, and now he was but the helpless game.

Alex clenched his fist around the handle of his knife. The grim prospect of being eaten alive by wildlife gave him a new sense of urgency. He remembered the lighter in his pocket. With it, he could start a fire. Or at least grab a tree branch and turn it into a torch. Slowly and painfully, he resumed crawling toward the tree line.

Next, the determined raven cawed right behind him, ready to peck at his stump again. Alex turned his head little by little. His neck felt rigid, like after a period of intense head-banging. He rolled over on his back and made a stabbing motion at the bird. This time the plump raven flew away a few yards before landing and resuming its wait.

Alex looked at his white, livid hands and a new dark realization hit him: he was bleeding out. His Aryan blood no longer pumped through his veins. He was now a nobody, out of touch with his ancestors, out of touch with his source of power. How could he trust his own thinking anymore? He needed to self-destruct as soon as possible. But how? How

Chapter 7 The Wild Hunt

can you kill a body that has already bled out and is medically dead? His brain cramped on the question.

He looked at his knife. He could cut his jugular and stop his breathing. But how could he be sure that would kill him? There was no blood flowing to his brain, and yet he was still able to think. What if his consciousness would remain even after he stopped breathing?

Should he burn himself? The thought of the immense agony knotted his stomach. It was one thing to extinguish a cigarette on your arm and another to set fire to your whole body. And how long would it take to die? And how was he to be sure his mind won't survive inside the charred skeleton?

As if to emphasize his psychological vivacity, a host of thoughts and images rushed into the stage of his mind. He remembered Hitler's suicide. How he shot himself as he bit down a cyanide pill. Alex used to find that tragic, but now he thought that Hitler had it easy. He was able to exit without significant complications. An abrupt cut of the tape of his consciousness. No double-takes. No trial and error.

Did Hitler go to Valhalla? Did he gloriously die in battle?

Tudor's questions echoed in Alex's mind and gave rise to another one: do suicides go to Valhalla?

The youth's panicked psyche spit out another disturbing notion: people of various ancient cultures believed that the soul resided in the bones. That's why the Druids got the skulls of their enemies and kept them as trophies. And that's why torching himself would probably not work. Will Tudor come back to take his skull and hang it on his belt? Drink beer from it like Vikings used to? Would Alex be conscious the whole time, staring out through the empty orbits as through the windows of a prison?

These morbid ideas weakened Alex's already lethargic resolve. As his mind was hunting for a solution like a frantic rat in a maze, his muscles were becoming gradually more stiff, as if he were buried in hardening concrete. He recognized the symptoms of *rigor mortis* from readings he made about human decomposition. He got curious about the subject after they'd killed Mr. Oprea. He needed to know if the police would be able to establish the exact moment of death once they found the corpse.

Decomposition and *rigor mortis* went faster if the body was outside.

So, he didn't have much time left before he'd get trapped in his body forever.

His soul, Alex reflected, was caught inside his body. He had no clue why this happened. Was it because George extracted his inner-eye, which was supposed to catapult his spirit out? But that small, stinky lizard couldn't have been responsible for his ecstatic experiences. And that led Alex to another idea. Maybe he was imprisoned in an alternate reality created by Tudor. Maybe Tudor somehow got access to magical powers and was thus able to control Alex's mind. What else would account for the suspension of the laws of physics and biology in this hellish dimension, if not an act of vile sorcery?

Tudor seemed to be king of this entire dimension. Alex recalled the lyrics of their favorite Grave song: *"In my dominion/ Blood will always rain/ I damned your soul/ To everlasting pain."*

Damned your soul. To everlasting pain. The words hammered in Alex's mind. Tudor must have repeated the incantation so faithfully that he was able to enter the interdimensional labyrinth and then create his own world like a computer game programmer and make Alex inhabit that twisted universe. This explained how everything here bent to Tudor's will, how there were probably whores waiting for them at the Poenari Castle although Alex knew that, in the real world, the castle stood empty. Somehow, on his way here, Alex recklessly entered through a hidden portal, and now he needed to find the exit.

Only an absolute concentration of his psychic powers could release him from this mental possession. Alex needed to focus on freeing his soul from the cage of his illusory broken

Chapter 7 The Wild Hunt

body and retrace his astral steps back to the actual world where his real body stood unharmed, probably immobile as if in a trance. His rattled mind instantly leeched to the hopeful idea. His real body was out there, unscathed. His Aryan blood still fed his mind through a transdimensional umbilical cord. He just needed to find the channel that would lead to his rebirth.

Alex put the knife on the ground and straightened his upper body. He folded his intact leg under him and rested his left hand on it palm up. His right went to the raw stump in the same position.

He closed his eyes.

He filled up his abdomen with air and exhaled slowly, through pursed lips. Breath, *pneuma*, his self was coming together, centered, focused. His will and purpose clear, laser-like.

Deep breath in. Slow breath out.

Alex began whispering under his breath.

I am the first Aryan man
I am this mountain, my fortress,
the center of the Earth.
Its forests and soil are my flesh,
and my bones are carved in stone.
My blood rushes
through underground caves and waterfalls.
The mountain peaks pierce through the clouds of my thought,
upper and upper,
onto the gates of Valhalla.

As Alex recited his incantation, a fly landed on his head and entered the bloody crevice on top of his skull. Others followed and began sucking hungrily on the decaying neural tissue. They would thrive and multiply between the walls of this forsaken castle.

Would you consider giving it a review?

Reviewing an author's book on primary book sites such as Amazon, Kobo and Goodreads drastically help authors promote their novels and it becomes a case study for them when pursuing new endeavors. A review can be as short as a couple of sentences or up to several paragraphs, it's up to you. You can find review options for the novel on Amazon or Goodreads.

Made in the USA
San Bernardino, CA
28 November 2019